Acting Strangely

I hope you enjoy Acting Strangely

Best wishes

Andy T.

Andrew Trim

Honeybee
Books

Published by Honeybee Books
www.honeybeebooks.co.uk

Printed in the UK using paper from sustainable sources

ISBN: 978-1-913675-08-0

Author: actingstrangely@gmail.com
Artist: Sam Zambelli (@Thatsrichartwork)

This book is dedicated to my dear wife Shareen,

My editor, my rock and my best friend.

(Just for the record, that's not four people, just one very busy lady)

Contents

1

The Opera House

It was 5 am in Holeford and Peter had just started his milk round. The sun was just peeping up over the eastern horizon – something it does routinely every day but today it was particularly beautiful. Its golden rays illuminated the fields south of the town. The shadows of the trees resembled barcodes radiating across the verdant meadows which were crisscrossed by the ditches and sluices of an ancient and neglected irrigation system.

The Long Horn sheep, seemingly oblivious to the beauty of the dawn, chewed rhythmically on the grass whilst looking up vacantly at the hilltop town as it slowly awoke to another working day. As Peter Goodall turned the corner from Princes Road into the High Street he braked suddenly, his clipboard slipping off the bench seat into the foot well and his cargo rattling and chinking together in protest. He stared intently at the window of the unopen supermarket. He was sure he had seen a movement inside the shop, which struck him as unusual for this time of the day. He watched a while for any further signs of life but nothing stirred. It must have been a trick of the light he concluded, but a shiver of doubt ran down his spine.

A figure inside the store had watched as the vehicle stopped abruptly, it now turned casually away.

Before moving on, Peter mused over the reflection on the window of the water meadows laying below the town. The idyllic vista reminded him of the reason he had moved his family to the South of England and away from the dirt and grime of smoggy London.

The window belonged to Price Low, the supermarket that had been built on the site of an old theatre which had burnt down in mysterious circumstances many years ago. Peter knew a little of the history of the town and the building that once stood on that site. There had, in fact, been a theatre in Holeford since 1783. The original being built by a wealthy Exford sheep turner for his friend, the actor/manager Bertram Briggs who operated several theatres on the south coast.

Many illustrious figures had performed upon that stage in multiple roles. Peter Kemble first appeared in 1794, returning nine years later as Richard the Third, Hamlet and Othello. Bill Vine first appeared in 1809 as Felix Don in *The Wonder* and the great Edmund Keen himself had also trod those boards in *Henry IV Part One*, returning in 1811 to conclude with *Henry IV Part Two* and *Henry V*. 'Not before time too!', reported the local press, having been left with a two year cliffhanger!

After Bertram Briggs' death, the theatre passed through several hands, whereby its decline began. Amongst its more interesting re-incarnations were a beer house and music hall before it closed altogether and was eventually purchased by a local wool merchant, one Tobias Pullover. It was reopened as the Royal Opera House, only to have its licence revoked after six years on the grounds that its many structural defects rendered it unsafe for public use. The last performance was *The Fall of the Mighty* on the 10th of October 1892.

Pullover then decided the best course was to demolish the entire building and replace it with a new, bright modern theatre. He gave the commission to local architect and specialist designer Compton Deverill. The existing theatre was therefore demolished in 1894 and the new one, costing £13,000, was built to much public excitement. The new opera house opened in 1894 with Norman Lustrum's Comic Opera Company performing the burlesque opera *Sister Penguin*. However, due to its popularity, the site proved to be too small and the adjacent property was purchased and the theatre was enlarged.

The new theatre was described in the town's pamphlets as follows:-

'The front of the theatre, to Princes Road, has a handsome facade of local red brick and cast concrete dressings of warm cream colour.

It carries up with a large, bold gable with scrolls and ball terminals. Between the windows are niches containing busts of local authors and composers and above these is a frieze containing the words Opera House.'

Through the doors you entered a beautiful vestibule with Portland stone stairs with red carpet walk centres and embellished with brass rods and handrails leading to both sides of the circle. The circle itself was furnished with red velvet covered flip seats and a large promenade to the rear. The stalls were raked seating with two separate exits to the street. The auditorium was decorated in the French Renaissance style, predominately in blue and gold with figures of the Muses painted inside oval panels. The ceiling was truly magnificent, being decorated to represent the sky with the sun being held in place by a pair of golden sheep, in acknowledgement and gratitude to the source of the finance to build this magnificent playhouse.

The stage was large for a provincial theatre and was equipped with a trapdoor and rising platform from the basement store under the stage itself which enhanced many productions. It was widely used in pantomimes for the arrival and disappearance of characters, much to the surprise and delight of the audience. Electric light was introduced in 1898, primitive and misunderstood but nevertheless a wonder of its age. Box office takings soared as people came from far and wide to experience the wonder of this modern miracle.

Early cinema was making its presence felt during the summer of 1916 when it replaced many of the live shows. The theatre did, however, continue live performances, with touring companies satisfying the demand for plays and musical entertainment. The theatre was finally sold to the Empire Playhouse Company in 1946, who converted it into a picture house, with the proviso that opera would continue to be performed on its well-maintained stage, hidden behind the Cinemascope screen when not in use.

In 1955, The Opera House was to host The Trolley Cart touring production of the comic opera *The Pirates of Penzance*, by W.S. Gilbert and Arthur Sullivan. It was a lavish production which had a successful run in London before touring the provinces.

The lead roles were as follows:-

Major- General Stanley ....Arthur Lawrence

The Pirate King..........................Wilfred Trunnion

Sergeant of Police .... George Shakespeare (no relation to William)

Samuel..Andrew Peverill

Frederick......................................Sutton Pointing

Ruth..Florence Bingham

General Stanley's daughters:

Mabel..Annie Pike

Edith...Evelyn Meade

Alice..Ruby Manville

Isabel..Alice Bennett

With all the actors came a support team of stage managers, lighting, props, box office, make up, dressers, and an eight piece orchestra led by their conductor the fearsome Colonel Sir Edward Sykes.

The Colonel was very much in charge of the whole team. "This is a musical and I make the music!" was his battle cry at every rehearsal. He had recently retired from the army following a successful career in the Second World War. He had inventively managed to avoid any combat whilst leading his concert party to entertain troops all over the world under the banner of ENSA (Entertainments National Service Association or Every Night Something Awful, as it was lampooned by the troops). He had served in Egypt, India, Italy and Germany, returning to England in time for his knighthood for Services to the War Effort, without having taken his pistol out of its holster, nor looking the enemy in the eye or from any distance for that matter.

He now controlled the orchestra with a rod of iron. The actual rod of iron he used as his baton was picked up from the ruins of a bombed-out theatre in Dresden. "A sobering reminder of the terror of war!" he would explain solemnly to anyone who would listen as he tapped the lectern for attention with the resultant wood splinters inevitably spraying the lead violin.

As they moved around the country, the touring company became a tight team and despite their moans, there was an underlying respect for each other's talents. A happy band of strolling players. Certainly no one could be accused of doing it for the money. Digs were provided with B&B's or rooms in the cheapest areas of town paid for by the Trolley Cart along with a small living allowance to buy food and clothing. Their costumes, make up and laundry were also provided by the company. As they spent nearly all of their time travelling between towns or in the theatres setting up and rehearsing, they had little opportunity, money or energy to waste on frivolities.

The Trolley Cart Company was a chance for new talent to be discovered and rise up the ladder to top billing and all the rewards that followed. This point was not missed by the managers and was used to exploit young hopefuls before the days of instant stardom provided by talent shows on the television. Talent certainly abounded in the company. All were very capable and were able to understudy several parts in case of sickness, even a stage hand stepped in one night when one of the pirates went AWOL.

On the evening of the 21st of August 1955 the show had finished to roaring applause. The local papers had declared the production

'Outstanding. A triumph, how lucky the town was to have the chance to see a West End production in their humble little theatre.' Back stage things had gone quiet. The adrenalin produced by the actors was beginning to wain as they cleaned off their makeup and carefully hung up their costumes ready to do it all again the next evening. After the applause of the audience and the sound of music and song reverberating around the auditorium, all was silence. There was a feeling, however, that the walls had absorbed the sounds of it all and retained them, so that maybe one day it would all be played back again. The building undoubtedly had a soul, built up in layers as it had soaked up the atmosphere of a thousand performances gone before. A patina of the performing arts.

The doorman, Billy Barnett, a short stout gentleman in his late sixties, had seen it all before. The companies came and went and then he returned to cinema projection until the pantomime season when the owners could be sure of a good return for live theatre for a short period. Billy's uniform was a bit too big for him as he only stood 5' 6", giving him the appearance of having very short legs. But the bright red coat embellished with gold braid and black trousers with red piping gave him the authority and stature of a much taller man. Following the show it was his job to ensure all the patrons had left the building and that the usherettes had tidied up and cleaned the auditorium, with especial attention being paid between the seats. It was not unusual to find the odd coin that had fallen from a patron's pocket, so it was no hardship for them to carry out this particular chore. In fact, there was usually a race to pack up the ice cream trays, close the bar and sweet stand, quickly change out of their uniform, don their old clothes and clean the floors in the hope of hidden bounty.

Billy changed, hung his uniform on the hook behind the Stage Door reception desk and prepared to go home. All the back of house staff had departed and he moved to the auditorium to ensure the building was empty. The orchestra had gone early, they always went early. They only had to pack their instruments away before making a dash for the nearest pub before closing time. The stage hands and lighting team were ahead of them and on their first pint by now.

Billy went from the wings down to the doorway of the dressing room checking for any stray personnel. He found Mr Trunnion.

"All gone dear, they've all gone," cried Wilfred Trunnion looking forlornly towards Billy, whilst holding his hand across his forehead in an overly dramatic gesture.

"Fine, I'll be off then and be sure to pull the door to when you go. It locks itself, so you won't be able to get back in again till the morning when

I get here," instructed Billy. He was supposed to ensure that he was the last to leave but over the years had grown to trust some of the performers to lock the door behind them so that he could catch the earlier bus home.

Wilfred smiled, he had no intention of getting locked out, but every intention of being locked in. He was weary of staying in the cheap digs provided by the management. The theatre was to be his bed and board. With fellow actors George and Alice to keep him company, this week they would sleep in the relative comfort and warm surroundings of the prop room under the stage. The room was full of props and furniture from old productions and Wilfred had claimed a four poster. It was actually a mattress laid on the base of the trapdoor but in the half-light with the guides for the rising floor, it took on the appearance of a magnificent bed.

George and Alice both had large sofas with soft cushions as pillows and heavy blankets which were being employed as dust covers to protect the delicate fabrics. It was by far the most luxurious accommodation they had found with this touring production since leaving London. Before settling down they made their way to the Circle bar for a nightcap. They sat for an hour listening to Wilfred while he regaled them of tales from his early days in the music hall. George, six years his junior, was sure most of them were made up or stolen from other performers but nonetheless it made for an entertaining hour and he was happy to humour him in this. Alice was in her early twenties and this was her first professional tour, she loved listening to the old stories and experiences. It was a hard nomadic life but a great adventure. Her parents had, surprisingly, encouraged her in her ambition to become an actress and were proud to support her as her star began to ascend. One day it would be her name at the top of the bill. She had already secured a summer season in Bournemouth with Harry Worth and Billy Dainty. Her career was on the up.

The adrenalin of the performance had subsided. Tired and weary after the day's excitement, it was time for sleep. They left the bar and headed back to their improvised digs for the night. George had checked that the doors were locked, the auditorium was dark and bar lights turned off.

"Good night," chorused Wilfred and Alice.

"Lights out," George announced and all went dark apart from the candle he used to make his way back to his sofa. Being careful to extinguish the flame between wet fingers he pulled the blanket over himself and fell quickly into a deep sleep.

High above them in the roof void of the theatre, things were not so good. Years of dust and mice activity had built up a layer of tinder around some of the original cabling which had never been removed. The production now performing was the largest the theatre had ever put on and with it came new technology direct from the West End. The lighting and sound system was powerful and drew more electricity than the old wiring had originally been designed to handle. This was not a problem, as the theatre had been re-wired for the cinema installation and was more than capable of sustaining the needs of this production. What no one realised was that one of the circuits still had some of the old redundant cables connected. In normal circumstances it was only used by the cleaners to vacuum the circle but was now being utilised to power a spotlight. The cable had got red hot and the rubber insulation had melted away.

The dust around it had begun to smoulder. By the time the three thespians had gone to sleep that smoulder was hastening into flame and beginning to spread through the roof void un-hindered. The intensity of the fire was increasing, unabated and unseen.

In the prop room under the stage, doors closed, lay George, Wilfred and Alice, in the dark, in a deep sleep whilst the building around them developed into an inferno. They had no idea of the blaze raging overhead, and now starved of oxygen, in what would become their mausoleum, they fell deeper into a sleep they would never wake from. The curtain had fallen on their last performance.

The fire raged well into the morning. The fire brigade, twenty five men strong with six tenders brought in from nearby towns, battled hard to bring it under control and stop it spreading to nearby buildings. The area around had been evacuated and the surrounding streets cordoned off by the police. A large crowd had gathered at the barriers to see what was happening. Dave Spokes from The Chronicle was at the front, camera in hand to record the demise of the town's historic theatre.

By sunrise all that was left was a distorted iron frame standing in a sea of smouldering rubble and timber. The fire brigade continued to damp down the wreckage well into the following afternoon. The smell of the fire had engulfed the whole of the town centre; it had penetrated the fabrics of houses and the clothes of residents. The town was in shock. The building, that had been at the centre of their community's life for generations, was now gone. Suddenly and without warning they had lost a beloved institution. As the three actors' bodies were never discovered and nothing more was heard of them after the dreadful day, it was accepted that they had died in the fire. The town was horrified at their loss but as travelling players they had had little association with the residents and no strong bond with the community. Only their families truly missed them. Without evidence of their remains it was difficult for them to obtain closure. Part of them kept the forlorn hope of their reappearance.

The Exham Chronicle recorded the disaster with a four page special fronted by a large picture of the smouldering ruins. Inside were details of past productions illustrated with old poster sepia pictures and a long editorial about the tragic loss of the cinema and theatre. Little mention was made of the tragic loss of life as it was too soon for the final statement from the fire officer. The leader of the council closed the article with promise of a new beginning. A new state of the art entertainment complex would rise, phoenix like, from the ashes of the ruins.

That was in 1955. The ashes soon cooled, along with that promise when they realised how much it would cost for the new venture. The owners were not in a position to fund the rebuilding; they had poor insurance which had just about covered the cost of the fixtures and fittings. Within a year the site had been fenced off and a for sale notice posted on the side of one of the distorted rusting steel columns. Alice's family had pasted posters on the hoarding appealing for any information on their daughter. These were now torn and faded like their hopes of ever seeing their child again. The Doorman Billy moved away a week after the disaster to seek work in Australia. He had to live with the fateful memory of the three actors he had, unknowingly, left in the theatre that night.

The ruin remained a blot on the landscape of the town centre until 1962 when the supermarket chain Price Low took on the project of adding the building to its growing portfolio of shops. The news was welcomed with open arms. The Exham Chronicle celebrated with the headline 'Holeford Town Centre Saved!' The local councillors, excited that they may get re-elected on the back of the news, assisted Price Low with its ambitions by reducing their business rates and giving the application an easy passage through the planning process.

That was many years ago and the supermarket was now in need of further modernisation. The faded paint peeling off the rotten timber windows was a sign that a refurbishment was long overdue. The rise of out of town shopping, the popularity of the weekly market and mail order shopping were beginning to impact on its profits, there was little in the budget for a fresh coat of paint. The town centre had not fared much better. Following the arrival of Price Low there had been a marked increase in shoppers but these had now decreased. They were managing, just, but it was a precarious way to earn a living. Some empty units would reopen for a few months selling kitchenware, art materials, second hand clothes etc. but few stayed long. New entrepreneurs trying to make their way in the world, only to have their dreams and ambitions severely dented by reality.

2

Holeford Awakes

1975 was a time of change to the way the British thought, worked and played. The freedom of the sixties post war baby boom was now giving way to the hardship of recession and a fluctuating economy. The Conservative party elected their first female leader, Margaret Thatcher, turning the conventions of the male dominated parliament on its head.

By contrast Charlie Chaplin was being knighted by the Queen while Led Zeppelin, at the height of their fame, played to full houses at Earls Court for five consecutive nights. The unrest about the future was causing turbulence, sparking protests about European integration and high unemployment. The unions were bringing the country to its knees with miners, bin men, car plants and even ambulance crews striking. Football hooligans turned the beautiful game ugly, resulting in Leeds United being banned from European competitions. Then the IRA bombed the London Hilton and Green Park underground station. Dark days indeed.

Even the weather was troubled, for the first time since 1761 it snowed in London in June!

But the stoic British public took it all in their stride and looked forward to more peaceful times. The Vietnam War ended and Russia worked with America on a combined space mission showing glimmers of hope for the future. The BBC broadcast new comedy shows like *Fawlty Towers* and *The Good Life*. At the cinema, *Monty Python and the Holy Grail, Jaws* and *The Towering Inferno* were premiering. Queen released 'Bohemian Rhapsody', changing the landscape of popular music. Glam rock was at its zenith with Bolan, Bowie, Elton and Slade at the forefront. As a reaction to the pretensions of Progressive Rock from the likes of Genesis and Pink Floyd, The Sex Pistols arrived performing their first gig. A prelude to the punk revolution which was going to impact the fabric of youth culture with its aggressive chords and belligerent attitude to society. Away from the seats of power and industry the sleepy West Country market town of

Holeford carried on its daily life, aware of the turmoil but buffered by its distance from it all.

Peter Goodall's milk round started at the Arlington Dairy, a converted stable yard in Grove Street on the edge of the town centre. His trusty vehicle nicknamed Trigger, was a Morrison Electricar 20cw milk float, manufactured in 1961. The float was heavy, slow and timeworn but after it had negotiated the old cobbled stone yard, originally designed for horses rather than electric vehicles, it settled happily into its task of delivering the daily 'pintas' to the good citizens of Holeford. The route was familiar. Designed to be completed before breakfast time and thereby missing the ever-increasing commuter traffic. Sadly fewer residents were getting their milk delivered to the doorstep now due to the intrusion of the town's supermarket and its cheaper produce. Arlington Dairy could not compete with the bulk buy, pile high, sell cheap ethic of the multi-nationals but at least, for the time being, still had a strong and loyal following eager to keep Trigger and his stable mates in work. Luckily some people still appreciated locally produced milk delivered to the doorstep in time for breakfast.

At Neil Armstrong Close, Molly Goodall awoke to the sound of the kettle's whistle from the kitchen as her mother Joan prepared breakfast before they went their separate ways to school and work. Ironically Joan worked at Price Low. Not the most popular place in the Goodall household and certainly not for Mr. Arlington at the dairy, who teasingly accused Peter of selling out to the competition. Peter would see to his own breakfast when he returned from his round and they would all catch up with the day's events over the evening meal. Their house was recently built and stood in a new development on the edge of the town. The estate, known collectively as Apollo Park, was named after the Nasa Space Missions. A popular choice, for the beginning of the 1970s had already seen the first man on the moon and further exciting space missions kept the street names fresh in the memory.

Theirs was a two-storey semi, set in a small garden with a drive and garage for their green Morris 1000. The ground floor consisted of a lounge, overlooking the front lawn, with a dining room separated by a glass screen and doors. The kitchen was accessed off the hall to the rear, with a serving hatch to the dining area. The floral carpeted hall had a staircase rising to an open plan landing with horizontal balustrade in varnished pine. Off the landing, to the front, was Joan and Peter's bedroom with two further bedrooms and the family bathroom to the rear. Molly's room was the smallest but had the best view over the open countryside towards the ancient earthwork of Monkton Hillfort. On the horizon she could see the outline of the redundant MOD radio aerials from a World War Two transmitter station and the mounds of ancient burial grounds. Looking south there were also glints of light reflecting off the windscreens of cars parked in the grounds of Holeford Golf Club perched high on the hill outside of the town.

Molly washed and dressed then joined her mother in the kitchen where she filled her bowl with Price Low Cornpops, added 'Arlington' fresh dairy milk and sat at the table in the dining room. Joan produced a fresh pot of tea and they sat eating their breakfast together as they did every weekday morning. Accompanied by the soundtrack of the Radio 2 breakfast show, they chatted about their plans for the day, washed up and departed. Joan went early to the supermarket where she would help at the tills selling the morning papers and Price Low Everyday Milk to the same group of patrons that came in each day for their fix of gossip and lunch supplies. As she entered, she was still humming the latest Tammy Wynette song which she had just heard on the radio.

Molly left the house about half an hour later, walking round to meet her best friend Kate who lived across the estate in Buzz Aldrin Way. From here they both headed off to Holeford Secondary Modern School for another day of education delivered alongside classroom crowd control.

What had begun as a normal day was descending into farce at Price Low. Jack Bonfield, the store manager, was in a fuming temper as he stomped around the store rearranging the displays as he went and dislodging much other produce in the attempt.

"This is ridiculous!" he exclaimed. "I spend all night setting up a new display of Price Low Super Energy Baked Beans only to find this mess in the morning!" The fact was that he had ordered Joe, the store's stockroom assistant to do the work 'under his supervision' whilst he stayed in the manager's office drinking coffee and dealing with the mundane task of reviewing the stock control report from Joan. "Just you look at this!" he continued. The tins of beans were not at the end of the freezer cabinet as instructed but were, instead, located in the domestic goods area between the mops and disinfectant. "Who in their right mind would put beans with the household materials? THAT BOY WILL HAVE TO GO!"

"But didn't you put them there?" Joan asked innocently, "After all, you spent all night putting up the display, didn't you?"

"No, I didn't!" replied Jack, now even more upset at that jibe. However he had no intention of dismissing Joe. How could he? He was his son after all and Jack knew very well that the display had been in the correct place the night before and perfectly aligned, labels out. Joe may not be the brightest spark but he was conscientious. Besides Joe was also careful to do what his father requested, reluctant to make his life more difficult since his parent's recent divorce. "And, what is more," Jack continued to rant, "THEY ARE ALL UPSIDE DOWN!"

The customers were greatly amused at this. Joan was looking up at the ceiling trying to hold her giggles in whilst the other staff moved behind the shelving away from Jack's gaze. He was in no mood to be messed with. If nothing else this morning, the activity in the shop had lifted the spirits of those in the supermarket. There was even a small rise in the sale of tinned beans for a short period, which helped to placate the situation for Jack.

The working day then settled into its regular pace with a steady stream of customers.

Joe re-positioned the display the right way up and in the correct place, confused as to the reason why the display had been moved. Someone must be playing a practical joke, he concluded…He had his suspicions.

Just after midday, regular as clockwork, the Smith twins dropped in to collect their copy of the Holeford Evening Chronicle. Dressed identically, their mirror appearance was uncanny. No one knew which was which and some even debated if they themselves knew!

"Good afternoon Joan," they greeted in unison. "The Chronicle please. My, oh my! Look at that, another depressing headline. I don't know why we buy this rag, can't they print some good news?" they chorused. They said the same thing every day but always returned without fail, rain or shine.

George Zimmerman, the local butcher four doors down, popped in for his usual cake, biscuits and chocolate bar. Every day the same purchases and his figure confirmed that he ate every morsel of them. The workers from the building site down the road, always good customers, loaded up with sandwiches, crisps, various snack bars and the usual boobs and bunkum newspapers.

By late afternoon the school children headed home, spending the days remaining dinner money on penny chews, sherbet dabs, sweet cigarettes, comics, etc. The evening paper distribution began with the small army of paper boys and girls collecting their prepared bags of papers for delivery on their way home. Jack took pride in sorting the delivery sacks which were emblazoned with the Chronicle logo. Each with its relevant delivery list placed on the top so that each could deliver the evening news on their particular route home.

Molly was amongst those returning from school. She would wait each day for her mum to finish her shift at 6pm. Jack gave her permission to use the stockroom to do her homework whilst waiting. Amongst the goods stood a well-worn old oak desk with one drawer missing, its veneer peeling and leather insert curling at the corners. A tired squeaky wooden swivel chair fitted neatly into the knee hole. She liked sitting here, it was quiet in the late afternoon. The creaky chair was comfortable and agedly reassuring despite the horse-hair stuffing hanging through the faux leather in several places. She never lost the fun of occasionally spinning round on the seat even though she was no longer considered a child, now in her teens. A bare light bulb hung from the ceiling giving a stark light and creating a myriad of shadows amongst the stock. She was surrounded by shelves stacked to the ceiling with large brown boxes of products waiting for their turn in the spotlight of the shop floor. The aroma was an intoxicating mix of cleaning materials, cardboard, sweet smelling foodstuff and fruit and veg, all concentrated in the enclosed space of the stockroom, a cardboard lined cavern which was strangely comforting and familiar.

Joe had popped in a couple of times to restock the sweet display following the swarm of liberated and excited children who had stripped the shelves almost bare. Molly was now alone. She had been sitting quietly for about half an hour studying the Kings and Queens of England for the conclusion of her history project. The gentle hum of commerce coming through the half open door acting as soothing background noise.

Suddenly a cold gust of air brushed her face, hinges creaked and the door gently closed behind her. Without looking up from her work she spoke. "I assume it was you who moved that bean display? You're going to get Joe into serious trouble one day." Molly then sat back, and turned around on the swivel chair. There, stood defiantly in front of the closed door, arms folded, was a young Victorian lady. She remained silent but the glint in her eyes and her guilty grin left no doubt as to who exactly had been responsible for the contentious display of beans that morning!

3

Home again

It had been the end of the previous Easter term when Jack had first agreed that Molly could use the stock room desk to do her homework whilst waiting for Joan to finish her shift. The desk was worn but serviceable and after a tidy up the room was spacious enough for Molly to sit quietly and study. Molly soon became used to the noises and smells around her. With the door left ajar she could hear the murmur of voices from the shop which was comforting but not distracting. Occasionally Joe would pop in to grab goods to bolster the depleting displays. She realised that when he felt comfortable with someone he relaxed and chatted easily. She found him thoughtful and intelligent and she enjoyed his company. He evolved into an unexpected mine of information for Molly to tap into when she became stuck with her studies.

This particular Thursday had been horrid. She had just finished hockey practice in the pouring rain, dried off and then ran to the shop where she was again dripping wet from the relentless storm. She was behind with her history project and not in the best of moods. After dumping her bag by the desk she shook out her wet coat and placed it on the radiator to dry, and slumped in the chair. The room felt cold, it did sometimes, that was not new and covering the radiator had not helped. She shivered, grabbed her books from her bag and laid them open on the desk. She started to read and make notes on her new project 'The English Civil War'.

"I played Cromwell once."

Molly heard a hollow voice just to the left of the desk. "Is that you Joe?" she whispered. "Stop messing about."

"She can hear you, Wilf," exclaimed a female voice to her right.

"Look, I am not in the mood for your games. Joe, I warn you now." Molly swung round violently on the creaky swivel chair.

The apparition of a young Victorian girl flinched at the sudden movement.

"Who the hell are you?" said Molly.

"Hi, I'm Alice. I'm sorry, we didn't mean to surprise you but usually no one can see or hear us."

"What do you mean, we?" exclaimed Molly, not fully comprehending the situation.

"Uhh… hello, Wilf at your service."

She swivelled round to be greeted by a tall mature vision dressed as a pirate. "OK, Joe, you can stop your silly game and come out now. Ha-ha, I don't know how you are doing this but I get it, nice trick."

"Joe's not working today," the pirate informed her politely.

Molly didn't say anything for a few seconds while she assessed the situation. Not known for histrionics she took a deep breath and looked at the two characters in the room with her. "Right, let's get this clear," she announced, like a detective unravelling the plot of a murder.

"The room is cold, I am looking at two transparent projections called Alice and Wilf who have just spoken to me and know the movements of the supermarket staff, this is not normal," she concluded, putting her head in her hands.

"You're telling me it's not!" exclaimed Wilf." This is extremely rare. How come you can see us? You must be the seventh daughter of a seventh daughter or some such thing. Very rarely can anyone feel our presence let alone communicate with us."

"What do you mean? Of course I can communicate, I'm not stupid. What are you doing here?" Molly was still coming to terms with what her senses were trying to tell her and was in no mood for games.

"We live here, this is our home," the girl replied quietly and calmly.

"OK, I get it, you are pretending to be two of the actors who were apparently killed in the fire. That's a bit sick, but you've done your research well. Joe told me all about the history of this place and if you think this is going to scare me you are very much mistaken." Inwardly Molly was confused and uncomfortable about the whole thing but she had no intention of showing it.

Alice sat on the edge of the table. "Look we're not trying to scare you. Wilf is right. You must be especially gifted if you can see us. You must understand, this is so exciting for us. I haven't had a female to talk to for years, please say we can be friends."

Molly was surprisingly not scared, confused, yes, but scared, no. "OK…

I understand this is not normal but suppose I am willing to accept that for some inexplicable reason I am able to communicate with your spirit world. We will just have to see how this develops."

"Blimey!" exclaimed Wilf, "you're made of strong stuff, most people run away screaming."

"Have there been others then?" Molly said.

"Oh, there have been a few others, mostly cranks who think they can get in touch with, 'The Other Side'," Alice said, in a melodramatic voice. "Wilf and George usually deal with them, a couple of door slams, a kick of the rocking chair and they're soon fleeing, screaming for their lives!" and she laughed.

"George? How many of you are there?"

"Just the three of us here in the remains of the theatre," Alice confirmed.

"Thank goodness for that but who are the cranks you're on about?"

"Well, there's the hotel on the High Street which is reputedly haunted. That's where we had some fun, we read in the paper about a ghost hunting group who intended to spend the night there and went along to give them value for their money. They even had a TV company there once doing a supernatural investigation programme. Their so-called psychic didn't pick up on us at all. He said the honeymoon suite was haunted by a 'grey lady' who had lost her lover and would not leave without him. He soon left though when Wilf and George ruffled the curtains and tipped over a candlestick… you're not the same as those other psychics though. I have never met anyone who can see us the way you do. Some sense us but don't communicate with us properly," Alice said thoughtfully.

"You're a bit transparent but other than that you look perfectly normal to me," explained Molly.

"Well, thank you I am sure!" she said and curtsied dramatically.

"Secondly," Molly added as an afterthought, "what do you know about the Civil War?"

Following this first encounter the relationship between the four of them developed. They became Molly's source of historical information. She got an 'A' for her essay on the Civil War and praise from her teacher Miss Jenner.

It was now a year later and she had become good friends with the ghosts. Molly was well into her last history project before the summer holidays. Kings and Queens of England. This was of great interest for Wilf and George who had played several of them over the years, coupled with the fact that they also had 'friends' they could call on for further information to assist her if and when she needed it. Joan would sometimes enter the room when Molly was talking.

"Who are you talking to, dear?" she asked looking around the room.

"Oh, no one Mum, just thinking out loud."

Alice or Wilf would usually sit on the chair opposite Molly, invisible to Joan and anyone else for that matter that came into the room. Joan got used to her daughter talking to imaginary friends, after all she still talked to her teddy bear and they were both nearly fifty!

On another day Joe entered and sat on the chair occupied by Alice who giggled. It tickled her as Joe passed right through her and landed with a bump on the seat.

"Oh! It's flipping cold in here," he said. "I don't know how you can stand it in this draughty hole." He left immediately, having been distracted from the reason for his visit.

"I seem to have that effect on most men," and Alice giggled again.

At six o'clock Joan finished work, hung her overall on the hook by Molly's desk and they headed for home. Molly did a discreet wave to Alice who then sank through the floor into the basement to catch up with her fellow ghosts.

As they strolled home Molly told Joan about her day at school and her last history project of the year. *She appears to have an in-depth knowledge of English history,* Joan thought and was proud of her daughter's A class student status. Molly never mentioned her friendship with Alice to anyone, it was her secret. She didn't want to be thought of as different, she would never live it down at school if it got out that she thought she could see dead people.

At home Gran was visiting and joined them for tea. Peter had just got in from collecting the milk payments door to door and preparing Trigger for the next morning and was now upstairs having a wash. After eating in the dining room, they moved to the living room where they just had time for a game of Cluedo. Peter then gave Gran a lift home and returned in time to watch *The Sweeney* on their black and white television. Joan joined him on the sofa and after Regan and Carter had satisfactorily rounded up the bank robbers they talked about the day's events over a cup of tea and a garibaldi biscuit.

Back at Price Low the store had been closed up, lights turned out and all made ready for the paper run. Jack had placed some large sheets of plywood on the top of the freezer cabinets ready to lay out the piles of papers for the boys and girls to place in their bags and distribute in the morning.

This was the time Wilf, George and Alice liked to come out and go for a stroll around the store. There had been a daytime incident when an old lady fainted after seeing Wilf in the wines and spirits area. A quick dose of smelling salts soon brought her round. An ambulance was called and the paramedics checked her blood pressure which appeared normal but recommended that she make an appointment to see her doctor. After a cup of tea in the staffroom she was taken home in the ambulance.

She told Joe, "It was not nice, to see a pirate suddenly appear through the floor." It had given her a terrible shock and if Price Low want to play silly jokes on old ladies she would "take her business elsewhere". The staff were glad to see her off the premises. She had caused a bit of a stir in the shop but things soon got back to normal and everyone dismissed her as a bit of a crank. The ghosts decided to only venture into the store in the evenings from then on.

Wilf and George did their usual tour of the aisles and after an hour Wilf settled down in the till area with a copy of the evening paper while George, dressed in his policeman's uniform, practiced his levitating skills on the tins of beans.

Alice went back to the staffroom where she sat at the table and flicked through a copy of Tit-Bits that had been left there. It was full of celebrity tittle tattle, cartoons and a special section on the summer blockbuster *One of Our Dinosaurs Is Missing* which included an interview with its star Peter Ustinov.

Wilf, dressed in his full pirate costume including hat with skull and cross bones, looked up after a while and watched George resplendent in his period police uniform practising his levitation.

"Why always beans?" Wilf enquired.

"Well, they're a good practice object. Not too heavy, yet difficult to damage and with a strong psychic presence," Alice said as she re-joined them in the shop to see how her apprentice was progressing with his practice.

"I wish I had your natural gift at moving things Alice. You took to being a ghost very easily. Moving the odd rocking chair or swinging a creaking door is very amateurish by comparison with your skill level," sighed Wilf as they both watched George practicing.

George continued moving the tins with increasing skill. He was now floating them around for several minutes and able to place them back on the shelf where they came from in a neat row.

"Well done!" Alice said, clapping, as she made her way towards aisle four, "You're improving. All this practice is beginning to pay off. You'll soon be ready for the strawberry jams," she closed the door to the staffroom behind her without looking around or even attempting to touch it.

"Wow, Alice! How did you do that?" George was very impressed.

"I learnt I could do it the other day in the storeroom while talking to Molly. Someone was walking by and I just willed the door to close and it did. I think my powers are getting stronger."

"How's Molly getting on?" asked Wilf.

"She's fine, busy studying for her history exam. But she could do with more of your help, after all you've played a few kings in your time," said Alice.

"And a few queens," put in George, losing concentration and dropping a tin of beans on the floor.

"Serves you right," laughed Wilf as George looked dejectedly at the dented tin on the floor then began to raise it back onto the shelf.

They all moved to the window to see who was about. It was now 11 pm and the pubs were closing for the night. It was entertaining to see who was out on the street at this time. A small group of lads wandered past, deep in conversation about the football match at the weekend. Two well-dressed men, who had obviously been at a meeting, passed with brief cases in hand. Occasionally George would go out onto the street and follow someone for a while to see if he could get a reaction. There was the odd success when the victim would look around and speed up, feeling as if they were being followed. There was one incident where a very drunk man took a swing at him, which was unnerving. He kept a safe distance after that.

The last bus of the evening left from the stop opposite. A car drove past slowly and turned into the carpark stopping in the 'deliveries' area at the side of the shop. A taxi picked up the two business men sheltering in a doorway opposite and the street soon went quiet again.

"Well, that wasn't very interesting," sighed Alice. "I'm going back to my magazine."

George and Wilf also returned to their previous pastimes.

"George, did you just drop another tin of beans?" asked Wilf a short while later.

"No, why?"

"I thought I heard a thud over by the staffroom," said Wilf.

Alice moved across the store and looked through the door into the staffroom without opening it.

"I do believe we've got burglars!" she exclaimed excitedly and moved back across the shop to join the others.

4

With Cat-like tread

At 11 pm on Sunday the streets were quiet. Brian and Charlie Clarke drove the Hillman Avenger down Princes Road and pulled in alongside Price Low's service entrance. Brian turned off the lights and they both sat quietly considering what they were about to do.

No more petty shop lifting for them. They had seen how to break and enter on the TV and this was their grand leap into the big time. The car was stolen by Brian earlier that morning from a car park in a nearby town. He had been practising on his own car by lifting the door catch with a binding strap to gain entry which he could neatly push inside the car around the door seal. Getting it started or 'hot wiring' as they call it on the telly was a hit and miss affair. The stolen car's dashboard was now in pieces with wires hanging down and a smell of burnt plastic from his failed attempts. However he had finally managed to find the right wires and start the car without use of the key. They were in business.

Brian broke the silence. "Well, this is it, all our planning has brought us to this moment."

"I'm not sure about this. Look, we can just dump the car and go home now. No more said. Game over," Charlie said hopefully.

"Too late, Charlie, there's no turning back now. Just this once, a big job, then no more. The week's takings are in the safe just waiting to be collected. We'll be set up for better things."

"What if it goes wrong?" Charlie really didn't want to do this but Brian was his big brother. He looked up to him and wanted to please him.

"That's just nerves but that's good, they'll help keep you sharp and focused. Just like actors before they go on stage, it's natural… have you got the tools on you?"

"They're in my pocket Brian, I don't need many."

"Don't use my real name, stupid!" snapped Brian revealing he too was nervous. "We've rehearsed this. You are Bill and I am Ben. If we are overheard no one will know who we are."

"OK Brian," said Bill.

"Idiot," said Ben, shaking his head.

At that moment a car drove along Princes Road, its headlights illuminating the carpark. Brian and Charlie hunched down in their seats to hide. The tension heightened as the car drove slowly by. Brian wiped a bead of sweat from his brow as they sat back up.

"Right you know what to do Charlie."

"Yeah! But don't forget I only have thirty seconds."

"So you keep reminding me. The coast is clear, let's go."

They removed stockings from their pockets, pulled them down over their heads and climbed out of the car quietly shutting the doors. Brian opened the boot, pulled out a large crow bar and lump hammer. Charlie took a small screwdriver from his pocket and felt for his pliers.

Using only the illumination from the nearby streetlight Brian located the locking point on the staff entrance door and pressed the crowbar against the join in the door and frame. Charlie watched the street.

"All clear."

Brian struck the end of the bar with one almighty blow. The frame split and splintered against the force and the door swung open. All was silent again.

The red light on the alarm case high on the outside wall started blinking.

Charlie moved into the store.

"One elephant, two elephant."

"What are you talking about? Charlie. It's not a bloody zoo."

"Shush, I am counting the seconds – five elephants, six elephants…" He located the control panel on the wall just inside the door where a second red light was flashing on a panel along with a high pitched, angry whine. He unscrewed the front cover.

"Sixteen elephants, seventeen elephants…"

He allowed the cover to hang from the wires connected to a printed circuit board which was now accessible. He then began to unscrew the board from its mounting being careful not to touch any contacts.

"Twenty-four elephants, twenty-five elephants…"

The cover was connected by three wires to a black box deep in the panel.

"Twenty-six elephants, twenty-seven elephants…"

Charlie took the pliers from his pocket. The sweat from within his stockinged head was running down and stinging his eyes. Brian held the torch steady.

"Twenty eight elephants, twenty nine elephants."

SNIP!

The light on the panel faded and the whine stopped immediately. They both paused and took a deep breath. Charlie, struggling to breathe, pulled off the sweat soaked stocking, cleaned his spectacles and wiped his eyes. He was not enjoying this. It wasn't like on the telly, this felt very real and uncomfortable.

"That was brilliant Charlie."

"Don't ever expect me to do this again Brian and I'm not wearing this stupid nylon mask." He stuffed it disgustedly in his pocket.

They moved quickly into the room closing the door to the yard behind them. They both felt a little more comfortable now they were safely inside the building. Using their torches to find their way, they crept into the lobby and onward into the Staffroom which led to the manager's office and the safe. Once in the windowless office Brian was able to turn the desk light on and set to work on the safe with his stethoscope. He surprised himself when he was able to break the code in less than five minutes. He had been practising on an old safe in his garage at home. He had perfected the skill of listening very carefully to the clicks of the cogs by holding the stethoscope just above the dial on the front of the safe. He had seen this in a TV drama a year ago and whilst buying spares for his car at the local scrap yard, he spied the safe and decided to have a go. For £5 the safe was his! It was very heavy but with help from his mate Chris, with his pick-up truck they had managed to get it into his garage. It came with a combination which made it particularly desirable for his experiments. The stethoscope was obtained from the local hospital whilst he was visiting a friend. It 'fell' off the trolley as he was passing and found its way into the holdall he was carrying. He was in business!

"Come on, grab these," whispered Brian hastily pulling out large bags of change and tin boxes filled with notes. The door to the lobby at the other end of the staffroom slammed shut. They both stopped. "What was that?"

"Just a through draught I expect," assumed Charlie. He looked back into the lobby where the door to the yard was still closed and went to investigate.

"The door to the car park must have blown open and slammed shut because you broke the lock," he reported. "I slid a box of washing up liquid against it, just in case it does it again."

They placed the money up on the table in the staff room. Heavy sacks and several long flat trays neatly stacked with one, five, ten and even a small wad of twenty-pound notes ready to load into the car.

"Wow! There must be over a thousand quid here. We're rich!" Charlie whispered excitedly.

"Not exactly, not yet, but let's see what else we can find in the shop," replied Brian. His nervousness now gone, he realised this was going well and they could make a one off killing here. His greed got the better of him. He opened the door to the shop floor and crept out. There was low background illumination provided by the streetlights and a glow from the freezer cabinets. His eyes adjusted to the semi darkness and he was able to negotiate easily around the displays and shelves. Charlie remained in the staffroom running his hands across the loot. He had never seen so much money in one place, just touching it gave him a thrill and it was all theirs. It was like taking candy from a baby, he thought. They had never had much in life since their dad had done a bunk and now he would be able to buy his mum something nice and pay the bills.

Brian made his way to the tills at the front of the shop, being careful to stay in the shadows of the displays in case anyone should be passing. Wilf stood by the tills watching Brian's approach.

"I like the stocking mask, very effective," Wilf said appreciatively to George, who was now stood at the end of the freezer cabinets so he could get a clear view of the burglar.

"How many are there, Alice?" asked George.

"Just the two, the other's in the staffroom playing with the money. He's taken the stocking off his head," she replied. It was Alice who had re-closed the damaged door when she found they had two guests. She now came through the wall from the lobby into the store and joined George by the dairy products.

They all watched as Brian crept forward towards the tills. A car drove by, its lights casting exaggerated shadows on to the rear wall. Brian instinctively ducked down behind a display of cornflakes. The light flickered across the wines and spirits at the back of the store. This gave Brian a bright idea to stock up with drink whilst they had the opportunity. They could sell that easily nearer Christmas and keep a few nice bottles for themselves.

Charlie came through into the store and stared across the shop directly at Wilf.

"Who the hell are you?" he asked in a startled voice.

"Sssh, what on earth are you talking about? It's me." replied Brian, concerned about the sudden raising of Charlie's voice.

"No not you, the bloody pirate stood by the tills!" exclaimed an alarmed Charlie.

"Good evening. My name is Wilfred Trunnion. Pleased to make your acquaintance," Wilf said politely and waved. "It seems we have a psychic with us."

"What's this, a flipping fancy dress party?" said Charlie, well and truly out of his comfort zone now.

"Keep the noise down Bill! What the hell are you talking about?" Brian questioned, while secretly congratulating himself for remembering to use the alias name.

Charlie whispered across the room. "There's a pirate called Wilfred stood by the tills. Can't you see him?"

"No I can't, are you losing your mind?" replied a now worried Brian.

"I'm not staying here! Something's not right," Charlie turned to leave but froze when he caught sight of George by the freezer.

"Bloody hell it's the fuzz!"

"Charlie calm down, there is no one in the store but us, just look around," said Brian, worried that the stress of the robbery was playing tricks with his brother's mind.

Charlie was now beginning to tremble with fear. "What don't you understand? Can't you see them, a pirate and a copper are here with us."

"Hello," said George and Alice in unison.

"Argh! There are three of them now!" Charlie screamed. "They're in the room and they're talking to me! "I'm off. Come on let's go." He ran for the outer door giving no thought to their hoard on the staffroom table.

Before he could get there the Staffroom door slammed shut trapping them both on the shop floor.

"Nicely done, Alice," congratulated George.

"No problem. I'll teach you that one as soon as you master the beans," Alice replied.

Brian was watching the action unfold in front of him but could only see Charlie mysteriously talking to thin air and running to the door which slammed shut in his face. There seemed no discernible draught, so what had caused it to swing shut so conveniently?

Charlie grabbed a cricket bat from the toy display alongside him and walked menacingly towards Wilf. He was now truly frightened, this was new territory for the brothers. He wanted out. This was too much and if he had to use force he would. As he approached Wilf, he raised the bat above his head. "I don't know who or what you are but you and your friends had better let us out now or I'll let you have it." The bat waved about in his unsteady hand.

George, with encouragement from Alice, manipulated a tin of beans high up into the air which then floated above Charlie as he walked menacingly towards Wilf. Before he could reach him, George blinked and the tin fell.

There was a dull thud and Charlie stopped in his tracks. His knees crumpled and he collapsed onto the floor knocking over a pyramid of washing powder. A lonely dented tin of beans rolled unsteadily down the aisle away from where he fell.

"Sorry about that," George said, with only slight concern in his voice.

Wilf looked on. "Thanks, George, he was really going to try and hurt me. He has no idea what we are."

"I didn't mean to knock him out, though. I guess I dropped it from slightly too high."

George, Alice and Wilf moved and stood around the prostrate burglar.

Brian ran over to Charlie's side. The area around him was freezing cold as he leant through George to try and rouse Charlie. "What happened, are you alright?"

Charlie opened his eyes and looked up to see the three ghosts stood around him. Brian was reaching through the pirate now and grabbing his shoulder and shaking him.

He closed his eyes again and whispered. "Get off, stop shaking me. Can't you see them? For goodness' sake, three of them, in fancy dress, stood with you and they're transparent. You're even leaning through one of them." Charlie felt faint again. This time it was disbelief at what he was seeing and saying. "I don't feel well," he moaned. He prayed he would wake up and find out this was all a horrible dream. George bent down to look him in the face.

"I am terribly sorry for knocking you out young man but you were going to hit Wilf and I couldn't allow that."

"Get away spook! You're not a real copper, are you? You're not even dressed right," Charlie could now see he was wearing an old-fashioned uniform.

Brian looked on in disbelief. "Who the hell are you talking to? What do you mean fancy dress? You really are losing the plot, mate."

Charlie, still lying on the floor looked up at Brian and talked in a slow controlled whisper.

"Something hit me on the head. I think it was a tin of something."

"It was beans, actually" Alice interrupted.

Charlie stared at her. "Beans whatever!" He then looked back at Brian. "I was hit on the head… we're surrounded by three transparent people, a pirate a policeman… and a young woman. They're talking to me, can't you see them?" he asked Brian, incredulously.

Brian was getting really worried and confused. The atmosphere had turned cold, he could see his breath just like a freezing winter's morning. Something was very wrong. He recalled the door slamming in Charlie's face and the door to the lobby closing when he was raiding the safe and suddenly felt ill at ease. This caper was turning into a nightmare. He just wanted to grab the money and leave. "Something is definitely not right, I think we should just get out of here." Brian grabbed Charlie by the shoulders and started lifting him up onto his feet.

"You don't need to tell me, let's go!" Charlie staggered forward steadying himself on the display unit, and with the help of Brian they headed for the staffroom.

"I'm sorry but we really can't allow that," Wilf said calmly as he stepped in front of them.

"They're not going to let us leave Brian, what the hell are we going to do?" asked a panicked Charlie. Brian glanced at him and looked around again. There was still no one there. He needed to take back control.

"Here's what we're going to do. We're going to grab the cash, walk out of here, get in the car and drive away. You're concussed. I don't know how you banged your head but we are going now," he said determinedly. He grabbed Charlie by the back of his shirt and guided him towards the closed door of the staffroom.

Alice had anticipated this and as they moved towards the door the chest freezer slid gently across their path as if on rails.

"What the hell!" Brian exclaimed.

They both froze and Charlie, now past caring said, "I told you so, this place is haunted and we are in deep poo."

Wilf, Alice and George stood behind the freezer looking at the two brothers who were staring back. Charlie, who could see their jailers and Brian, still wearing his stocking mask, seeing nothing but an obstacle that had mysteriously moved by itself to block their way. He conceded now that something was really weird.

"Are they still there?" Brian whispered, with a tremble in his voice.

"Yeah, looking right at us," answered Charlie, not taking his eyes off them.

"Ask them if they're going to call the police," Brian whispered into Charlie's ear.

"We can hear you perfectly well, Brian. We are not going to call the police," said George.

Charlie, whilst puzzled, felt some relief at this and turned to Brian, "No, they're not going to call them."

Brian was still trying to comprehend the fact that his brother was talking to a ghost and things were moving round the room on their own.

"No, we are not going to call them. But you are!" George continued.

Charlie's face drained, "They want US to call them!"

"Don't be stupid," Brian said defiantly. "Let's go."

A line of fruit then drifted into view at shoulder height, half lit by the glow from the freezer cabinet. Oranges, bananas, apples amongst other assorted fruit, floated across the store and then flew towards them with some force. Alice was in her element. A pear glanced Brian's head whilst an over-ripe plum hit Charlie on the nose.

"Sorry!" apologised George by the fruit stall, "I'm still learning!"

Brian was now beginning to tremble uncontrollably with fear but Charlie, wiping plum from his face was relieved. He was not going mad. The place was haunted and Brian was now in the front line. Brian lifted his arms to protect his head as a cabbage hit him on the shoulder knocking him off balance.

"Make it stop." Brian cried out.

All the fruit, now enhanced with assorted vegetables, stopped in mid-air and hung there, gently swaying as if held by invisible hands ready to fling them at the first provocation.

George addressed Charlie. "Right, listen young man, this is how it works. There's a phone on the wall over by the tills. The number is 9…9…9."

"There's the phone, on the wall over there," Charlie said pointing towards the till on the left. "Phone the police, it's the only way."

"Not a hope, we're getting out of here!" Brian ran for the till, grabbed the heavy swivel chair from behind the checkout desk and ran towards the street entrance doors holding it legs outward in front of him like a battering ram.

George and Alice were prepared. Just ahead of him four bags of frozen peas fell from the ceiling, bursting onto the floor and, acting like ball bearings, turned the area into an ice rink. Brian lost control and slid into the magazine stand by the door. There was an almighty crash as he tangled with the chair and lay on the icy pea strewn floor whilst papers and magazines avalanched down on him, followed by the display unit burying him.

A muffled voice of defeat came from under a pile of *The Peoples Friend*. "OK, get the phone, Charlie!"

Charlie walked past the tills using the half-light from the street to negotiate the obstacles. He reached the wall mounted phone and lifted the receiver. Wilf came across, stood next to him and just nodded. Charlie lifted the receiver and put his shaking finger uneasily in the nine on the dial and turned it clockwise. It seemed to take an eternity for the dial to return so that he could again repeat the operation. He could hear Brian at the other side of the store stirring under the pile of papers. Charlie held the receiver to his ear, aware that he was now being watched by all three ghosts.

"What service do you require?" the detached voice asked.

"P…Police."

There was a pause, then bleeps and clicks as the connection was made.

"Holeford police, how can we help?" came a formal voice through the speaker.

"Uhh…Mmm…"

Wilf leant forward "Go on tell them, Charlie."

"We're stuck in a shop," stuttered Charlie.

"Please state your name and location."

"Price Low, we can't get out, please help."

"What is your name and who is with you?"

Charlie remembered his script, "B...Bill and B...Ben," he said unconvincingly. "Look we're trapped in the High Street shop, one of us is hurt."

"A patrol will be dispatched, stay where you are. Do you need an ambulance?"

"I don't think so."

"Very well, I'll send a patrol car." The phone went dead. It all seemed so matter of fact, Charlie looked at Wilf and felt very small and stupid.

"There, that wasn't so difficult was it, Charlie? Now you had better go and see to Brian. We'll let the police in when they arrive," Wilf said. He was feeling some sympathy now for the two confused and defeated lads.

Charlie pulled Brian from under the pile of papers, magazines and bent shelving and sat him up against the vegetable stand. The floor was now wet with pulped and melted peas. Brian looked up at Charlie and wiped the soggy green mess from his trousers. He then pulled off the stocking mask and stuffed it under the stand out of sight.

"Don't say anything when they arrive Charlie, leave it all to me and don't forget you are Bill, I am Ben and we just found the store open and came in to see what was happening in case someone was in trouble!"

"I remembered that bit when they asked my name, OK, Bill."

"No, you're Bill, you twit!" Brian shook his head.

They could now hear an approaching siren.

"OK, look just forget that bit for both our sakes. Say nothing, and just agree with me."

A police car drew up outside the front of the store, it's flashing lights illuminating the shop like a cheap village disco. The blue strobe created an unearthly effect in the semi-darkness. They heard the car doors open then two beams of white torch light emanated from outside the glass entrance doors penetrating the dark within. They could just make out the faces of two officers peering inside, their streams of light swaying to and fro across the inside of the store like aliens seeking their prey. The floor inside the door resembled a dew-covered lawn. The once frozen peas had now thawed and covered the lino in a green hue, complete with footprints from the two bungling burglars. The spotlight settled on the two men.

"Here we go," sighed Brian.

The officers tried the doors, they rattled but stayed firm. They moved away and headed for the rear of the building but not before gesturing to Brian and Charlie in no uncertain terms to stay exactly where they were.

Alice, George and Wilf looked on from the fruit and veg aisle. Charlie looked across at them occasionally to see if they were still there or if his mind was just playing tricks. The three waved back each time to reinforce their presence.

"They're still there, Brian."

"Just say nothing, Charlie." Brian sighed. "You're losing your mind. When we get out of this, we will have to take you to the doctor. You're not right in the head!"

They could hear movement coming from the Staffroom. The two officers found the rear door open and one was calling the station on his radio for back up.

The officers tried the door to the shop floor from within the staffroom, it was still blocked by the freezer that had prevented the escape. Alice stared at the blockage and waved her hand gently in a sweeping motion. The freezer gradually slid back into its original position allowing access for the police.

Sergeant Montgomery led the way, resisting the urge to say 'Ello, ello, what's going on here, then?' He loved watching crime dramas on the TV, if only to be critical of the accuracy of the scripts. He did however treat *The Sweeney* as a training aid. That to his mind was real gritty policing with car chases, loose women and tough criminals being brought to justice.

Montgomery was a man of diminutive stature for a policeman. He had joined the force fifteen years previously by lying about his height. His pale complexion and mousy hair he put down to too many years based in the station behind a desk pushing paper. His recent promotion to sergeant saw him finally fulfilling his ambition for proper police work out in the field dealing with real criminals and bringing them to justice.

"Good evening, officers," Brian said as he stood up, bracing himself against the fruit stand, peas dripping off his shirt. "We were just passing the store when we saw someone moving around and as good honest citizens we came in to investigate but they ran off."

"Yes, that's right," agreed Charlie, immediately breaking the 'stay silent' agreement.

Brian turned and glared at him. Charlie got the message and put a finger over his mouth.

"Is that your Hillman Avenger parked around the back by the service door?" enquired Police Constable Dexter.

"No," replied Brian truthfully, he had no idea whose car he had stolen!

From outside they heard another panda car arrive with flashing lights and two-tone horn shattering the silence of the night. Doors slammed and two further officers entered the store.

"The car is registered to a Mrs. Nottley and was reported stolen three days ago, Sarg," informed the incoming officer.

"Are you sure you know nothing about the car?" Montgomery looked accusingly at the two men.

"Oh no, officer, we have no idea what you are talking about," Brian replied putting on his best innocent accent.

"And what of the bags of money, drawers of notes and large boxes of tinned beans in the boot?" Montgomery continued.

George looked quizzically across the aisle. "What have you been up to, Alice?"

"I was just helping them out, while they were busy in the store. I levitated the money into the boot of the car and added some tins of beans for good measure!"

"The beans were a nice touch," agreed Wilf, clapping his hands together in silent applause.

"I left them bags on the table honest!" Charlie said to Brian without considering the magnitude of his words.

"Idiot," Brian scowled back at him. Montgomery raised his eyebrows.

"That's good enough for me." He resisted his urge to say, "You're nicked!" Instead he pointed two of his officers towards the criminals. "Read them their rights and take them to the station for further questioning." This was what he had been waiting for. "I want dabs taken tonight, this caper has been broken. I'm going to throw the book at these two." He could not contain the clichés any longer.

"Well done Bill!" Brian kicked Charlie on the shin.

"I think it's time for us to leave, our work here is done," Wilf said. The three of them then simultaneously descended through the floor of the wines and spirits area into their back stage home. As they did so Alice looked over at Charlie winked and waved goodbye.

Charlie watched as they descended and pointed towards them "Bri…. Ben" he quickly checked himself. "There they go down through the floor, I'm not going mad!"

All the men in the room looked to where he was pointing. They had no idea what he was talking about except Brian who was shaking his head and staring at the pea strewn floor. '*We will never live this down,*' he thought.

Two officers came over and fitted handcuffs, read them their rights and escorted them out of the building into a waiting police car. Charlie still had his stocking mask hanging from his pocket.

As they left, Jack and Joe arrived to survey the scene. As principal key holders they had been called from the station to meet the officers at the store. As they entered, escorted by Montgomery, they turned on the lights from the switch panel in the manager's office. The sudden illumination made them all blink and the scene of devastation was now there for all to see.

The safe door remained open with its contents missing, the stethoscope lay discarded on the floor along with paper and other stationery that had been knocked off the adjacent desk. They then entered the store itself, to be greeted by the provisions and magazines all over the floor and fruit splatted against the wall where it had missed its target and what appeared to be a green slime all over the floor near the entrance. As they inspected further, they discovered it was the thawed and squashed peas, wet and soft, and spread in a wide arc where they had hit the floor with some force after being dropped from such a height.

"What the hell has been going on here? It looks like a bomb's hit the place! We need to get cleaned up for opening," exclaimed Jack.

"I'm sorry sir, I can't allow that until we have completed our investigations," said Sergeant Montgomery. "This is a crime scene now and we need to dust for prints and take photographic records before anything is disturbed. The 'scenes of crimes' officers, will be here soon." He was enjoying this. This is why he had joined the force, solving crime and apprehending criminals was so much better in real life than on any TV show. "The kitchen in the staffroom has not been affected though, sir, if you were thinking of making a cup of tea," he hinted expectantly.

On Monday morning customers found the shop surrounded by 'Police no entry' tape hastily wrapped around bollards to cordon off the crime scene and two officers standing behind them to ward off anyone attempting to cross the barrier. Jack and Joe had spent the remainder of the night with the police team helping with their questions, making tea and watching the SOCO team, photographing the scene and dusting for prints. The money was checked by Jack and returned to the safe, it was all there.

"I tell you what Joe, when I report this to head office I'm insisting on a new safe and a proper alarm. I've told them for years this could happen but they don't want to put their hands in their pockets," Jack said stifling a yawn. It had been a long night.

'But why the tins of beans in the car. It doesn't make sense,' thought Joe, this was not the first time beans had featured in strange events at the shop. While talking to the officers over a cup of tea in the staffroom one mentioned how Charlie had pointed to an area of the floor as if he was seeing something.

The barriers were finally removed and staff were allowed in at twelve-thirty. Jack explained, to the best of his knowledge, what had happened overnight and asked them to help clean up and prepare to reopen as soon as they were able. There was much gossip and excitement about what had happened, expanding on the brief explanation of the two bungling burglars who had broken in and made a terrible mess. They hastily erected a temporary magazine rack made from an old table and empty boxes from the storeroom and after a quick wash and brush up, the store was ready to open.

Normal service at Price Low resumed at 3 pm. There was quite a queue at the door, not so much to shop but more to find out what had happened. The local reporter Dave Spokes was first in and Jack escorted him into the staffroom where he gave an outline of what he knew before the stories from the staff got out of hand. This was then followed by a series of pictures being taken for the evening edition with Jack holding several tins of beans by the entrance doors.

Over the next few days takings went up as Price Low featured regularly in the local paper, Radio and even some national papers had picked up on the news. Stories of the burglars being locked in the shop, slipping on their own mess and the attempted theft of beans gave the quiet news room light relief dreaming up new headlines.

'BEANS MEANS CRIMES'
'BURGLAR BEAN BUNGLE'
'TINS THWART THEFT'

Jack was not slow to pick up on the swell of interest and got Joe to reinstate the upside-down tin display from the earlier incident, along with the addition of posters in the window deliberately fixed upside down. The rumours of the store being haunted only helped to swell the interest. Local historian, Joseph Robinson, wrote an article for the Chronicle telling the story of the theatre fire and the disappearance of the three actors.

Could it be their spirits now manifesting themselves after all these years? This theory was mainly dismissed as nonsense. If there were such spooky goings on in the building why did they only happen now?

The press soon lost interest in the story and didn't appreciate being used as free Price Low publicity. Life moved on and the Chronicle went back to headlines about changes to bus timetables, council decisions and an occasional police incident.

All this time Charlie had been in the police cell wrestling with his conscience. After three days he decided to come clean and tell the truth about the events of that evening.

The interview room in the station was small and rectangular with a barred window at high level. It was decorated a rather sickly shade of yellow with a dark green dado rail. There was a badly scratched grey Formica table-top with laminate broken off in one corner supported on black metal legs with two wooden chairs facing across the table towards a single chair where Charlie now sat. Opposite him on the wall was a large mirror. In it he could see his diminutive reflection and imagined officers assessing him from behind the two-way glass, he had seen this in several TV dramas. He could sense their calculating beady eyes staring at him. Sergeant Montgomery had also seen the same TV shows and arranged the installation of the mirror, just like in The Sweeney. It was, in fact, only a large wooden framed mirror from the local DIY store screwed onto the solid brick wall. But it looked convincing. In fact, the adjacent room was the gent's toilet. But it looked good and it fooled all that sat facing it, Charlie was no exception.

Montgomery entered the room accompanied by PC Dexter and they both sat opposite the fatigued Charlie who was now wearing a light blue police custody overall.

"Right Sunshine, what have you got to tell us?" Montgomery asked, in a strange cockney accent.

Dexter looked round at him not sure if it was the same man he had just eaten breakfast with in the canteen. Why was he talking in this peculiar drawl?

"Come on, we haven't got all day, you said you wanted to make a statement." He banged the table with his fist and the plastic ashtray leapt onto the floor. Charlie winced. PC Dexter replaced the tray and prepared to fill in the duplicate confession form.

"Well… it's like this," Charlie started nervously. He then went on to explain in detail the events with the pirate, the policeman and the girl, the door slamming, the flying fruit, tins and frozen peas, the sliding freezer cabinet and finally the phone call.

Montgomery was not amused.

"You brought us in here to tell us all this guff. Do you take us for fools?" He paused for a moment to think. "I get it, you think you'll get a lighter sentence if you get sent for a psychiatric evaluation don't you? I have never heard such nonsense in all my life!" He stood up, turned and faced the mirror, gesticulating as if there were men observing from the other side of the glass.

This worried Charlie, he was telling the truth. What else could he do? There were obviously doctors watching from the other room ready to put him in a strait jacket and take him away. Why had he thought the truth was going to help? Brian must be sticking to his idea of disturbing a break-in.

"It's true," he exclaimed.

"Dexter, lock him up till he is ready to corroborate his story with Brian's, this is a waste of police time!" The sergeant swivelled on one foot and marched purposefully to the door, opened it and slammed it behind him theatrically.

The empty room rang like a bell and the door rattled in the frame, causing flakes of plaster to dislodge and fall as dust to the floor. Dexter brushed off his jacket and hair with his hand, sighed and gestured to Charlie, who stood and was escorted back to his cell. Charlie protested to him that he was telling the truth but Dexter said nothing as he guided him by the arm along the corridor.

5

Having a Ball

Holeford Secondary Modern School was a typical 1950's functional school building. Long and low, built of red brick with big Georgian style windows which allowed plenty of light in, and in return were good for looking out of and day dreaming whilst lessons were being conducted. It was surrounded on three sides by playground, tennis courts and a sports field with the fourth side reserved as a staff car park.

Theirs was not the raggle-taggle mess of old wooden huts and inadequate brick-built class rooms with assembly hall of the much older, rival grammar school next door. Its pupils and staff had to cavort all over the town using other, not necessarily functional, buildings for art, domestic science and PE. The pupils could regularly be seen running around the town to and from lessons whilst the rain lashed down splashing their trousers and tights with mud. Art work got ruined and an occasional stew got upturned onto the pavement on its way back from domestic science – much to the delight of the local wildlife. Time was wasted on these inconvenient trips along with the disruption of putting outside coats on and off. How they managed to still produce good exam results was beyond the comprehension of the headmaster of the modern school, who himself often struggled to get his pupils to attend, despite the more up to date facilities they enjoyed.

The school term was nearly over and the long summer holiday beckoned. English and history teacher Carolyn Jenner had worked at the school for nearly ten years. She was now in her mid-thirties, tall and slim with dark bobbed hair, she had a pale complexion from spending most of her time indoors. She was well respected amongst her peers and was dedicated to trying to instil a love of their native language and history to her charges. Despite several romantic attachments she was single and living at home with her retired mother. One of the reasons she stayed at Holeford Modern was due to her family tie with the town. Staying with mum saved her money, as her salary was not enough to allow her to buy a home of her own but she was able to save a little every month and hoped in the future to be able to buy a small flat or house in the newly built Apollo Park. She had, occasionally, considered getting a transfer and moving to a bigger school elsewhere but, truth to tell, she liked the town and knew her mother liked having her around too.

Carolyn's dad had died when he was only fifty-eight and they both missed him terribly. He used to spoil her, while her mum used to be the disciplinarian but now seemed increasingly less confident and relied more on her. She had no burning ambition except to enjoy her work, which, in the main she did. She had seen stories in the national press and in the union newsletters that came periodically, of teachers in inner cities getting abused by their pupils or being so harassed that they had nervous breakdowns and never worked again.

At least things like that didn't happen at Holeford Modern... at least not yet and hopefully they never would. Maybe one day she would find something more challenging which would spark her ambition and interest but she was content for now.

Her favourite thing was her beloved pale blue Vespa scooter which freed her from the hassle of relying on the infrequent rural public transport system or lifts from the few friends and colleagues who could afford a car. It also allowed her to escape the confines of home and allow her to explore the local area. With her white helmet, goggles and leather gloves she loved nothing more than buzzing around the country lanes at the weekend or popping down to the nearby coast. She would visit relations, meet up with friends or just go for a spin for the hell of it.

The previous weekend the school had held its most successful fete ever as it continued to raise money for a new swimming pool. The original pool had sprung a leak and it was not economic to repair it. Most of the pupils were not sorry, as it was outside and not heated. There was no pleasure in jumping into freezing water, trying to learn to swim whilst the cold was draining away the will to live, let alone make it to the other end of the pool. As in all these things there was the exception. Up until recently leaving the school, Joe Bonfield had risen to become swimming champion and had a successful period competing in the county championships, returning with some silver ware which sat proudly in the display cabinet outside the headmaster's office. Carolyn had her own method of successfully raising money at the fete.

Two years previously she had been looking through the attic at home to find items suitable for the white elephant stall. This consisted of old clothes, a suitcase full of her toys and a cardboard box full of old china carefully wrapped in newspapers to protect it, all of which were still there from when her family moved into this house in 1957. She knew this from the date printed at the top of the Holeford Evening Chronicle carefully placed in the top of the box. All now yellow with time but a fascinating read nonetheless. The papers were a window into a time more innocent and apparently more formal too as all the people in the photographs were wearing suits, ties and hats, even at the funfair and on the beach! This was before the Beatles, flower power and glam rock. The TV was only on for a few hours a day and radio still remained as the main source of news and entertainment in most households.

Amongst the dusty containers in the roof Carolyn found an elaborately decorated wooden box. It was not much bigger than a large shoe box but was very heavy. She carefully brought it down from the loft along with the items for the stall. The box was very dirty but she could see floral patterns and strange entwined symbols on all its sides.

With a damp cloth she wiped the surfaces clean, revealing brightly inlaid veneers, brass and mother of pearl all skilfully turned into roses, orchids, and other exotic flowers all amongst and bordered by strange twisting and weaving shapes and patterns.It was beautiful; she could only wonder why her mother had left it in the loft and why she had never seen it before.

"Mum, what's this box?"

Carolyn's mother Monica entered from the kitchen wearing a flour-dusted apron. "Is that old thing still about? I thought we had lost it years ago," she said unconvincingly.

"What is it?" Carolyn repeated, now getting more curious.

"Press the brass compass in the centre of the panel and it should open."

Carolyn did so and the top of the box dutifully clicked open. She lifted the hinged lid and looked inside. There was a silk scarf also exquisitely decorated with the same motifs as the box. She carefully lifted it out and held it up to the window expecting it to be full of holes and stains from its years of neglect in the roof. But no, it was in a beautiful condition as if it had just been made. It was as light as gossamer, made of the finest silk with bright and vibrant colours showing off the floral patterns of stemmed intertwined roses and images of assorted symbols. She could make out a ships wheel, the compass again just like the front of the box, and other shapes which she assumed must indicate the signs of the zodiac.

She carefully placed the scarf on the back of the chair and looked into the box. It was no wonder it was so heavy for inside was a large glass ball about the size of a large grapefruit. She carefully lifted it out whilst Monica came back from the living room with a cushion to place it on.

"Mum, is this a crystal ball like you see in the films, you know like gypsies use to look into the future? It's beautiful!" The light from the windows radiated rainbow colours around the room from the perfectly spherical crystal globe.

"Your great grandmother was a traveller and used it to tell fortunes at county fairs to earn a living. They say she was truly gifted but I think it was just a family myth."

"Can I borrow it? I have a great idea to raise money for the school swimming pool. I could pretend to tell peoples fortunes. What do you think?" Carolyn asked excitedly.

Monica looked apprehensive. "No, I don't think so, dear. You shouldn't dabble in things like that. You don't know where it might lead. We had better put the old thing back up in the roof again, for safety and peace of mind."

"Oh, come on, Mum," cajoled Carolyn. "It would be great fun. I could use my acting skills to great effect and it would be more enjoyable than just selling draw tickets. It's for a good cause, after all and part of my job as a teacher is to do my part raising some money and at the moment, I haven't thought of anything else."

"Well, I suppose it'll be alright but you must be careful with it, and when you have finished put it straight back where you found it. Don't leave it out on display. You might catch the curtains alight if it magnifies the sun's rays."

Carolyn laughed. "So that's why fortune tellers always sit in a dark room or caravan, to prevent fires!"

Over the next few days Carolyn's imagination went into overdrive with ideas for the script and how she could dress, where she could 'perform'. She quickly made some notes whilst they were fresh in her mind. Then, when she was ready, she pitched the idea to the headmaster.

"What a novel idea!" he exclaimed and she was officially an added 'attraction'. The Art Department was duly tasked with making decorations and signs to adorn the new caravan that he and his wife had recently acquired.

The head, Mr Wade, was proud of his Eldis four-berth caravan and took no little joy from being able to show it off at any opportunity. Soon the school was to break up for the summer and he could start his three-week tour of Wales with his wife Edith and their two children but in the meantime, everyone could see it and marvel at how well he had done to acquire such a vehicle. He brought it to the school on the morning of the fete and positioned it by the edge of the field in the car park close to the tea and beer tents where it would be seen by all. A perfect spot to attract the thirsty parents and excited children. It looked wonderful. The door to the van was held back and over the opening draped a dark blue curtain decorated with the moon and stars. Above was a sign written in the style of a travelling circus, 'Gypsy Carolyn Fortune Teller'.

Inside, the cupboards and cooker had also been disguised with decorated curtains and the blinds to the windows drawn to create a suitably subdued and mystical light. Carolyn had written several scripts by cribbing ideas from the astrology columns in the papers and cobbling together very loose but convincing nonsense to entertain and impress her clients. *'Cross my palm with sliver', 'You'll meet a tall dark handsome stranger', 'You're going on a long journey'*, etc. All harmless fun.

Amongst the clothes she found in the roof was a long dark floral dress which coupled with the scarf, lots of bangles and several necklaces gave her the appearance of a gypsy.

It was strange though, the glass ball, although perfectly round, when placed on any surface stayed perfectly stable. No matter which way up it was put down, it would sit there gyroscope still, but it didn't look right without a pad under it and she needed to be careful she wasn't responsible for scratching a family heirloom. Therefore, the cushion from the sofa in the caravan, which she had thought of using, was replaced with a red velvet one made by Miss Baker in the needlework class. It was now in pride of place on the table with the ball resting carefully upon it.

The 1973 fete was a huge success. The weather was warm and sunny and all the arena events were well attended. The coconut shy, bric-a-brac, tombola, dunk the vicar, guess the weight of the cake etc. all reported a good days trading. The cake stall and the ice cream man ran out of stock and both had to close early. The tea tent adorned with flags was happy to pick up their trade instead. The red and white striped beer tent was profitable and very welcome, despite one of the parents having a little too much. Mr Wade soon dealt with the incident, escorting the man off the premises with minimal disruption to the proceedings. They had all their efforts well rewarded, raising well over four hundred pounds that first year towards the pool.

Carolyn was astonished at how well received her novelty act had been. Quiet at first but by the end of the afternoon there was a queue gathering outside and an anxious Mr Wade stood by his caravan acting as doorman in order to protect his new acquisition. The scripts she had written helped her with the first half a dozen clients but she wasn't prepared for the number of visitors.

After the first hour she stopped for a cup of tea as her voice was beginning to dry up and she needed refreshment and time to think up some more lines. When she started again it all seemed so much easier and she was enjoying making up new fortunes to tell. Somehow by looking into the crystal ball, shapes would form caused by the trick of the light and give her new ideas. However, she still ensured all the predictions were very loose, although strangely, sometimes she felt something else pop into her head but decided anything unscripted and out of the ordinary was best kept to herself. It was exhausting but rewarding and she was on a high when the day finished. The adrenalin from her acting and the response from her customers had given her a real buzz. She left the caravan which Mr Wade then immediately secured after having carefully checked for scratches. He then joined Carolyn and her mother for a well-earned drink in the beer tent to toast their success.

Back to June 1975…

This year was no different, it had again been a huge success. Gypsy Carolyn was more popular than ever, gaining in confidence and no longer needing scripts; it just flowed naturally. Some customers even asked if she did private readings! Maybe she had inherited some of her great grandmother's powers!

The school term was nearly over. However Carolyn had something she wanted to try over the school holidays and she had an idea how to achieve it.

It was the end of the history class, the bell had rung and the children were packing their bags ready to move onto their next lesson.

"Leave quietly and don't run in the corridors," instructed Carolyn in time worn fashion. The classmates had heard it a thousand times before and ignored the direction immediately they were in the hallway. "Molly Goodall, please stay behind. I want to talk to you in private."

Molly anxiously looked around as if Carolyn was talking to someone else. She certainly wasn't. As they hurriedly left the room all the other pupils looked back at her and speculated amongst themselves on what terrible crime Molly had committed. She apprehensively walked up to the teacher's desk which was mounted on a raised solid oak podium with oak panelling to three sides. The desk had an ink stained top with a hole where the inkwell had historically been sited. The desk stood like the keep of a castle, the last bastion of security when all order had collapsed in the classroom. She looked up at Miss Jenner who stood some three feet taller, due to the height of the platform above the classroom floor, like a judge about to pass sentence. The sun was beaming through the adjacent window so that her frame was silhouetted against the blackboard mounted on the wall behind her. Molly could not make out her expression as the light was creating too much shadow but with her hair in a tight bun and wearing a severely cut suit she looked formidable.

"Yes miss?" she asked timidly.

"Molly, I have to ask you about your homework on the Kings and Queens of England. It's exceptional and very originally written. How did you manage to achieve such detail? It goes beyond the text books we've been working from and I didn't notice you in the library doing research".

Molly felt she was being interrogated. She had help right enough but not from books. It was George and Wilf who had given her a dramatic insight into some of the royal characters, having played them on stage many times. Joe had also given her some tips. He was surprisingly knowledgeable on the subject. However, Molly could not admit any of this. "Oh, well I spent a lot of time reading about them while waiting for Mum in the shop," she quickly improvised.

"Well, it's exceptional and you're to be rewarded with the school prize for history this year. Congratulations!"

Molly now felt as tall as Miss Jenner. She had never won a school prize before. Carolyn moved off the podium down to her level and shook her hand. Molly's apprehension melted away as she saw her warm smile, illuminated by the light from the window.

"On another subject, Price Low has been in the paper a lot lately following the break-in. I know your mum works there, is Jack Bonfield still the manager?"

"Yes," said a puzzled Molly. "Why?"

"I taught his son Joe, he was a bright child. I expect he has gone on to great things, is he at university or college? Do you ever hear about him?"

"I see him most days when I am in the shop, he stacks the shelves and gathers the shopping trolleys," she replied, a little puzzled. Was Miss Jenner talking about the same Joe Bonfield? It's true he had been helpful with her homework on several occasions but he didn't appear to be the exceptional pupil that was being discussed now.

"Stacking shelves! I must be slacking, I had no idea. That's no way for a young man with his potential to develop!" Carolyn was shocked. "Thanks, Molly, you've been a great help, I think I need to pay Price Low a visit. You'll receive a special invitation to the end of term prize-giving along with your parents, where the mayor will present you with a certificate and book token." Carolyn shook her hand again and Molly left the room to be greeted by several of her class mates in the corridor who were eager to find out what she had done.

Carolyn was already thinking about Price Low. Good, she thought, this was just the opportunity she needed to go and see the manager. The next afternoon she had a free period. It only took ten minutes to walk to the store, where she bought the evening paper and a bag of dolly mixtures. As it happened, she was served by Molly's mum. This was a sheer coincidence but perfect for her scheme.

"You must be very proud of Molly," said Carolyn. "She's done some very good work".

Joan's face lit up with pride as she recognised Miss Jenner, and reached out to shake her hand.

"Oh, yes we are, and we're looking forward to coming to the prize-giving. To think we have a genius in the family, I don't know where she gets it from!"

"I thought I might see Joe Bonfield here," continued Carolyn looking around the store. "I used to teach him and understand he works here?"

"It's Joe's afternoon off. He'll be out on his bike I expect."

"Is his father working today? I'd like to see him, if I could."

"He's in the office; hang on I'll lock the till and show you the way." With that Joan swiftly closed her till. The other two tills would be able to cope for five minutes. She led the way to the manager's office via the staffroom. They had to negotiate around a pair of steps and avoid the drums of cable and boxes on the floor. "Sorry about this, please be careful. The electricians are fitting a new alarm system following the break-in. They must've gone for their lunch. It's a pity they can't be tidier!" she added crossly." Joan knocked on the door and entered. "Jack, I have Carolyn Jenner here to see you."

Jack looked up from his paperwork and frowned. "I'm expecting a new rep but she's early."

Joan looked confused. "She's not a rep, Jack."

Carolyn overheard the conversation and felt uncomfortable. "Don't worry Joan, if he's busy… it was just on the off-chance."

Jack heard the voice and was intrigued. "Please come in." Joan beckoned Carolyn into the office. He stood up, moved to the front of his desk and held out his hand. "Good afternoon," he said. He shook Carolyn's hand and then offered her a seat. "Joan, could you please bring two teas and see if you can find some biscuits?" Without taking his eyes off of Carolyn, he moved back to his side of the desk. Joan left the room leaving the door ajar.

"Your face is familiar. Are you from Percy's Potted Meats? No hang on, I've got it, Firkins' Frozen Fish," he said, pleased with himself.

Carolyn smiled. Jack was not how she remembered him from a parent's evenings two years before. He now seemed more relaxed and friendly, the stiffness and reluctance to engage had gone. He was smartly dressed, clean shaven and hopefully would be receptive to her proposal. "No, Mr Bonfield, you've got it wrong."

"Call me Jack."

"Jack," she continued "I'm from Holeford Modern School."

Jack went red in the face. "Oh God, I'm so sorry, I thought you were a sales rep. How embarrassing. Let me think… Carolyn Jenner," he paused thoughtfully and scratched his head. At that moment Joan returned with two cups of tea and a saucer with a mixture of bourbon and digestive biscuits. "Do you take sugar?" Joan enquired.

"No, thank you," replied Carolyn. There was an air of tension in the room which was suddenly broken by an animated Jack Bonfield.

"I have it!" he cried. "You taught Joe geography. There you are, I never forget a face!" he looked very pleased with himself.

Carolyn laughed, nearly spilling her tea.

"That's close, I did teach Joe but it was English and history."

"I'm sorry, I shouldn't try and guess, I'm not very good at it. Now what can I do for you? I'm afraid, if you are looking for school sponsorship that will not be possible. Our MD, Finbarr Lowe, has frozen all charitable support for the foreseeable future."

"No, that's not the reason for my visit. I'm after a more personal favour," replied Carolyn. "You may remember when we held the school fete, I did fortune telling in the head's caravan by the beer tent."

Jacks eyes now opened wide as he remembered in detail the events of the school fete two years previously.

"Gypsy Carolyn," he recalled. "Yes, well, I can only apologise for my behaviour in the bar that day, I'd just received some devastating news and rather let myself down."

Carolyn looked puzzled. "I'm sure I don't know what you're talking about, I can't recall any disturbance."

Jack blushed with embarrassment. "There I go again, making assumptions. I'm sorry. Please how can I help you?"

"I've read a lot about the break-in and the stories about spirits haunting the store and even a theory that they were responsible for the capture of the villains."

Jack sighed, "We've had several cranks and weirdos coming into the store claiming all sorts of strange sensations in here and offering to rid us of the ghosts, please tell me you're not one of those. You're far too respectable to be involved in that sort of goings on."

Carolyn tried to reassure him and explained about the fortune telling and the crystal ball then came to the point of her visit. "I wondered if you might allow me to spend an evening in the store to see if my powers go any further?" she asked, hopefully.

"Well, I understand your interest but I'm not sure you should be doing things like this. It's one thing having a side show at a fete and quite another trying to contact the spirit world." Jack finished his tea as they sat in silence. He studied Carolyn thoughtfully. *She was attractive and intelligent but here she was in his office asking to talk to dead people! What a shame. She certainly hadn't seemed like the others that had made similar requests and there was an innocence about her that he liked. So unlike a lot of the women he met.* Outside the office there were loud voices and the sound of a drill starting up; the electricians had returned.

Jack walked across the office and gently closed the door. "Sorry, we've got the electricians fitting the new alarm. Now where were we? I must admit this is not what I was expecting today. You're asking a lot of me, you know, to trust you with my store overnight. It's not something to be entered into lightly. You have no experience of what might happen, if anything, or how you'll react to things that go bump in the night." He was rather hoping this would put her off as he was not sure that this was something he wanted to get involved with. It was all a bit weird and he did not like to think what head office would say if they got wind of it.

Although a part of him was reluctant to disappoint her. He went silent and scratched his head.

"Are you saying no?" Carolyn looked disappointed, looking over her spectacles deep into Jack's brown eyes. "I hoped that you had more of an open and enquiring mind than some of the people around here. I'm sorry to find out I was wrong."

Jack became aware he appeared provincial and dull to this attractive lady and found himself regretting his hesitation. "Not necessarily," he replied. Mesmerised by her blue eyes he reconsidered. "Yes, why not?" the words just somehow fell out of his mouth. *'I've just agreed to this stupid idea,'* thought Jack. *'I must be mad. What's come over me?'* But it was too late to back down now. He could see she was thrilled and he hadn't the heart to disappoint her again.

"Thank you so much… When can I come?" Carolyn was hardly able to contain her enthusiasm. She had thought this was a complete shot in the dark and not for one minute did she think Jack would agree. To think she nearly walked past the shop too nervous to enter for the fear of refusal!

Jack opened his desk diary and ran a finger down the page studying the appointments.

"Well, how about Saturday the fifth? The store will close at seven."

"That's perfect, the last day of term is that Friday."

"Very well then," Jack made a note in the diary "If you meet me here at six-thirty we can get you settled in before closing." He thought he may as well get this whole ridiculous thing over and done with as soon as possible.

Carolyn stood up and held her hand out to him, determined to go quickly before he could change his mind. Jack stood and they shook hands, the event had been secured.

"I hope you know what you're doing Carolyn."

"So do I, and thank you again for this opportunity… and the cup of tea," she added as an afterthought. "See you on the fifth!" She turned and headed out of the office resisting the impulse to do a little skip.

Jack closed the door and sat down again. *'Oh boy, what have I done?'* he groaned, not quite understanding what had come over him to agree to such a ridiculous idea.

There was a knock at the door and Joan entered. "Shall I clear the cups? Isn't Carolyn nice? She's teaching Molly at the moment, she's done really well, won the school prize you know, we're ever so proud of her."

Jack looked up in a bit of a daze. "Yes, thank you Joan. School prize, eh? Very good." His mind was elsewhere at that moment in time.

One week later…

Thursday the 3rd of July was the evening of the school prize giving, held on the day before the end of term to ensure all the teacher, staff, pupils and parents were available before they started their summer holidays. It was a warm summer's evening as they all gathered in the assembly hall and the doors to the playground were left open to give plenty of ventilation. On the stage the headmaster introduced his staff and congratulated all the invited pupils on their outstanding achievements and told the parents about some of the activities that had taken place. The mayor, the Right Honourable Mr Mane, was invited to say a few words and then proceeded to hand out the book tokens to each individual as they climbed the steps onto the stage. He whispered congratulations to each of them which sounded increasingly insincere as each pupil came onto the stage to receive them.

This was then followed by an informal cheese and wine party offering the chance for the parents to mingle with the teachers. It also gave an opportunity for the teachers to drum up support for the next year's activities. The proud parents were so full of enthusiasm that they willingly volunteered to help at the fete, to assist with the outward-bound trips, take on carnival float duties and help backstage at the school play. The more help they could muster the less out of hours work the staff would have to do in the coming term. The parents were high on the success of their offspring and in the euphoria were vulnerable to persuasion. They would lament over the true measure of their generosity when the elation and the effect of the wine subsided.

The next day was the last day of term. The walls of the hallways were free of displays until the new term, the pin boards had been emptied awaiting a fresh display for next terms events and news and the sounds of shoes squeaking on the freshly polished lino echoed around the passages.

After the prize-giving of the previous evening Molly seemed to feel a closer bond to Carolyn. They met walking down the corridor and Carolyn confided in her that she had been to see Jack. This was not news to Molly, as her mum had told her all about it and the strange disposition that had befallen Jack after their meeting.

Carolyn went a step further and told her in confidence of her plan to try and contact the now legendary ghosts within the shop.

"You don't seriously believe they could possibly exist, miss?" she casually replied, while inside she was thinking, '*I have to tell them they're going to have a visitor and that they must behave themselves just in case Miss Jenner is able to sense them in some way.*' "Well good luck Miss, have a nice holiday," she threw back at her as she hurried out of the now sparse, unadorned school corridor.

Molly had never run so fast in her life. When she got to the store she was out of breath.

Joan saw her from across the fruit counter as she charged breathlessly into the shop.

"Whatever's the matter, you look exhausted. Are you being chased by a tiger?"

"No, I just have some homework to finish before I can start my holiday," Molly said between deep breaths.

"Homework? But I thought you'd broken up today?" quizzed Joan.

"Yes I have, sort of, but Miss Jenner needs some help with her history project," Molly fibbed. Well, it wasn't exactly a lie, thought Molly. It could certainly have an effect on Carolyn Jenner's history if she was able to contact George, Wilf and Alice.

She entered the stock room carrying her satchel for effect, she had no intention of getting any books out. She closed the door quietly behind her, checking she was not being followed.

"Alice," she whispered. "Alice, can you hear me? I need to talk to you now, urgently!"

6

Time to go

Montgomery sat in his office at the end of a challenging week. The lino-floored room was a mass of desks and filing cabinets. Its pale green walls mostly hidden by incident boards and police notices. It had a distinct smell of a public building; disinfectant and books. He was mulling over the situation of Brian and Charlie. He stood up and looked out of the large iron-framed window, turning his back on the pile of paperwork on his dishevelled desk. He hated office work. He was here to catch criminals and put them behind bars or give the orders and watch the constables actually apprehend them and deal with any punches that came their way.

Outside it was an overcast afternoon; '*a depressing afternoon*', he thought, as he looked down onto the grassy area surrounded by high walls with the houses beyond separated from the police station grounds by the cutting of the railway line. It made a formidable defence to the rear of the estate, but this was not a fortress. To the right lay open ground bordered by mature trees that formed the corner of an area of common land. The smoke from a bonfire in one of the gardens of the houses opposite hung in the still air as he thought carefully about the Price Low robbery. Below him the dog team were taking a new recruit through its paces on the obstacle course set out on the lawn that resembled a miniature show jumping ring with the trainer encouraging the enthusiastic young Alsatian to jump the fences and come to heel with the reward of a biscuit. He wasn't as hopeless as some of the young dogs he'd seen but he had a long way to go before he would be successfully bringing down a criminal. Mesmerised by the activity below Montgomery's mind was beginning to wander. '*Back to work*,' he thought, chastising himself for being distracted.

The only thing actually stolen in the robbery was the car and although he was convinced that the two brothers were intent on stealing the money from the safe they hadn't, in fact, left the grounds of Price Low with anything. *OK, the money was in the car along with some wine and several tins of beans but it hadn't been driven away. The shop was a real mess, though, as if there had been a drunken party in there or they had been chased by one of his dogs. Why would they waste time messing up the store? They had the money. Why hadn't they just made their getaway? It didn't make sense. But Brian had to be telling him a pack of lies. There was no evidence of the other burglars that he is suggesting they disturbed, no footprints or fingerprints, nothing that convinced him there was anyone else in the store that evening but the two of them.*

Now, Charlie was a different kettle of fish. He was living in a fantasy world. He professed to be telling the truth and every time he was interviewed the story remained exactly the same. All the disruption to the store, the scratches on the floor from the sliding freezer cabinet, the carpet of frozen peas, the damaged tin of beans he claims hit him on the head, they all made sense in his story. There is no doubt that he also made the phone call. His fingerprints were all over the receiver by the tills and the telephone records also confirmed the time and duration of the call to the emergency services. However, the ghosts of pirates, policemen and a young lady causing the chaos and forcing them to contact the police was just too much. If this went to trial, he would be laughed out of court and spend his remaining years back pounding the beat and he had no intention of doing that. He wanted to see out his career in a senior position with a nice fat pension at the end of it. The papers had already had a field day with the stories that had leaked from the station and it had also attracted interest far and wide from some of the odder members of society.

Price Low weren't complaining though. Jack Bonfield had bragged to him that their takings had rocketed since the incident. Now wait, that's a thought. *Perhaps it had all been planned as a publicity stunt and he was being used and taken for a fool. But no, the two brothers he had in custody were not clever enough for a stunt like that and they would have come clean by now.*

Dexter entered the room. "Afternoon, Sarg. Do you want a cup of tea?" he enquired.

Montgomery turned from the window and looked back into the room across the desk towards his colleague. '*Let's see what we can stir up*,' he thought. "I've made a decision, Dexter. Get Charlie Clarke into the interview room. I want another word with him. Oh, and get his belongings taken along to the front desk, he'll be needing them very soon. But first, yes, tea please and two sugars. Oh, and see if you can find some of those nice garibaldis we had yesterday. I have a particular liking for them. Come to think of it, so did Charlie, so bring him a couple with a nice cup of sweet tea," He grinned as he said this, looking rather pleased with himself. He was up to something, thought Dexter as he left the room.

Half an hour later Montgomery entered the interview room clutching his cup of half-drunk tea and with a few biscuit crumbs scattered on his otherwise spotless suit. He was followed by Dexter who was also clutching two cups of tea and a plate with three Garibaldis on.

Charlie was sitting despondently in the now familiar chair, prepared for yet another cross examination. He looked into the mirror opposite. He looked older than when he had first seen his image in that glass a few days earlier. He also looked tired, there seemed to be more lines around his eyes and was that a few grey hairs? *When will this ever end?* he thought. I wish I had never agreed to help Brian. The criminal big time was not for him. He had made a decision. He was going to get a proper job after this. Being a simple, honest electrician was just what he needed after this experience and his mum would be relieved. He had worried her enough. To his surprise Dexter placed a cup of tea in front of him and offered him a biscuit.

"Now my lad," Montgomery commenced, with his faux cockney accent in full flow. "You're a bit of an enigma to me, you know. Your story, which you so convincingly tell, is nothing but a fantasy. However, I believe it to be your version of the truth which leaves me with two choices; one: do I get you sectioned under the mental health act, or two: do I let you go home. What do you think, constable?" He turned and looked enquiringly at Dexter.

"Well, Sarg, I…"

But before he could continue Montgomery held up his hand to interrupt him. He turned and looked in the mirror, with Charlie reflected behind him, he spoke as if the men in the imaginary room could see and hear all the proceedings.

After a long pause he turned back and leant on the desk close to Charlie. "I'm going to let you go," he stated, somewhat surprising the other two in the room.

Charlie nearly choked on his tea. He could not believe it. "Thank you," he spluttered as tears of joy and relief started to run down his grubby face.

"On the understanding that you don't leave Holeford and you report to the station once a week until further notice. PC Dexter will fill you in with the procedure."

"Brian?" Charlie managed to say at last and with some concern. "What about Brian?"

"Ah, I'm afraid he'll remain here whilst we continue with our enquiries. We've solid evidence of the car theft and tampering with the safe and due to his fingerprints being found at the scene we can definitely lay those crimes at his door. Now get this waster out of here before I change my mind, Dexter. Take him to the front desk where his belongings are waiting." With that Montgomery strutted out of the room relieved to get this story telling idiot out of the station. He certainly hadn't relished the idea of all the paperwork entailed to get him sectioned. It was now time to pursue a new line of enquiry.

Charlie swigged back the remaining tea and walked out of the room accompanied by the constable. He took one last look at the large mirror and was convinced he could see two men moving on the other side.

Half an hour later he was outside breathing fresh air, his few belongings contained in a brown paper bag. The world seemed so big and bright and smelt so fresh. He just wanted to run and shout at the top of his voice. *Freedom is a wonderful thing*, he thought, as he watched people going about their normal lives. They had no idea how it felt to be incarcerated. He walked into the town with a huge grin on his face. '*Please God, don't ever let me end up in a place like that for a second time*.' Again the tears welled up in his eyes. *Time for a Mars bar then home*, he thought, and this time I am paying cash for it. He stopped for a moment looking at the barred windows high up on the police station and sighed. He wished he could buy one for Brian, too.

7

Is anybody there?

Despite all the activity of the final days of the term and with all the excitement of breaking up for the summer holiday, Carolyn's mind was on one thing. Tonight's experimental séance. She was having butterflies as she mentally prepared for the evening. It felt like she was backstage waiting for her entrance in the School play, nerves and excitement all contributing to a physical feeling in the pit of the stomach.

Had she done the right thing?

How does the crystal ball work?

Would it work?

What on earth was she thinking?

Could she stay awake?

How dark would it be?

What if the burglars came back?

She wished she had asked someone to go with her. She tried to keep her mind off the subject by planning the next terms projects and tidying up her paper work from last year. She had some new reference material to read and had arranged to visit Stratford-upon-Avon during the holidays and see a play at the Royal Shakespeare theatre with her long-time friend and fellow teacher Isabella Constansa. She loved Stratford. It was touristy, but in a nice way and she never got over the excitement of taking her seat for the start of a production in the hallowed theatre.

Carolyn's mother, Monica, was very concerned what she was getting in to with potential dangers of the occult. It brought back to her stories of poverty and immorality that her mother had told to her. She thought of her ancestors who had travelled from Eastern Europe to escape persecution and find a new home and freedom in England at the turn of the century. They had lived through troubled times earning a living at travelling fairs and seasonal farm work. The generations had come a long way from those dark days, evolving into accepted members of society. She was worried for her daughter. She wished that she had sold that bloomin' crystal ball when she had the opportunity years before. "You shouldn't meddle in things you don't understand," she warned.

But despite those warnings Carolyn was determined to carry out the experiment. She felt she may have some kind of flair for this sort of thing. She had always thought of herself as '*ordinary*'. There was nothing wrong with '*ordinary*,' an awful lot of people are and they seem to lead perfectly happy lives. But truth to tell, she rather hoped she did have an extraordinary gift. The very thought of it gave her a warm feeling. She knew her mother was unhappy about her discovery of the ball in the loft, and she seemed increasingly alarmed about her apparent inherited affinity with it. Carolyn didn't want to upset her but something inside was driving her on to discover more about the object. Monica wouldn't tell her the full history of it. *Was it so terrible that she couldn't speak of it? In which case why was the ball still in her possession?* So many questions. She only hoped she could handle whatever and whoever might happen!

At six-thirty on Saturday she arrived at Price Low with a large holdall containing her paraphernalia for the evening. Jack was in the store to meet her, took her heavy sports bag and escorted her directly to his office. The staff were not slow to pick up on the jaunty mood of Jack. He had his best jacket on and what looked like a brand-new tie with Price Low written boldly on the diagonal yellow stripes. He hadn't told anyone about the proposed evening's activities. In fact, he had told all the staff at a briefing just after the robbery on no account to fan the flames of rumour by talking about the haunting stories. This was made more difficult by the fact they were openly selling the mysterious upside down tins of beans that they had acquired from the incident. They all tried their best but it was too tempting not to comment on the subject when confronted by the press or questioned by paranormal investigators desperate for it to be true and happy to buy actual souvenirs from that fateful evening.

They both sat in Jack's office. Joan brought in cups of tea (she knew exactly what was going on as Molly had told her in some detail but she was sworn to secrecy). The large holdall sat on the floor next to Carolyn. She had removed her coat to reveal a long flowing dark blue floral dress. It accentuated her slim figure and gave her a nymph-like quality. Her long hair now hung down over her shoulders framing her face that gave away none of the nerves she was feeling inside. She also noted that Jack seemed different tonight. Maybe it was the aftershave or had he had a new haircut? He wore a well pressed, if old fashioned jacket and was that a new Price Low tie?

"Right then Carolyn, the store will close in about twenty minutes at seven and the staff will all be gone by quarter past. Have you a plan?"

"Err... no, not really, perhaps we could have a look around. I may get a feeling for the best place to set up."

They walked out of the office, through the staffroom and into the store. All the time Carolyn was looking for the best, most comfortable place to sit for the evening rather than what she might consider the more psychically receptive. After all it was going to be a long night.

The staff watched as Jack and Carolyn looked around the store. Joan mentioned to them that Carolyn was researching for a School project for the coming year. This seemed to satisfy their curiosity, they carried on cashing up and preparing for re-opening in the morning. Although why she should want to do this at the beginning of the holidays they couldn't imagine. *Didn't she have a life?* Closing down the store was a well-rehearsed routine and at seven o'clock the doors were locked, tills closed and balanced, all money deposited in the new safe then it was coats on and out the door. Jack wished them all a goodnight and locked the staff exit behind them. They were finally alone.

"I'd like to use the staffroom if you don't mind, Jack." It had a good-sized table with comfortable chairs but not so comfortable that she might fall asleep. "I'll go and get my stuff from your office." She went back into the room and recovered her holdall. She removed the wooden box and opened it. Jack looked in excitedly. She removed the silk scarf to reveal the crystal ball beneath.

"Wow!" exclaimed Jack. "That's beautiful, I've never seen one before. Is it a genuine crystal?"

"I believe so," replied Carolyn. They both gazed in wonderment at the object. She never tired of the excitement of looking into it.

"Well then, perhaps I should've had my fortune told by you at the fete a couple of years ago. It could have saved me a lot of grief."

Carolyn smiled politely but was too distracted by the task in hand to question Jack further on his statement. She took the handmade silk cushion out of her bag and placed it at the end of the table then carefully placed the ball upon it. Then she folded a silk scarf diagonally and put it over her head tying it behind her hair. "I know what you are thinking, it's a bit over the top, but the scarf means a lot to me and I seem to be able to concentrate better while wearing it."

"Not at all, it suits you," Jack replied diplomatically.

"Why, thank you kindly, sir," she replied in a jokey Romany accent.

"Now, are you sure you are going to be OK alone? I'll be back in at six to sort the morning paper delivery."

"Yes, I'll be fine. I have your phone number if I get bored, or want to call it a night."

Jack tidied his office desk ready for Monday and headed for the service door. "The door will be locked from the outside but if you have a problem just push the fire escape bar and it'll open. I've turned off the new alarm system so it won't go off should you want to move around the store. Feel free to help yourself to tea and coffee from the cupboard above the sink, the milk is in the fridge."

Carolyn followed him to the door. "You've been very kind. I can't thank you enough for this opportunity. You must have had quite a few odd requests since the break-in, it was very good of you to agree to mine."

"Not at all. I hope you find what you are looking for, you seem to have a real interest in all this stuff. You know there used to be a theatre on this site, the supermarket is built within its footprint. It burned down in 1955 and three actors lost their lives. That incident has fired the imagination of all sorts of strange types. But you're different, you're not a professional paranormal investigator." He noticed her quizzical look. "Yes, believe it or not such people do exist, they even have business cards!" They both laughed. "Good luck but if you need me at any time, just call."

It was now eight o'clock and the sun was turning a glorious orange as it began its descent towards the horizon.

"I'll leave you to your task. Are you sure you won't be frightened? I can stay here with you, it's no problem. The building can feel strangely unnatural when you are the only person here."

"No, I'll be fine. I think I'll have the best chance of success if I'm on my own, anyway I have your number."

"As long as you are sure." He picked up his briefcase and turned for the door. "This is our little secret. If head office find out, I'll be a laughing stock and the owner, Finbarr Lowe, will have me stacking the shelves."

He gave her a discreet wave and was gone.

She was now alone in the empty store. The echo of the door closing reverberated around the room and then all that could be heard was the gentle hum of the freezer cabinets emanating from the shop floor. Carolyn went to the staffroom and sat there unsure about what to do next. '*Come on,*' she thought, rallying herself. '*I have rehearsed this over and over in my mind for the last week.*' She opened her holdall and pulled out a plain purple velvet table cloth and laid it over the table-top in front of her. "That's better," she said to herself. "Get myself into the ritual." She then repositioned the cushion at the end of the table and, trembling with anticipation, lifted the crystal ball and placed it carefully on top.

'*Now, time for a drink, I think.*' From the bag she produced a flask and poured herself a strong black coffee. This was part of her plan to help stay awake. She'd deliberately napped in the afternoon and was determined to stay alert. There was plenty of time for sleep tomorrow. It would be just her luck to drop off at the exact moment something happened.

In her mind it was still early for anything to kick off so she relaxed with a magazine until the night drew in and a veil was drawn over the daylight. Jack said it was fine for her to wander about, the alarms were off and it might help for her to walk around and keep active. She read the notices on the canteen wall that contained career opportunities, jobs at other branches, safety notices and proposals for the Christmas party. She shook her head, *it was only July for goodness' sake.* She then wandered into the store itself and walked around the aisles which were illuminated only by the blue standby lights of the cold cabinets and the warmer orangey glow of the street lights shining through the windows. '*This is how it must have appeared to those nasty burglars. How can they sleep at night having caused so much damage and disruption, and what of their families? What had it done to them to have their loved ones arrested?*' She shivered at the thought of all the trouble they had caused everyone.

Time was ticking by slowly. Apart from the whoosh of the occasional car driving by and chatter from pedestrians passing near to the store, it was getting distinctly quieter as Holeford settled into its Saturday evening routine. Carolyn kept away from the windows in case she was seen and moved back to the staffroom. She didn't want to be mistaken for another burglar and have her vigil disturbed by police sirens and blue flashing lights. She settled back down at the table, wiped the sweat from her hands and placed them palms down on the table. '*Right, now I'm ready,*' she thought and felt much calmer and focused.

She imagined she must look like the fairground gypsy teller she had been at the fetes and although Jack had been amused by the headscarf, for her it was like putting on a uniform. When she did her fortune-telling she didn't feel properly dressed until it was on. It was important to look the part and for some reason it felt right, it certainly gave her more confidence. *It may be a comfort blanket but it works for me,* she thought defensively, and anyway, Price Low didn't waste heating at night when there were no staff and customers to accommodate. The room was certainly getting distinctly colder now the night was drawing in.

The room was well lit from the overhead fluorescent light. It was too bright and the atmosphere felt all wrong to Carolyn so she stood up, opened the door to Jack's office and turned on his table lamp. She then turned off the staffroom lighting. Immediately the mood changed and she resumed her position at the table, the half-light now created was far superior as the room was now submerged with areas of darkness. She could see the shadow of her seated figure projected against the back wall. From her bag she produced a candle and some matches and placing the former in its holder on the table, she lit it and the scene was complete. The flame flickered and danced, giving an ethereal quality to the mundane room and gave her reflection the appearance of swaying slightly, like a waiflike companion at the table.

George, Wilf and Alice were sitting at the other end of the long canteen table.

"That's a nice scarf," Alice complimented. George looked quizzically at the crystal ball. "Well, she hasn't seen us yet, that's for sure. I thought you said she was a medium?"

"No I didn't. Molly said she was a fortune teller at the local fete and had asked if she could spend the night here to see if she was able to contact the spirit world."

"She's a brave girl" exclaimed Wilf. "Why are you staring at that ball so intently, George?"

"Because my dear fellow, I believe that is a Petrolingo Crystal Ball," George said excitedly.

"What're you talking about?" Wilf replied as Alice looked on, also puzzled.

"I used to trade antiques between acting jobs and specialised in magic and theatrical props. I know my stuff."

"Well, you're a dark horse. I never knew you were a dealer," said Wilf. "But what's a Petrolingo?"

"They're incredibly rare. I've only ever seen one before when I was on tour with 'Charlie's Aunt.' In Delhi, of all places, it was. And, boy was that a hot and tiring tour, let me tell you. Anyway, the legend has it that they were cast from the glass taken from the basilicas of Byzantium following a raid by the Mongol empire."

"Yeah right, pull the other one," Alice said scathingly. She had heard many of his tall tales before but this topped the lot.

"No, I'm serious," George replied earnestly. "This is the Stradivarius of crystal balls, unless I am very much mistaken."

Wilf was unimpressed. "Well, it doesn't work. She has no idea we are here. Look at her. She hasn't a clue. I know what we'll do..."

"Don't you dare make anything move," Alice said quickly interrupting. "If you scare her, Molly will never forgive us," she cautioned.

Carolyn sat gazing hopefully into the ball, unaware of the interest around her. It was now one o'clock in the morning and she had to admit she was getting tired and a bit bored. '*This was a daft idea,*' she thought miserably. '*I must be mad to think just because I told a few fortunes at a side show that I have some sort of gift for contacting the spirit world. I might just as well put this useless bauble away and go home.*' She reached forward and as she touched the globe a dim light appeared deep inside it, like a distant flame. "Funny, I hadn't noticed that before," she said out loud. "It must be from the candle."

"No. Actually, I think it's down to us," George said.

Carolyn, startled, quickly pulled her hand away from the globe as if she had just received an electric shock.

The glow faded as the hairs on the back of her head stood on end and goose pimples rose on her skin. She caught her breath. '*I'm sure I heard a voice,*' she thought. Her mind was in turmoil. "Is that you, Jack? Have you come back to see if I'm OK?" There was silence.

"Oh, for goodness sake," George said crossly. "She's let go! She's never going to contact us if she let's go. Doesn't she know the basics?"

"Wow, did it actually work?" Alice now leaned forward to look closer at the crystal ball.

Carolyn slowly and carefully placed her right hand on the globe and the glow returned.

"Good evening," George said politely.

"G... Good... evening!" Carolyn replied softly.

Wilf and Alice stood with their mouths wide open, flabbergasted at the conversation now taking place in front of them.

George continued to talk in a slow, calm voice so as not to frighten Carolyn. "Molly said you were going to visit us, so... welcome to our humble abode!" He gestured flamboyantly around the room.

Carolyn was feeling tearful. She was not sure if it was joy or fear. She replied in a trembling voice, "Molly told you? You know Molly?"

"Oh yes, she's a good friend. That's a fabulous crystal ball you have there. How did you come by it? Is it yours? You obviously have no idea how to use it, do you?" George questioned.

"N... no not really, although I have told a few fortunes with it as a prop. I found it in the loft."

"Yes, Molly was telling us all about the fetes and how you found it easier and more instinctive as you got used to doing it." George commented.

"Molly's told you a lot!" Carolyn was losing her fear now and feeling more confident. The voice seemed friendly not threatening and the fact that it knew Molly gave her some reassurance.

"Do you trust me now?" George asked.

"I don't know. I mean, well you know Molly, so I suppose so." She was nervous again but her hand remained on the ball.

George signalled to the others to go into the store and leave him with Carolyn, which they did but concealed themselves behind the door where they looked back in at the proceedings.

"Now, all you have to do is place both hands on the globe." George instructed. "It's that easy."

"Well, OK," Carolyn nervously did as instructed and George immediately materialised at the end of the table. Dressed in tweeds, he somewhat took on the appearance of a Sherlock Holmes character, making her jump. "Oh wow!" She took a deep breath and managed to ask, "Are you really a ghost?

"You could say that. I must say you're unusual, you haven't screamed or fainted. That's usually the reaction."

"I'm sorry, it's just that I came here not truly expecting anything," Carolyn continued. "It was a foolish whim, really, I suppose. Just because I told a few fortunes I got the idea I was psychic or something and now, well, here you are!" Carolyn let go of the ball, reached into her bag for a tissue and dried her wet eyes. George immediately disappeared. She quickly put her hands back on the globe and George reappeared exactly where he had been before. "Oops, sorry. That's better I can see you again now."

There was a cough from behind the door to the room and George decided he had better move things on. "As you are at a disadvantage let me introduce myself. I am George Shakespeare. Actor, singer, impresario and player to the royal family. It is now my great pleasure to introduce to you my dearest friends and fellow thespians, first, MR WILF TRUNNION," he announced with a satisfactory air of expectation.

Wilf entered from the store dressed in Elizabethan doublet and hose, with a large ruff collar and floppy felt hat. He executed an exaggerated bow towards Carolyn and in a loud voice, as if addressing a crowd, said, "Good evening, Miss Carolyn, it is truly a pleasure to meet you. I have heard so much about you." As he bowed again his hat fell off which somewhat ruined his entrance and he scrabbled around the floor, retrieved it and plonked it back on his head. He then shimmied sideways to make some space.

George then continued. "And last, but no means least, please welcome the voice of a linnet herself, MISS ALICE BENNETT!"

Alice opened the door wide and pirouetted into the room joining the others at the end of the table. "Hello, Carolyn," she sang.

Carolyn sat, speechless, looking at the three of them, her mouth wide open and hands firmly placed on the globe.

"Now, I know what you're thinking," George began.

"Well, that will be a first," said Wilf. "This could be a whole new mind reading act!" George just glowered back at him.

Carolyn plucked up courage and spoke before George could say any more. "It's true then, you're the actors who died in the theatre fire. I always thought it was just a story. It's been all over the papers since the break-in."

"We are one and the same, my dear. Stars of stage and screen and in recent years, forced retirement in the basement of the theatre. Doomed to walk the aisles of Price Low," replied Wilf in an appropriately melancholy voice.

"Don't be so dramatic, Wilf," Alice interjected. "We chose to stay here. It's quite nice and we can always look at other alternative career prospects in the future."

Carolyn was now very confused. "What do you mean career prospects? No, hang on a minute, while I think about it have you been helping Molly with her homework?"

"Oh, was it that obvious." George looked a little embarrassed.

"Well, she didn't get it all from her books and if you know her so well it does seem plausible."

"Well, we may have given her just a few pointers," interjected Wilf. "But most of it was more earthly than that. Joe's been helping her a lot more than us."

"Does Joe know you as well?" asked Carolyn incredulously.

Alice stepped forward. "No, he has no idea we exist. He is a bright lad but he's not sensitive to us at all. We've spent many hours in his company while helping Molly but he's never once noticed our presence. He's a typical boy!" she finished, somewhat ambiguously.

Carolyn was full of questions. "So what about these career prospects of yours." She swiftly returned to the original subject.

The trio were somewhat taken-aback by the relaxed acceptance from their new-found friend.

"George, do you want to answer that one?" Wilf mischievously asked as he and Alice turned to face him, awaiting the explanation. It was like being interviewed on a chat show but George was up for the challenge and immediately started.

"Thank you, Wilf. When it all happened, we were visited by…"

"The Grim Reaper?" Carolyn interrupted excitedly.

"Well, sort of," George replied, surprised yet again by the easy questioning from Carolyn.

"Eric, that's his real name." Alice jumped in to help. "He's really nice, he wears a black cloak and carries a sickle which at first is a bit unnerving but once you get to know him he's great fun."

"Yes, Eric to his friends," continued George, unimpressed with the continual interruptions. "You see we passed over as a result of an accident which gives us certain options. We are not doomed to walk the earth for an eternity, condemned to the fires of hell or even to go direct to Heaven. It is our choice. We are able to hang around as long as we like and as we three have a bond through our shared experience and are very fond of one another, we have chosen to stay together for the foreseeable future in what is left of our theatre, relax and enjoy the peace."

"But what about the prospects?" Carolyn quickly added before George went off the subject again.

"Ah, yes there are many options, especially as we are actors," George continued proudly.

Alice interrupted enthusiastically, "I want to audition for a place at the Tower of London. It's a great gig and central to visit all the places of interest, and you get to keep pets. I would love that. I had a dog once you know – a little terrier called Ralph – and there's the ravens, of course. But unfortunately it's a popular job and places do not come up very often. The

Bloody Tower is fantastic, we've visited there a few times. Still, you never know, one day…" Alice trailed off with a dreamy, far away expression on her face. "I wonder exactly how many ravens there are. I would have to name them all, of course, but then maybe they already have names. Still, I could rename them. I might call two of them Wilf and George… my favourite ones, of course," she emphasised, looking at her fellow ghosts affectionately.

"Thank you, Alice," said George in a patronising tone. "I'm sure one day you'll be ready to go solo but until then 'we happy band' must stick together. There are lots of other transfer options. We're also able to apply to stately homes, old creaky pubs and hotels, caves, woods, etc. Trouble is most of them are cold and draughty. We haven't heard of anything as nice as this yet. It's warm, cosy, full of memories and we have all our costumes to hand. We can practically be anything we like."

Carolyn got in quickly whilst George paused for breath. Not that he needed to, of course – at least she assumed not. "The papers reported a pirate, policeman and young maid. Was that you?"

Wilf answered. "Alas, yes. I think our cover was blown by that burglar Charlie. He must have been born with the gift of second sight. He saw us all dressed up in our *Pirates of Penzance* costumes from our last production. They're very comfortable and so beautifully tailored for us in London for the West End production. It confused the hell out of Charlie but we couldn't just do nothing and let him and his brother steal from the shop. It did get a little out of hand though, and the police station is not the best place to try and keep a secret. Since then there have been all sorts of clairvoyants, mediums and spiritualists visiting to try and find us. We've had to lie low but it is different with you. Thanks to Molly we were expecting you, although we had no idea you possessed such a magnificent tool and would prove so successful. A genuine Petrolingo Crystal Ball! That's just amazing."

"What's so special about this ball? I found it in the loft. It was my grandmother's. It is very fine with a beautiful box but that's all."

George looked horrified."All? My dear, not so, this is truly a rare thing. There's one way to confirm my suspicions once and for all. Why do you place it on that cushion?" he finished unexpectedly.

"In case it rolls off the table," Carolyn said.

"There's no need to worry about that," George replied. "If you will trust me, I can prove to you the magic it contains."

"What do you want to do?" Carolyn was nervous. She didn't want it to come to any harm.

"It's very simple. We'll stand aside and you push the table up against the wall," George instructed.

"Well OK, I don't see that that'll do any harm." Carolyn pushed the long table across the room until the far end touched the wall. "What now?"

George looked at Alice. "Alice, will you kindly fetch several bails of toilet roll from the shop and place them on the table against the wall?" He then looked over to Carolyn. "You'll like this bit. Alice is a master at levitation, unlike Wilf and myself who are still learning."

"That's right, tell everyone," Wilf scolded.

Alice stared through the door into the shop and slowly several packs of toilet roll floated into the room and landed on the table against the wall. Carolyn, forgetting herself, clapped her hands in appreciation and the trio disappeared.

"Whoops, sorry." She placed her hands on the globe again and they returned.

"Oh, for goodness' sake! You can't keep your hands on the globe for this experiment," George exclaimed.

"Sorry. Then what exactly do I do?" she asked sarcastically. Carolyn felt like she was being told off and it rattled her.

"I'm sorry. You didn't know… there was no need for me to be short with you. The experiment will be pointless anyway if there's not another ball in the box."

"Another ball?" Carolyn questioned. "But there's only room for one."

"I don't think so. Have a look in the box. Is there a small shelf inside where the scarf is usually stored? Under that there should be a false bottom. There should be a velvet ribbon sticking out and if you pull it, the bottom will lift out and inside should be a small sphere about the size of a marble."

Carolyn let go of the crystal ball and lifted the box onto the table. All three of them, although invisible to Carolyn, gathered around watching closely as she followed the instructions. True to George's directions, in the corner, just exposed, was a small ribbon. She managed to tease it out with her fingernail, then pull up the velvet floor revealing a compartment containing a small globe. "That's amazing!" Carolyn was beside herself with excitement. "You're right. It's there, I never noticed that before."

Wilf and Alice were just as impressed. George was turning out to be full of surprises. Why had he never mentioned his antique dealing before?

"Stand back!" George warned Alice and Wilf. "Carolyn is in for a surprise!"

Carolyn lifted out the glass ball with her fingers. The three ghosts suddenly appeared right beside her.

"Oh, gosh!" she exclaimed jumping back. "I didn't expect you to be there."

"Sorry. I wasn't sure if it would work." George was now convinced about its authenticity. "I have only seen this once before. It is a concentrated crystal and saves you having to always use the large ball. There can't be many of them left now. The legend says that only six of these were ever made. If you are truly gifted just having this close to you, say in a pocket, should be sufficient for you to contact to the other side, as it is so crudely called."

"What next?" asked an excited Carolyn.

"Well, it's almost irrelevant now. I think there is no doubt about it but still, perhaps we ought to be sure. Take the ball off the cushion."

Carolyn lifted the ball and Alice carefully removed the cushion.

"Now place it on the table," George instructed.

It now sat on the table-cloth with nothing to prevent it rolling off. Carolyn held her hands close by just in case it started to move. She would never forgive herself if it fell to the floor.

"You have to trust me," George reiterated. The other two held their breath (figuratively speaking). They too had no idea what George was up to and were as excited as Carolyn. "Now, move your hands under the table and lift it so that the ball will roll towards the toilet roll."

Carolyn anxiously did as she was told and lifted the table at first by barely an inch. The ball did not move. She lifted it a little higher until the table was six inches off the floor. By now and by the laws of physics, the ball should have rolled down the table and landed amongst the tissue. It didn't. It just sat there exactly where she had placed it.

"That will do I think," George said smugly.

Carolyn gently lowered the table and stroked the ball with new admiration. The room was silent. They were all awe-struck by what they had just witnessed.

"My dear, not only is THIS a Petrolingo Crystal Ball, YOU also are a Petrolingo descendent. There is no other explanation. No one else could have done that. You are an exceptional person, you know. You have a mystical blood-line and have inherited a tremendous gift." George solemnly bowed to her in reverence. "I suggest you research your family history, it's going to be fascinating."

Carolyn's eyes welled up. "Mum knows something about our family but when I ask her, she changes the subject."

Alice levitated a tissue to her right hand and she wiped away the tears.

"I never imagined this when I came here tonight…" she paused and wiped her eyes again. "I never dreamt such a thing was possible. I felt there was this… something deep inside me when I started the fortune telling. I imagined it was some kind of instinct for it, but not this, not in a million years."

Alice cleared the toilet tissue back into the store and Carolyn slid the table roughly back into place, no longer worrying about the cushion. The ball sat solidly on the table-cloth.

Clunk!

They all heard a car door closing just outside the back door.

"Someone's out there!" Alice exclaimed and looked through the door into the yard. She quickly turned back into the room. "It's Jack, I bet he has come to see if you're OK."

Carolyn looked at the clock on the wall. It was four o'clock. '*Much too early to open up,*' she thought. *He must be wondering why I'm still here.*

There was a metallic sound as Jack turned the key in the door and pushed it open calling out, "Carolyn, are you OK, are you awake? Boy, its dark in here." Jack entered the room wearing a wet mac. It was obviously pouring with rain. "Hi, is everything alright?" he said, seeing Carolyn in the glow of the candle-light.

The three actors looked across at Carolyn, smiled, waved their farewell and appeared to slide across the floor through the door and into the shop. Carolyn did a discreet little side smile and waved back with her hand just above the table-top, obscured by the ball. Her feeling was that this was not goodbye but the beginning of a new adventure.

However the spell was broken for now. "Hello, Jack, I was just beginning to pack up, I'm getting tired now."

"I'm not surprised. Do you know it's four o'clock?" Jack was astonished that she was still wide-awake sitting in the gloomy light.

"Is it really four? I should be going. Why've you come back anyway? It's a bit early to be opening up yet, isn't it?" Carolyn asked.

"Well, yes it is but I was worried about you. Anyway, I am curious.

What happened? Did you see anything? Are you shivering?" Jack could not hold back his curiosity.

"It's just a bit cold in here, it's nothing."

She was expecting questions about her evening, but now was not the time. She was still in a state of shock and hadn't had time to gather her thoughts together. Never in her wildest dreams could she have predicted the events. If she told Jack all that had happened he might believe her or, more likely, think of her as another of the weirdo psychics that have been bothering him, or worse still, just humour her as some neurotic spinster who had to make up things to appear interesting. *'Calm down,' Carolyn thought. Just play it cool.'* She was trembling with excitement but her school training and amateur dramatics would have to help her out now. "Well, it's been very quiet. I thought I sensed something but can't be sure, it may have just been a draught."

She hurriedly started packing away the globe, scarf and newly discovered crystal marble into the box and along with her flask and candle placed them all carefully in her bag. "I've troubled you enough tonight, Jack, I should be getting off home," she said through a well-constructed fake yawn. She wasn't tired at all. In fact, she had never felt so awake. The adrenalin from the meeting and its revelations was coursing through her veins. Jack looked at her sympathetically.

"It must've been a bit of a disappointing evening but I'm going to provide one last service and give you a lift home. It's pouring with rain and you'll get soaked if you walk."

She could see from Jack's coat that it was very wet outside and would welcome a lift home with her valuable cargo. "That's very kind of you." She smiled.

Within five minutes they were on their way, sat in the warmth of Jack's green Austin Allegro. "I hoped to see Joe when I came to the store the other day," Carolyn said diverting the conversation from her evening adventure.

"That boy," Jack said wistfully. "He's a mystery to me. I don't know what he's going to make of himself. He's a drifter. After leaving school I was able to give him a job in the store but it's not exactly a career. I tried my best when Fiona left me for that greasy Spanish waiter from the Kings Head but I may have let him down," he reflected.

Carolyn was unprepared for this revelation and couldn't think of the best way to answer. "Well, here we are, thank you for the lift. I would have been drenched. As for Joe, I'd be happy to talk about his prospects but not now. I'm feeling very tired. How about meeting up for coffee and we can discuss this further?" She looked at Jack and smiled encouragingly.

"That would be great. I'll give you a call to arrange something," he replied thoughtfully. This was an unexpected turn of events.

"Never mind calling. I'll meet you in Tony's Café at 1pm next Tuesday to discuss Joe."

Carolyn was on a mission to save Joe from a life of shelf stacking and anyway she was just returning a favour after the evening she had just experienced.

"OK…," Jack was lost for words but the idea pleased him.

"Goodnight or rather good morning," Carolyn said hurriedly as she climbed out of the car and rushed to the shelter of her porch, bag in hand.

The rain was still falling heavily although the morning sun was starting to overwhelm the dark night sky. The puddles took on a luminescence as the light tried to push its way through the grey haze of the rainclouds. As she fumbled to put the key in the lock, she hoped her mother was still asleep. She would be bound to quiz her over breakfast. But what to tell? "Don't forget next Tuesday", she called back to him and opened the door and disappeared inside.

"Good morning!" Jack called back to the dark and empty porch and drove away rather pleased by the turn of the evenings events.

8

Porridge

Brian woke up on his hard bed covered with one blanket, his head resting on a pillow stuffed with gravel, or at least it felt like it.

In his cell only the grey light from the high-level window lit his face. All he could spend his time doing was muse on his situation. Firstly, why didn't they fit curtains in prison cells to make them more homely, after all he hadn't been convicted of anything, well not yet anyway. Secondly why was it always porridge for breakfast? He used to like porridge but now he was sick of the sight of it. What he wouldn't give for a bacon sandwich. The police had worn him down and he had decided it was time for him to tell his true side of the story. After all his 'dear brother' Charlie had and now he was back at home with curtains on all the windows and bacon on his plate. With that, the slot in the door slid open with a metallic clang and a bowl was passed through.

"Breakfast," was the only word to emanate from the corridor but it seemed to reverberate around the sparse room as if sung by a choir of wretched angels. Brian took the red plastic bowl of porridge with blue plastic spoon and then bent down to the slot in the door and addressed the server.

"I want to speak to Sergeant Montgomery."

"I'll see if he's available, sir," the reluctant waiter sarcastically replied and slammed the shutter with enough force to shake loose the flaking paint on the steel door frame.

'*Well, he's not getting a tip*,' Brian thought, looking into yet another grey bowl of gruel, his spoon standing to attention in the emulsified oats.

Several hours later Brian was escorted to the now familiar interview room. He sat staring at the large mirror wondering who was watching this time. The room was cold despite the summer sun now radiating through the window. After ten minutes Sergeant Eric Montgomery entered the room and looked across at the seated Brian.

"This had better be good, sunshine, I've just about had enough of your tall tales and nonsense. I have a mind to throw the book at you regardless and let the courts sort it out." Montgomery resisted the urge to follow up with 'you horrible little man', after all, even he was able to resist a cliché sometimes.

"Well, there was someone else there that night, but I didn't see them," Brian began.

Montgomery sat down opposite him. "OK, well that's better but wait there," with that, as if on cue, PC Dexter entered with a statement form and sat at the end of the table. '*So*,' thought Brian, '*that's who was behind the mirror.*' "Carry on then. I ain't got all day."

"Charlie saw them. They must have been in the shadows. They attacked him and then started throwing stuff at both of us."

"Is this before or after you broke into the safe."

"After," Brian replied, understanding the significance of this confession but going on anyway.

"Now we're getting somewhere. So you admit you were on a blag, you had a fair old bundle in the car." Montgomery smiled and rubbed his hands together with pride, the clichés were now coming quick and fast.

"Charlie said one was a policeman and the other a pirate, I didn't see them so I don't know about that but it was utter chaos. I was pinned down by the paper stand and the door was blocked by the freezer. We were trapped. Charlie had no choice but to call you. That's the truth, honest!"

"Good; you got all that, Dexter?" Montgomery had him. He was singing like a canary.

Dexter lifted the statement form to confirm it was all written down. Montgomery stood up.

"Dexter, I want a word with you in private. Clarke, you stay here and don't try any funny business." He indicated to the mirror implying that he was being watched.

Brian looked into the mirror. He had aged ten years in the last few days. He had all but just confessed to the robbery but he didn't care. He needed to get it off his chest. He felt a weight lift but a new one took its place. He was now going to have to face the consequence of his ill-planned caper. As he looked at his reflection he swore something moved behind the mirror. That must be cheap two-way glass he thought, convinced there were officers looking at him deciding his fate.

On the other side of the wall the Twyford high level cistern made no judgment. At regular intervals it just loyally discharged two gallons of water down its highly polished copper pipe into the porcelain urinal below, causing the aroma of Scandinavian pine forest to be discharged from the disinfectant blocks laying in the gutter. Beyond, PC Shackleton flushed his WC, opened the heavy Formica-clad cubicle door, adjusted his uniform and headed for the wash basins. The door automatically closed behind him causing the room to vibrate slightly.

"There, I heard the door bang," Brian said loudly to the imaginary officers through the mirror. "You must think I'm stupid."

As PC Shackleton left the gents he passed Sergeant Montgomery and PC Dexter in the corridor. They were deep in conversation.

"This is all starting to make sense, Dexter. But it is more serious than I thought," said Montgomery. "It appears there is a vigilante group wearing fancy dress on our streets. We have to stop this now. We can't have the public taking the law into their own hands, it would also appear that at least one of them is impersonating a police officer. That cannot be tolerated. This story more or less fits with his brother's and is far more feasible than the stupid ghost stories that have attracted the attention of the press, psychics and weirdoes with nothing better to do. You get him back to the cell while I go and see the chief!"

At 2 pm Brian was returned to his cell and he lay on the bed going over and over his confession. They would throw the book at him, that's for sure. He may never see his home and family again. '*What an idiot I was,*' he thought. He was not cut out for a career in crime. What had he been thinking? He didn't have to wait long. At 4 pm he was escorted back to the interview room. '*Well, this is it, where will it be? Princetown, Pentonville, Wormwood Scrubs, Alcatraz.*' The names of numerous prisons were rolling around and around in his head. It was making him dizzy and giving him a headache.

Montgomery entered the room, stern faced and ready to give sentence. Or so Brian thought.

"Now then, lad," he began somewhat more friendly than before. "You're not out of the woods yet. Your paw prints are all over the car and the safe. You'll be charged with auto theft and breaking and entering but thanks to your guardian angels, in the eyes of the law you never actually stole any money. It was in the car with the wine and beans but the car didn't leave the premises."

Brian was confused, he could see Montgomery's lips moving but his mind went into overdrive. '*How did the money get into the car? He had left it in the staffroom and Charlie was in the store, he certainly hadn't gone outside with anything. What guardian angels? The policeman and the pirate? Angels certainly hadn't been described like that at Sunday school at All Saints. Not that he always listened that hard to Mrs Pike the Sunday school teacher. He had been too busy flicking bits of screwed up paper at that snooty girl Catherine Miller but he would have certainly remembered hearing something cool like angels looking like pirates. What next? God looking like Elvis? Was he getting off lightly? Who was watching in the other room behind the mirror? Why do they have plastic ash-trays which melt when you stub out your cigarette? Beans, what beans?*

Montgomery banged the ash-tray on the table abruptly, jolting him from his daydream.

"Are you listening to me?" Montgomery shouted. Brian looked up from his daze. "Good there is someone at home," the sergeant said sarcastically. "As I was saying, you are free to go for the present but do not leave town and report to the front desk once a week until further notice. You'll be hearing from the Crown Prosecution Service who will advise you when your preliminary hearing will take place. But one false move and I'll come down on you so hard you'll have to reach up to cut your toenails." He leaned across the table menacingly, emulating his hero Jack Regan. "Do I make myself clear?"

Brian was waking from a nightmare. "Free to go?" he queried.

"Yes, now get out of here, before I change my mind. Dexter, show him the way. His possessions are at the front desk for him to collect." Montgomery was already heading for the door and stomped off down the corridor, on a mission now to stop the vigilantes.

Brian didn't need any further encouragement. He collected his things from the front desk and high-tailed it out of the station before anyone had time to change their mind.

9
The Arrival

The summer holiday had begun and for Molly that meant the chance to join her dad on the milk round. Strangely enough she enjoyed the early mornings. The streets were quiet, the only sound the rhythmic clink of the bottles in the back of Trigger. She also liked seeing the sun rising and feeling it warming the fresh invigorating air of the new day. It also gave her time to spend with her dad. Peter loved having Molly along with him, too, riding shot gun. It gave them time to discuss school, television, the break-in at the shop, where they would like to go on holiday. Just anything that was the topic of the day. Molly would help drop off the milk at the doorsteps and into the corner shops and offices where she had gotten to know a lot of the customers and they welcomed her like a friend. The round was quicker with her help too and he would reward her with extra pocket money at the end of the week. It was a routine they both loved.

As they drove by Price Low at full speed, which amounted to all of four miles an hour, Molly would sometimes see Alice, Wilf or George looking out of the window to see her go by. They would wave at her and she would wave back frantically.

"Why do you always wave at the shop when we go by? You can't like it that much even though Mum works there," Peter asked one morning.

Molly giggled. "Oh, I can see my reflection with me in the cart, it's just fun," she quickly responded.

Peter was sceptical. As they trundled round the streets, Trigger's electric motor whining away under their seat, he would regale Molly of tales of times when he was a stage magician. That was how he had met Joan. Although Molly had heard it many times previously, she never tired of hearing it – it was so romantic.

Joan was a dancer in the chorus during the Ted Ray summer special at the North Pier in Blackpool. 'The Great Avanti' (Peter) was the second act on in the first half between the opening chorus dance and Georgina

Sparrow ('The Nightingale of Worksop'). They were into the second week of a six-week run when Peter's assistant Samantha ran off with the musical director. Without an assistant he couldn't go on. Fortunately Joan had struck up a friendship with them and was familiar with the act. With a short rehearsal she migrated from the chorus to join Peter full-time and by the end of the run they were an item.

"She used to be sawn in half six nights a week and twice on Thursday and Saturday," he would recall. "She's only half the woman she was in those days!"

Molly grinned she had heard all the jokes before but it didn't matter. There was something comforting about the familiarity of it all.

"I remember when the theatre stood where Price Low is." He sighed. "It was a sad day when it burned down, three actors were killed you know, they were sleeping in there when it went up."

"Yes, it must have been terrible," reflected Molly. "Did you know them?"

"No, not personally. They were part of a touring group from London, we didn't move in the same circles."

She was so used to seeing them that she tended to forget the tragic circumstances of their death. She didn't see them as ghosts but as friends she could share time and confidences with. After all, it was largely due to them that she had won the school prize. She was so grateful for their help. She wondered where they would be now if the fire hadn't ended their careers and what would become of them in the future. Were they just going to haunt the shop forever? This seemed hard to contemplate. A tear trickled down her cheek as she thought of them. She blew her nose and wiped the tear away quickly, she didn't want her dad to see.

The round was completed at around 8 am just as Holeford woke up and Trigger was taken back to the stables. They then went to the corner café for their treat of bacon sandwiches with big mugs of tea.

After breakfast Peter would assist with the run to the dairy to collect and sort the products for the next day and transfer them to the cold room ready for loading the next morning. Once a week he went door to door to collect the weekly payments from his customers. Molly would pop in and see Joan then go off out with her friends or back home to read a book or watch summer TV. The BBC would show extra children's programmes during the holidays. This would include *Flash Gordon*, originally produced for children cinema clubs in the fifties and some dubbed black and white series from France. Whilst it was a mixed bag, often with a lot of repeats, there was usually something to keep her amused. Mostly it was just the novelty of television being broadcast during the day instead of just the test card.

At Price Low, life had returned to normal after all the upheaval of the failed robbery, and thanks to that they now had a modern safe and a state-of-the art alarm system. The previous one had been fitted cheaply and had never worked properly from day one, a fact that had been brushed under the carpet during the internal enquiry that conveniently the MD himself had conducted. Jack was in the office preparing the quarterly reports for head office and arranging restocking orders with help from Joan who would also deputise if he was out of the store or on holiday.

Joe was in the store tidying the baskets by the entrance doors when he saw a large black Jaguar car mount the kerb outside and park half on the pavement, much to the surprise and annoyance of the pedestrians. The driver's door opened and out stepped a large middle-aged man wearing a sharp cut suit. He took on the demeanour of a long-retired rugby player chewing a wasp, the once toned muscle now deteriorating into fat. He had a full head of long dark hair hanging over his overly sun-tanned face and wore more rings on his sausage-fat fingers than were in a jeweller's window display. Joe recognised him as the owner of Price Low and ran quickly to open the door. Finbarr Lowe entered the store, stepped inside and surveyed the scene.

"Where's the manager? Fetch him at once."

Jack could feel Finbarr's overpowering presence from the office and went into the store to see what was going on.

"Ah, Barnfield," Finbarr called out on seeing him enter.

"Bonfield, sir." Jack replied. "This is a pleasant surprise," he lied. "Would you like to come through to the office?"

"Don't give me that, Bonford. I know you're thinking, *what have I done wrong to deserve a visit from him?*" Before Jack could reply Finbarr continued. "I am a man of few words and quick actions, Barnford and I hear good things about you. Your takings are well up since the break-in and that must be down to you taking advantage of the free publicity and heightened public interest in the store. I want you to know you'll always have a place at Price Low."

Jack was somewhat taken aback by this unexpected opener. '*What was coming next?*' he thought. "Can I get you a tea or coffee, Mr Lowe?"

"Call me Finbarr, coffee black, strong and no sugar."

Joan was already at the door and put a thumb up to Jack and scuttled back into the staffroom. The kettle was already on and waiting.

"I have plans," Finbarr announced, wedging himself into the chair opposite Jack. "As a company we are going big with huge out of town stores selling everything. Food, clothes, electrical goods and records. We'll have a chemist, coffee shop, optician, you name it and we'll have it all. In one big Price Low store. Our customers will never need to come into town again. Just imagine that. Convenience shopping just got a lot more convenient."

Jack was horrified at the idea but kept an unemotional face.

"I hope to have you on board," Finbarr continued, as the coffee arrived. Joan brought it in on a tray and did a sort of half curtsey as she delivered it to the desk and reversed out of the room trying to work out what was going on. As she returned to the shop floor the other staff pumped her for any information on the boss's visit.

"Next Monday my surveyors will be visiting you to assess the buildings and car park and prepare a feasibility study. We're going to apply to flatten the site and build flats so we'll have even more customers for our new flagship store," Finbarr continued.

Wilf was having an afternoon nap when he heard all the commotion above. With encouragement from the others he passed up through the floor and stood in the corner watching the proceedings. He did not like what he was hearing.

"I've come to see the place for myself before we flatten it all and move the whole kit and caboodle out of town." Finbarr slopped coffee over the table which dripped onto his trousers. "Are you with us, Brownfield?" he asked as he hit his fist on the table. The crockery did a little jump, more coffee was spilt, and a tea-spoon leapt out of the sugar bowl onto the floor.

Jack was ashen faced as he stuttered, "Err, yes, sir. I mean Finbarr."

"Is it me or is it cold in here?" Finbarr shivered and looked around the room for the source of a draught. He shrugged. "This place is getting tired, but never mind it won't be here for much longer," he laughed. It was the sort of hollow laugh that didn't indicate humour but would scare children and shake china from a mantelpiece. "I know it is a lot to take in but wait till you see the plans. You'll be managing a retail revolution. There are exciting and profitable times ahead, Bonfield, for all of us. Play your cards right and you could soon be driving around in a new Triumph Dolomite. How about that, then?" With that he eased himself, with difficulty, out of the chair and shook Jack by the hand, crushing and cracking his joints in the process.

Jack retrieved his hand and gave it an involuntary shake to get the blood moving again. '*Well, at least he got my name right eventually*,' he thought, following Finbarr out of the room. The staff who had migrated close to the staffroom door quickly scattered around the aisles when they heard them coming.

Finbarr paused and surveyed the shop. "A brand new dawn," he exclaimed theatrically for all to hear and walked out of the store. The parking ticket that had been placed on the windscreen during his visit held no fear for him. Finbarr pulled it off and handed it to Jack. "There will be no parking problems in the future, Bonfire, you mark my words!" He then climbed back into the car, bumped down off the pavement and drove off without any regard for the pedestrians who scattered in his wake.

Jack watched the car disappear round the corner and walked back into the store. The staff had all turned to look at him, hoping he would enlighten them as to the reason for the unprecedented visit from Mr Finbarr Lowe himself. He held his hand up and they all waited with baited breath. "Staff meeting tomorrow at 11 am." They all simultaneously breathed out. "Sorry, I can't tell you any more at the moment," he added and headed back to the office. "Joan, can you come with me please?" She followed, eager to hear what was going on. The truth was, Jack had to work out what to tell them and how, but he had just bought some time and tomorrow they would close for half an hour for a short meeting. They both entered the office and he shut the door. He then talked through the revelations from Finbarr. Joan, sat quietly with a note pad jotting down the salient points. He was relieved to be able to share her confidence, one of the few staff he could trust to keep things secret until tomorrow's meeting. Between them they prepared the briefing and Joan then got in contact with all the staff not working that day to invite them along.

Unbeknownst to them, in the remains of the props room under the wines and spirits area a meeting was already taking place.

Wilf was lounging on the sofa while George and Alice sat on the raised wooden surface of the stage lift, suspended below the sealed trapdoor.

"I don't believe it!" George exclaimed having heard word for word Wilf's dramatic re-enactment of the meeting between Jack and Finbarr.

Alice sat with her head in her hands. "We need to do something, but I've no idea what."

"Brilliant!" George said sarcastically. "That's very helpful."

"Well, what can we do?" Alice asked, a little annoyed at George's outburst. "There must be some way to stop this."

"We'll have to wait until the surveyors come, follow them around, and hope they give us some ideas." Wilf said.

The Next Day

The shop went quiet mid-morning. It was the usual lull between morning papers and lunchtime shopping. At 11 am Joan closed and locked the doors, fixing on them a sign saying, 'closed for stocktaking - open again at 11.30', then turned out the lights to the front of the store. All the staff working that morning gathered along with the part time, weekend and shift staff who had been invited to come in to see what this was all about. The staffroom was far too small for the group of twenty-seven to assemble so they gathered at the rear of the shop near the wines and spirits.

Jack entered with an empty milk crate and plastic file in his hands. He placed the crate upside down on the floor and stood on it to address the meeting. He opened the file and read the prepared statement.

"First, thank you all for coming. Those who were unable to join us today will be contacted individually but I am pleased to see that most of you are here."

There was a palpable silence in the room, all faces staring up at Jack expecting to hear the worst. The room was unusually cold which was put down to the proximity of the cold cabinets close by. They were unaware of the three residents standing amongst them who were also keen to hear more.

Jack did a little nervous cough into his hand to clear his throat and continued. "As you all know our owner and Chairman, Mr Finbarr Lowe, visited us yesterday. He was very complimentary about our store and has asked me to pass on his thanks to each and every one of you for your professionalism and dedication following the upset of the break-in. In fact, since the incident, our takings have risen to their highest position since Christmas and a lot stronger when compared with the turnover for the same period last year. The incident, although unfortunate and disturbing for us personally, resulted in considerable publicity which was unintentionally good for business. I'm pleased to report that, following the investigation, we found nothing was actually stolen, as all the money and goods were recovered from the car, which they conveniently parked by our back door. What actually happened that night will no doubt come out following the trial of our two bungling burglars. I've spoken to Sergeant Montgomery this morning, who has confirmed that the two men apprehended that evening have been charged."

The group were immediately restless at the news and started to talk amongst themselves. Jack could make out odd words. 'Bonus, bang them up, redundant,' among them. Joan passed Jack a glass of water, he took a sip. He then held up a hand for silence and continued. "We at Price Low are at the cusp of a new adventure. We will be expanding in Holeford in the near future. From Monday you'll see men around the store surveying our building, this will be for potential redevelopment of this site into new homes."

The muttering grew louder. He could feel he was losing his audience but he ploughed on as best he could. "We will eventually be moving to brand new premises on the outskirts of town and I can assure you that all your jobs are safe. More positions and exciting opportunities will, in fact, be created by the first in a chain of Price Low superstores. The programme for the building of the new store and the date for our move are still in the planning process. As things progress, I'll personally keep you informed. I do ask for your discretion at this time however, as what I am telling you is confidential, for the ears of the employees of Price Low only and, in fact, you are the first staff outside of the board room to be privy to this information. However, due to the unprecedented visit by our owner it would be unfair of me not to give you an insight into what'll be happening." He paused, pleased to have got through it. "Do any of you have any questions?" He sincerely hoped they didn't.

There was silence as the staff tried to digest the news.

"I do!" cried out Alice lifting her arm.

"Put your arm down," Wilf scolded. "They can't see you and if they could, you would've scared most of them away!"

"But it's not fair! This is our home. They don't seem to realise that. We could lose our lovely dressing room and I don't want to haunt an apartment block. That would be horrible… All those stairs!"

"Then we'll have to do something," George interjected firmly. "We just need to wait for the right moment. It will come, mark my words."

The girl from cold meats held up her gloved hand. "When is this shop closing?"

"That's a good question Maureen." Jack replied, "It will not be in the near future, there are a lot of details to be finalised and a new store to be built."

Following this there were questions on job losses, where the new store would be built, why this store had to close, how secure were their positions, etc. Jack wondered if he had been wise to inform them at this early stage.

He tried to answer as truthfully as he could. At least when the surveyors arrived everyone will more clearly understand what is happening and it will answer a lot of their questions then.

The meeting had over run by a quarter of an hour but the staff had now had their fill of information and settled into mumbling amongst themselves. Jack looked around the room somewhat relieved. He knew they would moan and ruminate amongst themselves, but that was inevitable. "Right then, if you can't think of anything else now don't worry, just come and see me at any time, my door is always open to you and I'll do my best to answer your queries. Joan, if you would be so kind as to reopen the store, please."

As they were turning to go back to their stations Alice lowered her hand, as she did so a packet of '*Price Low Everyday Cornflakes*' slid from the shelf and fell to the floor directly in front of them. The group stopped in their tracks as Joan, who was leading them, swiftly bent down, picked them up and placed them back on the shelf. "Oops! Clumsy me," she said. Those close by were not convinced it was her fault. Joan was at least two paces from the shelf when the box fell.

"I told you we were bloody haunted!" a lone voice came from within the crowd.

They all laughed and went back to their places, quietly mulling over the recent revelations and not quite sure how a carton of cereal had appeared to move unaided.

Wilf looked across at Alice. "You did that deliberately."

Alice grinned. "Maybe, shall we go and make our battle plans then?" The three of them returned to the comfort of their lair.

Jack returned to his office and Joan came back as soon as the store was up and running again. "Well, that went quite well, I think. Thanks for your help. I am now going out for an hour to meet someone for lunch," he announced. "You're in charge."

"You. Going out for lunch?" She was surprised. "You never go out for lunch!"

"Well, today is different, Joan." Tuesday had come round so quickly. He straightened his tie, slipped on his best jacket, smiled at Joan and headed out of the rear door.

'*There are some funny things going on around here today, and that's a fact.*' thought Joan as she sat down in Jack's chair to reflect on the morning's events.

Princes Road was beginning to fill up with office staff heading out to buy lunch or do a bit of shopping in their lunch hour. Jack headed directly for the Corner Café which, puzzlingly, was halfway up the street and about as far from a corner as was possible. Historically though, it had been at the junction of Princes Road and the High Street and when it moved to larger premises in 1961 the then owner kept the name, a tradition that remains to this day. He entered through the pale blue glazed door between the bay windows to the sound of a single 'ding' from the overhead bell. The room was old and beamed and of floral décor throughout. The tablecloths had flower prints and each table held a glass vase with a fresh bloom. Around the walls were historic pictures of Holeford town and surrounding countryside. Waitresses wore crisp flowery aprons over their black dresses. The smell of roasted coffee and freshly baked cakes was homely and comforting and in essence gave the atmosphere of a village tea room rather than a town centre café.

All the tables seemed to be occupied and at the sound of the bell the diners stopped for a fraction of a second, with cakes and sandwiches halfway to their mouths as they fleetingly inspected the new member of their group before resuming eating and carrying on their conversations. Carolyn was sitting at a corner table for two under a sepia picture of The Opera House. As soon as she saw Jack she stood and waved him over.

Jack made his way to the table through the maze of chairs, shook her hand and they both sat down.

"Sorry I'm late," he said.

"No, not at all. You're dead on time," Carolyn corrected, grinning as she realised the relevance of the remark.

Jack sighed. "It's been quite a morning. We had a staff meeting this morning following a visit from our managing director yesterday."

"Nothing serious, I hope?" Carolyn asked, genuinely concerned.

A young waitress approached them, looking slightly nervous, a note pad in hand. Her hair was scraped back and woven into a neat plait. Her uniform wasn't a perfect fit. "Hello miss."

"Hello, Hazel, how are you? How's the new job going?"

"I'm getting used to it now. It's been three days. I can't believe how tiring it is being on my feet all day. By the end of it I'm worn out. I'll be glad to get back to school!"

Carolyn laughed. "Welcome to the real world! You'll soon harden to it and the experience along with the extra money will make up for it. Sorry,

Jack, this is Hazel Wood, one of my pupils. I'm afraid it is an occupational hazard bumping into pupils and parents when you live in a small town."

Hazel was looking at Jack trying to work out his relationship with Carolyn as he smiled, nodded and said, "Hi." She took their order and went back to the servery. This was one order she was determined would be perfect.

Carolyn leaned forward, keen to hear a bit of gossip. "What was the meeting about or is it a secret?" she probed gently.

Jack was terrible at keeping secrets. He would be no good working for MI5 so it was just as well he was a supermarket manager. He then told Carolyn in a feigned whisper what had happened the day before, holding his hand to shield his mouth from the fellow diners, indicating that this was not to be shared.

Carolyn went pale. She was in shock. "No, they can't do that, not now… not ever!" She was quite agitated.

He was stunned at her reaction, after all she could not be that fond of Price Low and as a shopper, the new, bigger store would offer her more choice. "Sorry, I shouldn't have told you, but I didn't think it would matter to you so much. It was a shock for me too and I know it'll have an effect on the town centre but that's progress. I'm afraid we'll all have to embrace it. It won't just be Price Low expanding to out of town stores, our competition will and we have to be ahead of the game."

"But what about George, Wilf and Alice?" Carolyn blurted out.

"I'm sorry Carolyn did you say, George, Wilf and Alice? Who are they?"

Carolyn was looking down at the table. She had said too much. '*Ooh! The cats out of the bag,*' she thought, knowing there was no turning back now.

Jack paused for a few seconds to gather his thoughts then continued. "Oh they're the names of the three actors who were killed in the theatre fire. You must have read about them. Why would they matter to you?" Then the penny dropped, he leant forward and whispered. "You contacted them the other night didn't you? I can tell by your face that I'm right! You actually saw them, didn't you?"

Carolyn was red faced and ill at ease at this deduction. "Well, it's more like they contacted me," she said, trying to play down the situation.

Jack was now on the edge of his seat, all thought of food gone. "You have to tell me more now, this is amazing!"

Carolyn held a finger to her mouth to silence him. The room had gone quiet as the other tables had noticed the intensity of their conversation and were trying to pick up any snippets they could.

"Not here, too many ears," she said, aware of the attention they had attracted.

"Now, let's talk about Joe," she continued, changing the subject and speaking naturally again, her complexion returning to normal.

Jack didn't want to talk about Joe. After that revelation he wanted to talk about his store being haunted. He was, however, aware of the interest from the other diners in the room so he played along.

"Ah, yes Joe," he responded. The volume of the conversation in the room returned to normal, '*nothing worth hearing there*,' was the consensus.

Hazel served the tea and cheese sandwiches from a tray, then with a polite, "Miss," and little curtsy, returned to the counter.

Carolyn continued, "You underestimate Joe. He achieved good grades at school and deserves a chance at a proper career. It's my opinion that he is just needs a bit of a push." She paused, detecting his unease. She'd probably overstepped the mark and certainly didn't want to offend Jack or question his parenting skills but a part of her wanted to push on for Joe's sake.

Jack looked thoughtful. He had never been lectured about Joe before, '*was she criticising the way he had brought him up? What did she know about their past and why should she care so much? Granted, Jack had been in a bad place when Joe's mother ran off like that and deserted them both. He had also taken little interest in the last year of Joe's schooling but, no, Joe was just a normal lazy teenager with no direction in his life*.' Before he could gather these thoughts and reply, Carolyn continued the conversation.

"He needs help, your help. He's not idle and certainly not stupid; he needs stimulating, if you can give him the opportunity to stretch himself, he'll respond I'm sure. He really is much brighter than you give him credit for."

Jack was confused and defensive, he was beginning to feel guilty that he might have neglected him at such an important time in his development. "First of all, you don't know what it has been like for us both and, anyway, why do you care about what becomes of him? I made sure he has a decent job, I don't see what more I can do."

She was prepared for this, she'd heard it many times during careers evenings in the school. Parents who thought it was the responsibility of the teachers not only to give the children knowledge but to mother them and decide what their children do with their lives, often failing to see what was right under their noses. Carolyn relaxed, she was on familiar ground now. She adopted her teacher demeanour and started, "Well, I care about Joe because he was one of my pupils and I would be failing him if I didn't try and help him onto a career path that would suit him and bring out the best in him. You can help by offering him a route through the Price Low Management Training Scheme. I saw the poster the other night in your canteen. It's tailor-made for him and he has more than enough qualifications to apply. In fact, I have a copy of them here for you, together with a copy of his last school report which might have passed you by somehow," she finished diplomatically.

Jack looked keenly at her. He could see that she was sincere in her belief in his son and had gone to some effort on his behalf. "My…you have been busy!" He scanned through the evidence that had been placed in front of him. "No, not Joe, not my Joe surely? These results are excellent."

"Yes, they are. Just try him, give him this chance, please." Carolyn stared hard and pleadingly into Jack's eyes. She knew then she had won him over and hoped she had given Joe a future. Also, she had carefully steered the conversation away from the psychic evening.

"OK, Miss Jenner, I'll take you at your word," Jack said, checking his watch. He finished off the tea and cheese sandwiches quickly. "I'm sorry but I have to get back to the store, my lunch hour is nearly up. I'll have a look at the poster this afternoon. I'll get the bill and, thank you for your honesty and sincerity." He stood up and Carolyn followed suit. He held out his hand and she hers. They shook but their grip held slightly longer than the polite handshake when they had first greeted one another. "One other thing, Carolyn, you have a story to tell me and I am not going to let you off that lightly. Would you be available one evening to tell me about your ghost hunting and I'll update you about Joe? Is that a deal?"

"It's a deal", she replied. She checked the pocket diary in her handbag. "How about Tuesday the fifteenth when I return from my holiday?"

Jack felt surprisingly pleased at how keen she was to meet again and how she had not hesitated to agree to his invitation. "Fine, seven at the Gorgonzola then, my treat."

"It's a date," Carolyn replied.

They both left the Corner Café a little wiser and happier that afternoon. Hazel was also happy. She had received a large tip.

Jack headed back to the office, read the poster Carolyn had referred to and phoned the training department. He was going to try and give Joe his chance.

Carolyn went shopping to buy some essential items ready for her trip to Stratford and then home to start packing her bags. She had done all she could for Joe and it was up to him now. Time would prove whether her confidence in him was justified. She was also looking forward to sharing her ghostly experiences with someone else. She felt relaxed now and ready to enjoy her holiday.

10

Mango's in the store

The next morning Jack received a call from the training department to confirm a place was available for Joe. They were impressed by his exam results and were able to offer a fast-track scheme to store manager status in three years if he was willing to study hard and put in the necessary work. The course started in September so they would need an answer by the end of the week. He would be based in the London office for the first six months and would need time to find accommodation. Jack thanked them for their prompt reply and hung up the phone with mixed emotions. He mourned the fact that the depression he suffered following the break-up of his marriage had clouded the joy of watching their boy growing up. There had been dark times but they had got through it together and now the fledgling had an opportunity to fly the nest. He had no right to stand in his way. He would be the better father for giving him this chance. He had to do it even if it was the hardest thing he had ever done. He would somehow manage without him.

Jack walked into the store to look for Joe. He watched him in a new light as he was busy stacking the shelves and enjoying some cheery banter with the customers. He was about to call him over when he noticed Sergeant Montgomery enter the store and head over to him. He held out his hand and Jack shook it; the firm grip made him wince.

"Good afternoon, sir, may I have a chat with you in private."

Jack wondered why it was that when approached by a police officer you immediately felt guilty and tried to work out what you might have done wrong.

"I want to bring you up to date on the robbery case, Mr Bonfield. May we go into your office?" They headed directly through the staffroom while Jack could hear the murmur of speculation spreading like a wave across the store behind them.

They entered the office and Jack closed the door behind them.

Montgomery sat down and Jack joined him across the desk. The sergeant explained what had transpired from the interviews with Brian and Charlie and outlined the next formalities regarding the prosecution and court appearances. "Of course, this all takes time," Montgomery continued. "In the meantime we are investigating the whereabouts of a vigilante group who are taking the law into their own hands. The evidence points towards three men who wear fancy dress and in this case succeeded in thwarting the robbery from your store. Whilst doing so they inflicted grievous bodily harm on one of the intruders and held them against their will. This is the job of the police!" Montgomery slapped his hand down on the desk. "Not the business of causing bodily harm to criminals, of course," he quickly corrected himself. But the thought of others taking the law into their own hands was making his blood boil. Arms flailing and with a loud, forceful voice he continued. "We have to track them down. This could be the thin edge of the wedge and could lead to a lawless society. This is Holeford, not the Wild West." Montgomery stopped to take breath. He was overexcited and close to hyperventilating. His face had turned bright red with exertion.

Jack looked on a little shocked at the outburst and was desperately fighting the urge to laugh at the absurd idea that there would be such a movement anywhere, let alone in Holeford. "So you want me to keep an ear to the ground for any information leading to a fancy-dress vigilante group, and report to you?" he confirmed.

"Exactly that, sir. A man in your position may overhear something or see something unusual. This has to be stopped and if we need the public's help, then I am not too proud to ask for it. As long as law and order is maintained." Montgomery had returned to his normal complexion and was calm again. "Now, thank you for your time. I have here a poster, I would appreciate it if you could display it in your store. It may help jog someone's memory. Also you'll be hearing from the Crown Prosecution Service regarding the court case. Remember, if you hear or see anything give me a call." As he stood up he handed Jack a business card with his direct phone number and the poster. "I'll see myself out."

As he turned to leave the room Wilf, dressed in his Victorian policeman's uniform, stood to attention and saluted. He had been in the room all the time, amused by the conversation. He could not wait to tell the others. Then it got even better. Jack unrolled the poster which showed photo-fit image of the three characters in question. Wilf looked over his shoulder and pulled a face. "We look nothing like these pictures, that's an insult!" He wasted no more time and descended back into the dressing room.

Joe came into the office immediately after the policeman had left. Jack closed the door and burst into laughter, showing Joe the poster. After calming down and drying the tears from his eyes, he explained what had just transpired. Joe hadn't seen his dad laugh so much for years. It was unexpected but nice.

"Were you looking for me earlier, before the copper came in?"

"Yes, I was, take a seat."

Joe's mind drifted back to the robbery. "Do you think the burglars are going to get away with it?"

"I really don't know, Joe. The thing is, they didn't actually steal anything from us, but they did steal a person's car. They forced entry into the store and broke into the safe but on paper that is all they did. Car theft, forced entry and vandalism." Jack paused. "On the bright side, we now have a new safe and a state-of-the-art security system that I've been pestering head office about having for years, so it's not all bad. Now sit down, I want to ask you something."

Joe glanced at the desk and noticed a copy of his school report and exam results. He was puzzled now as to what was coming.

"Where do you see yourself in three years' time?" Jack unexpectedly asked.

"I don't know. What's going on, Dad, are they closing the store? Why three years? Why are you suddenly concerned about my future?"

"It's nothing to worry about. I realise the way I behaved when your mother left and regret it. I showed little interest in your long-term welfare and education. I was primarily concerned with my hurts and sought solace a bit too often with a bottle. But between us we managed to get along OK, I hope." Jack looked anxiously at him.

"Dad, what's this, some kind of confession? We coped OK, yeah. What Mum did was inexcusable, dumping us both for her slimy boyfriend. I don't care if I never see her again!"

Jack held up the exam results. "I can understand that but we're getting off the subject a little. The fact is, I've had my eyes opened to your potential and have been in contact with head office with the details of these exam results. They're in a position to offer you a place on their management training scheme. It is a three-year course which commences with a six-month placement at head office before going to college, coupled with in-store training. Ultimately, you would, all going well, qualify as an under-manager and within five years, progressing through the ranks, you'd be eligible for your own store. What do you think?"

Joe was stunned. "What are you saying? Me a manager? Are you serious?"

"Yes, I am serious. Your results put you on a fast track to a managerial position. You have a bright future ahead of you if you want it. You'll have to work hard and study well but it is certainly within your capabilities. I'm only sorry I didn't see it earlier."

Joe stared across at Jack trying to read his expression. *Was this a wind up?* Then the penny dropped. "This is Miss Jenner's work! You have been seen out talking with her and she's planted this idea in your head, that's who you got the copies of the results from."

Jack blushed slightly. "Yes, I have and, yes, she did enlighten me to your potential. Is that so bad?"

Joe shook his head to clear it. "You really are serious aren't you? This is not a wind up?"

"No, it's not a wind up. This is for real. The place is waiting for you if you want it but I have to tell them by tomorrow. I know this is short notice and it's all been a bit of a shock but it starts in September so there's little time. All you have to do is say yes or no."

Joe was stunned by the sudden offer. He would have to find somewhere to stay in London. His first time away from home and it was London! Scary! But, then who knew what? One minute stacking shelves, the next on the ladder to middle management. Could he afford to miss this chance? "Blimey, Dad, I wasn't expecting this. It's a lot to take in."

"It's your choice, do you want to think about it?"

Joe looked across at his dad thoughtfully. Jack had been through hell over recent years trying to balance his work and maintain a home life for them both while coping with the grief of losing Mum to that horrible waiter. He had been susceptible to the odd bout of drinking too much to try and ease the pain and frustration but they had got through it. Joe noted the odd grey hairs and lines of age starting to appear for the first time. They had been so close yet he had never really looked at him, not like this. They had both needed one another, but now he appeared to be moving on; maybe it was time for him as well. He was bored with the mundane jobs he was doing around the store but was apprehensive about change. He took a deep breath and said, "No."

Jack was stunned. "No? You need to think about this opportunity, Joe. Is that really your decision? I am sorry to hear that."

Joe interrupted him quickly. "No, Dad. I mean no, I don't need time to think about it. It's amazing. Yes please, Wow this is fantastic; a proper career."

They both stood up and spontaneously hugged across the table.

"I am very proud of you, son, you go and show them what you're made of and make your old dad proud!"

They stood back from one another, shocked and a little embarrassed at the sudden affection they felt and had shown to one another. Neither could remember the last time they had shook hands let alone hugged one another.

"Let's call them now, shall we?" Jack lifted the receiver and dialled as Joe looked on in disbelief. "Hi, is that Sarah? Good. Jack Bonfield here. We spoke about Joe…Yes, that's right. Just to confirm he wishes to take up the offer…Yes, he's with me now…of course you can." Jack held his hand over the receiver, "This is Sarah Pitkin, Head of Training. She wants to speak to you."

Joe fumbled with the receiver and held it to his ear. "Hello…yes, this is Joe Bonfield…thank you. Dad, I mean Mr Bonfield just discussed it with me. It's all very exciting."

Jack slid a note pad and pen towards Joe as he continued the conversation. He grabbed the pen and the new trainee manager started making notes for his future.

Jack quietly walked out of the office and closed the door behind him leaving Joe to his phone call. He walked through the staffroom and out into the car park to get some fresh air. A lump in his throat, his eyes welling up with pride. He hoped no one would see him in this state, he took some deep breaths and tried to calm his feelings. 'Well,' he thought, '*God moves in mysterious ways. His son was growing up, moving to London, then who knows where? He was going to miss him but it was the right thing. He has been given the chance to fly and all because of a fortune teller entering their lives on the back of a fumbled robbery. Life is strange indeed.*' He gathered his thoughts and headed back to the office.

Joe had finished the call and told Jack all the important points, unable to contain his excitement. "They've got some flats near the office. I'll be sharing with three others and we can go up and look around before I start. Can we go next week, Dad?"

"Why not? I have a day in lieu due, so how about Friday? Joan can take the helm while we go and sus it all out."

"Great, Sarah is sending through all the paperwork. I have to write a

CV covering my store experience which I can take with me and we need to sign some forms. We can take those with us. Can I tell the others?"Joe was breathless with all the details and all the excitement he was feeling inside.

"I don't see why not, they're going to find out soon enough," Jack proudly replied. It was lovely to see Joe this excited and share it all with him.

Joe hurriedly headed out of the room, turning at the last second to say, "Thanks, Dad, I won't let you down."

"Get out, you're getting embarrassing!" Jack said and pointed out into the staffroom.

Joan entered the room as Joe left, looking back at him over her shoulder. "What's the matter with him? I've never seen him so animated."

"I need you to cover for me next Friday, if that's OK. I am taking Joe up to head office to meet the training staff and sort out some details with him. He's going to become a trainee manager." Jack smiled and watched Joan for her reaction. He knew she would be surprised by this revelation.

"Friday's fine: after all, we may be working for him one day." She smiled and winked.

"Not too soon I hope, I've got a few good years left in me yet!"

Monday 14th of July

The day started perfectly normally but Jack knew there was change in the air and today would be the beginning of a new chapter for Price Low. Carolyn was back from her holiday and while doing the shopping had popped in to remind him about their meal on Tuesday. The long wait to hear the full revelations about her séance were nearly over.

Jack was checking the stock control forms when Joan entered the office.

"There are two men here to see you. They say they're surveyors and you're expecting them. Is this to do with the new store?"

"I am afraid this is just the beginning. You had best hold on tight, Joan, I think we're all in for a long and bumpy ride. Show them in, please and, thanks, I appreciate all your help. We'd also better start advertising for a new storeroom assistant, can you start the ball rolling while I deal with our visitors?" He gave her a broad smile.

Joan gave a knowing smile back. She could see Jack was more like his old self. With the prospect of a new store as well, maybe things were looking up for them all.

"This way, gentlemen." She beckoned the men into the office. The two surveyors entered. Both were smartly dressed, wearing plaid jackets over white shirts with red ties and black trousers. They appeared to be in their early thirties, one tall and carrying a briefcase, the other of slighter, stockier build carrying a clipboard.

"Good afternoon," they said in unison.

Jack stood up and welcomed them. "Hi, I'm Jack Bonfield, I've been expecting you." They shook hands. "Please sit down. Would you like tea or coffee?"

Joan assumed her tea lady duties and headed to the staff kitchen.

The taller man with shoulder length dark hair did the introductions. "Pleased to meet you, Jack. I am Michael Jones and this is Mango Peters."

Jack couldn't contain his surprise at the name Mango and broke into a smile.

"His mother had a passion for fruit!" Michael explained, picking up on Jack's amused expression.

"If I had a pound for every time he'd cracked that joke I'd be a wealthy man," the shorter, more portly, surveyor replied amiably.

Under the guidance of their new financial backer, Mr Finbarr Lowe, Michael and Mango had recently set up their own company, breaking away from their previous employer. They had, up until recently, been working for Arkwright and Smith Surveying Ltd who, up until two months ago, had worked exclusively for Price Low. Finbarr had suspected that ASS Ltd had been overcharging for their services and when their MD arrived at their head office with a better car than his, he took that as confirmation and took decisive action. A week later he stormed into their board meeting as the partners sat on their leather-backed chairs around the long, narrow and expensive mahogany table in the oak panelled room. Finbarr, using somewhat colourful language, pointed out the error of their ways and tore up their contract throwing it up in the air like confetti whilst across the table his audience watched in stunned silence. No one got the better of Finbarr Lowe!

He had planned the moment carefully by already tempting Michael and Mango from ASS Ltd to setting up their own practice. He would fund them initially and be a silent partner while they did work exclusively for Price Low. It suited both parties, the two surveyors would now have their own company with a better salary and Finbarr had full control over his developments, with two men he trusted. He could also use them as spies. They were under orders to probe the managers and staff during their visits and report everything back to him directly. He would not put up with dissenters and was ready to ruthlessly weed out any weakness or disloyalty in his team.

Joan returned with a tray of coffee and biscuits. Jack asked her to join them, she would need to know all the details to help him with the proposed changes.

The four of them sat in Jack's office enjoying a cup of tea and looking at the draft proposals for the new superstore. Jack was fully aware of their relationship with Finbarr Lowe. He had guessed correctly that they would not only be reporting back about the building but also about staff morale. He was careful to hide any reservations about the impact the new store would have on the town's shopping streets. He figured he could do more to help the situation and reduce the risk, by maintaining his position and becoming manager of the new store.

Jack finished his drink and was now keen to get on with his stock orders. "Well, thanks for showing me the details. These are exciting times for us all and for Holeford."

"Yes, we think so too," replied Mango, relieved that they had received a positive response from Jack. It was much easier and less stressful for them to return to Finbarr with good news on the reaction of his staff. Mango shivered. "The heating in the new store will certainly be better than here, your office is freezing!"

"Oh, it comes and goes. I think our boiler's on the blink. Joan, will you please sign in our two visitors and issue their ID badges then give them a whistle-stop tour of the premises to familiarise them with our layout."

Michael stood up, happy to bring this initial meeting to an end. "We've taken up enough of your valuable time and will now carry out a full survey of your buildings and grounds. These are the original conveyance drawings and some historic information but we need to compile a full report and double check the dimensions for the architect to draw up his proposals for planning office approval."

Mango held up the briefcase rather like exhibit A in a court case. "We'll begin this afternoon and return tomorrow to hopefully conclude our work. We will need access to all areas but will try to minimise any disruption to the day to day running of the store. Incidentally, did you know there used to be a theatre on this site until it burned down? You never know, we may find some evidence of it while we probe around, it seems the store was built directly off the original foundations."

"Yes, so I understand. That must have been a sad day for Holeford when it went up in smoke," Jack said. He remembered with sadness about the three actors who lost their lives in the tragedy.

"Not as sad as it was for us," said George to Alice who had come to observe the proceedings from the corner of the room.

"Well, times move on, that's progress. No one wants theatre any more when you can go the cinema or watch TV from the comfort of your own home," replied Mango.

"Heartless bugger," reprimanded George.

"George, your language is awful," scolded Alice but tittered all the same. "I think we're going to be busy following them around for two days!"

Wilf came through the wall into the office. "What's happening? Have I missed anything?"

"Not a lot, they're just about to start the survey and they will be back again tomorrow," replied George.

Joan led the way to the customer care desk, issued their passes and took them on a brief tour whilst introducing them to any staff that they came into contact with. The two men then left the store and went into the yard where they had parked their car. They returned with more clipboards, torches, tape measures and a camera.

They started at the top of the building in the roof space, inspecting, checking measurements against the drawings and recording the condition of the structure as they worked meticulously from room to room down through the building, unaware that they were accompanied the entire time. The store was only thirteen years old and in reasonable condition which made their task relatively easy for the first afternoon. They worked until six o'clock in the evening.

"That's enough for today Mike," Mango said. "Let's get back to our B&B have a wash and go get something to eat." They returned to the office and saw Jack who was finishing his stock returns. "Sorry to disturb you, sir. We will be back in the morning to survey the ground floor and externals."

Jack looked up from his desk. "Please call me Jack, there's no need to be formal here. Hang on to your passes and don't forget to sign out. See you in the morning."

Alice started to fret. "Well, that was a waste of time and effort, Wilf, there was nothing learnt from that tour that we could use to save our home. The way they're talking it sounds like Finbarr has already decided to knock it down and build flats. What are we going to do? Our lovely home will be destroyed."

Wilf tried to console her. "Don't worry, old girl, something will crop up."

Alice was not convinced that he was right but there was nothing more they could do tonight. Their evening routine went as normal, patrolling the aisles, checking the local news and following the odd person down the High Street just for fun but it wasn't the same, George was not in the mood and their hearts just weren't in it. All of them were quiet. A cloud of uncertainty and fear hung over them. Alice was unable to practise her levitation or teach Wilf, following the fitting of the new alarm system. It was too sensitive and after setting it off twice, which was put down to teething troubles, they decided to stop until they could work out a way around it.

The next morning the surveyors arrived at nine to continue their investigations. They were now on the shop floor prodding and poking around behind the displays and freezer cabinets.

"Why do you think it's always so cold in here Mango? The staff don't seem to notice. It's like it's following us around."

"Don't be daft, Mike. You've been reading too many of the ghost stories about this place, and anyway, they don't heat the storerooms and you are currently standing next to the freezer cabinet!"

Mango tapped the floor with a small hammer. The floor responded with a solid thump as it struck the concrete slab. Mango continued the process moving towards the back of the store into the wines and spirits section when the sound changed to a hollow echo. "This is where the timber floor starts."

Michael carefully measured the position while Mango continued the rhythmic banging.

"What on earth are they doing up there?" George looked up to see dust falling from the ceiling of their basement.

Wilf looked at the dust drifting in the air. "I think they have started early."

"Right, action stations!" cried Alice.

The three of them rose through the floor to find Mango on his hands and knees tapping away with the hammer while the other surveyor stood behind with a clipboard.

"Well, really. This is too much!" Alice was in a rage and frightened. They were too close to discovering their home. She stared at the shelves and with a wave of her hand a bottle of wine fell from the lowest shelf and smashed on the floor.

"Alice!" George exclaimed.

"Well, they have to be stopped," she said with no remorse.

Chaos ensued as the staff ran up with paper towels to stem the flow of the red liquid across the floor. Joe came over with dustpan and brush while Joan followed with mop and bucket.

"I'm so sorry, Joe. We will pay for any damage," said a distraught Mango.

"Never mind that, just be careful where you wave that hammer around. Banging the floor must have dislodged the display," Joe replied shortly.

Mango put the hammer back into the holdall and Michael made notes about the condition of the floor.

"Well, that stopped that. Well done, Alice! First blood to us today. Now where are they going next?" said a proud George.

The surveyors moved through to the storeroom, staffroom and office, being more careful not to disturb any goods on the shelves. The three actors followed to ensure there was no more damage to their ceiling and try to find a weakness in their plans.

They eventually moved to the rear yard and car park. Michael took a theodolite from the car and set up a tripod, carefully screwing the revolving sight to the top. Mango went round the area with a tape measure, marking crosses on the tarmac with chalk at equal distances. He then took a measuring staff from the car which telescoped out and eventually stood considerably taller than him. He took it across the road to a little arrow carved in the plinth of the museum and held it against the wall.

"What is he doing?" enquired Alice of the other two.

"Well, that arrow on the wall is a bench mark. It's a known position above sea level and they're going to check the levels of the car park against those on the record drawings, then he will record the angles between the corners of the car park and buildings so that he can plot them against the earlier drawings," said Wilf.

"How come you are the expert?" George questioned.

"Well, while you were busy buying and selling other people's junk between acting jobs, I was labouring on wet & windy building sites, if you must know."

"Never mind that, look up at the window in the museum," Alice said. "Someone else is watching them."

They looked up to see where Alice was pointing. Sure enough, in the round window on the upper floor a man with wild grey hair and horn-rimmed glasses was watching them intently.

George recognised him, "That's Professor Halford, the curator. He is showing a lot of interest in the surveyor's work."

"Perhaps he wants to buy one of the flats," Alice said sarcastically.

Professor Dominic Halford stood on the galleried landing of the Victorian Gothic library in the museum. The room was a splendid cathedral style space with soaring wooden arches, elaborately carved mouldings and medieval style floral decoration of dark red and deep greens highlighted with gold leaf. It was one of the finest examples of the ornate Arts and Craft style to be seen outside of London. The walls were lined from floor to ceiling on three sides with dark oak shelving containing thousands of leather-bound books covering history and antiquities.

It also featured collections of local history, literature from Holeford's more notable sons and included many original manuscripts and first editions. The rear shelving was reserved for volumes concentrating on natural history both local and worldwide.

The gallery surrounded the cavernous room twelve feet from the ground supported on ornate stained wooden columns with further Gothic arches and brackets to brace the construction. The long elevation overlooking the street was glazed from floor to ceiling with small diamond shaped leaded lights framed by a border of brightly coloured stained glass all mounted in tall Gothic stone frames.

The Professor watched closely as the surveyors began to check the levels of the car park. As well as being curator of the County Museum, he also held the position of consultant archaeologist to the local planning department and was aware of what was transpiring below him across the street. He had no real interest in the fate of the supermarket. He would prefer to see a theatre return to its rightful place at the centre of the community where he dreamed he could give lectures on ancient history to an enthusiastic audience. He had long had a love of theatre having spent the majority of his career in London after leaving Oxford with his doctorate. He excelled in his subject of ancient history and had worked his way up to Director of British Antiquity at the British Museum.

He moved to Holeford two years ago to take the place of the previous curator, Sir James Randall who, before his death, had done little to popularise the museum, preferring to preserve it as a Victorian mausoleum full of old, dead and dusty exhibits. He also maintained a staff of old, dusty retainers and volunteers with no desire for innovation. Professor Halford, however, saw it as his calling to breathe life back into the building and inspire a new generation to venture through the doors and discover the wonders within. He wasted no time in rooting out personnel with no passion for modernisation. This caused a lot of friction with the board of governors but he stuck to his guns and dragged the museum kicking and screaming into the twentieth century.

He had been inspired by his father, Sir Mortimer Halford, when he had spent the summer with him here just outside the town at Monkton Hillfort. His father had been in control of a large excavation to try and discover the story of the people who had lived in the Iron Age hillfort and discover how it was overthrown by Roman invaders. He had been on holiday from boarding school and had helped with the cleaning and washing of artefacts from the dig. Some of these were still on display in the main hall.

He was proud of his dad and excited to be able to continue his work in the area that he knew so well. He had done extensive research on the whole of the county highlighting numerous settlements, hillforts, burial traditions and farm systems. This county, more than most, was blessed with ancient ruins, man-made contours, mounds and hills telling stories of the ancient people for him and his fellow archaeologists to discover and interpret for a new generation.

Following on from his father's studies, he was aware of the town's history and what lies beneath the modern buildings. Even the road system through the town followed the Roman lines linking Monkton Hillfort to the west with London to the east, the coast to the south and the ancient settlement of Sarum to the north. However, the area under Price Low was an enigma. No study had been carried out in modern times. This would be his chance to fill in a gap in local history and hopefully make some new discoveries. He watched with great interest the surveyors carefully mapping out the levels of the car park. 'Soon Dominic, soon, it will be your turn,' he said to himself, rubbing his hands together in anticipation.

Mango and Michael finished making notes in their book and did a visual study of the external facade of the building. They then leant on the bonnet of their car and contemplated their next move.

"You would never know this used to be a theatre, Mike. Even the shape of the footprint doesn't give away the history."

"Tell you what, Mango, we've got a bit of time so I want to go back to the area at the back of the store where the floor sounded hollow. There's something I want to investigate. Other than that, we'll have to commission an archaeological survey of the car park as there are no existing records at the planning office. Did you notice the old chap in the museum watching us from the window? I bet he can't wait to get his trowel out and have a poke around!"

They both laughed and went into the shop to study the floor area to the rear.

"Did you bring the endoscope, Mango?"

"Yeah, I'll go and get it from the car."

Jack came out of the office and saw Michael. "How are you getting on?"

"We are nearly there. But I do want to make a small hole in the floor below the wines and spirits and check the condition. We'll lift and replace the floor covering in the corner, then make a very small hole that won't do any damage. We have a small probe which will enable us to look underneath."

"Well, if you must, you'd better carry on. We want Finbarr to have the full report don't we?"

Michael looked at him wondering if he had heard a hint of sarcasm. "I'm afraid it doesn't end there. We'll complete our work shortly but have to recommend a further archaeological investigation in the yard to conclude the report for the planning office."

"What, dig holes in the ground outside?" Jack asked in surprise. "Blimey, I didn't expect that. What about my deliveries?"

Mango returned with a toolbox and joined the conversation. "They're not big holes, well not initially anyway. They'll dig some strips up about four feet wide and as deep as needed to inspect the strata. It shouldn't inconvenience your deliveries too much. I'm sure they will take that into account and try to avoid disturbance to your supplies. Your parking area will be somewhat reduced, though."

Jack wasn't reassured and was resigned to accept that there would be more disruption, despite what Mango was saying. "OK, well, hopefully it'll all be over quickly. Are you doing the floor now?"

"If that's OK," Michael said, opening the tool box and removing a brace and bit. "We'll then be on our way."

"Carry on, but make sure you leave it tidy," warned Jack, who was now getting a bit fed up with surveyors poking around in his shop disrupting the usual flow of the day.

Wilf, George and Alice looked on horrified. They were about to drill a hole directly into their dressing room. Wilf stayed in the shop while the other two descended through the floor to watch from below. Michael pulled back the vinyl floor, exposing the wooden planks below. He knelt down and positioned the drill bit and leaning gently on the brace with his shoulder, slowly rotated the handle. The thread on the bit grabbed the fibres of the wooden board and pulled the cutting edge into the grain.

"Look out below," bellowed Wilf who was watching and commentating on the procedure to George and Alice. "He's started boring into the floor."

From the props room they could hear the wood being cut away above their heads, then a small screw appeared and suddenly the whole drill bit came through. The tool had drilled a neat hole, causing wood dust and shavings to land on the sofa below.

"Oh, look at that mess on my bed!" George said disgustingly.

Michael withdrew the drill and assembled a bright steel tube into an eyepiece and connected it to a battery and tested the light. The end glowed, resembling a very thin, long, torch.

"Look out!" Wilf shouted. "They've got an eyepiece on a rod, it looks like a very small periscope."

From above, a shiny metal tube about eighteen inches long descended into the room then, without warning, it lit up, shining a light into the void and illuminating the darkness below. Like an alien trying to find its prey in a deserted house, it turned and twisted, the narrow band of light probing the dark revealing their furniture and costume rails.

"Hello, what have we here? It looks like a junk room," exclaimed Michael.

"Let me see," said Mango excitedly.

There was the noise of hurried feet and the two men exchanged places.

In a flash, Alice raised her eyebrows and the fire bucket in the corner of the room raised off its wall bracket and revolved in mid-air emptying its sand.

George was not amused. "Oh, that's great, now we have sand all over the furniture to add to the sawdust."

"Just watch", Alice said impatiently, "and shut up, you are putting me off!" The bucket flew up to the ceiling, covering the probe.

"Brilliant!" yelled George, now understanding the manoeuvre.

Mango knelt and looked in the eyepiece. "What are you talking about? There's nothing there."

"There is. You can't be doing it right, give it here." Michael knelt again and grabbed back the scope, swivelling it wildly, trying to focus on the view he had seen before. "There was a junk room, I swear there was," he said, doubt now creeping into his voice. "I've had enough of this! Two days creeping round this old building and now I am seeing things. Let's pack up and go back to the office. We have enough for our report for Finbarr." Michael pulled the scope out and handed it to Mango then laid the vinyl floor back over the hole.

Wilf descended into the room. "What did you do? I thought our cover was blown, then it was pandemonium and they packed up!"

George pointed at the bucket on the ceiling while Alice did a little bow.

Wilf was impressed. "You little angel, that's brilliant! But you can take it down now they have covered the hole."

The bucket made a controlled descent landing on the sofa. "Phew! That was getting heavy," said Alice.

"All we have to do now is clean the mess up," George added, still smarting about the sand all over HIS bed.

Mango replaced all the tools in the bag and returned them to the car while Michael went to see Jack.

"Thanks for your help. I hope we didn't cause too much disruption. The office will be in touch about the arrangements for the archaeologists to come and do their investigation."

They drove off leaving Jack to ponder on what was going to happen next. His mind however quickly moved onto this evening's plans. It was late on Tuesday afternoon, Jack had so much to tell Carolyn about the visit and was looking forward to hearing about her experience with the ghosts… Oh! And her holiday of course.

Below ground Wilf had started plotting. "Right, George, what do you know about Professor Halford? We need to find out why he is so interested in the shop."

"All I know is he came to Holeford a couple of years ago to replace Sir James when he died from a mosquito bite while cleaning an Egyptian artefact. The museum has since become more popular."

Wilf smiled. "Great, that's a good start. I know Sir James Randall. I sometimes see him at the club. I'll try and get in touch with him. But what about talking to the Professor. How can we do that?"

Alice's eyes lit up excitedly. "Can I come with you to the club? You did promise I could one day. I need you to introduce me to the secretary so that I can get membership."

George had lost interest in *The Ghost Social Club* and seldom visited now despite being a past president. It was in the basement of the District Council's Social Club close to their offices on Grove Street. The basement had been sealed off from the building many years ago but was linked to many of the older buildings in the town by a series of tunnels. No one knew the origin of the network which ran under the roads and prominent buildings linking them together. Many legends had been passed down through the generations suggesting they were used during the Civil War to hide the Royalists during raids and the judge from the Bloody Assizes using them to get from his lodgings to the court room without being seen. They had been linked with smuggling, storing the town's treasures during the war and more recently, as a nuclear bunker in case the Russians dropped The Bomb. That at least was true. The section under the council offices had been lined with concrete, blast doors were added and they were equipped with air pumps and filters along with a large store of provisions. In an emergency the Great and the Good of the council had planned to descend into the vaults with the more attractive secretaries and wait for the all clear when they could emerge and assess the damage. The bunker was linked to Westminster and a network of bunkers around the country by an elaborate and very secret telephone system. There they could set up committees to deal with the aftermath, hoping there were some survivors able to do the work while they directed it all and set about repopulating the country.

Alice wouldn't let it rest. "Go on Wilf, you need me to help you with this."

Wilf thought for a minute.

"OK, I'll introduce you but you have to talk to Molly, she could go and see the Professor. With the right questions she could probably find out why he is so interested."

"That's a deal!" Alice replied and rose up into the storeroom to await the arrival of Molly who would hopefully be in to meet her mum that evening as usual.

11

The Gorgonzola

It was Tuesday evening at last. Jack hadn't been out on any sort of a date since his wife's departure and felt nervous. '*This is silly*,' he thought. '*It's just a meal with Joe's teacher. Why am I getting nervous? I feel like a teenager.*'

Joe was sitting in the living room when Jack entered. "Blimey, Dad, you look smart, are you going for an interview?"

"Ha, ha! You think you're so funny."

Since the promotion to trainee manager, Joe had become more buoyant, he now had a goal and if he knuckled down the possibility of a good career with Price Low. They had exchanged ideas on how Price Low could expand and what would be good for the town. He had suddenly grown up, in his own mind and his dad's.

"Now, don't wait up," Jack said, sarcastically.

"No, Dad. I'll be in bed with a glass of milk by eight, don't worry." He waved him out of the door. "Oh, and have a nice time!"

Jack had arranged to call for Carolyn and walk into town together, saving any uncomfortable solitary waiting at an empty table. Carolyn lived on a direct route from his house towards the restaurant in Queens Road so it was not an inconvenience. It was only a short distance and on a warm summer's evening made for a pleasant stroll in the shadows of the chestnut trees along the leafy avenue.

Jack arrived and rang the bell. The door was opened by Carolyn's mother Monica who was wearing a floral-patterned dress under an apron dusted with flour. Patch, their pet dog, was also intrigued to see who the stranger was at the door but was being restrained by a hand round his collar. Monica studied Jack closely before addressing him. "You must be Jack," she said somewhat coldly. "Please excuse me. I'm just finishing some baking. Do come in. I'm sure Carolyn will be down in a minute.

Don't mind Patch. He's a bit lively but he'll settle down once he gets used to you."

"Sorry, I'm nearly ready," came a voice from upstairs and seconds later Carolyn descended the stairs wearing a tight-fitting pencil dress with bolero waistcoat trimmed in red. Her hair was tied back and hung down over her left shoulder and she carried a small glossy black clutch bag which matched her shoes whose high heels helped to accentuate her slim figure.

"Blimey!" Jack exclaimed and then hastily followed up with, "Sorry, I mean good evening I wasn't expecting…I mean you look lovely!"

"Well, thank you, Jack, I'll gladly take that compliment. It's really just something I threw on," she laughed, pleased at the response from Jack. "I hope it will be suitable for the restaurant." The truth is she had been scouring the shops in Stratford to find a new dress especially for the evening much to the annoyance of Isabella who wanted to spend more time sightseeing. They both stood in the hall while she double-checked her hair in the mirror. "OK, I'm ready now."

Patch ran back into the hall excitedly gripping his lead in his mouth.

"Sorry, not this time Patch, stay and look after Mummy." She patted him on the head and he sauntered reluctantly back into the kitchen and settled down by the warm oven. "Bye Mum, don't wait up." Her mother shut the door without a word. Patch whimpered, disappointed at not being invited out for a walk.

They stepped outside into the warm evening air walking side by side towards the town centre talking about her holiday.

"You know, Jack, you really should go, Stratford-upon-Avon is lovely. It's a bit touristy but that's to be expected; there are some lovely shops and restaurants. We visited Shakespeare's birthplace, it's right in the middle of the High Street and close to the theatres." She went on to explain in infinite detail the plot of Henry IV part One. Jack listened interestedly.

He hadn't seen any Shakespeare plays, having been put off at school by being forced to study 'Troilus and Cressida' and finding it dull and tedious. The way Carolyn explained it though, her Shakespeare sounded epic. Full of action, adventure, intrigue, comedy and to top it all, sword fights. Perhaps he had been missing the point all those years ago or maybe it was the way it had been taught. He understood why the children at the school learnt so much under the tutorage of Miss Jenner. Her enthusiasm for her subject was mesmerising. He too, was falling under her spell.

They arrived at the Gorgonzola restaurant and were greeted by a young man dressed in a sharp Italian tailored suit with white shirt and red tie. "Good evening, miss."

"Good evening, Enzo," Carolyn said, surprised to see another of her ex-pupils.

"Do you know all the waiters and waitresses in Holeford?" questioned Jack.

"No, I shouldn't think so," she laughed. "As I said, it is an occupational hazard."

Enzo led them down a steep staircase into the basement and showed them to their table which, unique to this restaurant, was in the cellars, under the kitchens. The walls and vaulted ceilings were of exposed brickwork. Tables were positioned down the centre and into the alcoves to the sides. Subtle lighting in sconces on the walls and candles on the tables placed in wine bottles laced with old wax dribbles, created an intimate atmosphere. Fresh roses in thin glass vases complemented the simple décor. The tables were laid with silver cutlery on red and white chequered cloths with red cotton napkins neatly folded. Enzo showed them to an alcove and held Carolyn's chair as she sat down while Jack made himself comfortable opposite her. They had a good view down the length of the restaurant which was beginning to fill. About half of the tables were now occupied and there was a gentle hum of subdued conversation with Italian music playing softly in the background.

"So, tell me, Enzo, when do you start your training? He's going to be a great chef one day, Jack," Carolyn explained proudly.

Enzo looked a little embarrassed. "I am off to Sicily next week to work for my uncle and I'll see what happens from there. We have many restaurants in the family and Dad has a half share in a vineyard. In fact, some of their wine is on our list here. Can I interest you both in a glass?" Enzo handed the wine list to Jack and menus to both of them.

"You'll go far, I like the way you promote your family's wine with such ease," Jack said laughing and took the wine list.

They agreed on a bottle of Sicily's finest Nebbiolo. Enzo left them to look at the menu, returning after a few minutes. He poured a small sample of the red liquid into a glass for Jack's approval. He raised the glass, swirled and sniffed the wine, sipped it and nodded his approval. Enzo poured a measure into both glasses placed the bottle on the table and raised his note pad and pen. They both took an appreciative sip of the dark red liquid, gave their orders and Enzo left them.

"How is Joe getting on? Did you manage to get him on the course?" asked Carolyn.

"I managed to reserve a place for him and offered it to him the same day. I must admit I was sceptical but you were so right. He accepted there and then and we're going up to head office next Friday to sign the papers and sort out his digs. He is a changed boy; hell, he is a changed man! He already seems to have matured, I can't believe what a difference it's made already. I don't know how I can ever thank you for your advice. His results were so good he's been fast-tracked into the Management Training Scheme and if he studies hard could be running a branch in five years. I may end up working for him!"

He raised his glass to hers and they chinked them together.

"All in a day's work, you might say but it's really just that I noticed the poster in the staffroom. If you hadn't put that up and allowed me access to the store that evening his future may have been very different."

The conversation paused as Enzo returned with a bread basket and bottle of spring water. As soon as he moved from the table Jack leant forward and whispered, "That's what I want to know, what actually happened that night? You wouldn't tell me in the café for fear there were people eaves dropping."

Over the meal Carolyn went through all the events of her evening in the store while Jack listened in amazement and disbelief. For Jack it answered many mysteries from his tenure in the store. The old lady in the cereal aisle, the saga with the beans, the robbery, the cold spots in the storeroom and around the store generally.

"So are you really a descendant of the Petrolingo family? Have you done any research?"

"I raised it with Mum but she wasn't very forthcoming. I think there must be something in our family history she wants to keep secret but I'll keep trying."

Back at the store Wilf and Alice were preparing to go to the club.

"Come on Alice we have to get going if we want to meet Sir James," Wilf complained.

"I don't know what to wear," she said anxiously from behind the screen in the props room. "Is it formal or casual there?"

"Does it really matter, for goodness sake?" replied Wilf. That was the trouble with women. They could never just go out. They always had to fuss around trying this outfit then that outfit and the hair wasn't quite right and then lastly there was the small (or often large) question of accessories! It gets to the point when you wonder if it is worth going out any more.

Alice could tell Wilf was getting impatient. "It's like this, Alice, there will be people there from many different periods of history and they all dress from their era. Everyone will look different and out of place to everyone else. That's the beauty of it, no one is going to judge you."

"What, not even the judge from the bloody assizes, you said he is sometimes there?" she said sarcastically.

"Lionel's a nice bloke, actually. He had some bad press following the rebellion, when all he was trying to do was restore law and order for King James. You might say he was just following orders. OK, you may think he was a bit heavy handed but you have to remember those were different times with different values. He let a lot of them off but you never hear about that. He had a job to do or it would have been his neck on the block, quite literally. Now come on or I'll never offer to take you again!"

Alice emerged from behind the screen wearing a costume she selected from a production of *The Importance of Being Earnest*. It was a brown suit with knee length skirt, white blouse and large brimmed buff coloured straw hat, with large floral bow on the side.

"How do I look?" she asked, giving them a twirl. "I wore this when I played Sissy."

Wilf glanced at her impassively. "Yeah, you look fine… now come on, we have work to do."

George watched from the now clean sofa, amused by what he had witnessed. "You two sound like an old married couple."

Wilf did a little tut and looked up at the ceiling. Alice said nothing and joined him by the stage lift and they set off.

"Don't be late home," said George sarcastically, settling down for a nice quiet evening in on his own.

"How are we getting there?" enquired Alice as they went up into the shop.

"We need to go across to the museum and then we'll drop down into the basement and use the old tunnel network. It's easier than above ground just in case there's anyone taking their psychic dog for a walk!"

Alice laughed.

"I'm serious! It does happen, sometimes the dogs go mad when they see us. That's OK and fun when we interrupt a guided ghost walk, but we don't want that tonight."

Alice wasn't convinced. They crossed the road and went through the museum doors. Alice paused to look into the main hall. "Wow this has changed! It's so clean and spacious."

"Never mind that now. You can come back another time and look around."

Wilf led her through a narrow door and down some steps into the basement. They were now in the archive room. Long rows of wooden shelving contained hundreds of cardboard boxes all carefully placed with labels on their ends noting their contents. On tables by the wall some boxes were opened and items placed out for inspection and cleaning. Angle-poised lamps peered down at relics as if studying them. Tools and note pads lay alongside waiting for the return of the historians. At the end of the room was an ancient bricked up opening. They both went through the wall effortlessly and entered a network of tunnels.

"This is amazing! I never knew this existed." Alice's eyes were wide open with excitement.

Wilf looked back at her. "Come on, this way."

Alice, behaving like a tourist, followed her guide down a narrow passage for about a hundred yards until they came to another bricked up opening in the side of the wall.

Wilf waited for her to catch up. "Now, this is a tricky bit. We have to go through a restaurant basement. It's normally fine but if they're busy there is a risk of being seen, so we need to be quick and no tricks. We go in through this wall and straight through the wall at the other end as quickly as possible."

Alice was intrigued, this was better than she had expected. First the tunnels, now this and they hadn't even got to the club yet! "Right, I'm ready, Wilf, let's go."

They went through the wall and emerged in a restaurant, and were greeted by the sound of Italian music and the sights and smells of a busy trattoria.

"This is amazing! Where are we?" Alice asked.

Wilf was surprised at the number of diners and babble this early. "I think it's called The Mozzarella or something. Never mind, let's get through here quickly. You see the wall at the end? Well, we go straight through there. Come on!" urged Wilf.

"Oh look, there's Carolyn with Jack," Alice cried out excitedly. "I didn't know they were an item. How sweet."

Wilf looked around and saw Alice heading across the room towards the two diners.

"Hello, Carolyn," she called and her movement caused the candle flames to flicker as she passed the tables.

Wilf was beside himself. "ALICE, COME BACK… She can't see you. She hasn't got her crystal ball."

Alice approached the table where the two of them were deep in conversation.

"Hello, Carolyn," she repeated, somewhat louder this time.

Carolyn didn't react. She continued her conversation with Jack as if she wasn't there.

"Oh, you're right," Alice said disappointedly. "Carolyn needs her ball to hear me."

Carolyn continued to look at Jack. "Hello Alice, I do know you're here. Is that Wilf over there with you?"

Jack looked at Carolyn as if she had suddenly gone mad. "What? Carolyn… are you alright?"

"I'm fine. We have just been joined by Alice and Wilf is on the other side of the room, he's looking very annoyed."

"No! You're pulling my leg. What? Here? Are you mucking about?" He looked quickly around the room but to no avail.

Wilf had now come over to join Alice. "Come on! We've got to keep going!" he urged.

"Hello, Wilf," Carolyn said, whilst still looking at Jack as if continuing their conversation to avoid strange looks from other diners.

Jack was totally bemused. "This is ridiculous!" he exclaimed but then he felt the temperature drop considerably.

Carolyn continued to address the two ghosts. "Why are you two here? Have you come out for a meal?"

"No, we're on a mission to save the supermarket from development. How come you can see us?" Alice said excitedly.

"I've got the little crystal in my clutch bag, which is on my lap and here you are in the Gorgonzola. Isn't that amazing?"

Wilf was trying to draw Alice away. "Carolyn, it's lovely to see you but we are in a hurry. Can we have a chat with you tomorrow night in the shop? There are some things we need to discuss with you, also we need to get someone on the inside at the museum but we must go now."

Carolyn looked confused but an idea dawned on her, "Jack, can I come to the store tomorrow night? I'd like to introduce you to your residents, they seem to have a plan brewing."

Jack was completely lost for words. This was not turning out to be the evening he had expected. A nice meal, good company and an explanation about the séance would have been fine. This was beyond belief and now Carolyn was inviting him to meet the ghosts who apparently were stood next to him in an Italian restaurant, of all places!

He was still trying to get it all straight in his head. "Do you really mean they're here now and can hear everything we say?"

"Yes Jack, haven't you been listening?"

"It's a bit hard to take it all in."

"Well, they're here but are in bit of a hurry, so is tomorrow ok?"

"Yes, of course. It will be a pleasure." Then Jack whispered to Carolyn, "They're not really here are they? You're winding me up."

"Alice, can you make a little sign of some kind and then you had better go? I can see Wilf's getting agitated and we are making a bit of a scene. We will see you at seven tomorrow night."

Alice pointed at the candle in the middle of their table.

"Watch the candle Jack," Carolyn whispered.

Alice stared at it intently and then blinked. The flame increased slightly then lifted away from the wick but still burnt. It hung there for a few seconds then went out leaving only a tail of smoke rising to the cellar ceiling. There was no draught nor did the flame flicker. It just went out, like it had been switched off.

"There, Jack, how about that?"

"Ooh!" was all he could mutter.

"See you," Alice said, waving goodbye airily and headed through the wall at the other end of the cellar with Wilf, who turned and put a thumb up as he too passed through the wall.

Enzo came over to them and re-lit the candle.

"I'm sorry. It must be draughty. Do you want to move table?" He was embarrassed that they might be uncomfortable.

"No, not at all. Everything is fine here thanks, Enzo… Just fine." Jack couldn't hide his joy at being out with Carolyn and the candle trick was the icing on the cake.

"Would you like to see the dessert menu?" Enzo asked.

They shared one portion of tiramisu and followed it with coffees and mint chocolates.

As they headed home Carolyn looped her arm in Jack's and he felt on top of the world. Carolyn felt at ease in his company, they just seemed to gel somehow and she had so much she wanted to share. She sensed the beginning of a new period in her life and it felt good.

"Wilf said that we need someone on the inside at the museum, do you know anyone that works there?"

"No sorry, Professor Halford asked me for sponsorship once but I can't say I know him personally. They're always looking for volunteers though."

"Of course, why didn't I think of that? The school's been doing history projects with him. I know just the person to introduce to him for the summer if she'll do it."

They stopped at the gate to Carolyn's house.

"This is normally the bit where I ask you in for coffee but we've already had some and I know you have to get up early."

Jack interrupted her. "I've had a wonderful, entertaining evening, but you're right. I do have to be up early, so I'll bid you farewell until tomorrow night."

Carolyn stepped close to him. "It has certainly been an eventful evening and tomorrow can't come soon enough for me. I know Wilf and Alice were up to something, hopefully then we will find out their plans," she said, then leaned forward and kissed him on the cheek.

They looked deeply into each other's eyes and parted. Nothing more needed to be said.

Carolyn noticed the curtain in the upstairs window had twitched as she headed down the path. '*Mother, do go to sleep.*' Shaking her head, she pushed the key into the lock. Jack walked down the path, turning back to watch Carolyn go safely inside where he could hear Patch barking at her safe return. '*Life is good,*' he thought and strolled off home.

Wednesday started normally, a regular flow of familiar customers came in to buy the papers along with the usual milk and bread, etc. This morning was Joan's turn on the rota along with Joe who was sporting his new lapel badge with the words Trainee Manager. Jack was more upbeat than usual greeting everyone with a cheery good morning.

"What's up with your dad, Joe?" Joan asked "Whatever he's on, I want some! He's in an exceptionally chirpy mood. You wouldn't think the future of the shop was on the line!"

"He went on a date with Miss Jenner last night. He's been up beat for days now and I think he's smitten. She prompted Dad to get me on the training scheme. I owe her a lot." Joe gently polished his new ID badge with his sleeve.

"Carolyn Jenner; well, I can see the attraction. She's very attractive. I'm amazed she's still single. She's Molly's teacher, you know. In fact, she phoned us this morning during breakfast and Molly's going to see her about a possible summer holiday job that has suddenly come up at the museum."

After breakfast, Molly left her dad reading the paper and went on her mission to see Carolyn. Alice had already explained the mysterious face at the museum window and Molly was intrigued at the connection with the phone call. She was not one to refuse a challenge and if she could help her friends in any way to stay in their home she was willing to try. She arrived at Carolyn's house and paused at the gate. Gathering her thoughts, she walked up and rang the bell. Carolyn answered the door closely followed by Patch, hoping for a walk.

"Hello Molly, you're very prompt."

Molly caught her breath. She had run all the way from Armstrong Close. "Hello miss. Is this to do with Alice, Wilf and George?"

Carolyn looked out into the garden to see if anyone was listening. "I'll get my coat, let's go for a walk."

She opened the cupboard under the stairs and put a light blue bomber jacket on over her Che Guevara printed red tee shirt and scruffy jeans. She also had Patch's lead in her hand. "Mum, I'm just taking Patch for a walk."

"OK dear," cried a voice from the top of the stairs.

Patch heard the word 'walk' and needed no further invitation. He ran up the hall, ball clamped firmly in his jaws and stood patiently by Carolyn while she clipped on his lead.

"Let's go over to the park, I think whatever we have to discuss is for our ears only, don't you?"

"Yes, miss," Molly replied, enjoying the intrigue.

They strolled across the road towards the green where they could talk in confidence. Patch strained at the lead, he knew play time was only a few steps away. Carolyn looked down at the bright, intelligent girl who reminded her of her younger self.

"Now, first things first, please call me Carolyn. There really is no need to be formal out of school."

"OK, Miss… I mean Carolyn, thank you."

They found a park bench in the shade of the trees and sat as equals, sharing knowledge about the tenants of Price Low. Patch was allowed off the lead, he dropped the ball to the ground ready for the games to begin. Carolyn threw it across the open grassland and off he went.

Molly opened the conversation. "You know they're planning to knock down the shop and build flats? Well, the surveyors have been measuring up already and Alice is afraid they may have to move out, and they don't want to."

"Yes, I'm aware of the plans. Jack told me all about it," Carolyn said.

Molly gave her a knowing look. She had heard her mum telling Dad all about Jack's meetings with Carolyn.

"What does that look mean?" Carolyn enquired defensively and with some embarrassment.

"Well, you've been seen out with him. Is he your boyfriend?" she enquired bluntly.

"Not exactly. I have been pushing him to arrange a promotion for Joe. Now, enough about me, what about these surveyors," Carolyn hastily added to change the subject.

"They've arranged for an archaeologist to come and dig up the car park. The thing is they, I mean Wilf mostly, think the man in the museum opposite was showing a lot of interest in their activities and I think you may be able to help us find out what his interest really is. Maybe that will help in some way? Can I get the summer job there? I could do some investigation," Molly added excitedly.

Carolyn threw the ball again for an impatient Patch and turned to face Molly. "You're thinking along exactly the same lines as me. I saw Wilf and Alice last night. They passed through the walls of the restaurant where we were having a meal. They said they were off to a club of some kind. I think they may already be doing some investigating themselves. However, they did say they needed someone on the inside at the museum."

"Were they going to the Collington Club? That's where all the ghosts hang out. It's a sort of social club for spirits. Alice has been on about wanting to go there for ages." Molly talked as if it was normal to know the business of the spirit world. "I think it would be fun to go there too. Maybe a little scary though, don't you think?"

"That could well have been it, then," Carolyn decided. "They were in a bit of a hurry." She realised she had a lot of catching up to do. Molly was way ahead of her with knowledge of the three ghosts' activities. "Did Wilf say what the man at the window looked like?"

"He said he had glasses and wild grey hair."

"That sounds like Professor Halford. He's the curator of the museum. I know him quite well. He has helped with some school projects, he's a very nice man. He's done a lot of work to improve the museum presentation, it gets quite busy at times now, much more than it used to. I think he brought a lot of ideas from London. We need to act fast and if you are up for it we could go and see him this morning."

"Are you sure it's that simple? There might not be a job." Molly said.

"By the time we have finished this morning there will be, Molly. He's always keen to encourage potential young historians. He won't be able to resist."

Molly's eyes lit up. "Can you really do that, so soon? That would be brilliant."

"Never mind that, are you sure you want to do this? It really is going to be a bit like spying, what if you get found out?" Carolyn looked apprehensive, what was she getting Molly into?

"I don't mind at all, it will be fun. I get to go behind the scenes at a real museum, do a bit of espionage and meet a real professor. I can't wait!" Molly said excitedly.

"Well, as long as you are sure, shall we go and talk to him now?"

"Is he expecting us?"

"Well sort of, I did phone and say I may pop in with a potential volunteer. There's no time to lose, if you're happy to try, let's go. I had better drop off Patch and smarten up, we need to impress!"

"Cool, it's nice to have someone to share this secret with. Most people would think we're a bit bonkers," replied Molly.

They then walked back to Carolyn's house. Half an hour later they emerged with Carolyn dressed in her best suit. Out to impress.

They soon arrived at the museum and stopped outside.

"Now, are you sure you want to do this? It's a big step you are taking and no one will blame you if you back out." Carolyn wanted to be absolutely sure that Molly knew what she could be taking on before they crossed the threshold. "Don't forget we will need to get permission from your parents before you can start, assuming we can charm our way in. I did call your mum this morning so she's aware that I am going to try and talk to the museum for you."

"That's fine, we can see Mum later. I am really looking forward to it, come on let's go in." Molly eagerly pushed the heavy Gothic oak door open and led the way into the foyer. Immediately to the left was a glass cabinet with a selection of exhibits displaying what visitors might expect or want or investigate further as they explored the main hall. On the right wall was a section of a Roman mosaic alongside an information board explaining where this had been found in the town and a selection of leaflets giving information on visitor attractions in the area. As they moved forward, the short corridor led them into the entrance hall with its impressive sweeping stone stairwell. To their left was the deliberately small reception counter, to leave as much room as possible for their vast collection of exhibits to be displayed. Even so, there was an enormous amount of them stored in the basement, off-site in a building to the rear and in a disused church down the road. The reception staff would have liked a little more room. It was a tight squeeze for two of them to work in and was especially restricting when there was a queue of visitors and only the one till, which was no longer a rare occasion since the new curator had taken over and made the exhibits more dynamic. Thankfully at this time, Carolyn and Molly were their only visitors. The museum, like lots of other small town public buildings, could not function without the help and enthusiasm of a willing band of volunteers like the mature lady stood behind the desk today who welcomed them both with a warm smile.

"Good morning, will that be one adult and one child?" she asked politely.

"No, not exactly," Carolyn explained. "We haven't come to look round. I'm from Holeford Modern School, Professor Halford should be expecting us."

From the room behind the counter a distant voice was heard.

"Carolyn, is that you?" They were in luck. The Professor was sorting through some papers in the office. He dropped them onto an already overflowing desk, and came through immediately into the reception hall. Molly was unprepared for the tall, wild haired man who now looked across the counter at her. "Ah, you must be Molly." He held out his hand to her encouragingly and Molly shook it tentatively. '*He knows my name. He looks very clever. Wow! Does he know everything?* she thought.

"Good morning, sir," she said politely.

"Carolyn has told me so much about you. I'm looking forward to showing you around and if you like what you see I would be pleased to give you a holiday job. There's no pay I'm afraid and you may end up making the tea at times but I can assure you there won't be a dull moment. We have so much to do and it does get busy when the tourists come out of their lodgings and even more when it rains and they can't go to the beach. Now come on up to my office where we can discuss the details. How much time can you spare us? I hear your history results have been very good. Carolyn is such an inspiration to her students." The Professor had hardly taken a breath. Carolyn gave her a reassuring smile and before she knew what was happening, they had all ascended the stairs, walked across the gallery of the library and into his office through a secret door in the oak panelling. The Professor sat at his large mahogany desk which was covered in files. All the surfaces around the room were piled high with books and more files tied together with string to prevent the contents escaping.

"Now first things first, young lady. You're to address me as Prof; everyone does, there's no airs and graces around here. We're all a team, trying to drag history into the present day to entertain and inspire the masses." He rang a bell on the desk and the lady from reception entered. "Beryl, this is Molly. She will hopefully be joining us for the summer, now be a dear and make us all a nice cup of tea."

Beryl nodded politely. "Hi Molly. Welcome to the team." She shook her hand and left to get the refreshments.

"Thanks for this, Prof. I think Molly will gain a lot of useful experience over the next few weeks, due to your generosity." '*This is going really well.*' she thought.

"Not at all, Carolyn. I am pleased to help and encourage potential historians."

Molly couldn't believe this was happening. Carolyn had obviously paved the way and now she was going to join a team, not as a school child but as an equal, in an adult world. She felt grown up but a little apprehensive too. It was all happening so quickly.

During their tea, they agreed that Molly would initially join them for afternoons only, from Monday to Friday and if it all worked out then they would increase the hours. He then took them on a behind the scenes tour of the museum through all the exhibition halls into the offices and storerooms, down into the basement archives and finally into the library. They sat there for a while on large red leather chairs in front of an imposing fireplace which had exotic animals intricately carved into the stone surround.

The Professor could see Molly was overwhelmed with information. "It's a lot to take in, but don't worry. At least you now have a vague idea of your way around and the other staff will help you." He was keen for Molly to start as soon as possible. He handed her a parental consent form which had to be signed and suggested that she return after lunch to see Beryl and fill out some other forms.

Carolyn and Molly went out of the museum and crossed the road to update Joan and asked her if she would be happy to give her consent.

Joan was surprised at the short notice but pleased that her daughter was going to work in the museum. She could see the excitement in Molly's eyes. "It will mean giving up helping your dad with the milk round, you'll need your energy for your afternoon shifts."

"Yes, I suppose I will, Mum. I hope Dad will understand."

Carolyn explained the arrangement to Joan and reassured her about what was expected of Molly. She pointed out that the Professor could be a useful contact if she wished to follow a study path in English and history over the next two years and possibly go on to college or university.

After lunch Molly returned to the museum with the forms and Beryl invited her behind the reception desk. She then presented her with a museum ID badge which read '*Molly Goodall, Volunteer*'. She suddenly felt very grown up and excited.

12

The Morning After

The ghosts were late stirring on Wednesday morning.

"We had a busy night, George!" pointed out Wilf.

"Never mind that. You haven't told me what happened. Come on, Alice, spill the beans," George pleaded. Wilf looked across the room at Alice, giving her a discreet nod of consent to tell the story of their evening escapade.

"Well, we met Jack and Carolyn in the Gorgonzola restaurant on the way. That was exciting. Jack couldn't see us but Carolyn could. She had the little crystal with her."

"That bit you've told me, several times already," George interrupted. "Now get to the good bit, what about the club?"

"Sorry, right to the point." Alice was excited and rushing her words. "Well the club… it's quite a long walk from here and there are so many tunnels I don't know how we didn't get lost."

"Yes, OK, I know what the place is like, but what happened?" George was getting impatient.

Alice carried on regardless. "Well, it was not what I was expecting. In fact it was rather dull really. The room was a big cellar, rather like the restaurant we passed through on the way. There were ghosts sitting around at various tables chatting and some stood at a bar, near the blocked off stairs. Lionel, 'the hanging judge', was showing off. Doing some tricks but they didn't work very well because we could see through his cloak at all the hidden cards. It was quite funny really. His patter was good though. There was a small group at a table that didn't appreciate his magic at all and one scowled at him. Wilf said they were the ones he sentenced to death, so it's hardly surprising they weren't amused by his act. I'm amazed they were in the same room as him but I suppose it's just as much their club as his. A couple of Roman guards from Monkton

Hillfort were there. Did you know Sir Mortimer Halford has a summer residence under the hillfort? He came back to see where he had been digging, just after he passed over and liked it so much he keeps coming back. He was a bit embarrassed, he said, because the Romans were really nice and hadn't actually slaughtered everyone like he had assumed from his dig in 1937. It turned out he had dug up the cemetery for the hillfort and not a battleground at all but they have forgiven him for the bad press and are now the best of friends. Oh, and there was a proper knight there! He said he was Sir Gawain and served at Arthur's round table, Wilf said he probably served the drinks! I think he was right, he wasn't very butch at all and I can't see him ever fighting any dragons, not even squirrels, come to think of it." She laughed.

George again interrupted, trying to steer her enthusiasm back to the subject. "This is all very well and I'm sure you had a lovely night out, both of you, but, what about the supermarket? Did you find out anything to our advantage?"

"Oh yes, well, we did meet the late Sir James Randall the previous museum curator. He's a miserable man and hates what Professor Halford had done to the museum. He reckons he's turned the place into a fairground freak show… Anyway, he did say he'd heard the Professor wants to carry out further digs in the area, carrying on his father's work. Giovanni… one of the Roman soldiers, quite dishy actually, told me he's very proud of his son's work at the museum." Alice went silent.

"Is that it?" George said indignantly. "After all that? Well, we haven't got much to tell Carolyn tonight. I hope she'll have some better ideas."

Alice was a bit annoyed. "Well, we did our best. There were no guarantees who would be there." She stood with hands on hips staring indignantly at George.

Wilf butted in quickly. "It wasn't a complete disaster. I did mention to Carolyn about getting someone on the inside at the museum. We just need to get close to Sir Dominic. Hopefully she will be able to help with that."

The day dragged for Jack. It was quiet in Holeford. It was a nice sunny day and most of his customers who were not working had gone to the beach a few miles away. After the initial rush there wasn't much to do in the shop, all his paperwork was up to date and there was no stock to order today. He did write the advert for a new shelf stacker and in line with new company policy, this was now to be a night-time job that would also include security duties. It was a relief that Joe had got his promotion as he wouldn't have liked the anti-social night working. He looked around the store, tidied a few shelves and even restocked some shelving himself, just to pass the time.

"Penny for your thoughts," said Joan, as she sat at the till with a copy of yesterday's Chronicle spread out in front of her.

"Life's a funny thing, Joan," he reflected. "There I was jogging along quietly and then suddenly Joe is off to college, the future of this store is in jeopardy and there's also the challenge of launching a new superstore."

"And Carolyn enters your life," Joan said, gently probing for information. "She's had quite an impact on you, I hear."

"Yes, you're right. But not like you're thinking," he added quickly. "We've struck up a friendship, that's all, and she's been very helpful to Joe but it's not like that. I do enjoy her company, though."

Joan looked disappointed. "Well, she's certainly put a spring in your step, which is good to see."

Jack blushed. "I have to admit, she's quite special."

The hands on the clock finally crawled round to six. One hour to closing and not a soul in the shop or even in Princes Road for that matter. It was like they were the only people in the world. Then Carolyn arrived, coming through the entrance doors backwards, carrying a box wrapped in a polythene bag.

"Hello Joan. Hi, Jack," she said in cheerful tone. "I know I'm early, but I had a hunch you might be quiet. It's like the *Mary Celeste* out there. I think everyone's gone to the seaside."

Joan gave Jack a knowing look, *just good friends eh,* she thought.

"Do you fancy an ice cream? The van is just down the road, if I'm quick I could get us a treat but I do need to be quick. He looked like he was packing up." Before either of them could reply, Carolyn put the parcel down on the counter and ran out the door returning five minutes later with three 99s, their chocolate flakes standing proud in the soft cold vanilla ice-cream balanced on the wafer cone. "He was going to drive off so I hope you both wanted one, you need to hurry, they're beginning to melt," she said feeling a drip of cold cream running down over her fingers.

At six-thirty Jack decided to close early. Joan cashed up while Jack locked the doors and turned out the lights. Carolyn went through to the staffroom to wash her hands and prepare for the meeting.

"Have a nice evening, you two," Joan said with a knowing smile.

Jack let her out and locked the door behind her. "Goodnight, Joan, and try to keep your imagination under control."

Jack re-joined Carolyn in the staffroom with Wilf, George and Alice already positioned around the table waiting for him. Carolyn had the crystal ball in front of her laid out on the velvet tablecloth.

Jack nervously rubbed his hands together as he entered the room. "Right, what do we do? Do we have to light some candles, do you have to go into a trance and summon them up?"

"Come and sit down, none of that will be necessary they're already here." She offered him a chair next to her, to avoid the problem of him sitting on one of the actors.

"It does feel cold in here. I do hope that tonight I may be able to meet them properly."

To be polite Jack turned and addressed the empty seats. "Well, good evening, you three. How are you all?"

"Good evening," replied George, Wilf and Alice in unison. "We're fine. How are you?"

"Nothing to say for yourselves, then?" exclaimed Jack.

"Well, that's charming," said Alice, waving her arms around frantically trying to get Jack's attention.

Carolyn held his hand and placed it on the crystal ball. "No, this isn't going to work," she said. "Sit in my chair." She stood up and Jack moved over. Carolyn stood behind him, leant over him and taking his hands she held them gently on the crystal ball. The three sat and watched. "Now, do you sense anything?"

Jack could feel the heat of her body as she leaned into his back and the tenderness of her warm hands touching his. Carolyn's head was alongside his and she whispered into his ear.

"Jack, you're shaking. Don't be nervous. I'm with you. There's nothing to be afraid of. Can you see or feel our friends around the table?"

"He can feel something," George quipped, "but I don't think it's us!"

"Shush George! This is serious," Carolyn said crossly.

"I'm sorry, there's nothing. This is very nice but I can't hear or see them."

Carolyn was disappointed. "Jack Bonfield, you don't have a psychic bone in your body! That is such a shame."

Jack felt like he had let her down. "I'm sorry I wish I could have sensed something. I do believe you and wanted to be able to share this with you."

Carolyn held his hand again to console him. "Never mind, it may just take time for you to adjust. In the meantime, Wilf has been practising a little display for you, to show their presence."

Wilf stood up, George moved over by the wall and Alice stayed alongside Wilf.

"Off you go Wilf," she encouraged.

Jack watched as a tin of beans entered the room from the store and landed gently in the middle of the table. "OH MY GOD! Carolyn, that's amazing. How are you doing that?" Jack was glued to his seat but reached out and grabbed her hand for reassurance.

"I'm not doing it, it's taken Wilf hours of practice. Now watch!" she ordered reproachfully, placing her other hand on his now shaking hands.

Another tin of beans floated in and landed next to the one on the table, closely followed by a third, this time controlled by Alice. It hovered above the other two then revolved to land upside-down forming a small pyramid.

Jack couldn't control his excitement and tears of joy welled in his eyes. He let go of her hand and took a handkerchief from his pocket and dried them. "I'm sorry. I don't know what's come over me. So it was them who moved the beans and all this time I blamed Joe. I feel so ashamed."

Carolyn comforted him. "Don't worry, Jack, it must be unsettling for you. I can assure you they're very friendly, if a bit mischievous sometimes but they've nothing but respect for you and your staff. One day you may be able to communicate with them. Now let's get on with the agenda for tonight's meeting to save their home. Don't worry, I'll repeat what they have to say to you." She got out a pen and paper and chaired the meeting. "Right, Alice, how did you get on with Wilf at the club?"

"Well, not as well as we had hoped. We did get to talk to Sir James, the old curator, but he was in a filthy mood about what the Professor has done to his museum. He said he's turned it into a fairground sideshow with loads of noisy children wandering through putting their sticky fingerprints all over the display cases. Half of the exhibits have been put back into storage and he's added colourful explanation boards." Alice put on a deep voice trying to impersonate Sir James. "*The man's a fool, whatever next? Before you know it he will add a café to finish off the cheap commercialisation of my museum!*" Alice was obviously incensed by the miserable attitude of the old curator.

Wilf butted in to get things back on track. "Frankly, it was a waste of time. All we do know is, there's a link between the Professor and his father's work done in the 1930s but that's it."

124

"Well, thanks for trying. That may be useful." Carolyn then repeated the news to Jack, who was trying to get his head around the fact that apparently there is a social club in Holeford for ghosts and it's located directly below the council's own social club in Collington House.

Carolyn could see the, 'little boy lost', expression on his face. "I know it's a lot to take in but bear with us. This morning I went with Molly to the museum to talk to Professor Halford. I know him from work with the school. It wasn't difficult to persuade him that a bright student with potential to go on to study history at university was looking for a chance to help at the museum in the holidays. He was impressed with Molly and immediately offered her a position as a volunteer starting straight away. Not only does she get a step on the ladder but she is now our girl on the inside."

George looked concerned. "You can't expect a young girl to infiltrate the museum and spy for us. That's too much to ask!"

Carolyn had been prepared for some resistance. "There's no need to worry. This was as much Molly's idea as mine. She is keen to help but it will also give her a huge opportunity to learn about working in a museum and hopefully the Professor will inspire her to further her studies. She's already interested in history and English so it may lead to a future career. Anyway, what is there to look suspicious? A young academic, introduced by her teacher, showing interest in the exhibits and local history is right up the Professor's street. He won't suspect a thing, I'm sure of it."

Jack looked admiringly at her. "That's terrific, not only are you trying to help our friends here but you're also helping Molly to a potential career. That's brilliant."

George was not so convinced. "I want to be sure Molly is happy to do this. You two have gone quiet." He looked accusingly across the table at Wilf and Alice.

"It's fine by us," Wilf replied. "Molly's a smart kid and she may unearth something that could help us."

"Good, that's settled then. Meeting adjourned," Carolyn said decisively, finished her note taking and put down the pen. "Just as well because she starts this Friday!"

Jack looked bemused. "Is that it then? Is it agreed?"

"Yes, that's it for now."

The three actors thanked her for her help and Alice returned the tins of beans to the shop, while Jack and Carolyn looked on appreciatively.

"Now, Jack, I suggest you take me to the pub for a drink and I'll fill you in on what is going to happen next."

Jack was thrilled at the idea of them spending the rest of the evening together and hoped to get a clearer picture of what exactly had gone on around him that evening. While Carolyn packed up the crystal ball he did the final checks around the store and they left together through the rear service door where he turned off the lights and set the alarm.

They headed up the road to the Royal Arms for a well-earned drink. Jack avoided going to the Kings Head despite it being closer because of its association with his ex-wife and her waiter there. They settled on the sofa in the lounge bar with a pint of Holeford Best and a Bacardi and Coke. They continued talking about the development of the store and ways they could help their ghostly friends. As the conversation moved to Joe, Jack had a bright idea.

"This may sound a bit forward but, as you know we're going to head office in London on Friday to meet the trainer, sign some forms and see his accommodation. Would you like to come with us? To be honest, we need to buy a new suit for Joe and I'm useless at choosing clothes."

"That would be lovely. I'm afraid that shopping, especially in London, is one of my weaknesses... well that and the theatre, so I hope you don't mind if I look for a few things for myself. I'll try to confine the expedition to Oxford Street, hopefully we will have enough time."

Jack was thrilled. "Fantastic, we're going to have a great day out, I can feel it. We should be done at HQ by mid-day and it's only a short trip on the Underground to Tottenham Court Road station."

They drank up and walked back through the park. The flowers were in full bloom, trees swaying gently in the breeze. The band stand looked resplendent following a fresh coat of paint. The open space was busy with people walking their dogs and children shouting with joy in the play park. They could hear the distant click of bowls from the green behind a distant hedge and the pit-pat of a tennis match on the hard court behind them. Everyone seemed to be out enjoying the sunshine. They sat on a park bench for a while by the Victorian clock and chatted, enrobed in the glory of a beautiful summer's evening.

Later that night Jack had an idea to add to their trip to London.

Next day Joe's forms arrived in the morning post and Jack started to fill them out. He called the trainer at HQ to check on a detail and confirmed the time of their visit on Friday. She also offered overnight accommodation for Joe to meet his fellow students for a 'bonding session' at the company flat. He then asked to speak to his friend Steve in promotions. He knew that Price Low sponsored some theatre productions and enquired about any available tickets. Steve called back an hour later with news of some returned tickets for the RSC production of *Henry V* starring Alan Howard, Charles Dance and George Baker. Steve told him these tickets were like gold dust so Jack couldn't believe his luck. He called Carolyn straight away; he had to confirm back within the hour or he would lose them.

She was amazed when he told her. "I can't believe it, that's fantastic, I just read the review this morning and it said that it's a sell-out."

"So, do you want me to say yes?"

"Oh yes, Jack, don't lose them. This is brilliant but how did you manage it?"

"I can't take too much credit for it, Finbarr is a patron of the arts. Who would have thought it? We have to pick the tickets up from the box office. Is that normal?" Theatre was not one of Jack's usual pastimes.

"Yes, that's fine," Carolyn reassured him. "You know that Charles Dance is in it? He's one of my favourite actors."

"I haven't been to the theatre since I took Joe to a pantomime when he was ten. It all sounds a bit highbrow for me. We didn't do much Shakespeare at school but when we did it was difficult to understand."

"You'll have to trust me with this one, Jack. Just relax and let it all flow over you and I guarantee you'll enjoy it. If not, I'll treat you to a meal at the Gorgonzola as compensation," she laughed. She was not surprised at Jack's fears. She had met resistance to Shakespeare often. In fact, all her pupils were pre-conditioned to hate the plays until she revealed the magic of his works to them. *Henry V* was a good all round one with lots of stirring speeches, fights, comic characters and romance thrown in for good measure.

"Well, it sounds OK when you put it like that. I'll call you back later to let you know how I got on."

No sooner had he put the phone down on Steve than it rang again. "Is that you Barnett?" From the phone line came the unmistakable loud hailer voice of Finbarr Lowe.

"Bonfield, sir. My name is Bonfield."

"Yes, right, Bonfield. I have been reading the report from the surveyor and it all seems in good order, apart from this archaeological nonsense.

I've told them to get on with it anyway and you'll have contractors with a machine there on Monday to dig up the car park while the archaeologist looks in the damned hole. Load of old baloney if you ask me but there you go!"

"How long are they going to be here?"

"They say three days should do it, so you'll have to work your deliveries around them."

"I'm sure we can manage," Jack replied, as his mind shifted into overtime trying to predict the disruption.

"Good, knew you would... Oh! And one other thing, Barnford, there has been a lot of rot talked about the shop being haunted, of all things. It's not done your sales any harm but may put buyers off living there so I'm going to put a stop to it. Have you seen that film *The Exorcist*? It was out a couple of years ago. Well a friend of mine knows a priest who does that exercising sort of thing for a few quid so he's coming over to you on Saturday night to clear out any evil spirits. At least we will be able to say it's been dealt with, should put people's minds at rest."

"You did see '*The Exorcist*,' didn't you, Finbarr? It didn't end well for the priest, you know."

"No, I didn't as a matter of fact, not my thing, but that's just cinema tosh. I'm putting a stop to all the rumours, Banfield, so let him in and let him do his stuff, alright?" Finbarr was sounding agitated at being questioned so Jack didn't push the conversation any further. "He'll be in touch with you," and with that the phone went dead.

"And goodbye to you, too, Fishbar," Jack said sarcastically to the vacant tone buzzing in his ear and replaced the receiver.

The impact of Finbarr's information then dawned on him. He hadn't met the ghosts properly yet but now their existence was under threat. Then he thought of Carolyn and Molly. They had a bond with them, how would they react? What if this priest could move them on, where would they go, what would happen to them? This could have terrible consequences. He lifted the receiver and phoned Carolyn immediately. There was no answer.

He walked out into the shop to find Joan and noticed Molly emerging from the stock room. She had visited under the pretence of looking for one of her school books to update Alice on her job at the museum.

"Molly, do you know where Carolyn is?" he asked urgently.

"She's in the shop talking to Mum."

Carolyn saw him and waved. He couldn't believe his luck. "Hi, Jack, how did you get on with the tickets?"

"Yes…, yes that's all fine but I just had a call from Finbarr, we need to talk NOW, in private."

Carolyn's excitement turned to apprehension. She could see something was wrong by Jack's expression.

"Come into the office."

"Jack, what's wrong? You're worrying me. You look like you've seen a ghost. Sorry that wasn't meant to be funny, are you alright? It's nothing bad to do with Joe's new job, is it?"

Jack closed the door. Wilf was also in the room closely followed by Alice. He had heard part of the call from Finbarr and had come up through the floor to see what was going on.

"Hello you two," Carolyn said. "Now, Jack, what's up? You look terrible! Whatever it is I'm sure we can sort it out."

"I don't know that we can. I've just heard from Finbarr. He's arranged for a priest to come here on Saturday night to perform an exorcism to rid us of our ghosts."

You could hear a pin drop in the room and they all turned pale as the shock hit them. All apart from Wilf and Alice who were pale already.

Carolyn was the first to speak. "What, like in that awful horror film that was at the cinema a while ago?"

"Yes, exactly!" Jack said agitatedly.

"What are we going to do? If that happens we will be out on the streets or condemned to infinite torment," Wilf said pessimistically.

Carolyn looked distraught.

Jack couldn't bear to see her upset. "Hold on Carolyn all is not lost… We all need to focus and come up with a solution a bit quick. Wilf, if you can hear me, what do you suggest?"

"Does exorcism actually work or is it just a gimmicky story?" Carolyn asked.

"Yes, it does work, and worse than that, I have heard some terrible stories of botched attempts at removing ghosts. I'll spare you the details but we need to be prepared to move on immediately," Wilf said, looking paler and more transparent than usual.

Alice felt like crying. "We'll be alright though… won't we?" she said in a shaky voice trying to reassure herself.

Carolyn gathered her thoughts and took control. "Jack's right, we need a plan. Wilf, can you talk to the Grim Reaper and find out what options there are? Is George here? He may have some ideas?"

"George has gone to the club, I'll see what I can do in his absence, try not to worry. We just need to be prepared for Saturday, whatever," Wilf reassured her. He signalled to Alice and they descended through the floor.

The phone started ringing, Jack nervously lifted the receiver.

"Hello, is that Mr Bonfield?" the voice asked.

"Yes, this is Jack Bonfield."

"I am Father Michael McManus. I believe you have a problem with a possession of evil spirits in your property and I've been asked by your owner, Mr Lowe, to come and rid you of your demons. I shall come to the shop on Saturday evening at eleven-thirty when I'll perform the necessary rituals and remove the paranormal beings. They will trouble you no more. I shall send them to a place from whence they will never work their evil on you, or anyone else, again," he finished reassuringly.

"Eleven-thirty this Saturday," Jack said vacantly, surprised at the speed of the events.

"Is that a problem? If it is, I'll contact Mr Lowe and say you are not willing to assist in this most serious matter," replied the priest sternly.

"No, no, eleven-thirty will be OK. If you come to the front door and tap the glass I'll be there to let you in. Is there anything you need from me?" Jack asked, far from happy about having to return to the store so late in the evening for this stranger to do something he wished was not happening at all.

Carolyn watched the helpless Jack agree to this terrible turn of events.

Jack concluded the call. "OK, see you on Saturday." He replaced the receiver and looked ashen. "Well, that's that then. Saturday it is and there's nothing we can do to stop it."

"Do you think we should tell Molly?" Carolyn said

"I'm not sure… would she understand? But if we don't she'll be upset that we haven't included her, after all she's going to spy for us in the museum. Oh God, this is getting deep, Carolyn. I'm not comfortable with this."

Carolyn remembered a speech by Lady Macbeth. They had gone this far and they couldn't turn back. It was time to 'screw their courage to the sticking place'. "I'll have to tell her, it's only fair, leave it to me, Jack."

"OK, as long as you know what you're doing."

"I'll try and catch up with her now."

Jack couldn't see but she had her fingers crossed and hidden behind her back. "I haven't got a clue what we can do to prevent this exorcism. I just hope Wilf or George can come up with something."

Molly had just left the shop and was heading home. Carolyn caught up with her in the High Street and broke the news to her of the danger their friends were in without sounding too sensational. Even so, Molly could not contain her anguish and began to sob. Carolyn sat with her on a bench in the precinct. She shared Molly's upset and also felt tearful. They both sat in silence for a short while. Carolyn eventually reassured her that they were doing all they could.

"Miss, I am glad you told me but I don't see what we can do? Does this mean I don't need to go to the museum?"

"No we must carry on, Molly, the battle is not lost. We must have faith." She touched her on the cheek. "Now dry your eyes and go on home, I'll keep you informed. Please try not to worry."

Fat chance, Molly thought. She could do nothing but worry!

Below the store, others were talking over their options.

"I wish George would hurry back, we need him here. Why has he gone to the club anyway? He hates it there. We only have till Saturday night. What are we going to do, Wilf?" Alice looked towards him for some comfort.

"The first job is to pack our bags ready for a quick exit, just in case. If we get caught up in the ritual it could be curtains for us. We have to be prepared to move on, Alice. George has no idea what danger we are all in yet. Where the hell is he?"

Carolyn returned to the office. She was considering the events of the past few weeks. How suddenly her new adventure was beginning to unravel and how cruel it was that Molly was having to deal with all this, too.

Jack looked up as she entered the room. "How did she take it?"

She crumpled into the chair opposite. "That was the hardest thing I've ever done Jack, I hate having secrets but sharing them with a fifteen-year-old... It's a burden she should never have to carry, it's not right, this is too cruel. I need to be here with you on Saturday... please?"

"I would love that. I don't relish going through this on my own but are you sure? I don't think it's going to be a pleasant experience."

"I think I owe it to Molly and the others and I was the one who involved you in all this. I feel bad about making you get to know them all and then having to oversee Saturday's events. Please, Jack, let me join you. I have to see this through." She reached over the desk and held his hands in hers. "It's the least I can do." She looked into his eyes, pleading with him to allow her to come.

"If you're absolutely sure. Your concern for others is an example to a selfish old sod like me. Of course you can be here. I'll be glad of your company. Thank you." He kissed the back of her hand. "Now, what are you doing for tea?" he enquired, trying to lighten the mood.

"I promised to be home by six, Mum is cooking tonight. We haven't had much time together since I got back from Stratford and I want to show her the photos. I'll see you and Joe in the morning for our trip to London, we can talk then."

Friday morning

The next morning Joe was up early, bags packed and ready in the hall for the trip. As he was now staying over after visiting HQ, Jack would have the rest of the day and evening with Carolyn and Joe wouldn't have to spend his time traipsing around the shops, which was definitely not his favourite pastime. They could sort out his new suit in Holeford before he started the course and moved to London properly.

After a quick breakfast they loaded the car and drove round to pick up Carolyn and headed to East Finchley in north London. The journey took only two hours. Jack parked at HQ where he would be able to leave the car for the day. They met the trainer, Sarah, in reception and after welcome coffees and filling out yet more forms, she took them on a guided tour of the training facilities where they joined up with several of Joe's fellow students. To Joe's obvious relief Jack made their excuses, leaving him to continue exploring his new surroundings and get to know the others without a parent in tow. Jack and Carolyn headed for the Underground station and within half an hour were in central London. Carolyn was in her element. She loved shopping in London and took Jack on a guided tour of her favourite shops. From Piccadilly they moved through Regent Street via Savile Row, headed east along Oxford Street and then westward back past Liberty into Carnaby Street, where they spent the remainder of the afternoon. Carolyn acquired several bags, which Jack chivalrously carried for her, containing a new dress, shawl, scarf and shoes. Along with aching feet and a desire never to enter another clothes shop, Jack, with his first dalliance into designer fashion, had acquired a Paul Smith jacket which Carolyn had persuaded him to buy, after insisting that it looked terrific on him. He had to admit he felt good in it while doing his best to ignore the price. He would certainly look the biz back in Holeford. They decided to eat in Carnaby Street as they were both too weary to go further and it was also a convenient stop-off before the show.

After a light meal and rest they headed to the theatre to see the Royal Shakespeare Company production of *Henry V.* Jack had to admit he had been dreading this part of the day and his feet dragged as they entered the foyer and he went to the box office to collect the tickets. It turned out that Finbarr was indeed a patron of the arts. The concierge came over to them and invited them both to join the champagne reception in the sponsors' lounge where, along with a small group of fellow supporters, they were presented with a copy of the programme and invited to return for complimentary drinks in the interval and again after the performance. Jack felt out of place with all the shopping bags encumbering them but that was soon taken care of as they were whisked away to be returned, by the cloakroom assistant, at the end of the show. Carolyn couldn't believe the treatment they were receiving and couldn't help but be impressed by Jack's contacts. The champagne had relaxed Jack's pre-theatre nerves and he was now relishing the experience. They were shown to their seats by the uniformed doorman, large comfy seats in the centre stalls. The best seats in the house! This date was going to be hard for him to top.

As the lights dimmed, Jack was totally unprepared for the spectacle that unfolded in front of him. The show began with the chorus setting the scene and instructing the audience to suspend belief and use their imagination. Jack felt as if he was talking directly to him. The less he concentrated the more he somehow understood everything, he relaxed and let the play engulf him. Perhaps this wasn't going to be so bad after all, he thought.

He was moved at times, he laughed, he cared about the characters and was shocked and excited by the realism of the sword fights as sparks flew from the clash of steel only feet from the audience. The sweat and fake blood as warriors fell was all so realistic. It seemed much more violent and real than watching such things on the TV at home. He could sense the energy of the anger and hatred emanating from the stage. He was completely won over. He had seen nothing like it before and as the curtain fell for the last time, he stood spontaneously with the whole audience clapping and cheering, emotion showing all over his face at the overwhelming experience.

He leant over to Carolyn and confided, "I didn't know it was like this, you were right, you've opened my eyes to a whole new world."

"I told you to trust me, Jack," and she held his hand, thrilled at the intimacy they both felt by sharing such a great experience.

They had been invited back to the lounge for a post-performance drink and to their surprise, Charles Dance came and joined them all. He thanked them for attending and raised a toast to the sponsors before meeting everyone individually and signing their programmes. It was now Carolyn's turn to be overwhelmed.

Neither of them remembered much about the journey home. The Underground was a busy whirl in their minds as they were carried along on the adrenalin of the evening's entertainment and, literally swept along with the tide of other theatre-goers making their way home. When they finally returned to the car they were suddenly brought back to normality. They drove home reminiscing on their day, each picking out their favourite parts of the play and agreeing this was definitely not going to be the last time they went to the theatre together. Jack, however, did point out that he couldn't always guarantee the special treatment they had received that evening. Carolyn didn't mind. She was happy to know that she would have her knight in 'shining Paul Smith armour' to share the experiences with and to remember this special time together.

As they drove home their thoughts soon returned to Holeford and, the impending threat to their ghostly friends brought them back to earth with a bump. Nothing could truly return to normal, whatever that was to be, until this horrible event was resolved. It was gone midnight before Jack drew up outside Carolyn's home, they were both tired and apprehensive about the coming twenty-four hours. They went to the back of the car and sorted out the shopping which Jack carried to the door that Carolyn had quietly opened, trying not to disturb her mum. Illuminated only by the porch light they kissed. A gentle warm lingering kiss of contentment, and Jack, still holding the shopping, felt happier than he had in a very long time. She eased back and they looked deep into each other's eyes. Words were not necessary but the spell had to be broken.

"Now try to get a good night's sleep, I'll pick you up at eleven, tomorrow night, I'm not having you walking around the streets on your own at that time," Jack said finally placing the bags in the hall.

"Thanks, Jack, it has been a wonderful day. The first of many I hope."

They kissed again and Jack quietly drove home his mind in a whirl of emotion.

13

There must be some way out of here

Saturday 19th of July

The store was opened by Joan this morning and she was surprised to see Jack come in at ten. They discussed how Joe had got on at head office and Jack told her all about the shopping and theatre trip. Joan hadn't seen him as animated for years, he was chirpy and amusing with an aura of contentment. This had to be Carolyn's doing, she was making her mark on him. In the basement below there was growing anguish amongst the ghosts. They had packed their bags ready for a quick exit.

George was remaining quiet about his trip to the club on Thursday. "Not just now, it's of no importance at the moment," was his stock reply whenever the other two tried to question him.

"Why don't we just leave now?" protested Alice. "If it's going to be that bad maybe we just need to get out."

Wilf was less sure. "Look, we don't know if he's any good yet and anyway, where would we go? We can't just wander into another building and settle. For us to have a new home we need to be invited. Otherwise the best buildings would be full of ghosts. I can't imagine spirits residing in a dungeon would not want to move to a nice comfortable stately home but you can't pick and choose."

"So we just sit here waiting to be exorcised? I don't like this, Wilf, it's like sitting in a waiting room, while your fate is being debated," Alice said defiantly crossing her arms.

Molly went out with her dad on the milk round trying to keep occupied and distracted from thinking about how the day, or rather night, may unfold. Afterwards she popped in to see her mum and caught up with Alice. This did nothing to ease her concern.

Joe returned home on the noon train full of enthusiasm following the time spent with his fellow students.

The day dragged. Each minute seemed like an hour. Evening eventually came and the sun reluctantly dipped over the horizon. The night drew in, streets went quiet and Saturday evening rituals began. Taxis moving into position, groups of friends and couples walking to pubs and restaurants. Queues trailed along the pavement outside the cinema to see the latest blockbuster. While feelings grew darker in the minds of those few with the knowledge of the impending event at the store.

At eleven Jack drew up outside Carolyn's house in his Austin Allegro. Carolyn was watching out for him at the window and ran out to join him. "Thanks for coming. I don't think I could do this on my own," Jack said.

"This is just so sad, Jack. I've just discovered these amazing powers and met some lovely spirits who've helped me understand my ancestry and now it's going to be taken away. I feel I'm only just starting out on this particular road of discovery. It's not fair. The worst part is the risk of losing contact with those lovely people for ever."

They travelled the rest of the way in melancholy silence until Jack pulled up outside the front of the shop, pulled on the handbrake and turned off the engine. He looked out at the dark supermarket.

"Well, we don't know for sure what's going to happen tonight, but while we have time there is hope and whatever happens I promise I'll always be here for you. At least something will have come out of all this, my getting to know you. Remember, don't put yourself in any danger tonight. You may think this sort of thing is now your area of expertise but don't forget you're new to this and anything could happen. We're opening the shop for the priest then keeping out of harm's way."

Carolyn looked across at Jack, his profile silhouetted by the street light. She could see he was anxious. "Thanks, Jack, our friendship means a lot to me, too." She took a deep breath. "Now shall we get this over?" He opened the store doors, turned off the alarm system and entered the gloomy cavernous shop floor.

Carolyn then followed him in. "Shall I make us a coffee?"

"Good idea. It will help us stay awake."

At 11.35 a dark shadow appeared at the window of the store and tapped on the glass door.

"Here we go," Jack sighed and went to let him in.

Father Michael entered the store. A short man, dressed in a black cloak covering a black cassock with a black fedora hat pulled down over his head. He carried in his hand a large black leather bag which he placed on the floor as the door closed behind him. He looked like a malevolent crow. "Good evening. I'm Father Michael McManus. I believe we spoke on the phone?"

Jack held out his hand and reluctantly shook the cold clammy hand of the executioner, at least that was how Jack viewed him. "Good evening, Father," he replied. "Would you like to come through to the staffroom? I'm just having a cup of coffee. Would you like one?"

"Yes please; black no sugar, thank you."

Jack led the way and the priest followed. As they entered the room Father Michael was surprised to see Carolyn sat at the table and gave her a quizzical look. "Good evening, my dear," he said in a cold impassionate voice. He shrugged. Another presence made no difference to his work here tonight.

Carolyn stood and offered their unwelcome visitor the cup of coffee, which he willingly accepted.

The room felt cold and the atmosphere between the occupants was even colder.

"What are you going to do, Father?" enquired Jack politely. "I mean, how do you go about the ritual?" He wished the floor would open up and swallow their visitor. He didn't really care what he was going to do and he just wanted him to go away. He was however conscious that Father Michael may report back to Finbarr, so he had to be polite. Carolyn sat watching as if in a trance. Her fury boiling away inside, frustration that this Irish priest could wreak such havoc to their harmless world.

Father Michael opened his bag and lifted out a heavy, polished silver cross standing about nine inches high, which he placed on the table, followed by a silver chalice and an unmarked glass bottle filled with clear liquid of some unknown kind. "Well, firstly I'll wander the building, all the time summoning up the power of the Lord Our Saviour to rid the place of its unclean spirits and bring peace to the hallowed aisles of Price Low," said the priest vaguely waving his hands around to indicate the route he was going to take.

"Do you issue a certificate on completion?" Carolyn asked sarcastically.

Jack looked across at her sympathetically, but his expression said, '*Stay cool, Carolyn, that won't help.*' Carolyn gave him a wry smile but she didn't regret the little jibe.

"This table will do as an altar. I'll sprinkle holy water around the building whilst reciting incantations from the *De Exorcisimis et Supplicationibus*

Quibusdam," he said in a matter-of fact-way. "This can be a terrifying ordeal for the inexperienced. While I do this ritual I can have no other people in the building, so I must ask you to leave, now. It'll take about an hour if the spirits are receptive, longer if they're not."

Jack and Carolyn were left in no doubt that this was a grim affair.

"What on earth is the 'de exosimist suplicatos Quibildam thing' or whatever you said?" enquired Jack.

Father Michael looked at Jack as if he was stupid, he then explained in a slow deliberate tone. "It's the rite of exorcism issued by the Vatican in 1614. It really is quite well known."

Jack was none the wiser but was now very aware that this guy was not messing around and the resident actors were in terrible trouble.

"Finbarr was wise to get me here. I feel a strong malignant presence in this building."

He took a gulp of the coffee prepared by Carolyn, who had added three heaped spoonful's of sugar. He winced and coughed. "Malignant indeed!" he repeated, looking across at Carolyn who remained impassive.

In the dressing room Wilf and Alice were doing some final packing as George, who had mysteriously disappeared again, came through the back wall. "What are you doing?" he exclaimed as he watched the two of them frantically trying to fit their costumes into small bags and cases.

"Where the hell have you been, George? We're in big trouble. The priest has turned up. Hurry, help us finish off the packing," Wilf said.

"It's terrible, George. He's really here," Alice added, frantically trying to stuff a large ball gown into a carpet bag, to little effect. "I can't believe this is actually happening."

"What, here? Already? You're kidding?" said George.

"No, we are not! Get packing. We need to go, now!" cried Wilf.

"Now, hang on a minute," George said bravely. "If there's a priest here, I want to see what he's doing. I've never been exorcised before. I'm interested to see which ritual he is using."

"Don't be stupid, you don't ask a firing squad what gun they're intending to use to shoot you! You can't hang around here to see how we meet our doom just because it might be a new experience for us! We need to get away, fast!" said Wilf now in a blind panic.

"Yes I can. I am not going to be held to account by a fear of the unknown, that's not rational," replied George casually.

"Who do you think you are? Spock from Star Trek? *Oooh that's not logical, Captain*," Wilf said in strange accent. "Pull yourself together, we have to get out of here," he pleaded.

George ignored him, rose up through the floor and into the Staffroom, where a man dressed in black robes was kneeling in front of the silverware placed on the table. He could see the back of Jack as he walked out through the door into the store with Carolyn in front, her head bowed, obviously in some distress. They had agreed with Father Michael to go and wait in the car while he performed the ceremony as he needed to be alone with the itinerant spirits.

They left the store and returned to the Allegro parked on the street at the front of the shop. He unlocked the passenger door and Carolyn got in as he went round and opened the driver side. Jack turned on the ignition to provide illumination. The radio burst into life just in time for the Radio Two announcer to end the days broadcast with the National Anthem.

"Turn it off please, Jack," Carolyn asked.

He leant forward and turned the switch on the Motorola radio. They sat in silence, too caught up with the imagination of what horrors may be playing out to talk. Jack held her hand to try and comfort her. She clutched a handkerchief tightly in her left hand ready to dry any tears that she could feel welling up inside her. The interior light glowed like a single candle, the smell of the plastic dashboard and faux leather seats permeated the air as the windows began to steam up from their breathing.

Back in the store, Wilf and Alice were again trying to persuade George to pack.

"George! Please come on, we can't stay here", Alice entreated, pulling at the sleeve of his pirate cloak.

Father Michael was uttering some incomprehensible gibberish then stood up and picked up the bottle of water, unscrewing the lid.

"I reckon that's the holy water," explained George, helpfully.

"I don't care if it's purified water from the deepest depths of Lake Titicaca, we can't hang around to find out!" said Wilf now getting really annoyed at George's seemingly blasé attitude to the danger they were in.

The Priest moved into the store itself and started to flick the water around in front of him. As he walked around the aisles towards the window, he could see Jack trying to console Carolyn as they sat in the car. Jack looked up and saw the silhouette of the priest walking past the window. Fortunately Carolyn was drying her eyes at that moment and missed the depressing sight of the water-flicking minister.

George was following Father Michael around the store with Wilf and Alice, trying to drag him back. "Will you get off?" rebuked George trying to shake free of their restraining arms. "I want to see what he's doing."

"It'll be the last thing you do see," Wilf said.

Father Michael moved towards the rear of the shop and as he passed the wines and spirits display, he reached out and selected a bottle of Irish whiskey.

"That's strange, why would he do that?" George pointed out to the others, intrigued.

Both Wilf and Alice were also surprised at the swift, deliberate and incomprehensible act. They stopped trying to restrain George and they too followed as the priest headed back into the Staffroom.

Once there he placed the whiskey in his leather bag and returned to his makeshift altar and began to recite. "I command you, unclean spirits, whoever you are, along with all the minions now attacking the servant of God, by the mysteries of the incarnation, passion, resurrection and ascension of our Lord Jesus Christ, by the descent of the Holy Spirit…"

Alice started to descend through the floor. "I don't know about you two but I'm going now. This is just too much."

"No, hang on, Alice," George said. "Do you feel anything? Do you feel tingly? Are you nauseous? Is there a feeling of wretched dread?"

"Well, now you come to mention it, no not really, apart from being scared stiff!"Alice replied.

"Nor me," Wilf butted in not wanting to be left out. "What's your point, George?"

"By now shouldn't we be starting to weaken or fade or something? I need a closer look at this chap," George added and moved opposite him at the table. "You know, there is something about him that is familiar."

The priest continued the incantation in a booming theatrical voice, unaware of his audience. "Depart then, transgressors. Depart seducers, full of lies and cunning, foes of virtue, precursors of the innocent. Give back this place to he, within whom you will find none of your works…"

"Alice? Can you please go and ask Carolyn to come back in, then stand by the stock control chalk board," George asked mysteriously.

"OK, but I hope you know what you're doing," she said and left the room.

"So do I George, what're you up to?" chipped in Wilf.

"You are guilty before his son, Our Lord Jesus Christ, whom you presumed to tempt…" continued Father Michael now getting into his stride.

Carolyn and Jack re-entered the room looking confused and apprehensive while Alice took her place by the chalk board. The priest was startled and stopped the incantation.

"What are you doing back here? I told you to stay away. I'll tell you when it's safe. Now be gone, you are ruining the ceremony." He pointed to the door, looking furious.

They both shrugged their shoulders and held their ground. They were not sure why they had been asked to return, but followed Alice's instruction.

"Stay there, Carolyn, you are in no danger, I need you to witness this," George said.

Carolyn held Jack's hand to reassure him and they stayed in the room.

Father Michael looked flustered. Why hadn't they followed his order? This was not going to plan.

"Alice, write on the chalk board for me the name Arthur Ray, please," said George calmly.

Alice concentrated really hard. It was one thing moving objects but another to steer a piece of chalk and spell a name. However a stick of chalk gently lifted from the small channel at the bottom of the board and appeared to be writing. Carolyn pointed excitedly at the board on the wall by the office door.

Father Michael watched in disbelief as the stick of chalk rose and started to write;

A R T H U R R A Y.

"What kind of trickery is this!" he demanded, standing and pointing at the board, trying to look authoritative but he could not stop his hand from shaking. The chalk continued to wave about as if considering what else to reveal.

"No trick," assured Carolyn still looking a little confused.

"Blimey, this place really is haunted! I'm not hanging around here," his Irish accent now descending into cockney. But the priest found it was not that easy to escape as Jack had quickly moved and now stood in front of the fire exit while Wilf stood in front of the door to the shop.

George moved forward. "This is Arthur Ray, Carolyn, and he most definitely isn't a priest. He is an actor. I worked with him in 1952 on the North Pier Blackpool where we appeared in *Aladdin*. At least until he got the sack for helping himself to the takings."

After hearing this, Carolyn needed no further prompting. She was furious at this charlatan for causing them all so much distress.

"Well, Arthur, do you want to come clean?" she said, her arms folded as if admonishing a naughty child.

"I'm sure I don't know what you mean," he tried to say innocently. "This is crazy you couldn't know that name!"

Carolyn had the upper hand of this creep now and she knew it… So did he. "Let's not play games, Arthur, you've caused too much distress already. Does Finbarr know you're an imposter? I am sure he doesn't and I'm equally sure he doesn't like being duped."

He stood in silence looking around the room for a means of escape. He spied the door to the shop floor unaware that Wilf was anticipating his move.

Without warning the silver cross inexplicably fell over and slid along the full length of the table. On reaching the opposite end it gently lifted, flew up into the air like a model aircraft and then traversed around the room doing a series of loops over Arthur's head.

"This is witchcraft! There really is evil here! You want to call a real priest," cried Arthur. "Make it stop…PLEASE MAKE IT STOP," he pleaded, as he dived for cover under the table. The others were transfixed by the aerial display, a level of skill and control from Alice they had never seen before.

The cross then stopped and hovered over the table, rotated into its vertical position and gently landed.

"Wow! That was your best yet Alice!" George said in appreciation.

"It wasn't me," she replied and all eyes turned to Wilf who was still standing in the doorway arms folded, prepared to block the sudden exit of the priest.

"As Alice says, practice makes perfect," he said, feeling pleased with himself and took a little bow. A ripple of applause came from his audience, apart from one member still huddled in a ball on the floor.

"What's going on? Has it stopped?" came a muffled voice from the sanctuary of the table.

Carolyn bent down, looked under the table and addressed the shivering cleric.

"OK, Arthur, I think I should now call you Arthur rather than Michael, don't you?"

"Yes, yes OK, call me Arthur, just make it stop!"

Carolyn held out a hand. "It has stopped. Now, won't you come back up and join us?"

George leaned over and whispered into Carolyn's ear. She nodded her head and mouthed *'thank you, George'*. Arthur clambered out from his haven and stood up.

"You're all mad... You wait till I tell Finbarr about this. You're all going to be in big trouble. I hope they pull this place down with you still in it."

"That's not very Christian of you Father, anyway, I don't think we are the ones in trouble, do you?" Jack said.

"How do you know my name?" he asked looking round the room suspiciously.

"I know a lot about you, Arthur. My ethereal friends here have just enlightened me. You've given us all a wretched time this evening. For a while we actually believed you."

Arthur looked around the room bemused. There was only Carolyn and Jack. "What friends? You've got nothing on me. I'm going now, my job here is done!" he said trying to regain some control.

"Would you like to tell us what is in your bag?" Carolyn asked.

"No, I wouldn't; now get out of my way." Arthur moved forward to grab his bag but as he did so the cross slid across the table to block his path. Arthur stopped as soon as he saw the movement.

"Jack, be a dear and open the bag please."

Jack picked up the bag and placed it on a chair. He slid the button on the fastener and it popped open revealing an unopened bottle of whiskey with the Price Low special offer sticker emblazoned on the front.

"Well, well, what have we here? How on earth did this find its way into your bag?" Jack questioned.

"That's been in there all the time. It's part of my payment from Finbarr," Arthur replied, desperately trying to cover his tracks.

"I don't think so. I only stocked the shelf with these this evening after we closed. They're a new consignment due to go on sale tomorrow," Jack said.

"He picked it up while going round the store flicking water around," Carolyn informed him.

"That's fine Carolyn, thank you. Fortunately it will all be recorded on the new state-of-the-art night vision CCTV that Price Low had fitted following our recent robbery, so I think the game is well and truly up, don't you, Arthur?"

Arthur looked angrily at Carolyn. "What are you some kind of mystic?"

Carolyn was thrilled at the idea. "Yes, I suppose I am."

"Well, what do you want?" Arthur replied, resigned to the fact that he had been exposed.

"Well, let's make a list," Jack replied. With the relief of the evening's events now empowering him, he was in control and could use this to his advantage. "Firstly, an apology to all those in the room for the unnecessary distress you caused them. Secondly, the return of the stolen goods. Thirdly, you'll return to Finbarr and tell him your mission was a complete success and his property is now free of evil spirits."

"I don't know what tricks you used this evening but you should be on the stage," Arthur said.

He couldn't hear the laughter from the three actors, just Carolyn sniggering. "I can assure you no trickery was used Arthur. You're indeed in the presence of the paranormal. Remarkable people who have spared you from a potentially agonising and humiliating evening. Now do you have anything to say?"

"Are you trying to tell me this place really is haunted and that display was their work?" Arthur replied, looking anxiously around the room for evidence.

Jack ignored the question. "Do you have anything to say?" he repeated.

Arthur was a broken man, he sat down and rested his head in his hands. "OK… if it makes you feel better, I am sorry if I caused you any distress. You have no idea what it is like for an out of work actor. I needed this job to pay for my digs or I would be out on the streets."

"You should've thought of that before stealing the takings from the North Pier Blackpool," Carolyn added. "Perhaps you would still be a respected actor with plenty of work."

Arthur looked stunned. "How on earth do you know about that?"

"As I told you, I know a lot about you, Arthur," Carolyn replied.

Arthur reached into the bag and handed Jack the bottle of whiskey. "I'm sorry, it was just too tempting. I'll tell Finbarr it all went according

144

to plan and his store is now cleansed of evil spirits."

"Thank you, Arthur, but remember, if I do hear anything I don't like, I'll show him the video of you taking this bottle. I know for a fact he does not like thieves. Now gather up your things and get out."

He needed no further prompting. Arthur quickly placed the props and empty bottle of water in his bag. He then fled out through the door as fast as his legs could carry him and disappeared into the night.

Carolyn re-locked the door and joined Jack in the staffroom.

Wilf, Alice and George waited for her return and sang, "For she's a jolly good fellow," at the top of their voices.

"What a night!" Jack said with relief.

"I think a stiff drink is called for." He went to his office and returned with a half-empty bottle of scotch.

"I keep this for emergencies," he joked, holding forward the bottle for Carolyn to inspect.

Carolyn took the bottle from him, placed it on the table, wrapped her arms around his waist, held him close and kissed him. Jack automatically held her gently and they relaxed into the intimacy of the moment. The three actors discreetly lowered themselves through the floor into their room, leaving them to their embrace.

"Boy, that was a close one!" exclaimed George as he sat on the sofa.

"Too bloody close," exclaimed Wilf.

"What a horrible man. Fancy impersonating a priest. He's certainly for the high jump when he finally passes over. Now we have to unpack everything!" Alice smiled broadly.

"It looks rather tidy in here," George commented. "Perhaps we should leave it like this for a while. I like it."

"I don't want to be the purveyor of bad tidings but don't forget there is still the plan to knock this place down," Wilf reminded them.

All the exploits of the evening had caused them to momentarily forget that the main threat to their home still existed.

Alice slumped down despondently onto the floor of the stage lift. George gave them both a thoughtful look. He was hatching a plan which required outside help but it was too early to reveal it to the others in case it didn't come off. That could wait until the arrival of the archaeologists.

Carolyn loosened her arms and whispered in Jack's ear. "I'll go and get two glasses."

"Mm-yes-good idea," Jack mumbled, still reeling from their embrace.

"That's probably the worst evening of my life!" Carolyn said, placing two glasses next to the bottle. She poured two generous measures. "That horrible man put us through hell. He cheated Finbarr and frightened us all for no reason. That is unforgivable." She took a sip from the glass and pulled a face. "Ugh, that's horrible! How can you drink this stuff?" she exclaimed, pushing the glass away. Her thoughts then went to Molly who needed to be told as soon as possible.

Jack took the glass and added a drop of cold water. "Here, try it now," he said, handing the glass back to her.

"Mm, well that's certainly better, thank you", she said. The whisky was now softer on her tongue and she could detect the aroma of peat and heather from the Highlands. "It's a good job you have that hi-tech, night-vision CCTV system. That burglary did you a favour," Carolyn said.

Jack remained silent, tipped his head to one side and looked sheepish.

"You haven't got a night-vision system, have you?"

"No, we haven't, but Arthur didn't know that!"

They both laughed and lifted their glasses in salute.

The adrenalin of the evening's events was beginning to subside and they were both in need of sleep. Alice popped her head up through the floor checking that the coast was clear and saw them both getting up to leave. She rose fully into the room and moved over to Carolyn. "Thank you both so much for your help this evening."

"That's not a problem," Carolyn replied sincerely. "We now need Molly's help to see if we can find a way to stop the demolition. This battle is won but the war is far from over."

"Who's there," Jack enquired.

"It's Alice, thanking us for tonight," Carolyn explained. '*The relaying of conversations was getting unexpectedly tiring*,' she thought, but there was no other way.

"I am sorry I can't see you Alice," Jack said, looking in completely the wrong direction. "But I can assure you we'll do all we can to help you."

Carolyn held Jack's arm and turned him to face Alice. "Alice is here, Jack. Hold out your hand." Jack did so and Alice reached over to grip it.

Her transparent hand passed through Jack's. He could see nothing but he felt the icy touch as their energies met. "I felt you, Alice, you touched my hand!" Jack said excitedly. "Please don't worry. We're going to safeguard your home! We'll think of something," he added, determinedly.

Having contact with Alice he felt closer to her. "I wish I could see you," he added wistfully.

"Come on, Jack," Carolyn said, putting her arm in his. "It's time we went home. "Goodnight Alice, and congratulate Wilf on his levitating skills!"

Jack set the alarm and they left the building. It was two o'clock in the morning, the clouds had parted and a full moon hung in the sky illuminating their way back to the car. The town was asleep, they saw no one on their journey home.

"We have to tell Molly about this, she'll have been worried sick." Carolyn said.

"It's Sunday opening tomorrow, I'll be in with Joan at seven-thirty. Do you want me to get a message to her?"

"No. I need to speak to her face to face. I'll pop round and see her with some excuse about the museum or something."

Jack didn't get much sleep that night. All the memories of the evening kept spinning around in his head. He was back in the store at 7 am to sort out the papers ready for the paper boys to arrive.

Joan joined him at seven-thirty to prepare for the 8 am opening. "You look terrible Jack, are you feeling alright?"

"I had a late night, Joan, but actually, I have never been better, thank you," he said smiling.

"I don't want to know about your nocturnal activities, thank you, Jack!" Joan replied totally unaware of the evenings events.

"It's all perfectly innocent," Jack added lamely, and was going to explain more when Joan interrupted.

"I don't want to know, really," she said holding up her hand to stop him saying anymore.

"OK," said a relieved Jack. How could he have explained all that had happened? "Have you seen the advert for Joe's old position? It went in the Chronicle last night," he said, changing the subject.

Carolyn took Patch for a walk immediately after breakfast and headed for Apollo Park to call at Molly's house.

Peter Goodall answered the door. "Hello, Miss Jenner this is a pleasant surprise."

"Please call me Carolyn, Mr Goodall."

"Peter."

"Thank you, Peter. I was wondering if it would be possible to speak to Molly regarding her work at the museum tomorrow."

Molly had heard the door and was rushing down the stairs. This had to be news about the exorcism. Carolyn look relaxed, could it be good news?

Carolyn gave a reassuring wink that told everything. Later over a cup of tea in the garden, Patch enjoyed a biscuit while she told Molly the whole story. The relief at knowing the actors were safe, for now at least, galvanised her determination to find out what she could about the Professor's interest in the shop when she started work tomorrow. Molly felt now that, maybe, they really could save the store.

She practically skipped all the way to the shop on the pretence of walking home with Joan. She got there at eleven-thirty just time to catch up with Alice before the mid-day closing. She waved at her mum who was busy on the till and went directly to the storeroom carrying a magazine to read. She tapped the floor and Alice joined her. Alice told her all the details of the evening. She was so relieved but surprised that the priest was a fraud. However, the threat of demolition was still very real. Alice explained that George was up to something but wasn't letting on. The store room door creaked open and they went silent.

Joan entered. "Who are you talking to, dear?"

Molly looked up from the magazine she was pretending to read. "No one Mum, I was just laughing at an article in the magazine."

Joan joined Molly at the old desk and sat on a rickety chair next to her. "Is everything alright, dear? You've not been yourself for a few days and it's not like you. Is it the museum? Is it too much for you? You can tell me."

"No Mum, everything is fine. It's just well… You know."

Joan misread this as Molly hiding the natural anxiety of the physical changes she was experiencing moving into adulthood.

Molly had to change the subject quickly. "Are Jack and Carolyn going out, Mum?"

"That's an interesting question… I don't know for certain, but they seem to be together a lot lately. Jack has certainly perked up. Did you see the new jacket he was wearing today? Very trendy! If you ask me there's something going on. I'm sure Jack will tell me in his own good time."

Molly had succeeded in diverting the line of conversation and Joan had to go and cash-up, giving her a chance to finish talking to Alice. The store closed at mid-day and they walked home where Peter was preparing the Sunday roast. Joan didn't interrogate Molly any further, much to her relief, and they enjoyed their meal with apple pie and custard for pudding.

14

What lies beneath?

Monday the 21st of July

On Monday, Price Low opened as normal but Joe had been busy putting out bollards to block the entrance to the car park. At eight-thirty a large flatbed lorry arrived with a small mechanical excavator on the back. The driver climbed down from his cab, confirmed with Joe that he was in the right place and pulled two ramps from the rear of the wagon. He unstrapped the wheels of the machine that had been secured to prevent the load moving, climbed into the cab and slowly reversed the machine down onto the road. Joe moved the bollards to allow access and it was driven into the car park where the driver stepped out of the cab, handed the keys to Joe, swiftly secured the ramps to his vehicle and drove away.

At eight forty-five Mango arrived with a young man in a beige duffle coat. "Hi, you must be Joe. You may remember me from the survey a few days ago."

"Yes, you're Mr Mangle," Joe replied holding out his hand.

"Close, it's Mango actually and that's my Christian name. Please just call me Mango, it'll be easier." They shook hands. "This is Archibald Strathmore. He's the archaeologist who will be attending the excavation and following up on any finds."

A rather sorry looking Morris 1000 van then arrived and a short, stocky man stepped or rather rolled out from the driver's seat. He was in his late fifties wearing a tatty donkey jacket, blue overalls and muddy rubber boots.

"Ah, no prizes for guessing who this is," quipped Mango.

The donkey jacket waddled over to them and held out a large rough-skinned hand to Mango. "Shaun," it said.

They shook hands, Joe handed him the keys to the machine and invited the trio into the staffroom to sign the visitors' book and meet Jack.

At 9 am, on the other side of the road Molly knocked on the door of the museum. It opened and she stepped inside. She couldn't help but notice the activity in the car park opposite. It was her first full day and the Professor had asked her to report to his secretary, Gwen, to assist with the morning post and filing. In the afternoon she would be assisting with a group of visitors from the 'Independent Order of Strange Fellows' who were coming for a behind the scenes tour. These tours were a new venture introduced by the Professor to raise much needed funds for his new antiquities exhibition.

Molly pushed open the heavy oak door into the library and headed up the stairs along the gallery to the Professor's office. She noticed him on the gallery looking out of the corner bay window toward the Price Low car park. "Morning, Professor," she called.

"Morning, Molly. Welcome to your first full day with us. Gwen's expecting you so go straight through." He spoke whilst maintaining his view across the road.

Molly entered the office. Its oak panelled walls repeated the elegance of the library but felt more homely. The large rug on the floor obscured most of the polished oak floor but made it more informal. The walls supported old faded photographs of expeditions, archaeological sites and groups of Victorians posing on the lawns of grand houses. Molly could make out that one was definitely taken in Egypt, as she could see a group of men in shorts, wearing pith helmets standing by the Sphinx, with a large pyramid in the background. Behind Gwen was a large dark oil painting of a distinguished looking man wearing mayoral robes looking down on them intently, his piercing blue eyes seemingly following you around the room.

"Hello, Molly, welcome to the inner sanctum," Gwen said smiling, as she rose from behind her solid oak desk. She came around it to greet Molly with a hand-shake.

"Thank you, miss. I'm really looking forward to helping you."

"Firstly, please call me Gwen. You're not at school now and you're hopefully going to be part of our team for a long while. The Professor has been impressed with you already, so take a tip from me. He's a very clever man and you can learn a lot from him, so be sure to make the most of your time here. He would be a very useful ally if you wanted a career in this business."

The penny dropped for Molly. *'Carolyn has been very clever yet again! I love this place already and the people in it. Could it be possible that I could go on to study and work in a museum or go on archaeological digs?'*

"Thanks, Gwen, what do you want me to do?" Molly was keen to get the working day under way and see what information she could gather. Firstly she had to find out why the Professor was so intently watching the work going on in the car park.

Jack greeted the team of men as they entered the staffroom and invited them into the office, where Joan brought cups of tea on a tray. Mango explained what was going to happen. He laid a drawing of the site and surrounding roads out on the desk. Two long narrow rectangles had been drawn in red ink over the car park. Mango explained that this is where Archibald wanted to commence the trench investigation. Archibald went on to explain that he would closely monitor the excavation and measure and record any changes in the strata of the ground and investigate any items of interest. They finished their teas, signed the visitors' book and headed back out into the yard, where Joe was redirecting a delivery van to the front door of the shop. Mango set up a tripod and mounted his theodolite on the top. With the assistance of Archibald they marked out the corners of the trenches to be dug and Shaun gathered a bag of sand from the back of his van which he sprinkled between his hands, onto the ground, to form a line as a guide for the bucket of his machine. He then climbed aboard, started the engine which spluttered into life, belching black smoke and moved into position.

The bucket mounted on the arm of the machine started to paw at the unyielding tarmacadam, the hardened teeth sliding without effect over the hard surface. Sparks and whiffs of smoke accompanied the angry screech of the steel against aggregate as it tried, vainly, to grip the surface. The sound of the conflict ricocheted off the walls of the surrounding buildings. The roar of the engine intensified and fumes bellowed vertically from the exhaust pipe until the determined teeth finally penetrated the surface. The machine then lurched forward as it gripped the crust, which started to rise and fracture into manageable pieces, revealing the compacted gravel below. Mango and the archaeologist watched intently from a safe distance at the edge of the parking area. This was going to be a noisy, slow, laborious business.

Also watching intently from on high was the Professor. He had borrowed the telescope from the *Battle of Trafalgar* exhibit and now stood at the window like a wild and windswept sea captain, his long unkempt hair kept marginally under control by his spectacles which he had pushed up over his head like a makeshift hairband. Molly had been watching from the open door of the office whilst opening, stamping and sorting the morning post for distribution. She spotted her chance and offered to make coffee for Gwen and also made a cup for the Professor.

She moved along the gallery, the polished oak floor creaking and squeaking under her feet as she moved to the Professor's side.

"Coffee, Professor?" she said, placing the cup on the table by his side.

"Ah, most welcome. Thank you," said the Professor, not moving from his position with the telescope still firmly held to his eye.

"What are you looking at?" Molly casually asked. She stood on tiptoe, leaning on the windowsill to see where he was looking.

The Professor glanced down at Molly, warming to the inquisitive new recruit. "My father carried out extensive investigations round here. He wrote several books on the history and antiquities of Holeford and surrounding area." He pointed down to a section on the lower floor near the entrance doors. "They're all down there on those shelves. He also carried out an extensive survey of Monkton Hillfort back in the thirties. It's still used today as a standard text for all archaeological students," he said proudly. "That's where it all started for me, Molly, I was younger than you when he was on that dig and I joined him in the school holidays where I helped with the cleaning of the artefacts that were dug up. It was a big job, there were over thirty assistants with him. Digging, and recording all the items he was uncovering. Some of those items are stored here and the best are on show at the British Museum. I'll show you our collection one day when we have some free time. I then went on to study ancient history, ending up as a curator at the British Museum. He was very proud of me. And now I have returned to where it all started to continue his work, fill in some of the missing pieces and try to inspire a new generation."

"I had no idea, Professor," Molly replied and looked at him with new respect.

"Why would you? They were some of the happiest days of my life. Spending time with him was not always easy. I was away at boarding school and in the holidays he was not home much. Usually off on an overseas expedition or too far away for us to see much of each other. I had to share him with his vocation. He was a wonderful inspiration to so many people, including myself." He looked through the eye piece again while Molly continued to look out of the window as the machine scraped away at the ground. "Did you know a theatre once stood where the shop is? In fact several stood there until the last one, The Opera House, burnt down. There's a lot of theatre information on the shelves over there… fascinating records, well worth a look," he said pointing to the leather-bound volumes close to where they were standing. Molly took note of their position so that she could investigate them later. "Sadly, things move on though, Molly, and now the shop is to give way for a new development and that's why I am watching closely. Come and look at this." The Professor put down the telescope and moved to a large table alongside the window where he rolled out an old survey map of the town.

Molly could make out the roads and the footprint of the buildings but superimposed over the modern layout were other lines and rectangles that made no sense to her.

"This is Holeford through the ages. You can see the shop and car park here." He pointed at the corner opposite the museum. "But also these lines indicate Iron Age paths and the route of the Roman Road, which is still the position of the modern-day streets. Look here, this circle of dots was the position of a prehistoric henge that predated Stonehenge. It was constructed from timber posts and aligned to the summer solstice in just the same way. They were remarkable people," he said, pausing to allow Molly to absorb the information. Molly was quiet, her mind trying to imagine the wooden circle.

"Now, look here," he continued, encouraged by a willing listener. "This is the position of a Roman baths," he pointed to a collection of squares and rectangles positioned over the large gardens of a private house, not far from the main street.

"What, like in Bath?" Molly said intrigued.

"Yes, exactly like Bath except there was no hot spring here. The water was brought in by the use of an aqueduct and then heated by means of a hypocaust system. This would have been the tepidarium." He pointed at one of the squares. "This would have been a warm room. Then we move on to the calarium which was hot, like a modern sauna, then here is the frigidarium where they would finish with a swim in cold water."

Molly looked up at him in total amazement. She had no idea any of this was under her home town.

"But, now here," he pointed to the area of the shop and car park. "Can you see that the lines of ancient buildings and road stop around the perimeter of this area? It's unexplored and this could be my chance to fill in a gap on this map."

Molly noticed in the bottom corner of the drawing, a name, below some faded text. "Is this your father's name?" she said pointing to the title box."

"Ah yes, you've spotted the main reason for my return to Holeford. I want to continue his work and part of that job is to fill in the gaps in this, his very map. It may seem a bit sentimental but I feel it's my duty to complete what he started."

"That's not sentimental at all, I think it's a lovely thing to do," she replied sincerely.

The Professor looked warmly at his protégée. They both returned to look out of the window and as they did so the men around the hole stepped back very quickly as a jet of water spurted high up into the air.

In the car park there was a sudden flurry of activity as the intrigued bystanders frantically tried to get away from the geyser that had erupted from the hole. Shaun leapt from the cab to survey the exposed pipe.

"What the hell is that doing there?" he exclaimed. "That pipe's not on the services drawing you gave me." He looked at them accusingly.

"Never mind that, it's definitely there!" shouted a soaked Mango over the noise from the jet of water. "I'll phone the water board before we all drown!" He rushed into the staffroom with his clothes dripping wet and asked Jack if he could use the phone urgently. He then called the water board from the list of contact numbers in his notebook.

Jack went to the door and looked out into the car park which now contained a small lake complete with its own ornamental fountain. The archaeologist had moved to the other side of the road, where he stood dripping and bemused.It took the water board engineer half an hour to arrive by which time the lake had overflowed from the car park and was running along the kerb into the nearest road gully. The engineer, wearing blue overalls, chatted to Shaun who had taken shelter in his van, and then casually returned to his own vehicle and extracted a long steel bar from the rear. He levered open an iron cover further down the road, inserted the bar, twisted it several times and the spout abated.

"What happens now?" Molly asked.

"Well, that will delay things for a while but when they finally get themselves sorted out, the gentleman in the duffle coat will report to the planning office and they will invite me as their consultant to review the initial findings and recommend any actions," the Professor said rubbing his hands together.

"So, it's up to you how much they dig up?"

"Precisely, Molly, exciting isn't it?"

As they watched, a more heated exchange was taking place between the engineer and machine driver which included a lot of pointing and gesticulation, much to the amusement of the Professor and Molly.

Molly returned to the office pleased with her morning's investigation and continued to help Gwen with the distribution of the post and filing. During her lunch break she decided to do some research of her own. She headed to the ground floor of the library and quickly located the books containing the records of the theatres in Holeford. She ran her fingers along the spines until she located The Opera House 1946–1955. She carefully lifted down the heavy leather covered volume and placed it on the reading table. She opened it up and soon found the 1955 section near the back. It told her of the cinema production shown for that year and then towards the end she read, '*Trolley Cart presents, The Pirates of Penzance*'. She paused for a minute, nervous about what she was going to find. It could prove that her spirited friends were false and all this was a waste of time.

She needn't have worried. She plucked up the courage to read on. It told her of the touring group who had come direct from the West End.

Then there it was; the cast list.

Major- General Stanley ....Arthur Lawrence

The Pirate King...........................Wilfred Trunnion

Sergeant of Police ....George Shakespeare

Samuel...Andrew Peverill

Frederick......................................Sutton Pointing

Ruth..Florence Bingham

General Stanley's daughters:

Mabel..Annie Pike

Edith..Evelyn Meade

Alice...Ruby Manville

Isabel...Alice Bennett

It was all true. Here, in front of her, in black and white, was the proof of her friends' mortal existence. She clapped her hands with relief and read on. It included the newspaper report about the production and when she turned the page a copy of the programme had been printed in full. She quickly turned to the cast information and staring out of the page at her were black and white pictures of her three friends along with some background information.

Wilf Trunnion

Wilf Trunnion was born in Birmingham in 1904. An outstanding all-round entertainer, his long experience in the business ranges from Cabaret, Repertory, Summer variety shows and Pantomime. He has also starred in something approaching 500 radio broadcasts. His West End stage credits include. *'Bigger than Life'* at the Duke of York's Theatre and followed a run in *'Call Me Sir'* and *'A Nightingale Sang in Pimlico'*. Wilf joined the Trolley Cart Company during the West End run and has made the part of 'The Pirate King' his own.

George Shakespeare

George Shakespeare is from the third generation of a show-business family. His grandfather was a music hall comedian and his mother a famous summer show comedienne in the 1920s. He played at the famous Embassy Theatre for many years. He served with the Fourth Hussars during the war with Hitler. On his return he enjoyed a successful run in the West End. A true impresario with numerous productions to his credit including Plays, Panto and Variety. In 1952 he decided to return to his first love of musicals and joined the Trolley Cart Company.

Alice Bennett

Alice was born in Coventry and studied music and dance at the York School of Speech and Drama. She made her debut playing Cobweb in *'A Midsummer Night's Dream'*. She followed this with a variety of parts in plays and summer shows. She played principal boy opposite Wilf Trunnion in *Puss and Boots* at the London Opera House before joining the Trolley Cart Company for this national tour.

On the next page she read some of the press reviews for The Pirates of Penzance;

Enough funny situations to blow theatre-goers off their seats with gusts of laughter. An outstanding performance from Alice Bennett with a top-

quality orchestra made for a magical evening.

Harrold Tinker – **Sunday News**

Wilf Trunnion... Like brandy flames upon a delectable plum pudding. Sublime.

Herbert Johnson – **Daily Press**

Wilf and George play effortlessly into each other's hands, proof that they can run rings round most actors on the London stage.

Georgina Bell – **Holeford Evening Chronicle**

She then read the newspaper report of the fire and tragic loss of life. This included photographs of a building in flames, the smoke hanging in the air and another of the bent and twisted steel frame of the once magnificent theatre. She couldn't imagine how it must have been for those involved, the pictures showed horrific scenes. How must it really have been for George, Wilf and Alice trapped under the stage? Did they really just fall asleep and not wake up? Suddenly the immensity of their experience became very real. Here it was laid out before her, in this book.

She heard the door open behind her as the Professor entered. "What interesting morsel have you found then, Molly?" He came to her and looking over her shoulder could see what she found so absorbing.

"Ah, the theatre, yes a fascinating story. I assume you'll see the shop a little differently now. That's what recorded history does, Molly, it changes our perception of life around us."

"And death," Molly added quietly.

"You're so right. You're a very perceptive young lady. I do hope you'll stay with us after the holiday, you're just what this place needs. You understand that the past is not just about dusty artefacts but what they can reveal about the lives of those gone before us... Have you thought seriously about what you are going to do when you leave school?"

"No, not really."

"Well you should seriously think about studying towards a history degree. Ask Carolyn. She'll have ways of putting you on the correct path and if I can help in any way, you only have to ask."

"Thank you, Professor," she said closing the book and placing it carefully back on the shelf. "I'm helping with a tour group this afternoon, wish me luck." She was feeling quite deflated after what she had just read but made an effort to perk up.

"You don't need luck, all you need is knowledge and confidence. Go and enjoy yourself," he said.

Molly went to the reception desk to join Gwen, where she was preparing for the group to arrive.

Gwen was ready with instructions and reassurance for Molly. "Now, don't worry. All you need to do is follow the group around and keep them together. They're rather like sheep so just need a bit of herding. Most probably they'll ask where the toilet is first so that's easy but it's important to make sure they stop at the shop and spend their money before leaving. We need every penny we can get to fund the Professor's plans for the new exhibition."

The afternoon went quickly for Molly. The 'Independent Order of Strange Fellows' were a group of retired professional types who definitely lived up to their name. They were certainly a bit strange. As they visited some of the back rooms, they seemed to be interested in the building as much as the exhibits. They did indeed need herding, as small groups started to break away from the rest at the least opportunity. Molly got quite proficient at keeping them together. She also learnt a lot more about the exhibits and managed to steer them all into the shop where they spent lots of money. Gwen had high praise for the new recruit as they returned to the office for a well-earned cup of tea.

At 5 pm she grabbed her coat and ran across the road to the shop, said a quick hello to her mother on the till and went into the staffroom where she knocked on Jack's door. Joan looked across at Audrey, on the other till. "That girl's grown up very quickly in the last year, before long she'll be running that museum and she only started properly today!" She shook her head and greeted the next customer.

Mango was just inside the manager's office explaining to Jack that the investigation would be delayed until Friday because the water board had to do a permanent repair to the water main.

"Come in, Molly, Mango was just leaving," Jack said seeing her hurried arrival into the staffroom through the open door. "We've had an eventful day here."

"I know," replied Molly, "we've been watching from the gallery in the library."

"I don't suppose you could've missed it from over there." Jack stood up and thanked Mango, they shook hands and Mango returned to the yard to make sure all would be safe till Friday.

"I have some news!" said Molly excitedly, as she closed the door so they could talk in confidence.

Jack tapped the floor three times with his foot and Molly looked at him quizzically.

Wilf immediately rose up through the floor to stand next to Jack. "Greetings, fair maiden," he said majestically and did a little bow.

"It's our little signal," Jack explained smugly, having noticed her bewilderment just a moment ago, "You wait, someone will be with us soon."

Molly laughed. "Wilf's already arrived," she said giggling.

"What news?" Wilf asked.

"What news?" asked Jack, unknowingly repeating the question.

"The Professor wants to lead the investigation of the area under the car park to complete some of his father's work. He showed me the original map and there's a big space where this area has never been surveyed and he's determined to fill in the missing information."

"Well done, that was quick work," said Jack, impressed.

Wilf remained silent he was rubbing his chin, deep in thought.

"There was nothing to it, really, but we need to let Carolyn know what I have discovered."

"I'll phone her now. Are you enjoying working over there?" Jack said as he reached to the phone.

"Yes, it's amazing! There's so much to learn. I get to go behind the scenes, the people are all nice and I have access to the library. I've been reading about the Trolley Cart Company today.

At that, Wilf stopped rubbing his chin and looked at her in surprise. "That's our company."

"And I've been reading about you, Wilf."

"What, there's information about me in the museum?"

"About all of you! And reviews of 'The Pirates of Penzance'. All good, too, I am pleased to report."

"I'd no idea, we never got to see a review. Sounds like we need to take a trip over the road ourselves. But in the meanwhile I need to tell the others about the results of your snooping. You've done well." With that he waved and descended through the floor.

Jack, who had been bemused by Molly's one-sided conversation, dialled Carolyn's number. "Hi it's Jack. I have some news." He started to relay the information from Molly. "Hang on, Molly is here, I'll hand her the phone that'll be easier." He passed the phone over and Molly outlined the day's conversations with the Professor. She went into intricate detail on the whole of the morning's events, including the water main and the delay till Friday. *'How on earth do women remember every single thing and even every word of dialogue?'* thought Jack in wonder. *'I bet she can even remember what everyone was wearing.'*

Molly then handed the receiver back. "Carolyn wants a word."

"Hi…Yes they know, Wilf's gone to tell the others. We'll have to see what they can come up with… OK, I'll see you later, bye." Jack replaced the receiver. "I'm meeting her tonight to see what we can do."

Joan entered the office. "Come on, it's time we went," she said to Molly. "You can tell me all about your first full day at work while we walk home. Bye, Jack."

Jack sat down and started to sift through the applications for Joe's job. Amongst the twelve applications he had received, one name seemed familiar. He immediately dismissed six as unsuitable and drafted a 'thanks but no thanks' letter to be sent to them in the morning. At 7 pm Carolyn arrived, as Jack closed up for the night.

Alice met her in the office as she waited for him to do his final checks. "George has an idea but he needs to see someone first, I don't know any more than that. He's keeping his cards close to his chest. I think he enjoys being a bit mysterious," explained Alice.

"OK, thanks for letting me know. We are going to discuss everything over dinner and if we think of anything else I'll let you know."

With that Jack set the alarm and they went to the lounge bar of the Royal Arms.

They settled at a table by the window overlooking the High Street and Jack poured two glasses of red wine from the bottle. "Now, what do you make of Molly's information?"

"Well, I saw Alice when you were locking up and she said George is up to something but needs to see someone before he tells us. It's all a bit mysterious but he won't tell her anything else."

Over dinner they talked about trying to change the mind of Finbarr in some way but couldn't come up with any bright ideas. The water leak had however played into their hands and bought them additional time. Hopefully George would come up trumps. They finished off the evening with coffee and Jack dropped Carolyn at home.

Tuesday was Jack's day off. Joan stepped into the role of manager and looked after the store. He had arranged to meet his friends for a round of golf, so he was up early. On the way he popped into the shop to collect his paper and some sweets.

Joan was surprised to see him. "You just can't stay away, can you?" she said as he entered the store.

"Hi. I'm not stopping, just picking up a couple of things." He'd forgotten to take home his new box of golf balls so he went into the office to collect them. He was sure that the afternoon before he'd put them out on the desk in plain view so he'd remember them, after a search he eventually found them under the job applications. He jumped back in the car and placed the box on the passenger's seat. The car felt cold despite the sun now rising for its daily journey across the sky. He turned on the heating and it soon started to warm up.

George, sitting on the passenger seat did not appreciate having papers, sweets and golf balls deposited through his lap. However, he secretly congratulated himself at getting Alice to hide the balls. It had worked just as planned and he had been able to hitch a ride.

Holeford Golf Club was only three miles from the town, perched high on the ridge of hills that separated the coastline from the agricultural heart of the county. From the clubhouse there were panoramic views over the lush countryside, the blanket of green interspersed with woodlands looking like heads of broccoli neatly squeezed between the straight edges of the fields. The sun glinted off the calm sea, visible only four miles to the south. It was even possible to see the Isle of Wight on a clear day and then follow the shoreline west to the Devon hills. Even when having a bad day's golf, the outstanding views were a reward for what sometimes became an unremitting slog of trying to get a reluctant ball into a small hole, hundreds of yards away. How anyone thought this game up was a mystery, but it was addictive.

The club was established in 1863 and boasted some notable historic members. One of the professionals at the club had played in the Ryder Cup and also in the 1920s it had been used as a host venue for Open qualifying tournaments. The course was built on poor farming ground, suitable only for grazing sheep, due to its undulating and hilly disposition. In prehistoric times the ridge of the hill, where the course now lay, was crossed by a pathway (the original highway), etched into the land by ancient civilisations. It was due to its strategic position that it had become a place of significance. It was an obvious route between fishing ports on the coast and various hill forts, including Monkton which could be clearly seen, four miles to the west. Numerous tumuli or burial mounds were constructed to contain and commemorate great chiefs. They had been buried with practical and valuable belongings to assist them in the afterlife which they awaited laying in peaceful state. The course, its Art Deco clubhouse and car park had been laid out to fit around the mounds which created some unique and unexpected hazards for wayward golfers.

Jack arrived and parked up. Some of his friends had arrived before him and were extracting their clubs from the rear of their cars. Jack removed his holdall from the back seat, added the balls and sweets from the passenger seat, greeted his fellow competitors then headed for the clubhouse. Although there weren't enough lockers in the changing rooms for all the members, he had recently been lucky enough to hire one. There was a waiting list and after three years finally one had become available. It was a case of waiting for members to retire their membership, or in some cases die, before these coveted closets became vacant.

As soon as the car had stopped George stepped out and stood by the first tee. He was not a fan of car travel, much preferring the train but he had to admit that modern motor vehicles had come a long way since the war. He stood by the side of the Allegro looking north. He marvelled at the view for a while. It was not often he got out into the countryside and on a morning like this it was a treat to see the local area in all its sun-drenched glory. He turned and watched a group of four men dressed in brightly coloured shirts and trousers tee off. They sprayed the balls in different directions in their attempts to hit them down the fairway. They then blamed the wind, new clubs and lack of practice for their poor efforts, picked up their bags and each wandered off separately in search of their next shot.

On the south side of the car park lay the eighteenth green and alongside that, a large grassed mound standing at least sixteen feet high and with a diameter of approximately a hundred feet. It formed a barrier between the green and the clubhouse, acting as a giant full stop at the end of the course. It was to this ancient burial mound that George now headed, having regained his composure after the car journey. He walked around to the eastern side of the man-made hill and then proceeded directly into it, as if through an invisible door.

"Hello, Charles, are you in?" he cried, being unable to ring a bell or knock on an actual door. (Both these inconveniences are worth bearing in mind should you consider designing your own burial mound.) George stood in a narrow passage formed by large vertical flat stones with another series of flat stones laid across their top, forming a primitive entrance hall.

"Hello, old chap, come on in," came a voice from the end of the hall.

George walked along and the passage opened out into a large room of similar construction, with animal skins hanging around the perimeter acting as dividers. There was a stone floor and a stone altar positioned in front of an alcove at the far end. He stood in the empty room.

"Hang on, I'll be with you in a jiffy. Make yourself at home," came the jovial voice from behind one of the curtains.

Charles was a Bronze Age tribal chieftain. His real name in modern English translates roughly as Wolf Gore. He was interred in the mound in 2100 BC. Being a great warrior and leader, he was given a ceremonial burial and deferentially provided with all he could need for the afterlife. All he could need, that is, except golf clubs. No one could have anticipated that! He had witnessed, from his elevated position, the Roman invasion, the rise of the Saxons, the arrival and disruption caused by the Vikings, the Norman invasion which descended into the Dark Ages, the medieval period and the arrival of the Black Death carried by rats from ships docking in the port below the hill. This led onto the Tudor and Stuart periods, the Civil War and finally the resurrection of the royal dynasties. But nothing had prepared Wolf Gore for the construction of a golf course around his home, a mere 112 years ago. It was at this time that he adopted the name of Charles; it seemed a more fitting name for the period. It also had a royal ring to it befitting his heritage.

The hide curtain to the left of George wavered and from behind it emerged Charles."Take a seat. It was good to see you back at the club the other night. You've been missed." Charles stood by the dais wearing a wide brimmed flat cap with yellow short sleeved jumper over a white shirt, plaid plus fours above striped socks and the latest in golfing spiked shoes on his feet completed the outfit.

George was slightly taken aback. "I must say you look rather dapper, Charles."

"Well, thanks, old chap, one does one's best."

"Where on earth did you get the outfit? It suits you to a tee! Sorry about the pun. But it's not exactly tribal chieftain, is it?"

Charles did a little twirl and then reached into the alcove and withdrew a full set of brand-new Spalding clubs in a leather carry bag.

"Ta-dah!" he sang with a flourish, rather pleased at so admirably having completed the look. By the way, you didn't happen to notice the flagpole by the clubhouse on your way in did you? Was the flag flying high?"

"As a matter of fact it was, but what of it?"

"When it flies at half-mast it means one of the members has passed over. That's my opportunity to obtain clothes and equipment from their locker, as their possessions by default, also pass if wanted into the spirit world. I did wonder whether one of them had come over. There was an old chap out on the fairway last week, struggling up the hill coughing his lungs up… Pity. Still, I'm sure it won't be long, I've got my eye on his new Scotty Cameron putter."

"Hang on, working on that theory, don't they want them themselves?"

"Some do. It depends if they remain earth bound, in which case they can become members of the Holeford Ethereal Golf Society, of which I just happen to be the current Captain," Charles said proudly. "Here, do you fancy a game?" he eagerly asked George and pulled back a drape revealing an alcove with a large amount of golfing equipment all neatly displayed on racks.

George sat down and tried to take in the scene around him. The inner sanctum of the Neolithic tumuli now resembled that of the pro's shop in the clubhouse. "So, you actually play?" he asked in astonishment.

"Don't sound so surprised, of course we play. It's great fun! Good exercise and we have the course to ourselves every night of the week." Charles was surprised that the question should come up at all. "We have leagues and weekly competitions. You really do need to get out more. It's doing you no good holed up in that burnt out theatre of yours. You're rather losing touch with reality, old boy."

"Who else plays?"

"Well, let's see. There are several other chieftains from tumuli along the ridge, a couple of Vikings who were slaughtered over by the main road. Oh, and there's also a group of Romans from Monkton Hillfort. There are so many of them that they have their own golf society but pop over once a week for a friendly. A few others you would probably recognise from the Collington Club. I haven't had so much fun in millennia. The past hundred years have been a revelation, they really have. You should give it a go." He beamed encouragingly. He pulled a club from his bag and handed it to George. "These clothes are also very comfortable, much better than the animal hides we used to wear in my time. They used to chafe one terribly."

George sat on a bearskin covered rock twirling the club in his hand, feeling the weight of it and gripping it like a fishing rod.

"No, no, old boy. Don't grip it like that!" Charles said appalled. "You look like one of those awful little pagan figures that sit in people's gardens by those grubby little ponds and pretend to fish! What Gods they're meant to represent I can't imagine. Frightful little buggers."

George sat in silence, club in hand his mind drifting back to the fate of Price Low. Charles studied him intently and could sense that something was occupying his mind.

"Anyway, enough of this for a minute, what really brings you here? I only normally see you at the club and not even there lately, something must be up."

George rested the club against the wall and slouched on the rock dejectedly. "Our home is under threat. It may only be a burnt-out theatre to you but to us it's home." He then went into detail about their dressing room residence, the supermarket, Finbarr's plans, the attempted exorcism and the threat of demolition hanging over them.

Charles was fascinated by the revelations and listened astonished as he poured it all out. "That priest must've got more than he bargained for, I wish I'd been there!" Charles said laughing at the thought.

George didn't join in and Charles stopped smiling. He could now see that his friend took this situation very seriously.

"OK. So in a nutshell, you want to stay in the store and think that the Professor somehow holds the key to stop the possible demolition?"

"Yes, that's it. Any ideas?" George said hopefully.

"Mmm… Let me think a moment."

They were both quiet whilst Charles gave it some thought. George hoped that with Wolf Gore's centuries of experience he would come up with some ideas. He was their only chance, that's why he hadn't told the others, he didn't want them to get any false hopes. At long last Charles looked up at George thoughtfully.

"Well, there is one possibility that occurs to me. What you need is something so important that makes them reconsider their plans, right? It's happened before. When they brought the railway through the town there was such a fuss that the line had to be diverted around the site of the Roman amphitheatre, hence the odd kink in the route." He grinned at George excitedly. "What you need, old boy, is treasure!"

A bemused George just sat there looking at him. "But won't that make them want to dig even deeper and further?" he asked at length.

"No, it doesn't work like that, you'll just have to trust me." Charles then reached over to another curtain, pulled it back and revealed a hoard of shining metal objects. Amongst them George could see gold rings, a necklace, bowls, bronze axe heads and other curious items too numerous to contemplate.

"Blimey, Charles, that must be worth a fortune!" exclaimed George.

"Probably, dear fellow, but to me they're just trinkets. Some were buried with me and others I have collected over the years," he replied nonchalantly, selecting a handful and placing them on the stone table.

"So, what do we do with them?" George asked somewhat puzzled.

"You do nothing, you'll leave it all to me. When are they due back to dig the car park again?"

"Friday."

"Right, leave it with me. But I warn you, there will be a price to pay," he added ominously. "Are you still willing to go with it?"

"Yes, you name it," replied George, determined to take any chance to keep their home but a little worried what Charles could possibly want in return.

"It's the Captain's Day competition in three weeks' time and I have to lay on entertainment for the players after the match. I want to do it at the Collington Club and my price is that you, Wilf and Alice provide that entertainment," he asked expectantly.

"It would be our great pleasure," George replied somewhat relieved. "What would you like? Songs from the shows, dancing, comedy? You name it, we can deliver it." Truth to tell he was delighted at the prospect of entertaining properly again.

"A nice variety show would go down well. I'll leave all the details up to your expertise. Now can I interest you in that round of golf?"

He thrust a set of golf clubs towards him. George instinctively grabbed the bag before it fell to the floor. "But I've never played in my life!"

"Well, perhaps you should start playing in your death!" Charles said with a grin and pulled the putter from the bag and placed it in his hand. "You've got time to kill before your lift back into town so let's have a go at some putting."

George reluctantly gripped the club and with a few minutes' tuition was tapping the ball along the entrance hall into a practice hole that Charles had concocted from an empty peach tin.

At 1 pm George said his farewells and sat back in the car, pleased with his day's work. When he had started out earlier, he hadn't really known whether Charles would be able to help at all but he felt the meeting had been constructive and he could report back to the others that he had a plan. They also had a show to organise.

His first attempt at hitting a golf ball had also gone well, Charles was a very proficient teacher. While he waited for Jack to return, he watched the members teeing off and tried to memorise their swing action. His brief introduction to the game had given him enough interest to come back and give it another try.

Jack returned after a successful and enjoyable day on the course. He again noted that despite the Allegro being exposed to the sun in the car park all morning, it felt cold. He made a mental note to mention it when he took it for its annual service. Maybe the heater was on the blink.

15

The Find

Friday 25ᵗʰ of July

It was early Friday morning and the sun was lazily rising, casting an increasingly orange glow over the beginning of the day. The greenkeepers on Holeford golf course had been busy, even before first light, preparing the course for the day's play. The fairway edges had been trimmed, tee markers positioned, bins emptied, bunkers raked, greens swept and holes moved to avoid excessive wear to the finely cut grass. It was now six-thirty and they had all gathered in the green keeper's hut for a well-earned cup of tea and a bacon sandwich. Two of them said their farewells and headed home, they would then return later to tend the fairways ready for the weekend competitions, while those remaining set about servicing machines and undertaking general course maintenance well out of the way of stray golfers and their errant projectiles. Peter Mounce, was one of those going home and unbeknownst to him, there was a passenger in his Mini for the ride back into town. On the back seat sat Wolf Gore wearing his impressive chieftain regalia. His long hair was swept back and held in place by a golden comb. His buck-skin robe hung from his shoulders over a thick woollen kilt with large leather belt fastened with a bright bronze buckle. Not afraid to modernise for comfort, he wore a pair of long *Pringle* socks and a pair of brand-new shoes he had recently acquired from a deceased member of the club. Alongside him on the back seat was a leather bag containing the necessary materials for his morning's work.

Charles greatly admired the modern horseless chariots. They were so much more convenient and comfortable than the ox-drawn carts of his youth, even if this one was a trifle cramped for someone of his stature. He knew from previous rides, that Peter lived close to the town centre in one of the old railway cottages and that Price Low was in Princes Road, a short walk over the railway line. He could remember when the Romans laid out the road system and most of the later town centre had evolved around their original street pattern.

At seven-thirty he entered the shop and headed to the wines and spirits area where George, Wilf and Alice were waiting to greet him. He advanced slowly, admiring the incredible variety of goods for sale. The pictures on the packaging looked appetising; what a shame he was unable to try them. '*Sometimes being a ghost sucks*' he thought.

"Wow! I love the outfit." Alice looked up in awe at the tall, broad shouldered handsome warrior chief. She had never met Charles before, she only had George and Wilf's description. They certainly hadn't done him justice, he was truly magnificent.

"You're early, Charles. I was going to meet you outside," George said stepping forward to shake his hand, closely followed by Wilf.

"Ah, this must be the beautiful Alice," Charles said not answering George and brushing the men to one side.

He lifted her right hand, elegantly kissing the back of it. "Delighted to meet you at last. I've heard so much about you but nothing prepared me for your radiance. We're very much looking forward to your performance at the Captain's Day celebrations."

If Alice could have blushed she would have done so; She didn't know that a prehistoric chieftain could be so charming. "We're all looking forward to the chance to perform for you, it'll be our pleasure," Alice said, feeling slightly overwhelmed.

"Do you need a hand with anything?" asked Wilf, keen to get down to business and probe him to find out what he was planning.

"Totally unnecessary, old chap. I arrived a bit earlier than planned so the deed is already done." He held up a now empty leather bag to indicate that he had deposited the contents.

"What have you done?" Alice enquired excitedly.

"Well, my little Nightingale, let's just say they're in for a bit of a surprise when they start their investigations. Now, are you going to give me a guided tour of your charming home? Quite frankly I could do with putting my feet up for a while."

"Follow us," beckoned George, and they descended through the floor into the basement.

Charles admired the prop-come dressing room and was particularly enamoured of the mechanism that operated the trapdoor and lift. "You have a cosy place here," he said, settling himself on the sofa. "Ah, that's better, I must say this is more comfortable than my stone bench," and he patted the arm of the chair producing a small cloud of dust. "I've had a busy morning, I don't usually do mornings. Night-time suits me better, when the golf club is quiet. I have to be very careful. There are a couple of members who are sensitive to the beyond. I don't want to attract the interest of those meddling ghost hunters!"

"They're alright," chipped in Wilf. "We have a bit of fun with them, sometimes. Being in the town centre, it's hard to avoid them entirely. There's a weekly ghost walk given by the official tour guide. We go and give them a bit of a scare sometimes, it livens things up for them, he can go on a bit at times." The three of them then told Charles stories of some of the tricks they had played on ghost hunters at the Kings Head hoping to see evidence of the *Grey Lady* and how they sometimes spooked the tour guide's audience. "He's no idea we're doing it, he thinks he's just a very good storyteller. Come to think of it he's probably built up his entire reputation thanks to our interference, we ought to charge him a fee!"

They all relaxed while Charles then regaled them with stories from his past. The actors were transfixed by his extensive knowledge and realised how inexperienced they were to ghostly existence.

At 9 am the archaeologist and machine driver arrived at the shop and signed in the visitors' book. After a brief meeting with Jack they resumed their task, being careful to steer clear of the newly repaired water main. The impromptu lake created by the incident had now soaked away and they were able to continue the laborious task of slowly scraping away the ground, an inch at a time. Closely monitored by the archaeologist. Occasionally, Archibald Strathmore climbed down into the ever-growing hole and carefully dug by hand with a small trowel and a dusting brush. This routine continued for an hour. The four ghosts came out to get front row seats and watch the proceedings. Charles had predicted something would happen soon after the recommencement and they wanted to witness it.

Molly had taken a coffee to the Professor and she used the opportunity to take a peek out of the window and see what was happening. She could see her three friends standing by the trench along with a strange man wearing a fur coat, a kilt and socks with sandals. It was very strange dress sense but he looked a bit of a hunk! This was a certain sign in her mind that something was happening. It was unlike the actors to come outside in daytime in case they were seen, and who was the person with them? She passed the mug of coffee over to the Professor who had remained perched on the edge of the table observing the proceedings closely.

"Thanks, Molly, nothing exciting to see yet, but keep your fingers crossed, you never know with exploratory digs."

She watched for a while then reluctantly returned to the office to sort the post ready for distribution.

In the car park Archibald suddenly held up his hand and instructed the driver to stop the machine. He jumped down into the hole and with a small trowel and dusting brush started frantically scraping and sweeping the ground. He then got down on his knees, his nose only inches from the base of the pit and carefully prised something from the ground. Holding it in his right hand he gently brushed more dirt off the object in order to get a clearer look at his find. He then climbed out of the hole where he was joined by the driver, who had turned off his engine and climbed out of the machine.

"What you got there, then?" he enquired.

Archibald did not answer. He was trembling with excitement and lowered the item into a bowl of water and gradually washed away more of the debris.

Charles gave George a conspiratorial wink and folded his arms smugly. "Here we go!" he said knowingly.

All four of them circled the archaeologist as he rinsed the find. Archibald pulled an eye piece out of his pocket, gripped it with his eyelid and lifted the object out of the muddy water into day light, where he could examine it closely.

"Well, what is it then?" the driver asked again impatiently. He moved in close to see what it was for himself and blinked as a shaft of golden light reflected into his eyes. "Cor, is that gold?" he exclaimed excitedly.

"I need a second opinion immediately, I need to go over the road, wait here."

Archibald gently wrapped the treasure in a cloth and headed quickly across the road towards the museum. Then suddenly stopped, spun on his heels and shouted back to the driver. "Make sure you don't let anyone near the excavation, and touch nothing yourself." He sprinted off again, crossing the road without stopping to look left or right. A blue Ford Cortina had to brake sharply and made significant use of his horn. Archibald was unaware. He had gone into the museum by then and did not see the rude gesture aimed at him by the irate driver.

The Professor had seen the sudden flurry of excitement from his vantage point and was already heading along the gallery and down the stairs when the excited archaeologist burst through the doors into the lobby clutching his discovery.

"Professor… Professor, are you there?" he cried out, looking in all directions for him.

Behind the reception desk Beryl was not amused. "Shhh! Please keep the noise down whoever you are. I'll see if the Professor is available, but only if you wait here quietly. Now what is your name?"

"No need Beryl," said the Professor entering the lobby from the library. "I know this gentleman, I'll take it from here."

Beryl returned haughtily to her post, aiming a withering look at the visitor.

"Hello, Archibald, What's all the fuss about? What's that you've got in your hand?" He asked, trying not to reveal the fact that he had been watching them all morning. "Come on through to my office, why don't you?"

Archibald, now trembling with excitement, followed him up into the library. At the desk he carefully unwrapped the cloth to reveal a muddy artefact with glimpses of metal concealed within its crust.

The Professor added a cautionary note to the proceedings. "I guess this is from the site opposite? You realise that bringing me this find is in contravention of the council's procedure? I haven't been given authority by the planning office to consult officially with you yet."

Archibald was taken by surprise at the official stance being taken by the Professor. "Yes, I realise that, but how do you know where it came from? Anyway, stuff the council, this is extraordinary and I must show it to you. We can tell them later."

"Couldn't agree more… Alright then, let's have a good look at what you've found. Come on, follow me." They headed quickly back through the library, up the stairs and through the outer office. They quickly passed Gwen's desk, careful to keep the find protected by the cloth.

Beryl, watching them, thought they looked just like two sneaky schoolchildren up to mischief.

They entered the Professor's office. "Right, let's have a closer look." He produced a large magnifying glass from the top drawer of his desk. Archibald unwrapped the object and placed it on a tray. The Professor studied it intently for a few moments.

"OK, let's go into the lab." He carefully carried the object through a side door into a small kitchen where Molly was washing up the coffee cups. "Ah, Molly, that's very fortuitous, you're in the right place at the right time to witness an exciting moment in the history of Holeford," he said, pleased to be sharing this with his new protégé. Be a dear and clear away the coffee cups, we need some space."

Molly did so and the Professor placed the tray containing the object on the draining board.

"I thought you said lab?" queried Archibald, looking round the small cluttered kitchen.

"Well, it is, just use your imagination," said the Professor impatiently. He emptied the sink and filled it with clean water. Then opened a wall cupboard and removed a roll of canvas which he placed on the worktop. It unfurled to reveal a series of small dentist-like tools contained in individual thin pockets. Molly and Archibald gathered round as the Professor carefully continued to clean and wash the object. Gradually, after an hour of painstaking cleaning, a large ring of twisted wire was revealed.

"As I thought. This is a Bronze Age Twisted Torc or Neck-Ring. It is formed by twisting a rod of bronze around its own axis and you see these rounded ends, these are what we call twisted terminals. That dates it to between the eighth and sixth centuries, probably from the Hallstatt period."

His companions both stood in silence. Stunned by the age and beauty of the exposed bronze artefact.

"This is extremely rare and I have to say this is a particularly fine example. In fact one of the best I've ever seen," beamed the Professor. "Archie, you have to get the planning office to authorise me immediately. We need to continue with the dig at once, this is too important to wait."

"Very good, Prof, I'll go now." He practically ran from the room, down the stairs and out through the front door of the museum. The sound of his footsteps still echoed in the cavernous library as the door closed. Much to the bewilderment of his audience in the car park he did not cross the road to re-join them as they expected but turned right and ran up the hill towards the council offices, where he could report to the planning department, without delay.

"Right, Molly, while he does the red tape stuff, let's have a look at my father's map again. I have a feeling I'll be able to fill in a missing section very soon now." They headed round the gallery to the table by the bay window where he'd been watching the excavation. Molly could see the four ghosts still in the carpark looking towards the museum. She moved close to the window and did a thumbs up, which Wilf acknowledged.

"Well, it's all looking good so far," Wilf said to the others. "I don't know exactly how you've done this, Charles, but it seems to be working."

"Let's just say I have a gift for making things happen, and this is just the beginning. Now I must be going. My lift back to the golf club in the Mini chariot leaves soon. Don't forget your golf lesson on Sunday night, George, and see you all at the Captain's Day dinner. We're so looking forward to the show."

Wilf and Alice looked at George. "Golf!" they exclaimed in unison.

"What about it? It is the traditional sport for us theatrical types." George said defensively.

"Yes, but this is George Shakespeare we're talking about," Wilf said. "You're hard put to go to the Collington Club let alone consider joining a golf club."

"Well, I thought I'd give this one a go, Charles can be very persuasive."

Archibald returned to the museum from the council office two hours later with the necessary duplicate form instructing the Professor to inspect and report back to them in his role as planning consultant. The Professor had anticipated the instruction and had already contacted the university to arrange for two students to join them on Monday morning to assist with the dig, cleaning and recording the other artefacts he was confident of finding.

The Professor, having changed into some old clothes he kept in the cloakroom for just such situations, was impatiently waiting for his return. "Good, you're back. Now come on, let's get started, no time to waste." He took the planning authority form and placed it in a tray on his desk. "We can deal with the paperwork later."

He picked up a rucksack containing his trowel and brushes and dashed out of the door, down the stairs, out through the entrance and across to the car park. Archibald had to run after him to catch up.

They continued to scrape away at the ground with their trowels late into the evening. Alice and George grew tired of watching two grown men scratching away in the dirt and returned to the props room. Wilf, however, continued to watch and would give them a report later. The two archaeologists made copious notes of their progress but unfortunately it was Friday so the dig would have to go on hold until they had additional help on Monday. Also, the machine operator was getting agitated. He just wanted to go home, so they agreed to seal off the area with temporary fencing. The machine was then shut down, its arm resting on the various sized digging buckets for safety and security until resumption the following week.

Monday 28th of July

On Monday the Professor and Archibald were joined by the two archaeology students and the dig began in earnest. Charles had done them proud and an assortment of artefacts continued to be sporadically uncovered. Molly assisted with the transporting of the finds across the road to the museum for cleaning and recording. Progress was so good that Archibald was able to return to the council offices to arrange an emergency meeting with the chairman of the Heritage Committee.

On the other side of town, Brian and Charlie arrived at the police station for their weekly visit to sign the register confirming their presence in Holeford. This was now routine and they were in no hurry. They wandered through the arched entrance into the courtyard, which had once stabled the horses and carriages. It was now a small car park for the constabulary's mixture of Ford Escorts and Austin 1100 panda cars, which all faced towards them, their vacant headlights looking on accusingly. They turned left and entered the public lobby where PC Dexter was on duty.

"Morning lads," he said greeting them amiably. He reached under the desk and produced the register for them to sign. "Big day for you both then," Dexter continued. "You'd better sit over there," he said pointing out the row of chairs opposite, positioned under a big poster informing the public to 'Lock it or lose it!'

They both looked confused. "What's so special about today?" Brian said.

"You'll find out soon enough, if you don't already know," added Dexter mysteriously.

They both sat down whispering nervously to each other. They had no idea what this was all about. However, they wouldn't have to wait long. On the opposite wall to the left of the enquiries desk was an information board containing various items of community news and useful contacts. In the middle of the board was a new poster with a picture of a pirate, policeman and a young Victorian woman. At first they thought it was a poster for a fancy dress ball.

Brian walked over to the display to take a closer look at the text below the picture. He read out loud, *"Have you seen these people? The police are seeking any information on the whereabouts of this group. They're believed to live in the Holeford area and are wanted for questioning regarding illegal crime prevention. Any information given will be treated in confidence. Call Holeford police station and ask for Sergeant Montgomery."*

"They don't look a bit like that," Charlie said.

Brian turned his head and looked directly at Charlie. "This is all your doing. You started all this with your stupid story. I hope you're satisfied!"

A door slammed shut in the room behind the desk and the building vibrated. They both looked around for the source, beyond the counter. The mood abruptly changed and a gloom descended over the waiting room. Brian returned to his seat quickly and quietly as if driven by a force greater than his will.

Behind PC Dexter, the door to the back office had opened and a very large woman stood framed in the doorway. She was built like a prop forward and waited, perfectly still. Her stern face was accentuated by her pulled back hair fastened into a tight bun. Not a single hair had dared to come loose and stray onto her expansive neck. She wore a steel grey suit, with the jacket hanging like chainmail over the plain cream blouse encompassing her ample bosom. Her head began to rotate, robot like, scanning the room with her beady laser eyes. Neither Charlie nor Brian would have been surprised if her head had rotated through three hundred and sixty degrees. Her glance finally came to rest on the two of them. They were paralysed by the gaze, seemingly unable to move while they remained in her vision. It felt like their energy was being sucked out of them, her presence absorbing the atmosphere leaving only an empty feeling of foreboding.

"Ah, good, you are both here," she said in a deep mesmeric voice. She then walked to the counter where Dexter quickly lifted the flap to allow her an unobstructed path to the public area. One felt she might have crashed straight through the wooden obstacle, reducing it to splinters without even missing a step. She turned sideways to negotiate the narrow gap, her stately frame brushing both sides of the opening. Once through, she turned and headed towards the two brothers who sat motionless under her spell. Dexter closed the flap hastily as if he had released a dangerous beast and wanted to ensure it could not return. Brian and Charlie could now see that where the chain mail suit stopped, two tree trunk sized legs protruded out, terminating in gleaming black size-12 Doctor Martin boots. She lifted her arm and with her banana fingered hand pointed at Brian. "You first," she boomed and pointed to the interview room on the opposite side of the public hall.

Brian gulped. '*What on earth was going on?*' he thought, as he reluctantly stood and walked unsteadily to the door, as if in a trance. Charlie felt no better as he watched his brother disappear into the room and the door firmly closed behind him. He wondered if he would ever see him again! Dexter breathed out and visibly relaxed.

The room was similar in décor to the interview room where they had spent many unhappy hours being interrogated about the robbery. The austere décor was the same but instead of a large mirror there were posters containing public information slogans. In the corner was a stand containing leaflets about home security, driver safety, witness protection, violent crime and Legal Aid.

The creature sat down and pointed Brian towards the chair opposite. "I am Sarah Cray, from the magistrate's court. You will have received a letter from my department regarding your court appearance on the eighth of August."

Brian was totally confused. "No… I haven't received anything."

The piercing eyes of Sarah seemed to darken in disbelief.

"I haven't… honest," Brian reiterated.

"Well, no matter," she said stonily while reaching into her briefcase. She removed a duplicate copy of the letter that was supposed to have been sent. She always anticipated the failings of her office and the incompetence of the people she dealt with, who would ignore officialdom at every opportunity causing confusion of the system and unnecessary delay. She could not abide such blatant disregard for The Standard Procedures. She slid the copy across the table to Brian. He could see the official nature of the document and feared the worst. "You have been summoned to appear at the magistrates' court on Friday of next week. You have been charged with: car theft, breaking and entering and attempted robbery. Do you have anything to say?"

Brian had had time to reflect on his misdemeanour after being released from the police cell. He had nothing to add, he just wanted to get through this and move on. He decided that he was not suited to crime. He would pay his debt to society and pursue an honest way of life, a life of crime was too complicated. It all looked exciting and romantic on the telly, beating the system and living the high life on the costa-del-crime, with dusky maidens bringing you cocktails by the pool. In reality it was hell. Trying to organise the break-in, working undercover to steal a car, getting attacked while trying to steal the money from the supermarket, which all lead to dank cells, itchy blankets, constant questioning, appalling cups of tea and the removal of his freedom. No, this was not for him. He was going to tread an honest path from now on.

"Well, do you want to say anything?" Sarah growled with growing impatience.

Brian seemed to have drifted into a daydream. He was snapped back into reality by Sarah slapping her hand on the table.

"No, nothing," said the dejected ex-burglar.

"Do you have legal representation or do you require Legal Aid?" she asked. Then without waiting for his answer, began reeling off a long list of what was going to happen next week, what was required of him and what to expect, dependent on the leniency or not of the local magistrates. She advised him to plead guilty, due to the strong evidence against him or he could face Crown Court, which would add months to the procedure and result in a more severe sentence. "Do you understand what I have said?" she concluded.

"Yes, I think so," he said unconvincingly.

"Good. Here is a transcript of the points I have raised." She also handed him a booklet.

"You may find it useful to read this before your appearance. Now sign here to say you have received and understood what I've covered in this meeting." She handed him a sheet of paper filled with small print, offered him a pen and pointed at the dotted line at the bottom of the page.

Brian signed without reading anything and then they both stood up. She opened the door and he returned to the public lobby, clutching the paperwork and looking totally shattered.

Charlie was pleased to see he was still alive, fearing he had been eaten by the creature. Brian didn't say anything, he sat down next to Charlie and just whimpered. His mind was in a whirl after listening to all the information he was supposed to remember for next week.

From across the room the gaze of the court official now rotated to Charlie. He could feel her eyes burning into him and he instinctively started to rise as the fog horn that was her voice, bellowed, "You next" The pink bananas now beckoned him too to the fateful interview room.

He entered and sat where indicated by the rugby player in drag. The door then closed on the outside world.

"I am Sarah Cray from the magistrates' court and I suppose you are also going to tell me you didn't receive a letter last week?"

"What letter?" Charlie felt it was his fault that he hadn't received any correspondence last week. Was this another crime?The only post he received was a *Reader's Digest* circular telling him he had won a full set of encyclopaedias. He'd thrown that straight in the bin.

Sarah sighed and again reached into her briefcase and removed a copy of the said letter and slid it across the table towards Charlie. "The charges against you for breaking and entering and attempted theft have been dropped. The prosecution service has taken into consideration the fact that it was you who called the police and coupled with your mental frailty, will not be pursuing your conviction. Your misdemeanour will be retained on record and may be reconsidered if you offend again. If you are happy with this conclusion please sign this form here and here." She indicated several dotted lines on the paper. "That done, you will be free to leave the police station and will no longer be required to sign in weekly."

She handed him the pen, which he quickly took and scribbled his signature along the dotted lines. They both stood up and Sarah opened the door. Charlie thanked her and walked into the lobby a free man. He carried his copy of the signed form and held it in front of Brian.

"I've been let off! They think I'm crazy!" he said, not sure if he should feel indignation or relief at the assumption but he wasn't going to argue the point.

"Well, at least it officially confirms that you're a mental case. You've got it there in black and white!" Brian remained seated holding his summons. "I'm pleased for you."

"Well now everything's sorted can we go?" asked Charlie.

"Yes, let's get out of here, but it's not all over for me. I am in court next Friday." He looked down forlornly at the forms in his hand. "She was on about a letter sent last week but we didn't get anything did we?"

"No, nothing, now let's go," pleaded Charlie who was afraid they would realise he had been given the wrong form. He was sorry for Brian as he assumed he had been free to go as well, but at the moment, his overwhelming feeling was relief for himself. He felt as if a great weight had been lifted from him.

As they walked back into town Brian started to quiz Charlie. "What did you tell them in your statement for them to come to the conclusion that you'd lost your senses?"

"I just told the truth. You know, about the pirate, the policeman and the girl and how they threw things at us and wouldn't let us leave, that's all. They made me tell them, I was trying not to, honestly, but they just wore me down."

"And now they're looking for a vigilante group who go around in fancy dress trying to stop crime?"

"That's not my problem." Charlie shrugged his shoulders. "I was only telling the truth."

As they walked through the town centre they passed Price Low and could see the excavation going on in the car park. It was attracting quite a crowd watching the proceedings in the hope of something interesting appearing out of the mud. They stopped and joined the group of onlookers. However, their interest soon waned, individuals scraping and brushing the ground could only hold their curiosity for so long.

"I've applied for a job." Charlie dropped casually into the conversation as they watched the archaeologists.

"A job? Where?" Brian asked.

"Here."

"What do you mean here? On the dig?"

"No, in the supermarket."

"Now I know you're off your rocker. You don't seriously think Price Low are going to employ someone who tried to rob them do you?" He looked at Charlie trying to read his expression. He had to be winding him up. This had to be a joke! Either that or he was incredibly stupid. Charlie looked back at him with a straight face, but said nothing. "You have, haven't you? What on earth are you thinking?"

"Why not? There are no jobs for electricians at the moment so I have to do something! They want a shelf stacker to work at night who can also take on the role of security guard," Charlie said.

"You, an attempted robber in charge of security at night! That takes the biscuit!" Brian laughed at the irony of it. "What about these ghosts you say you saw. Aren't you scared they may pick on you again?" he taunted.

"I don't think they would and anyway, I like them. They did me a favour. It was their action making me phone the police that got me off the charge," he reflected. "And anyway, one of them is standing over by that wall now, watching the excavation and I don't think he's so scary. How can someone dressed as a comic pirate be scary?"

Brian took one step away from Charlie. "What?"

"I don't think he's seen me," Charlie said ignoring Brian's dramatics.

"Why don't you wave him over? He may be able to put in a good word for you with the manager!" Brian said sarcastically.

"Shall I?" Charlie replied naively.

"No, Charlie, no! I was not being serious. Don't start attracting attention. Let's go before 'Long John Spooky' sees you," he said grabbing his arm and pulling him quickly away from the crowd.

"Seriously, it's worth a go," continued Charlie, feeling peeved at Brian's apparent scoffing of his attempt to rebuild his life. "It would keep me occupied while the dust settles and keep me out of trouble. I'd also be earning some cash and you never know what it'll lead to. Anyway, from today I am a free man and won't have a criminal record, unlike you!"

"Thanks for reminding me! You're a jammy sod, I hope you'll come and visit me in prison," Brian said half-joking. He was feeling annoyed at his brother being able to plan for his future whilst all he could think about was the impending court appearance.

"Well, that'll depend if visiting fits in with my working hours," Charlie mocked.

Brian just shook his head in disbelief and they headed home.

16

The Heritage Committee

Tuesday 29th of July

The Price Low storeroom was well stocked despite the restriction of bringing all the deliveries through the front door. Joe had done well at moving the stock in with minimal disruption to the customers. Jack was making himself busy sorting through the pile of applicants to replace Joe in preparation for a review with Joan on Wednesday. He even managed to spend some time on the till as light relief from the paperwork. He missed the interaction with the customers now that most of his time was spent in the back office. It was nice to meet and greet the regulars, pass the time of day and put the world to rights. In the afternoon Jack finished early and headed to the golf club for a friendly game with some of his mates. Unknowingly George again hitched a lift.

Carolyn was busy at home preparing for the new term in between shopping and household chores.

Molly was reading up all she could about the objects they had been removing from the trenches in the car park. She had spent most of her time in the museum helping to clean and log the objects. This was slow, intensive work, but what treasure they were finding. The Professor was over the moon with the finds and not a little perplexed about how such a mixture of valuable artefacts should be together in one trench. It supported his view that the hoard may be a private collection hidden during the Viking invasions.

Molly kept Alice updated with progress and Alice in turn reported on progress with the Captain's Day show.

"Wilf's going to compere, I'm going to sing and we are having auditions for some surprise acts. It's going to be a great evening," Alice said excitedly. "We haven't had a chance to perform since the fire. I just hope we can make it a regular thing."

"It sounds like George is using his impresario skills to recruit more talent, I read about them in the theatre programme."

Alice was touched by her research into their careers. All three of them were excited by the chance to perform in front of an audience once again. Molly wished she was able to see the show. She just hoped the supermarket would not be demolished, giving them somewhere to rehearse and revive their entertaining skills for future events. She didn't voice her fears as it might spoil Alice's cheerful mood although the worst scenario was probably not far from Alice's mind anyway.

Wednesday 30th of July

After the initial rush of customers, Joan brought tea into Jack's office and they sat down to go through the applicants for Joe's position, or rather the new role of shelf stacker/ security guard.

Jack had reduced the pile of applicants down to three plus one mystery contender who strangely kept appearing at the top of the pile. Unbeknownst to them, Wilf had also joined the review, after all, the choice would have a profound effect on his residency at the store.

Jack took a sip of his tea, put the mug down and began.

"Right, Joan, I've whittled it down to these:"

Stephen Small;

He works at the cash and carry on the industrial estate where he is already shelf stacking. He wants to further his career and would very much like to work for a progressive company like Price Low. His hobbies are going to the cinema, books and crochet."

Martin Jones;

Ex-army, retired prison warder. He is used to un-social hours and can turn his hand to most things. His hobbies are judo, snooker and gardening.

Catherine Butcher;

She has just completed her business studies at Exford College, has been working part-time at Asco's supermarket and would like the opportunity to work for Price Low. Her hobbies include music, reading and netball.

Charlie Clarke; qualified electrician. Looking for a change of direction. Hobbies include; self-defence, the theatre and visiting museums.

"I don't know about number four." Jack said, passing the applications across to Joan. "The name seems familiar? You know how you get a gut feeling about these things."

"Do you seriously not know who he is?" Joan asked.

"No, should I?"

"I should say so, he's one of the guys who tried to rob the place a few weeks ago. He's got a nerve," she exclaimed.

"I think he's perfect," said Wilf. "He knows we exist, so no problem for us and we can keep an eye on him. I don't believe he's a bad egg, just easily led by his brother." Wilf shrugged his shoulders. He might just as well speak to the angle poised lamp. They had no idea he was there and certainly couldn't hear him. Reshuffling the applications had worked though, at least they had noticed him now.

"Well, what do you think?" asked Jack.

"My order of preference is Martin, then Steve followed by Charlie." Joan was startled by what she had just said. '*OK, well whatever made me, I've said it now. Stick to your guns, girl,*' she thought.

"There you see! Even you're siding with our burglar. Why is that? I think we need to have a chat with him. There's something extraordinary about this but, right or wrong, I'm going to include him in the interviews and drop Catherine, I don't think, in hindsight, she is suitable."

"Well done!" Wilf said and lowered down into the dressing room for a rest before his afternoon stint on trench duty.

"Good, that's that then Jack. I need to go back into the shop. Candice is off sick today so we are short of numbers, I'll leave you to it." With that, Joan left the room astonished at the impulsive advice she had just offered about candidate Charlie Clarke. Jack thanked her and picked up the phone to call and arrange the interviews with the three remaining candidates.

By late afternoon they had finished the trenches in the car park which now stretched up to the side wall of the supermarket. They had revealed the red brick footings of the theatre on which the shop now stood. They counted up the number of finds from the three days of permissive work and listed:

Four neck-rings, four bronze ingots, twelve axe heads, five bracelets, numerous spearheads (which would need to be carefully separated as they had fused together) and several sickles.

It was an unprecedented discovery for the Holeford area and a joy for the Professor who could now conclude a section of the work he had inherited from his father. But the question remained, what could be done to preserve the site for the future?

Thursday 31ˢᵗ July

At ten-thirty on Thursday morning in the museum library the chairman of the heritage committee, Councillor Trevor Griffiths, called the extraordinary meeting to order. He was joined by the Professor, Archibald, the council chairman, the head of the planning department, the chief building control officer and Mango.

In the entrance hall a sign hung on the large oak door. 'No Entry. Meeting in progress.'

They all sat at one end of the long oak table in the middle of the room which was normally reserved for society members to spread out documents for study. Gwen sat with them at the opposite end of the table to take the minutes and Molly was allowed to join them purely to observe the proceedings. In the centre of the table the ancient map the Professor was using for reference was laid out along with a tray containing samples of the cleaned items.

"Well, what can be done, Trevor?" asked the Professor. "We have here one of Holeford's most significant excavations for a century. You have a duty to the town and its people to ensure this site is accessible." He found it difficult to hide his distrust of the snide little official opposite.

Lizard-faced Trevor showed no emotion. His greasy hair swept back over his head and he wore an ill-fitting crumpled suit with white shirt. His tie with council insignia shone from over ironing. The Professor was convinced he had cold blood running through his veins. "I see three options, Professor," he began in his nasally drawl. "I have taken advice from British Heritage who, despite the historical significance of the site, have no current funding available to assist. However, they suggest the following."

He opened his briefcase and handed out copies of the council directive for all to read. While they were passed around he removed a notepad and fountain pen, closed the case and placed it on the floor by his chair. He then read out the proposals.

"One; the site is purchased by the council or the museum, fully investigated and then turned into a visitor attraction. However, I believe neither has the funds available at this time to carry out such an undertaking.

Two; the planning office can put an order against the property to prevent any further development of the site. Effectively preserving the remainder of the site undisturbed until such times that the site may be sold in the future. At which time, if there are sufficient funds, a full excavation of the site can take place.

Three; we can put a covenant on any planning permission, thus compelling the developer to pay for the full investigation, gift a section of the land for a visitor centre, cover the cost of its construction and contribute a sum of money to fund the aforementioned centre including preservation and exhibition of any artefacts found."

They then debated each of the proposals weighing up the impact to the community and Price Low. Mango argued strongly against the punitive proposals for Finbarr while the Professor tried to impress the importance of the archaeology. After two hours the councillor officially closed the meeting. He promised to present the minutes to the next Planning Sub-Committee meeting. Mango thanked the Professor for his hospitality and left to report back to Finbarr.

The Professor sighed. "Well what a fiasco, Molly. I think it's time we had a cup of tea. I'll go and get the biscuits."

Molly went to the kitchen and returned with a tray of tea things and Gwen poured out the welcome brew.

"Why didn't we have a cup of tea during the meeting?" Gwen asked the professor. "I think everyone could have done with one."

"To tell the truth, Gwen, I don't like Gecko Griffiths."

"Who?" Gwen said nearly spilling her tea.

"That's what they call him in the planning office. He would sell his own mother to further his career. He came here from East Grinstead two years ago to work in the Highways Department where he was so useless, they promoted him to Heritage where it was assumed he could do less harm. He's got no knowledge of archaeology or heritage what-so-ever and lords it over the council offices as if he owns the place. He can go and get his own tea!" He paused for a gulp of the refreshing brew. "You can see what they're doing. This will drag on for years. He'll report at the monthly meeting, it will then eventually be passed to a further sub-committee who'll debate the options. If they're satisfied it will go to full committee again, for another debate before recommendations are put to a full council meeting. In the meantime there will be elections both local and nationally probably, then the whole thing will disappear in a filing cabinet and likely never see the light of day again. I'm sorry to be so cynical but

I have seen this many times before. I can't get my hopes too high. Local politics is just as perplexing as the archaeology we have uncovered and much less interesting. The good news is that we have some exceptional artefacts from our initial survey which will help with the ongoing work started by my father. Plus, there is enough material for a special display in the antiquities hall. I do hope you are able to stay and help us, Molly, as much as you can between your studies."

"Yes please, Professor," said the excited young apprentice.

"I am sorry we won't be able to pay you but the reward will be an exceptional chance to dip your toe into the wonderful world of archaeology. It'll be invaluable should you want to pursue it as a career. In the meantime we'll change your badge to assistant archivist, I think that'll be more fitting for your new role."

At lunchtime Molly ran over to the shop to report on the meeting to Carolyn and Jack who were waiting in the office. The three ghosts also joined them following Jack's tap on the floor. Molly joyfully repeated the proposals from the slimy council officer and showed them her copy of the meeting agenda that was being considered.

"I don't know what will happen next but it sounds like there might be another delay," she said clapping her hands.

Wilf looked at the proposal. "Charles was right. He's really come up trumps with his enhancement of the archaeology."

Carolyn added some words of caution. "We mustn't get our hopes up. There's a long way to go yet. It'll all depend on Mango's report and recommendations to Finbarr."

"They wouldn't demolish it now, would they, not after all this?" Molly said hopefully.

"Mango's back tomorrow to oversee the making good of the car park surface, I'll tap him for information," Jack said.

Carolyn took Molly to one side. "Now Molly, your help has been marvellous but you don't have to continue to volunteer at the museum. You're back to school soon and it will be a busy year for you." She had once again assumed the role of concerned teacher.

"But I need to carry on Miss. I know I'll have more homework next year but the Professor said I can help whenever it suits me. Can I do A level English and history? I'll need them both if I'm going to university." Molly had again resumed the role of pupil, so calling her Carolyn just didn't seem right.

"Well, you seem to have decided what you want to do. When we get back to school we'll arrange a meeting with the careers advisor and see what we need to do. I am very proud of you."

"We're all very proud of you," added Alice.

"Thanks but I have to go back now, I have lot of work to do." Molly got up, waved to them all and dashed back out of the office to return to the museum and carry on with the cleaning of the artefacts. She had certainly taken to museum life with gusto, she felt part of an adult world and to her amazement she fitted in perfectly. Her thirst for knowledge was being satisfied and she just wanted more. With the Professor's support and good exam results, a university life could be in reach for Molly, where she could progress her ambitions.

"Yes and we need to get back to our rehearsals for the show," added George. "We've got auditions tomorrow for the supporting acts so we need to be ready. This is going to be one night that the golfers won't forget in a hurry." With that, the three of them descended back to their room to review their costume choices.

"You've created a force of nature there. Molly will be running that museum in a few years," Jack said, unaware of the ghosts exit.

On Friday morning workmen arrived with the digger driver to backfill the large hole in the car park and return it to its normal use. They brought with them a lorry loaded with sand and crushed stone with a large roller. The sand was carefully spread over the areas where the artefacts were found, to protect the strata. Then the pile of excavated material was layered back into the depression and compacted with the vibrating roller. The new stone was then added to give a smooth solid surface for the final finish and surplus material loaded onto the empty wagon.

At 2 pm Mango arrived, signed in and formally reported to Jack. He then returned to the car park to monitor the conclusion of the repairs to the surface. At two-thirty another lorry arrived. Its open bed bulging with a hot steaming substance covered with a tarpaulin to stop it cooling too quickly. It reversed into the car park over the freshly compacted aggregate, the men removed the cover to reveal the tarmac and its sweet intoxicating bitumen smell filled the air. The lorry tipped up the load as the workforce gathered behind it to carefully distribute the hot sticky substance, filling the depression that had been left to receive it. They raked it into position and the roller then went to work, levelling and compacting it to a smooth hard surface. There was a large water tank mounted above the engine which kept the steel drum wet to prevent it sticking to the tar. Steam rose from the ground as the water hit the hot tarmac and the vibration of the roller became more intense as the surface hardened. The tremors were felt in the store where bottles and tins rattled on the shelves taking on a life of their own. This time without the assistance of Alice. Joe, along with the other staff, monitored the animated provisions to make sure nothing came to harm while Jack went out into the yard to join Mango and see what was going on.

"Hi Jack, nearly done," Mango shouted over the noise of the machine. He was checking the levels and quality of finish as the men moved close to the entrance off Princes Road. They had now stopped the traffic on the road to conclude the surface repair at the edge of the footpath.

"How's the shop, anything fallen off the shelves?"

"I hope not, it's like the place is haunted," Jack ironically shouted back.

"In five minutes I'll be in, any chance of a cup of tea?" Mango asked over the din.

"No problem, then I want to know what happened with the council recommendations." Jack shouted back.

"Deal," replied Mango.

Jack went back indoors to relative peace away from the machinery. The staff were poised on the aisles like a gathering of wicket keepers watching for any rogue produce to venture from its allotted place and quickly moving to push it back into position. Peace then descended, all went still and the wandering products rested once more on their shelves. "Damage report, Joe?" Jack enquired as he entered the store.

"One bent tin of beans but all other goods are fine," reported Joe. '*Why is it always beans?*' he thought.

In the props room, the dust from the last twenty years had been dislodged and was still raining down.

Wilf returned to report that the men had finished and were now packing up.

"Bloody good job!" exclaimed George. "It was like an earthquake down here."

Bottles had fallen from shelves and the tall mirror, once in the corner of the room had now repositioned itself under the trapdoor. Alice had been frantically trying to prevent items falling and had covered their clothes rack with a dust sheet to keep them clean. "Thank goodness!" she said.

"We need to get over to the club for the auditions. Come on you two, let's go, we can tidy this mess up later."

Outside the workmen cleaned up, the surplus spoil from the excavation was loaded on the now empty lorry, they swept the car park and placed their tools in the back of the van. Mango signed some paperwork, gave it to the foreman and they drove off. The steam from the tarmac was beginning to diminish but the strong intoxicating smell of hot bitumen hung in the air.

Joe came out to see what had happened and was surprised to be greeted by a pristine brand-new car park.

"Keep vehicles off it today so it can cool and harden, you can reopen it properly tomorrow," explained Mango as he headed for the service door and hopefully a nice strong cuppa.

Jack was pleased to see Mango arrive in his office thereby signalling the end of operations in the car park. He wasted no time interrogating the surveyor.

"Come on in, tea's made. Take a seat. Now tell me what is happening Mango, that looks like a permanent repair out there," he said hopefully.

Mango took a sip of tea and then went through the minutes of the meeting held in the museum and gave Jack a copy. Jack didn't let on that he had already seen the proposal given by Trevor Griffiths. The minutes detailed the facts that Molly had reported but did not give any further clue as to what may happen next. '*Was the store safe, would the demolition go ahead, when would the new megastore be built?*' All valid questions that he and his staff would like to know.

"This is all very well, Mango, but what happens next? This affects me and my staff and we have a right to know," Jack said, trying to contain his frustration.

"I'm sorry, Jack, I've reported to Finbarr and the ball is now firmly in his court. I guess he'll discuss the situation with his board, come up with a revised strategy and hold further dialogue with the council but I hold no influence over their decisions."

Jack was not impressed by the gobbledygook being spouted by the surveyor. "In other words, you don't know or if you do you are not at liberty to tell me," Jack said rising to his feet.

"As I said Jack…." Mango started, but Jack raised his hand to stop him.

"Oh, I heard you, Mango. I just hoped you would be able to give me some hint as to what might happen."

Mango was startled by the change of tone in Jack. It was clear to him that the fate of the shop was very personal to Jack, he admired that but at the same time made a mental note to report this to Finbarr. After all, he had been tasked with finding out what the staff thought of the new proposal for Price Low and Jack's true colours were now beginning to show. "I'm sorry, Jack, but I only report to Finbarr. It isn't two-way, he doesn't confide in me."

"I'm sorry too, it's just distressing for all of us here," Jack said apologetically, holding out his hand, which Mango shook. "You have to understand we are all worried about the future of our jobs and all this disruption only increases the anxiety for me and my staff. I'll be glad when we have a clear plan for the restructuring rather than this limbo land we seem to be in at the moment."

"I do understand," replied Mango sympathetically.

They both walked out to the car park where Joe was ensuring a refrigerated delivery van, supplying this week's dairy products from Price Low central distribution, kept off the new surface.

"Good timing, Joe," Jack said admiring the new surface. "They've done a nice job." He thanked Mango and watched him leave. Joe came over to him.

"Well, what have you found out, dad?"

"Nothing more than we already know, he's either playing his cards close to his chest or he genuinely knows nothing. We'll just have to wait for news from head office."

Joe shrugged his shoulders and went over to deal with the delivery and Jack returned to the store where Joan was waiting in his office with the same question.

17

The Audition

In the brick-lined cellar of the Collington Club the actors had rearranged the furniture for the auditions. A platform had been fashioned from some trestle tabletops balanced on an assortment of beer crates to make a crude but sufficient low stage. Under normal circumstances it would be highly unstable, but of course in the spirit world the ghostly performers had only to float above it, being careful not to drift through the boards onto the flagstone floor below. The makeshift stage was about fifteen feet wide and ten feet deep, plenty big enough for the performance they had in mind. Alongside an upright piano stood in a poor state of repair. The cover was missing, several of the yellowing ivory keys were sticking out at unnatural angles and the varnished wood had taken on a cloudy hue due to exposure to the damp in the cellar. However it was ready to provide accompaniment when required. A long table with three chairs faced the stage so that Wilf and his two fellow judges could confer as the contestants auditioned to win a place on the bill of the Golf Club Captain's Day festivities. The room was fit for purpose as a performance space.

George sat at the table in a daydream thinking of times past in London's smoke-filled basement jazz clubs where he used to play between engagements.

"George, did you hear me?" shouted Wilf.

"Sorry, Scats... just daydreaming," replied George, his mind shocked by suddenly returning to reality.

"Who's Scats?" Alice asked.

"Never mind, just an old jazz mate, I'm back now. What's happening?" George said.

Behind them a small crowd of budding performers was beginning to gather, waiting to be called to the audition. The poster that Wilf had displayed in the social club a week before had paid off and they were surprised at the number of hopefuls that had turned up.

"Blimey, this is going to take all day!" moaned George looking at the eclectic mix of ghosts, standing in expectation. It looked like a semi-transparent tableau of Holeford through the ages.

"There are some groups performing, so it's not that many individual acts," Alice reassured him. "It should only take a couple of hours."

George looked relieved. He was pleased to see the response but he knew how laborious these things can get. One act they were not surprised to see was 'The Hanging Judge'. He was always showing off his magic tricks when he came to the club and they had now given him the excuse to display them to a wider audience.

Wilf took to the stage. "Good afternoon, ladies and gentlemen. Thank you all for coming.

As you know, we're auditioning for an evening's entertainment to be held here following the Captain's Day tournament at Holeford Golf Club, hosted by this year's Captain, Charles, or as some of you will know him, Wolf Gore. There was some muttering in the crowd. Charles, was not that well-liked by some of the performers who felt intimidated by him but their egos were stronger than their dislike. They just wanted the chance to perform. "We're looking for three acts to join us for the evening entertainment but, please don't be disappointed if you are not chosen as we hope to put on other shows in the future, if this one proves successful. Now, down to business. I'll be the compere for the evening while George is the musical director. I believe Alice has taken all your details and will call you forward as your turn comes. After your audition you're welcome to stay and watch but please remain at the back of the hall and be quiet as some of our hopefuls may be a little nervous. Before we begin, I do have one safety announcement. In the case of fire please leave the room in any direction you like." Wilf then pointed randomly in every direction. His makeshift audience laughed politely and Wilf joined his fellow judges at the table.

George then stood up and addressed the group. "If you've brought your own music please pass it to me on the way to the stage or if you just require background accompaniment let me know and I'll do my best to oblige."

He then sat down again and Alice called the first act to the stage. "The Monkton Quartet please."

Four Roman soldiers marched forward. As they passed the table the leader handed a musical score to George and whispered in his ear. While they mounted the stage George took his place at the piano. The soldiers certainly looked resplendent in their uniforms. Their polished headgear and breast plates seemed to shine out like lanterns in the gloom of the room. Well maintained swords and daggers hung from their belts and the leader held a tall staff on which a golden eagle stood proudly holding a plaque with the letters SPQR emblazoned upon it. Underneath hung a makeshift sign which read 'The Monkton Quartet'. George placed the music on the piano, looked at the commander and, with a quizzical look, pointed to something printed on the paper. The statuesque soldier nodded. George shrugged his shoulders and pressed one key on the piano and returned to his judge's chair. The one solitary note rang out around the cellar and seemed to hang in the air. There was silence as everyone waited in anticipation. The four soldiers began to hum softly in unison, slowly raising the volume until their voices equalled the tone of the piano.

The commander began to sing, the other three joining in with the harmonies. Their voices melted together like cream on a warm dessert. There was a ripple of applause from the audience who were spellbound by the beauty of their syncopation. None of them had expected an acapella version of the Simon and Garfunkel's, '*Sound of Silence*'. When they finished there were roars of appreciation from the crowd, the soldiers saluted solemnly and marched proudly down off the stage showing no emotion.

"Blimey, I wasn't expecting that!" Wilf said in admiration. "Where on earth did they learn to do that?"

"Never mind that, are they in?" Alice asked her fellow adjudicators.

"Well, it's a yes from me," said George.

"And me," echoed Wilf.

Alice put a big tick against their name. "One down, two places left to fill," she said. "Are you ready for the next one?"

She looked round and signalled to the next contestant.

Lionel, 'The Hanging Judge', stepped forward from the waiting group. There was an audible sigh from everyone as they awaited the same old useless card tricks. Not at all put off by the reaction he stepped briskly up onto the stage and announced proudly, "I would like to perform some magic for you."

"I'm sorry to break this to you but your card tricks just don't work, we can see right through your cloak. You are just too transparent, dear," George said, as sensitively as he could.

"Never mind that, I have a new trick for you," Lionel replied excitedly.

He waved into the crowd and beckoned forward a forlorn looking man in scruffy clothing with a grubby cloth cap on his head carrying a fold-up card table and a box. The assistant was one of those condemned to death from the Monmouth Rebellion trials presided over by Lionel. Time had, however, been a great healer and Geever Wormspreader had forgiven the judge and become a good friend and confidant. Geever placed the table on the stage with the box behind. Due to the construction of the box it was difficult to make out what was in it other than some sort of hat.

"Thank you, Debbie," said Lionel. He had become a massive fan of the magicians currently performing on TV. The scowling Geever looked back at the judge then bowed solemnly to the audience and left the stage. There was a ripple of applause for Geever, more in sympathy than amusement. The judge flexed his fingers and reached into the box, lifted out a top hat and placed it on the table. The audience once again groaned for within the hat they could see a rabbit.

"I'm sorry Lionel, but we can clearly see the rabbit, which has rather ruined the surprise," Wilf said.

"Damn it!" said the judge as he reached in and pulled out a rather stiff inanimate animal.

"Where did you get the bunny?" asked Alice, trying not to laugh. "It looks stuffed."

"I borrowed it from the museum."

"Do they know you have it?" Alice questioned.

"Not exactly," the Judge confessed. If it was possible for ghosts to take a sharp intake of breath then the room would have been deprived of air. "But I am going to put it back!" he quickly exclaimed trying to redeem the situation.

"And you a judge. I can't believe it. Stealing from a museum!" Alice teased.

"I only borrowed it! Honestly," Lionel said passionately.

"Why bother to borrow one from the museum?" George interjected. "When you drive up to the golf club there are loads of ghost rabbits hopping around in the road where they've been accidently run over. You could have used one of those!"

The judge felt like he was now on trial, facing the jury. "I didn't think this through very well, did I? I just wanted to be in your show."

Wilf felt sorry for him. Lionel obviously just wanted to entertain people. It was probably a reaction to his days spent convicting and sentencing criminals. A psychiatrist would have a field day trying to unravel the inner workings of his troubled mind.

"Well, is there anything else you can do?" George asked sensing his disappointment.

"I can play the piano," he replied brightening.

"Go on then, let's hear you," George said, motioning to the upright by the stage.

There were mumbles in the audience as Lionel moved to the piano and sat on the stool. He placed his hands on the instrument and without the aid of any sheet music effortlessly moved his hands over the keys and played the opening opus of Rachmaninoff's Piano concerto No. 1. The room was silent, in awe of the beautiful, beguiling sound emanating from the old dilapidated instrument. When he finished the audience erupted into loud applause.

"Was that OK? I'm a bit rusty," Lionel asked hopefully. The sound of the appreciation had made his heart swell. He had redeemed himself.

"That was fantastic!" Wilf said and walked over to him. He leant on the piano and quietly asked him, "Do you know any Egyptian music?"

"No, I'm not that old!" Lionel responded, offended.

"No, sorry, I'm not explaining myself very well," replied Wilf quickly. "With you playing for us we, that is George, Alice and myself, would be able to perform our party piece to close the show."

"I can read music if you have the score," Lionel whispered, keeping his voice low as if this was a best kept secret.

"OK, you're on. We'll need to practise in secret. We want this to be a surprise for everyone on the night. It'll be more fun that way. We can make arrangements after the auditions, so hang around when they have all gone and we'll sort it out," Wilf said concluding the deal.

The judge returned to the back of the room and was greeted with further applause by the audience. Geever retrieved the magician's props and dumped them in a dark recess hoping never to see them again.

Wilf returned to the judges' table and whispered to Alice and George, "He's our man, this is going to be great show." Alice and George both had wide, satisfied grins. The missing piece of their show stopping grand finale was now in place.

"Right, who's next?" asked Wilf.

Alice looked to the back of the room and called, "Tom Harding, please."

There was movement from the back of the room and a small withered faced man in a crumpled brown suit and grey fedora hat, made his way to the makeshift stage.

"Blimey, I didn't expect him to turn up!" exclaimed George.

"Is that who I think it is?" Alice asked.

"It sure is but he's seldom seen out. He's a bit of a recluse. The last I heard of him he threw a tantrum because his library, desk, stationery and a chair had been moved from his house to the museum. He hasn't been seen for months. I don't know who he's trying to fool by using that daft pseudonym."

Tom stood on the stage facing the judges.

"Ok Tom, in your own time. What would you like to perform for us?" George asked.

"I would like to read a new poem I have been working on." Even for a ghost the little old man looked frail and unearthly. He cleared his throat, steadied himself and began;

"Greengage blossom all but gone,
Bluebell hue purple darkens to leave
Bower and bud. New green appears
To greet the summer sun.
Along the path through thick growth, fair maiden walks
Glimpse of petticoat neath black dress, bodice tight,
Milkmaid cap and apron white."

There was an audible sigh from the room. George turned and held up his hand to silence the audience. He turned and whispered to Wilf, "He's always writing about milkmaids. I think he has an unhealthy obsession with them!"

Tom continued, oblivious to the reaction in the room.

"Her leather boots depress the sod
To the parlour for an honest bob.
Twigs crack and brush aside

As the Baron's son stalks the path beside.
Dressed in tweed he doth quiver,
Concealing inside what he wants to give her.
She hears his breath and starts to quicken.

Slow down, young wench. 'tis only I
Just give me time on yonder bench.
Up ahead she rests her bones while Baronet atones.
They sit a while in contemplation
Hardly a word in their relation
He hands his gift before swift away.

From the distance Obadiah comes.
Was that his nib from the manor?
Shame he's got a little stammer.
Yes, it was she replied
Let's to the dairy swift and bold
The cows are waiting getting old.

What's that given in your hand?
'Tis a gift from the squire, never you mind.
You be careful, maid of mine
Twas only last week he gave of mine
Early sun golden and broad
Dew drop resolving on the sward."

Tom lowered the notes and looked out at the audience. "Personally, I think the end needs more work, but I can work on that." The little old man looked out forlornly at the judges as a polite ripple of applause more in relief than appreciation faded away.

"Thank you, Tom. That was beautiful. We'll let you know at the end of the auditions," Alice reassured him, slightly in awe of who she was addressing. Tom knew a polite rejection when he heard it and with bowed head floated down off the stage to anonymity at the back of the room clutching the now crumpled paper.

Over the next two hours the tireless judges saw another twelve acts which included;

A Viking knife-throwing act which, though very skilful, lacked any danger, as their targets were already dead. Also, it wasn't clear how close the knives were landing to their bodies due to their translucent demeanour.

A troupe of singing nuns from the convent cemetery sang a lamentation.

Angus Trenchard, Holeford Mayor in 1961 and 1967, told some after dinner jokes which made him laugh heartily, despite the cold reception from his audience.

A group of Irish labourers who died during the construction of the railway tunnel through the ridgeway to the coast, played their fiddles and did an infectious jig that had everyone tapping their feet.

A victim of the bloody assizes who sang a rather ironic version of '*My Way*'.

Without exception, all had put their heart and soul into their performances. It had been an exhausting but entertaining afternoon for the judges who were left with enough talent to put on several shows.

Wilf strode back on the stage and addressed the applicants. "Ladies and gentlemen, I hope you've all enjoyed this afternoon as much as we have. There's certainly some great talent in this room and we thank everyone for taking part and giving their all." He then announced the acts that they wished to use for the golf club show and took details of all the others, for future productions.

George asked Lionel to stay as they wanted to discuss the musical arrangement for their grand finale. The show was going to be a wonderful cornucopia of performers. Alice, Wilf and George were thrilled by the talent they had discovered, even though their own future in Holeford was still uncertain.

18

The New Recruit

A week had passed with still no word from head office or Finbarr himself regarding the fate of the store.

It was Friday the 8th of August. The day of the interviews for Joe's position. Jack had to admit he was leaving it a bit late as Joe was due to start his training the following Wednesday. Joan was dressed in her best suit and sat with him in the office to meet their prospective new recruits. Joe met the candidates as they reported to the customer service counter and escorted them into the staffroom. He was intrigued to see the people applying to replace him. The staffroom had to double as the waiting room, giving the other workforce a chance to take a sneaky peek at the possible new team members. Joe showed them in one by one.

First to arrive was Martin Jones who marched in wearing a neatly pressed pin stripe suit and highly polished black shoes, standing straight with shoulders back, thanks to his army training. He had little to say to Joe and sat bolt upright until called in to the office. He was followed an hour later by Stephen Small from the local cash and carry. He had an unkempt appearance, an ill-fitting suit and crooked tie. Rather in keeping with the pile it high in boxes, mass purchasing of the warehouse where he currently worked. He was chattier than the previous incumbent but Joe couldn't help thinking he was a bit downmarket. His language was colourful and manner too familiar for Joe's liking, he also smelt of cabbage.

At 3 pm it was the turn of Charlie. Not unexpectedly, he was treated with some suspicion as soon as he entered the store. The staff knew he was due and as he entered the shop he couldn't help noticing the increased chatter and finger pointing as Joe escorted him to the staffroom. Charlie was wearing his best suit and had a new haircut. This was a big chance for him and he was pulling out all the stops. Joe greeted him and treated him the same as the others while trying to work out why on earth his dad would even consider employing a criminal, even if he did look the most reasonable candidate so far. As they entered the staffroom Stephen Small lumbered out of the office. Joe held the door open and thanked him for coming whilst hoping never to see him again. Charlie was emboldened by the sight, realising at least one of the competition didn't appear to be up to much in Joe's opinion.

Jack came out of the office and spied Charlie. "Ah good, you're here. Charlie isn't it? Come on in." He followed him in and closed the door.

"Please, sit down," Joan said casting a speculative eye over Charlie. She had in her mind an image of burglars that she had seen on the TV and didn't expect to see a smart young man in a suit. It threw her a bit. She awkwardly shuffled some papers on the table while Jack came round and sat beside her.

"Charles Clarke. Are you related to Dave Clarke the singer?" Jack asked, trying to break the ice.

Joan winced.

"No, I don't think so," Charlie said uneasily.

He was feeling nervous now. He remembered the room from that fateful evening. He could see the new shiny safe in the corner.

Jack spotted Charlie's eye attracted to the safe. Charlie was beginning to doubt that he had any chance and he felt his optimism draining away.

"It's new. The other one was old and rather too easy to open," Jack said, giving him a knowing look.

Joan looked at him sternly. There was no need for that comment. She could see that the lad was nervous and that was quite understandable. She began to feel sympathy for him and wanted him to at least say his piece.

"I'm sorry. This is all wrong. I shouldn't have applied. I don't know what I was thinking of." Charlie started to stand.

"Sit down, young man," a voice commanded from behind him. Startled, Charlie swung round and saw George in his police costume standing by the corner.

"It's you!" Charlie exclaimed, suddenly glued to the spot. He instinctively looked up to check there was nothing over his head waiting to drop.

"Yes, Charlie, it's me, now sit back down, there's a good lad. We have an interview to do."

Jack and Joan were bemused by Charlie's behaviour and watched silently.

"What's going on?" Charlie asked. "If you've got him, why do you need a security guard?" he said, pointing at George.

"I don't know what you mean," Jack said.

Joan just sat impassively watching Charlie's unusual action.

"Him… there," Charlie said, pointing at the corner of the room.

"My name is George."

"OK, George, whatever. He's the one that hit me and made me phone the police."

"For the record it was Wilf who dropped the beans on your head, not I."

"You or Wilf, it still hurt!"

Jack was amused by Charlie's one-sided conversation and a little jealous that he could see and hear the ghost that had obviously joined them in the room. Joan remained quiet as if watching a play. "Say something, Joan. This is the quietest you've been all afternoon."

"So, you're a trained electrician," she asked, ignoring Charlie's previous one-sided conversation.

Jack looked at her, did she not see what had just happened?

Charlie smiled, he felt more at ease talking about his trade. "Yes, fully trained. I've brought my indentures if you wish to see them."

"That's not necessary at this stage but enterprising of you to bring them. What makes you want to apply for night shift work stacking shelves?" Joan enquired.

It was Jack's turn to be quiet, he was pleased by Joan's ease at taking control of the interview and was happy to take a back seat.

"Well, since the unfortunate episode with my brother I haven't been able to find any electrical work. Anyway, I want to put the past behind me and make a new start. They let me off, you know. I didn't get charged in the end. I'm ever so sorry for the problems it's caused you… My brother Brian is in court this afternoon…It's been terrible," he rambled on. "Anyway, I know I've no experience working in a shop but I am willing to learn. I'm a good worker and I'm trained in self-defence for the security bit."

"Unless you're attacked by tins of beans," added George, chuckling.

Charlie forgot himself and swung round to look at him. "That's not fair! You dropped them on my head. I didn't have a chance!"

"It wasn't me, it was Wilf! How many times do I have to tell you?" George protested. He drew a circle in the air with his finger indicating for Charlie to turn around and carry on answering the question.

"Yes… sorry… anyway," Charlie regained his composure. "Not only can I help with the stacking and security but if you have any wiring problems or electrical faults, I could sort that out too."

Joan made a note on a form in front of her.

"Can you see George?" Jack said. Joan was shocked at this strange, unexpected question but continued looking at Charlie.

"Of course I can, he's here behind me. Where are the others?"

"Others, what others?" Jack replied.

"Well, the pirate and young girl. They can't be far away."

"Are you telling me you've seen all three of them?"

"Yes, of course I have. They shut us in the store and kept throwing stuff at us. I didn't imagine it, you know. Look, I'm going to go, I'm sorry if you think I am making this up. I'll try to get a job somewhere else."

Charlie again started to rise from his chair.

"When can you start?" Jack said loudly, stopping Charlie in his tracks and startling Joan with his sudden decision.

"What?" Charlie couldn't believe his ears.

"When can you start?"

"Are you offering me the job?" Charlie dropped back down into the chair. "I didn't expect to know so quickly."

Joan rested back in her chair effectively handing control back to Jack, this was going to be good.

"Do you want to work for us, Charlie? You'll have to be prepared for a frosty reception from the staff, but I think you could win them over. I have a good feeling about you and I trust my instinct, now what do you say? How about next Monday? I'll get the contract drawn up for you to sign, if you still want to join us."

"Yes, please… I don't know what to say."

"Good, that's settled then. We need to go through the formalities and some form filling. Can you come in again tomorrow with these completed and bring the documents listed on Form A along with your indentures?" Jack handed him several official looking forms.

"Yes. Thank you. Thank you so much, I won't let you down."

"I know you won't, Charlie, after all you'll be working with our residents on night duty. They'll keep an eye on you."

"Good point." Charlie turned around to George. "Thanks, I'm sure you helped me with this but I can't understand why?"

"My pleasure, young fellow. It'll be nice to have someone new to talk to in the evenings." He saluted and descended through the floor to tell the others.

"Until tomorrow then." Jack and Joan stood up, shook his hand and showed him out into the store.

Joan grabbed Jack's arm and pulled him back into the office. "Jack, I hope you know what you're doing. The staff will take a lot of convincing," she said doubtfully.

"He'll be perfect. They'll soon come round. He seems a nice lad who needs some direction. We also have the advantage that he can see and communicate with our ghosts. That's a win, win in my book, anyway, he was on your short list too."

"Yes but…" Joan tried to interrupt.

Jack held his finger to his mouth. "You haven't been totally straight with me, Joan. You knew George was in the room, didn't you? Don't try to deny it, I could see your reactions. You didn't flinch. You knew there was a ghost in the corner of the room and you didn't blink. I bet you can see the others as well."

"I can't see them, not like Carolyn, but I sometimes feel a presence. Honestly, Jack, would you seriously have believed me if I'd told you? It's not something you shout about. Everyone would think I was round the bend!"

Jack sat down. "You're right. I wouldn't have believed you, but with recent events you could have told me. It's crazy isn't it? You go along quietly minding your own business then without warning the world throws up all sorts of strange things," Jack said.

Joan looked at him squarely in the face. "If it wasn't for Carolyn's antics and your blind faith in her, you'd still be in the dark. I've felt something was strange about this place since the beginning, but it's taken a long time to realise what it is. They do no harm. In fact, recently they did a lot of good, stopping the burglary."

"But I still can't believe you didn't tell me," Jack said, slightly upset… "I assume Molly knows about your sixth sense?"

"I've never told her. I'm not sure what I could tell her, it's just a feeling I get. It wasn't till your recent adventures with Carolyn that I started to understand about their presence, if that's what you call it."

"I think maybe you should confide in Molly. She's known for quite a while. She's been working to try and help them. You won't shock her, I can assure you."

"Molly's been helping them? My God." Then the penny dropped. "It's not just Carolyn, Molly is in on this as well. That explains her behaviour, I thought it was just ambition spurred on by Carolyn to work in the museum but it's all part of some grand plan mixed up with these ghosts. I wish I'd confided in you earlier. When I joined the staff your wife had just left you and you drank too much. You were not the most approachable man. So when I first felt their presence it seemed better to keep it to myself. As time went by it became second nature to maintain the secret. I didn't want to spoil anything or lose my job. I enjoy working here. But now things are different. Since Carolyn came on the scene and introduced you to her paranormal friends our relationship has changed. Look what else has happened. You've fallen in love, you now believe in ghosts, Joe's a trainee manager, and Molly seems to be on course for university. And to top it all you have just employed a burglar as a security guard, not even knowing if the store will even be here next year. It's been quite a summer!"

They both started to laugh out loud. Joe came in to see what was going on.

"Is that it, Dad? Just the three? Why are you laughing? Were they that bad?"

"You're not going to believe this, Joe," Joan said.

"I've just offered the job to our burglar!" Jack said trying to stifle his laughter.

"Are you mad?" Joe exclaimed.

"Far from it. He's perfect in so many ways. He starts on Monday but I'll introduce you properly tomorrow when he brings back the employment forms. Wait till you meet him, you'll like him."

"Well, I hope you know what you're doing. The staff are going to have a fit when you explain who he is! I'm off to my training course from Wednesday of next week so it's going to be a baptism of fire for him." Joe looked worried.

"You're just going to have to trust me on this one. But keep it to yourself until Monday when we have a staff meeting... Can you notify them please, Joan, let's have it at eleven o'clock. Usual routine. I'll call the other two applicants and let them know we'll not require their services. Now how about a nice cup of tea?"

Joan returned with the tea and the three of them talked through the best way to introduce Charlie to the staff. "Have you heard anything yet about the new store? It's not fair keeping us in the dark like this," Joan asked.

"As far as I know head office are waiting for contact from the planning office which could take ages knowing how speedy local government is, but I wish they'd get a move on. It's horrible keeping us in suspense."

Charlie returned home to break the exciting news to his mum that he was back in legitimate work. He went round to the back of the house and entered the kitchen via the back door. He was surprised to find Brian making a coffee. "They didn't bang you up then!" Charlie was overjoyed to see him back from the court but was loathed to show his true feelings.

"Not that you care!" Brian scowled.

"What happened then, tell me all the gory details." Charlie reached for a mug to make his own coffee.

"It didn't take long. I was summoned into the court by the female wrestler who saw us at the station. After one of the wigs read out the charges, Sergeant Montgomery went through the evidence and read out the statements. After that I had to stand in the dock. The Legal Aid lawyer told me to plead guilty, and say nothing else. So I did and then the magistrate adjourned the hearing for lunch. Two hours! Two bloody hours I waited for them to eat their sandwiches. It felt like a lifetime. Anyway, we were eventually called back in and I was ready for the worst. The magistrate gave me a good dressing down, something about disgrace, disrespect, letting my family down, unacceptable criminal behaviour, etc. I can't remember the full details but it was pretty grim. Then he said he wouldn't refer me to the Crown Court as it was my first offence. However, I would receive a six-month suspended sentence and £500 fine. He then went into detail about what would happen if I offend again. There's no messing about. I'd be thrown into prison, pronto. Here's the book telling me what could happen." Brian slid a thin information booklet across the table to Charlie. "I tell you what, I'm not going through that again. I've never been so frightened in all my life."

Charlie picked up the book and flicked through it, scanning the contents. It all looked very official and incredibly complicated. "I got the job at the supermarket," he casually added, wary of what reaction he would get. He felt guilty that because of his interview he hadn't gone to support Brian.

"You're joking! You're telling me the best candidate they had was someone who tried to steal from them? The others must have been really bad or the manager must be stupid!"

"George, you know… the ghost policeman… he was at the interview. I think he swung it for me," Charlie said, taking a sip from his hot mug.

Brian looked at him in total bewilderment. "I'm really pleased for you." Then he said calmly but seriously, "Look, I don't know what drugs you're taking but you have to stop now, you really must."

"Don't be daft! I'm not taking drugs. It's true. I have to go in tomorrow with my birth certificate, national insurance number and these forms filled out." He slid the employment forms across the table. "Exhibit one, I start on Monday."

Brian looked at the forms and then back at Charlie. "Well don't nick anything. It's not worth it."

"That's great advice, coming from you!"

On Saturday morning Charlie returned to the store with all the forms filled out, his national insurance number, tax details and other items listed on them.

Joe saw him enter and went over to greet him. He rather tentatively shook his hand. "Hello, you must be Charlie, I'm Joe. We'll be working together from Monday. It's going to be busy though. I'm off to London from Wednesday, but I'm sure we will be able to cover the basics and Joan will be on hand afterwards, while you find your feet." Joe was trying to weigh up the new recruit. He had never met a burglar before, he seemed ordinary. He had a natural warm smile and dressed smartly. Not at all what he was expecting, perhaps his dad was right after all.

Around the store other staff had seen Joe approach the man who looked a lot like the burglar they had seen in the paper. They were trying to assess the situation as he was escorted to the office. The girl on number one till rang the bell for a supervisor, knowing full well that Joan was on duty.

Joan walked across to the till holding the inventory of magazines she was checking. "Is there a problem, Charmaine?"

Charmaine beckoned Joan towards her and whispered, "Isn't that the burglar, what's he doing here?"

"Don't be so nosey and don't start spreading gossip, all will be explained on Monday at the staff meeting."

Charmaine was a conscientious worker but of all the team she was the one with her nose in everyone's business. She had her uses when Joan needed to know the background to any personal problems with staff but those facts tended to be embellished by her furtive imagination.

"So, I'm right aren't I?" she quickly deduced from the reply.

"Leave it till the staff meeting on Monday, all will be explained. I would appreciate it if, until then, you keep your thoughts to yourself." Joan then returned to the magazine rack, to leave Charmaine speculating.

Outside the store there was a flurry of activity as pedestrians scattered away from the shop front. There was a mechanical thump as onto the pavement, just in front of the window, a large black Jaguar screeched to a halt. The driver's door opened and Finbarr Lowe stepped out, slammed it shut and marched into the shop. He was not in a good mood. Red faced he stared straight ahead his eyes like lasers, fists clenched as if ready for a fight. Staff and customers in his path, parted to allow him clear passage as he headed directly to the office. He walked straight into the meeting with Jack and Charlie.

"Bonfield you're not going to believe this." He then saw Charlie sat opposite Jack.

"Who the bloody hell are you?" he said, directly to Charlie.

There was a time Charlie would have been have been frightened by such a sudden approach and blunt language from a complete stranger but, if nothing else, his recent experiences had made him more resilient. This imposing figure lacking in any social graces bore down on him with little effect. From his demeanour Charlie had assumed he was some sort of senior manager or mafia heavy.

"I'm Charlie Clarke," he stood up and held out his right hand.

This astonished Finbarr, who was used to people shrinking away in fear or awe at his presence. He automatically lifted his hand and shook the young man's without thinking. Charlie winced at the vice-like grip. "I'm the new night shift shelf stacker and security guard," he added still gripped by Finbarr's hand. "I start on Monday."

Finbarr was completely thrown off his train of thought. "Finbarr Lowe, Managing Director," he replied "About time we had someone like you here, we need good security and you look like the man for the job. This place was burgled only a few weeks ago, if I could get my hands on them I would give them what for!"

"Don't worry sir, your store will be safe with me," Charlie said pokerfaced.

"See you Monday morning, Charlie. Come in at ten-thirty and we'll introduce you during the staff meeting at eleven," Jack said trying to hide a grin.

Finbarr watched him leave. "Seems a good lad. His face seems strangely familiar, should I know him?"

"You must be mistaking him for someone else, would you like a coffee?" Jack said quickly, trying to distract Finbarr and get him on to the reason for this sudden visit.

Finbarr's fury began to subside. "Right, where was I Bonfield? Yes, a drink… good start. Never mind the coffee, got any whisky in the filing cabinet? I need a strong one and so will you when you hear what has happened."

Jack could see his hackles beginning to rise again. He reached into the filing cabinet, pulled out a bottle of Bells and two glasses. This was all too familiar territory for Jack, who in the past had been rather too partial to a large medicinal scotch himself. No longer though, that was all behind him, he had been given a second chance and he was not going to blow it this time.

Finbarr gulped down a generous shot of the golden liquor and held out the glass for a top-up. "Ah that's better… I've just come from the planning office where those trumped up civil servants have tried to scupper all my plans. The planning officer has told me if I want to develop this site for housing they want ridiculous amounts of money in the form of contributions toward a full archaeological survey, a new visitor centre and commuted sums to maintain them for the next twenty-five years. It's legalised robbery." He was beginning to raise his voice, took another swig and continued. "On top of that, the new out of town store can't have electrical goods, clothing or a pharmacy. Out of the goodness of their hearts they will concede to consumables and a café. Who the hell do they think they are?" He thumped the now empty glass down on the desk, indicating another top up. "Well, let me tell you I'm not giving in that easily, but I am certainly not giving them vast amounts of my hard-earned money to line their council coffers."

Jack poured a less generous tot in Finbarr's glass and took a small sip from his. Not one for half measures, Finbarr grabbed the bottle and poured an additional slug into his glass and leant back in the chair.

"I've got a new idea but I need your help," Finbarr was now beginning to mellow as the whisky relaxed his system. He leaned towards Jack as if to share a confidence. "What about this, we retain this store and take it upmarket and build the new out of town unit selling the Price Low regular affordable brands. I'm thinking out loud here, Jack. This could be a local convenience store selling local produce from local companies. A more traditional approach so it won't take trade from the new store but will pander to those with more disposable incomes who like to support the home-grown economy, not some national company who don't give a stuff. It can still provide convenience for shoppers but at slightly higher prices. How does that sound?"

Jack was taken aback by the change of approach suggested and also at being addressed by his Christian name. He took a large gulp from his own glass. "That's brilliant, Finbarr. We can keep this store in the High street and attract new custom with quality produce, it's a win-win situation."

"Good, glad you like it because I want you to head it up. Get together a portfolio of local companies where you can source produce, at good rates mind. You can use the resources at head office. Call my secretary Olivia tomorrow afternoon after I've briefed her and she'll sort someone in the office to help you."

Jack's mind was already a whirl with names of potential suppliers. Arlington Dairies, Ring's Bakery, Vine's soaps. Several of the local farms also came to mind including the Upper Parrot orchards and Singleton's soft fruit. But best of all the store remains and the actors' home is saved. He wanted to call Carolyn and Molly to break the news but Finbarr hadn't finished. "Right, let's have a think about this... How about Price Local, it can keep the same font but a more upmarket colour & style so it links with Price Low but with a bit more class. Get on to it, Jack. Now here's the catch, I want the report next Wednesday morning. We'll look at it together then you'll present it to the board in the afternoon. Are you up for it?"

"Am I sir? You just try and stop me." Jack felt like standing to salute his general. This was all his Christmases come at once. He felt alive again, driven to achieve a new goal, this time one he believed in with all his heart.

"You've only got four days, get your staff involved as well, they may have some ideas."

Again this was music to Jack's ears, he was wondering what he could tell the staff, now he had permission to share this with his team. Whatever next.

"Hear you like the theatre," Finbarr said, abruptly changing the subject.

Jack was taken aback by the statement. "Yes, I came up to town a couple of weeks ago with Carolyn to see *Henry V*... it was amazing."

"My wife loathes it, but it's one of my passions. That's why Price Low sponsor the arts. Look, if you are coming to London on Wednesday why

211

not stay over and come with us to the first night of Hedda Gabler. A couple of the board members are coming, it'll be good for you to meet them and why not bring your young lady with you. I have a box so there's plenty of room and the theatre will look after us like royalty."

Jack had no choice, not that it needed a seconds thought. He had the theatre bug already even if Carolyn couldn't come. What an opportunity to socialise with the board of directors, as well.

"Well, yes, Finbarr that would be fantastic. I'll check to see if Carolyn is free."

"Good, till Wednesday then." Finbarr rose from his chair, shook Jack's hand and spun around, pulled the door open and was gone. Jack followed on his heels to see him off the premises and flinched as he jumped in his car and pulled away. He beeped his horn at the pedestrians who were rude enough to walk in his path and disappeared round the corner at the end of the street.

Jack, still stunned by events turned back into the store. Joan was watching the action whilst pretending to reorganise the magazines by the doors. "Joan, can I see you in the office please." Jack practically ran back to the office, Joan had a job to keep up. They entered and he closed the door.

"Have you been drinking, Jack," she asked accusingly. The bottle was still open on the desk.

"Yes, a little tipple with Finbarr, but never mind that. Sit down, you are not going to believe this." Jack regaled her of the conversation he had just had.

"That's brilliant news. Carolyn and Molly will be so relieved."

"They're next on my list to tell."

"And what about the ghosts, are you able to communicate with them?"

"Sort of," Jack thumped the floor three times with the heel of his shoe.

Unusually all three ghosts rose up through the floor. "Good afternoon," they said in unison.

Jack and Joan felt the room temperature drop. "I think they're here. Can you feel anything?"

"No, not exactly, Jack, but it's suddenly very cold. The atmosphere is strange. It feels like there is a presence but I can't see anything out of the ordinary." She could however see her breath in the air, just like on a frosty morning.

"Then they must be here." Jack explained the news to the empty room assuming they were listening.

The news began to sink in and the trio were beside themselves with joy, Charles had been right. They couldn't believe their luck. Alice was jumping up and down with excitement which initiated the start of an impromptu dance from them all around the office. They were joined by a vase of flowers and several reams of paper that levitated and jigged around the room with them. Jack lifted his glass and toasted them all, while Joan looked on in amazement at the spectacle taking place around her. She sat down and poured herself a glass of scotch and took a hefty swig which made her cough.

"Yuk! I don't know how you drink this stuff," she spluttered. "Does this happen a lot in your office?"

"No, this is the first time. I guess they're pleased. Now I need to call Carolyn," Jack said excitedly.

"And I need to get back to the store." Joan gathered herself together and got up to leave the room.

"Don't tell the staff yet. I need to think about the changes and present it to them formally at our meeting on Monday," Jack cautioned.

"I'm not sure which bits I could explain, Jack. Your secrets are safe with me and good luck with writing your speech," Joan left the room.

Jack grabbed the phone and rang Carolyn, hoping she would be home. It was answered by her mother. "Hello, Holford 24019," she said in her best telephone voice.

"Hello. It's Jack here. Is Carolyn at home?"

"No, you've just missed her, she's taken Patch for a walk. Do you want me to pass on a message?"

Jack couldn't imagine how to relay this particular message through a third party. He could tell that Monica was wary about him ringing so often and his burgeoning relationship with Carolyn. He didn't want his sanity to come into question if he tried to explain. That would not do his case any good. "No, that's OK. Can you just ask her to call me at the office when she gets back? Tell her it's urgent."

"Very well," she said wondering what on earth could be so important. "I'm sure she won't be long. Goodbye Jack."

It seemed like hours till Carolyn called. Jack resisted the urge to have another sip of whisky and put the bottle back in the filing cabinet out of temptation's way. Ten minutes later the phone rang.

Jack quickly lifted the receiver. "Carolyn, is that you?"

"Jack! What on earth's the matter? Mum said it was something urgent. Are you all right?"

"More than alright. Finbarr has just visited. The planning office demanded too much from him to redevelop the store so he's changed tack completely. He wants me to head up a new, upmarket shop at this store. It's like he is sticking two fingers up at the council. The store is safe, Carolyn, everything is going to be alright!" The line went quiet. "Carolyn… Carolyn, can you hear me? It's alright. They're all safe."

Carolyn was in shock. She held the phone to her ear but her emotions were in overload. She didn't know whether to laugh or cry. Eventually she managed to talk.

"That's wonderful news. Do George, Wilf and Alice know?"

"Yes, yes… I summoned them by banging on the floor with my foot… you should have seen Joan's face when the room went icy cold."

"What? Joan was there as well? Did she see them?"

"No, but she couldn't miss the papers and vase of flowers jigging around the room." Carolyn was trying to imagine the chaotic scene. "Stay there, I'm coming down. I'll let Molly know. She will be relieved."

"There's more, Carolyn."

"Tell me when I get there, my love, I need to see Molly. I won't be long, I'm leaving now."

Again the phone went dead before he could respond. Jack was now lost for words. Had she really said, 'my love'? He replayed the tail end of the conversation in his head.

Yes it certainly sounded like it. Emotions welled up inside him. He had feelings for Carolyn the first time they had met but hadn't dared dream she could ever feel the same, could it be true?

He rose from his chair and walked out into the store. Everything was normal. Customers were walking the aisles selecting items and placing them in their baskets, there was the gentle hum of chatter and the satisfying ring of the tills.

The taped music was playing 'The Girl from Ipanema' for the thousandth time. Staff busied themselves, ensuring the efficiency of the sales floor, attending to the shoppers, aiding their shopping experience. Apart from Joan, no one around him was aware of what revelations had just taken place, how all their futures had been altered by a whim of the shop's owner. Everything felt good and he felt good, life felt good. He stood for a moment trying to imagine a revitalised store selling local produce rather than the pile high, sell cheap view he was looking at. Of course, they would need balance. After all, they still had to cater for all pockets, and sell a respectable selection of essential items. He mustn't alienate his regular clientele but perhaps he could open their eyes to alternative, quality products. Turning over ideas in his head, he returned to the staffroom and headed for the storeroom to share his thoughts with Joan while he waited for Carolyn to arrive.

He could hear Joan's voice as he stood by the closed door.

"Careful. When you've done that I need three boxes of toilet rolls from the top shelf."

Curious, he thought. He opened the door to find Joan in the middle of the room stood by the trolley used to carry stock to the shelves. Nothing unusual in that. He then caught a movement from the corner of his eye. He looked upwards and witnessed a box of cheese and onion crisps float down and land in the trolley.

Joan looked across at Jack and grinned. "I've recruited some new helpers," she said indicating the stock floating around and heading for the trolley.

"How long have you been using the ghosts to do your lifting?"

"I've just discovered it after the display in your office. I wish I'd known about their talents before. It's saving so much time. I could even give them the stock requisition sheets and let them do it whilst I get on with something else. Mind you, I think they need more practice."

On hearing this Wilf was momentarily distracted from his task. A multi pack of self-raising flour slipped silently from the shelf above Jack and struck him on the head. Jack stood perfectly still. Joan dropped her clipboard.

Alice screamed at Wilf. "What've you done?"

Wilf stood as if bolted to the ground, not sure what to do. He came over paler than usual as the shock of the blow sank in. Jack didn't say anything. He stared straight ahead with a stupid grin and fell in a heap on the floor, knocking over a stack of crisp boxes which conveniently broke his fall and then, unfortunately, burst open, sending small packets of Hoola-Hoops and Quavers in all directions.

Joan ran over to him as the bags popped and crunched under her feet and knelt down beside him. "Jack… Jack speak to me." She gently touched his head looking for a response. He was as white as a sheet, coated in the flour that had burst on impact.

"Say something, Jack!" He didn't move. She shook his shoulders. "Please open your eyes!" A cloud of flour dust rose in the air from around his mouth as he suddenly exhaled. "Oh thank God! You're alive!" Joan said.

The door opened and Carolyn entered, closely followed by Molly. They were greeted by a tableau resembling the Death of Nelson with Joan taking the part of Hardy. The storeroom was hazy with flour dust and the floor was festooned with crisps. Carolyn crunched and popped her way to Jack's side. Joan instinctively stood back and Molly watched as Carolyn knelt by Jack and gently caressed his head.

"It was an accident." Joan said beginning to shake, as the shock of the incident began to take hold.

Molly saw Alice pointing at Wilf who stood in the corner unsure how to react. "What have you done, Wilf?"

"He's moving," Carolyn exclaimed.

Jacks eyes momentarily flickered opened. "Carolyn… where am I?" he whispered weakly, as another plume of flour dust expelled from his mouth.

Wilf moved closer, relieved that his victim was alive. "I'm terribly sorry, old chap. I had a lapse of concentration. I feel awful."

Jack's eyes opened wider and he looked directly at Wilf. "What's a pirate doing here, Carolyn?" he asked confusedly.

"That's Wilf, Jack. My God!" she exclaimed. "Can you see him?"

Jack looked around the room, his eyes now half open. "Is that Alice?" he asked. "Hello", he said lifting a shaking hand as if to wave a greeting to her. His eyes closed again and he lost consciousness.

"Blimey, he could see us," exclaimed Alice excitedly.

"Never mind that now, what are we going to do?" Molly said.

Carolyn took control of the situation. "Joan, get me a bowl of cold water, towels and any blankets you can find. Molly, stand guard outside, we don't want to alarm the staff."

As she knelt by his side she gently rubbed his temples. "Oh, Jack. What have they done to you? It's such an exciting day and here you are in a heap on the floor."

Jack came round again. "I can see them. They're here now."

"He didn't mean to do it," added Alice pleading Wilf's innocence. "He was distracted."

"I understand, Alice, don't worry. You're all safe now, that is the most important thing but you need to give Wilf more training," Jack said looking directly at them for the first time. He began to regain full consciousness in the arms of Carolyn and as he did so the images of Wilf and Alice began to fade until he could no longer see them. Tears began to run down his cheeks, creating lines in the flour. "Carolyn! I saw them but they're fading."

Joan returned with the water and Carolyn bathed his face. His complexion was still pale despite the removal of the flour deposits.

As his condition improved Joan and Carolyn helped him up and took him to the office. He slumped in his chair and sipped on a cup of strong tea to assist his revival. The staff in the store had noticed the commotion and Joan had assured them there was nothing to be worried about. Jack had just slipped in the storeroom and knocked himself out. Carolyn continued to bathe his head with a cold compress.

"Ooh! That hurts."

"You've received a nasty blow. When you finish your tea, I'm taking you home where I can look after you properly. You might have concussion. Maybe we should go to Casualty to be sure. We can't be too careful."

"Thank you. I'm glad you're here. I saw them though… I definitely did… what about that?" Who's Hedda Gabler?"

"Are you fantasising again? That's a bit obscure even for you."

"No, it's something Finbarr said. I've got to go to head office next Wednesday to present a report on new ideas for the store and he asked if we would like to see *Hedda Gabler* with him and some of the directors in the evening. It's the first night and he's got a box and everything."

"Now I know you are hallucinating. You must have seen it advertised at the theatre. It's the new production by the RSC. Glenda Jackson's in it… and Patrick Stewart. It's been sold out for weeks, there was a feature on it in the Sunday paper."

"No, he was serious, and he suggested you come too and we stay over in a hotel."

Carolyn looked deep into his eyes, softly held his head and kissed him gently on the clearly visible bruise which had appeared on his forehead. "I think we should get you home where I can look after you properly. Where are your car keys? I'll drive, you're in no fit state."

19

New Beginnings

At 11 am on Monday morning Joan closed the doors to the street, locked them and displayed the 'Back at 11.30' sign. All the staff on the first shift gathered at the back of the store with most of the off-duty personnel who had come in to hear the news first hand. No one wanted to miss the latest announcement on the future of their jobs and the fate of the shop. She then re-joined Jack in the wines and spirits area where he was poised by his makeshift podium. By his side stood Charlie Clarke dressed in his new, fresh, out of the packet, sharply creased, Price Low overalls. His presence in the store was confusing some of the gathering, and causing some animated debate. Jack kept him close and constantly reassured him. Charlie was, to say the least, nervous. He felt like a fraud, out of place amongst the victims of his bungled crime. *Perhaps he should just run away now before it was too late,* he thought, but then looked across at George, Wilf and Alice who were stood by the cold cabinet to disguise their cool aura. Wilf stuck his thumbs up at Charlie to give him encouragement. That simple act galvanised his resolve and he straightened his back, standing tall and proud in his new uniform. Who knows, if it wasn't for Wilf he could have been wearing a prison uniform and staring at four walls by now. Even so he stood very close to Jack and tried to avoid eye contact with anyone.

Joan gave Jack a nod of reassurance and he stepped onto the rostrum. The crowd immediately fell silent. The atmosphere was a mixture of impending doom and confusion at the new man in overalls stood at the end of the room. Why a new recruit if the shop was going to close? He looks like one of the burglars? Why did Finbarr visit on Saturday? Why did the cold cabinet feel colder than usual? All these questions and more were to be answered any second now. Well, except the last one about the cold cabinet. Jack made sure his makeshift stage was stable by cautiously shifting his weight around. The thick wire basket creaked and grumbled under him but held firm.

"Good morning everyone. Firstly I'd like to thank all of the staff not working today for taking the trouble to attend our little gathering. After the meeting I'll immediately contact those unable to be here but I'm pleased to say, I only have two calls to make! No doubt your keen interest is due to concern over the future of our store. Before I go into detail, I'll just say, don't worry, I only have good news."

The tension in the store relaxed a little and there was a tangible change to the atmosphere. Jack held up his hand to again quieten the group who had started to whisper to each other and shuffle around.

"The past few weeks have been stressful for all of us and I thank you for your patience and support during the upheaval and uncertainty about our futures. As you know my son, Joe, is leaving us this week to take his place on the Price Low management training scheme. On behalf of us all I wish him all the best. He's been a real asset to the store and made his father very proud." Jack beckoned him forward while Joan picked up a heavy parcel from the floor and handed it to him along with a card signed by all the staff. She kissed him on the cheek. Joe went bright red, and thanked them all. "The parcel contains Joe's reference books to help him in the first year of his training and were paid for by your generous collection."

The staff spontaneously burst into applause, bolstered by cheers and whistles. Joe returned through the crowd to his spot and placed the package on the chest freezer. The room again became silent and all heads turned once more to Jack.

From the staffroom the now familiar frame of Carolyn appeared. She handed Jack a piece of paper and positioned herself at the back of the gathering with the three ghosts, to listen to the proceedings.

"I now wish to introduce you to our new recruit. Following the recent break-in and in line with new Price Low procedure, we are to have a security guard and nightshift shelf-stacker. This replaces the role that Joe has been doing. Some of you may recognise Charlie from the newspaper. I can confirm that he is highly qualified on the subject of the recent burglary as it was Charlie, together with his brother, who attempted to rob us."

Some of the staff stared daggers at Charlie while others were just confused at the logic of employing someone who had recently attempted to rob them.

Tom, the instore butcher and part-time wrestler, was not backward in making his feelings felt, and egged on by some of the more militant staff members, he raised his hand. "What are you playing at, Jack? We don't want thieves working for us, why not just leave the doors open at night and let them help themselves?"

"I know you think I have taken leave of my senses, Tom, but I must remind you that this appointment was made before I received the blow on the head!"

This raised a few confused but polite titters. "Charlie's brother Brian has been charged with theft and is paying the price. I can also confirm that it was Charlie who phoned the police on that fateful evening thus preventing the removal of anything from the premises. Due to this act he was cleared of all charges. I believe by giving him this opportunity he'll reward us with many years of service. All I ask of you is to trust my judgement and suspend yours until you get to know him. Therefore I ask you to extend a hand of friendship to our new team member. Charlie will be working on the shop floor with Joe until Wednesday and you'll all have a chance to meet him before he commences the evening shift."

Charlie still looked uncertain but now stood taller. Yes, it was his action that had stopped them both committing the crime. Thanks to Wilf who had caused the mayhem and forced him to the phone. He did a shielded thumbs up to the three actors who waved back.

Jack's audience quietened down and he hoped they had settled into an initial acceptance of the new intern, albeit a reluctant one in some quarters. Most were reserving their judgement for now. He continued. "As you know Finbarr has plans for this town, one of which is the proposal to build a new out of town store. This plan is still going ahead but the overall concept has changed. Originally this store was to be closed and we were all going to move to the new site but because of the amazing archaeology found during the survey, this plan has now changed... let me explain. The archaeology unearthed by the surveyors during their investigations was unprecedented and caused a few issues between the planning authority and Finbarr. As you know he doesn't like being pushed around by authority and so has changed tack. The result of this is that our store is not only to remain open but is to be rebranded as 'Price Local'. We are to be the first in a new concept of local stores with the emphasis on local. I have been tasked with engaging suppliers in the area to supply our shop and promote produce from our surrounding area thus reducing our reliance on the central depot. This is very exciting for us all but I need your help. If you know any companies or individuals who you believe could join in this new enterprise please let me know as soon as possible. I have very little time to prepare and have to present my proposals to the board on Wednesday, so I'm going to be very busy. Your help will be much appreciated."

Staff turned towards each other and started to discuss who they thought could possibly supply the shop. There was an atmosphere both of relief and excitement at the new prospect. Most of them had friends and family working on farms, in bakeries and dairies who would also benefit from a new local outlet for their produce. The meeting was getting a little out of hand as the volume rose.

Jack clapped his hands to regain their attention. "I'm pleased to note your enthusiasm but we need to reopen the store so please go and have a think then come to Joan or myself at any time with your suggestions. I have one last thing to add before we finish. During the research for the site Joan's daughter Molly started volunteering at the museum and under the guidance of Professor Halford she's discovered information on the theatre that once stood here. Amongst that material she found an old programme of the last production. It lists the cast which included the three actors who sadly died in the fire. They were Wilf Trunion, George Shakespeare and Alice Bennett."

These three were bewildered at their name call and unsure what was coming next.

"What's going on?" Alice asked

"Just listen," Carolyn whispered reassuringly.

Jack continued. "There's been rumour and speculation over the years that the spirits of these souls remain trapped within these walls and are directly responsible for a series of unexplained occurrences. I personally believe their spirits do live on in the fabric of this humble building." The staff seemed a little unsettled by Jacks comment and were unsure what this was leading to. "I know some of you may think I am losing my marbles. I leave you to decide individually if you believe that they maintain a presence here. Or in fact I am losing my marbles… however the history books do not lie and I feel deeply that it's about time these three actors were remembered." Joan started to clap and a ripple of applause silenced the mumbling of the perplexed staff.

Jack opened the paper that Carolyn had handed to him. "This letter comes from the Chairman of the Civic Society and confirms that a plaque is to be erected on the face of this building commemorating the site of the theatre and the lives of the three actors who'll be forever remembered for their contribution to the history of this site."

The staff then burst into thunderous clapping and whistles. This would certainly add some recognition to their shop and engage it further with the community. The letter seemed to be all that was needed to endorse Jack's theory. As the sound reverberated around the room the three actors moved to the wines and spirits section and bowed, soaking up the applause and adulation. It was a wonderful tribute and they milked the moment for all it was worth.

"Shame they can't see us," Wilf said taking one final bow. They then sank down through the floor into their dressing room, the sound of the ovation still ringing in their ears.

The meeting concluded, Joan reopened the shop and Joe took Charlie round to meet the workforce individually. After some understandable negative reactions from the more militant members of staff, they went to the back room to look at stock control. Charlie was prepared for a cold reception considering his past record. He knew it was up to him to knuckle down and win them all over through hard work. Joan, along with Joe, started reorganising the systems to accommodate the overnight working practice. They only had two days to go through the routines with Charlie.

20

Captains day

Midnight; Holeford Golf Club

The last of the members in the clubhouse finished their drinks and headed home at 11 pm. Keith, the steward, lowered and locked the clanking portcullis shutter to the bar, cleaned the glasses, tidied the room and replaced the chairs neatly round the tables ready for a new day. He secured the doors to the entrance, checked the fire exits and windows were all secure and stepped out onto the patio. He stood for a while looking over at the lights of Holeford in the distance. He took a deep breath of the fresh, still air that held the scent of the warm summer's day. The moon glowed like a celestial light bulb and there was not a breath of wind to rustle the leaves. He listened carefully to the sounds of the night, a fox cried out and rabbits scurried for cover. He was sure he could hear deer moving around in the woods off to his left. It was also not unusual to see badgers at this time if the moon was bright enough. It was always a thrill to see them but they did have the unfortunate habit of digging up the fairways in search of beetle larvae. The green keeper hated them but Keith had to admire their fortitude.

He stepped back into the clubhouse, closing and bolting the doors behind him. He then moved behind the bar, turned off the house lights and headed for the stairs to his flat which was conveniently included with the steward's position.

In the barrow Charles was preparing for the evening's competition. The conditions were perfect and he was expecting the largest number of entries ever. No doubt the promise of entertainment after the prize-giving had encouraged the members to put their names down. He wrote the starting line up on a parchment and pinned it to the notice board on the starters hut. As he was doing so the first of the competitors arrived in a coach mysteriously moving without the aid of horses. The ghostly coachmen climbed down from their seat, opened the doors and four more men stepped out dressed in their finest plus fours. They all retrieved their clubs from the rack on top of the carriage and joined Wolf Gore on the first tee.

Further transport had been arranged from Holeford and before long a ghostly double-decker bus could be seen heading up the hill towards the car park. Bert and Reggie's coaches still operated in the town but this example had long since been confined to the scrap heap. However, in the spirit world this was no barrier and it continued to provide a service for the ethereal, despite the ceased engine. Although the vehicle silently manoeuvred into the car park the passengers were far from quiet. Singing and laughter erupted from within. The bus drew up alongside the first tee and a cornucopia of historic characters stepped off carrying their golf bags. George was last off having been sat upstairs at the front for the journey from the Collington club pick-up point.

Charles was thrilled at their arrival. He had never in all his years seen such a turn out for the captain's night competition. The camaraderie was intoxicating. They were all having such a good time and the competition hadn't even started yet. The players all gathered on the first tee, Charles addressed them from the roof of the starters' hut and read out the starting sheet for those who couldn't read English. Amongst the group were Vikings, Romans, two other Iron Age chieftains, three convicts, the coach driver and footmen to name but a few. It was to be a shotgun start which meant groups of three players moved to their allotted tees and awaited the sound of the gun. The groups all teed off at the same time and would hopefully all complete their eighteen holes and return to the car park at around the same time for transportation to the club for the results and the cabaret.

In the flat above the clubhouse Jess could hear Keith locking up the bar and setting the alarms. She looked out of the window across to the first tee, it was a hive of activity. She watched a crowd wearing various regalia gathered around a man wearing a red Slazenger jumper and plus fours, reading to them from a scroll. She had seen small groups of players after dark before but this was unprecedented, there must be at least fifty of them. The gathering then split into groups of three and headed to all four corners of the course. Jess ran from window to window looking down in fascination. The groups then stood on the various tees talking and comparing their clubs while keeping an eye on the clock tower on the clubhouse roof.

On the first tee Richard Swede stood alongside Charles and their playing partner Judge Lionel, who coincidentally was tipped to be the chairman for the next season. Richard De Pearcy looked at the clock intently. In his hand was a loaded blunderbuss, once his implement of choice for his day job as a highwayman, now the improvised starting gun for the Captain's Day Competition.

Jess watched as at the stroke of midnight he lifted the wide barrelled gun, aimed it high in the air and fired. The resulting explosion was not heard by most of the world and their slumber was not interrupted, but for those attuned to mystical phenomenon there was an almighty bang. Deer ran for cover, curious rabbits ran out onto the course to see what was happening while the unconcerned badgers continued to turn over the turf on the fairways, looking for grubs.

Jess went wild as Keith got to the top of the stairs and entered the room. She ran around knocking papers and a glass off the coffee table with her tail, barking fit to burst and running from window to window trying to point out to Keith all the action taking place under his nose. The players on the tees all took their first stroke simultaneously, the spectral balls soaring off in all directions, mostly down the fairway but by no means all.

"Now then girl, calm down. What's the matter, have you seen one of those nasty badgers?"

Jess looked at Keith with bemusement. "Look for yourself, the course is full of ghosts playing golf… are you stupid?… and one of them is armed!"

Unfortunately this came out as a series of barks, whines and whimpers and Keith missed the point entirely. He looked out over the first tee but there was nothing there, the light from the full moon could only hint at the contours of the course and outline the trees on the far side. He patted Jess on the head, tidied the room replacing the papers on the table, turned on the telly and sat on the sofa. Jess mumbled at him in resignation at his stupidity and curled up alongside him. Why she chose to live with this dumb animal she sometimes wasn't sure.

After four hours of play the tournament drew to a close and all the players gathered back at the car park. Charles and Lionel collected all the scorecards and placed them in a box. They would take them back with them and check all the scores before the revelries began at the club. Bert and Reggie's coach was waiting along with two horseless carriages to take all the participants back to town. It had been a huge success. Without fail everyone had enjoyed the game. All were animated with stories of their best drives, their excellent approach shots and frustration at the lip outs and unfortunate kicks that had tarnished their score card. They would talk about this for weeks.

George was pleased with his first attempt and exhilarated by the camaraderie of his playing partners. He would keep trying and improve his skills before the next competition. His thoughts now turned to the evening's entertainment. He felt guilty at not being back at the club to help set up the stage but Wilf and Alice had assured him they could manage. He went back on the first transport available. He managed to hitch a lift with Lord Pitfall in his magnificent landau pulled by two ghostly skeletal stallions. He felt very grand as they pulled up outside the club. Wilf was there to greet them and escort them in. George needn't have worried. The room looked amazing. The stage had been extended with old tabletops to fill the alcove at the end of the cellar and old card tables and chairs had been laid out in a random fashion through the room. He imagined this was how a *speakeasy* would have looked during the prohibition in America.

Alice had brought the spare stage curtains from the prop room and draped them along the walls and either side of the stage to add a subtle elegance, hiding most of the bare brickwork. The piano sparkled to the left of the stage. By some magic they had managed to clean it up and it looked really smart.

Alice was on the stage checking the props ready for the show, she saw George enter and held out her arms as if to show off the refurbishment.

George applauded. "This is fantastic! You've been busy."

"Thanks, but we had some help, we can't take all the credit." She pointed to the small groups of 'The Great Fire' victims smouldering at the back of the room.

George turned to them. "Thanks guys, you've made an old thespian very happy, let's hope we can make more use of this facility after tonight. It would be such a shame not to."

Charles and Lionel were next to arrive; they were gobsmacked at the transformation but quickly found a table in the far corner and started analysing the score cards. They had work to do before they could enjoy themselves. Each score card had to be checked and the winners decided before the entertainment could begin. Before long all the players had arrived and the room was beginning to buzz with anticipation. In the meantime Alice was sat at the piano playing some light background tunes to add to the atmosphere. A surprise arrival was Sir Mortimer Halford who was with the contingent from the hillfort. Although he wasn't interested in golf he was the unofficial president of the Monkton Golf Society. Either way, he wasn't going to miss this show for the world.

Charles took to the stage and thanked all the competitors for their participation and after a brief speech read out the winners. The first place went to Maximus Gurillius from the Roman Legion based at Monkton Hillfort.

George was pleased at coming an impressive twentieth in such a large field on his first attempt, feeding his ambition to improve his handicap. No time to gloat though as he was backstage ready with the first of the acts.

Wilf opened proceedings, and formally thanked Charles for his assistance with the salvation of their home, all done within a short comedy routine which warmed up the audience nicely. The show then commenced in earnest with Alice singing a couple of songs accompanied by Lionel on the piano.

Then followed a jig from a group of Irish labourers, axe juggling by two handsome Vikings in full ceremonial regalia and Tom Harding read some comic verse. The evening then moved to its climax. The Monkton Quartet wowed the audience with their acapella singing, having to do an encore before the show could continue.

They had the room eating out of their hands as they moved to the finale.

Wilf, Alice and George returned to the stage to the accompaniment of Lionel playing 'The Egyptian Ballet'. There was no mistaking the opening chords of the sand dance made famous by Wilson, Keppel and Betty. Wilf and George were dressed in Arabic costumes, wore long moustaches and make-up to emphasise the sharp angularity of their features that made them appear almost identical. They demonstrated their impressive suppleness in adopting wild gestures and dancing in identical synchronised movements, while Alice, wearing a flowing Egyptian dress and veil, played the role of Betty. The dance itself was a soft-shoe routine originally performed on a layer of sand spread on the stage to create a rhythmic scratching with their shuffling feet. This was their technical problem, as ghosts have difficulty with friction. However, with help from Charles and a generous helping of sand from one of the bunkers they were able to manufacture the sound behind the piano, by sliding an old tea chest rhythmically over the grains sprinkled on the floor. It worked perfectly. The room erupted with laughter and applause and as the routine finished they received a standing or rather a floating ovation.

Charles came onto the stage to thank them for a wonderful evening and beseeched them to do more shows in the future. Alice was presented with a bunch of flowers with the memorial card discreetly removed. What a night!

The Evening shift

Charlie's training continued on Tuesday evening, but on Wednesday everything changed. Joe went off to HQ to start his training while Charlie worked the evening shift with Joan in support, to iron out any teething problems with the new procedures. From Thursday Charlie was on his own. Or rather he wasn't. The three actors had been watching very carefully and had also learnt the routine. Joan was aware of a presence, but didn't mention it to Charlie, she was interested to see how he coped in their company. She witnessed him talking to the ghosts on several occasions but pretended not to notice, they were obviously comfortable with each other, which had to be a good thing. She had underestimated Jack's instincts in employing the lad. He was hard working, good company and best of all, not scared of ghosts.

By Friday, Charlie had settled into a routine. A stock-control list was waiting for him when he arrived at seven, along with notes of other maintenance issues which could now be resolved without inconveniencing the customers during opening hours.

Between the building security patrols, he was assisted by Wilf and Alice while George was now at liberty to look at the papers and read out any interesting news while the others went about their business. Wilf was now able to hone his levitation skills without fear of alarm bells. This was a luxury that had stopped with the installation of the new alarm system as the movement detectors were very sensitive to floating groceries. Outside the nights were starting to darken earlier and nature's thermostat was beginning to lower as autumn's cooler hand began to beckon in winter's icy grip. The bright green flora was turning to a darker, fatigued hue with moth-eaten edges browning as the leaves anticipated their gentle fall to earth. At midnight the restocking was in full flight. The bell of the town clock chimed twelve times and fell silent not to be heard again until 8 am to start the working day. The streets were now quiet, just the odd straggler heading home. From inside the store the subdued light reflected back the image of the aisles in the large windows.

Charlie heard a metallic rata-tat-tat against the glass, he could also make out the vague shape of a man. He moved closer, leaving the trolley, walking past the tills and anxiously approached the window. He could now make out the face pressed against the glass, its features framed in the fur of a parka jacket hood. He imagined the underside of a limpet must look like this if you happen to be a rock. However the window was not a rock and this was no mollusc. He could hear a faint cry as the glass steamed up from the breath of the man looking in.

"Let me in!" came the plea from the limpet. It was Brian heading back from the pub and checking up on his industrious brother.

"No, go away you might nick something," Charlie replied.

"I won't, honest."

Charlie was not so easily persuaded. "I've heard that before, now go home, I'm busy."

Brian looked beyond Charlie. Deep into the store he could see in the half-light, a trolley of produce moving slowly down the aisle with boxes and tins appearing to hover across onto the shelves. "Well, it looks like hard work," he said sarcastically nodding towards the trolley. "That thing automated then?" he asked, not aware that Wilf and Alice were behind the trolley continuing the stacking while Charlie investigated the disturbance.

Charlie glanced over his shoulder to see the operation still in full swing. He grabbed his torch from his belt holster and shone it directly into the limpet's eyes temporarily blinding him.

Brian pulled quickly away from the window, shielding his eyes with his right hand. "What did you do that for?" he shouted, rubbing his eyes in a vain attempt to try and restore his sight.

"Go home, Brian," Charlie shouted through the pane.

"What did you do that for?" Brian repeated. "You could've blinded me."

"Well I haven't, now go home, you've been drinking. I'll see you for breakfast."

Brian stepped away from the shop front and blinking profusely, stuck two fingers up at the shadow in the store and headed on up the street, his peripheral vision returning but two bright green orbs remaining and obscuring most of his view.

Charlie returned to the others.

"That was quick thinking," Alice said admiringly as Charlie twirled the torch back into its holster, like a cowboy after a successful gunfight.

"What next?" asked Wilf.

Charlie lifted the clipboard and consulted the list. "Tinned fruits, assorted bread, washing powders, then a cup of tea for me before we do the dairy section."

"Very good, sir," Wilf said and saluted Charlie.

Both of them were happy with the new arrangement and were enjoying it immensely. For Charlie it meant regular work with his new friends who didn't judge him and make nasty remarks about his brush with the law. For Wilf it meant he could continue to practise his levitation skills under the watchful eye of Alice.

"Hey! We're in the paper, guys," shouted George. "Front page headlines *'PRICE LOW SAVED'. Sources have confirmed to The Chronicle that, following rumours of closure, the High Street store is to remain and sell an increased range of local produce. Also a new flagship out of town superstore will be built by Price Low. Wow! They don't hang about. The County Museum will be displaying a selection of the finds from the recent archaeological survey. Curator, Professor Dominic Halford, in an exclusive, told the Chronicle that the hoard of artefacts are unprecedented. Never has there been a more diverse collection of relics found in one small area from so many periods of history. There will be a new exhibition including previously unseen material from his father Sir Mortimer Halford's dig. The display will be opened on the 15th of September by TV star and pre-eminent historian Mr Shamus O'Flanigan.* I do hope Molly is invited."

"What about Charles?" asked Alice.

"Good point. I'll let him know when I have my next golf lesson, hopefully he'll be able to attend. As a matter of fact I think we should all go," George said excitedly.

As they all moved back towards the storeroom to reload the trolley a grey smog appeared from the wines and spirits section. It emanated from just above the vodka display.

"Look, smoke," cried Alice in a sudden panic. Memories of their death once again vivid in her mind.

Charlie ran for the fire extinguisher, grabbed it off of the wall and pointed the nozzle directly at the cloud. Just as he was about to press the lever Wilf intervened.

"Don't, Charlie, I can't smell anything burning, can you?"

Charlie paused, his hand still applying slight pressure to the lever on the red cylinder. He sniffed the air. There was no smell of smoke. It was more like the musty smell of old damp clothes. He relaxed his grip but remained poised, ready to react if indeed there was a fire. The cloud increased in volume, now filling the drinks section and became darker. It was now impossible to see the rear of the store but the cloud seemed to be contained. It didn't drift down the aisle as you might expect but seemed to be turning into a solid mass. It now smelt of almonds or perhaps maple, it was difficult to tell. Charlie showed no fear and remained in position. He was charged with protecting the store and its stock and he intended to do so.

"Stay calm, Charlie, you can put the extinguisher down now," Wilf reassured him with a calm voice. "There's nothing to fear."

The cloud then became disturbed and the shadow of a creature could be made out walking towards them. The four of them stood together at the end of the aisle mesmerised by the apparition in front of them. First they saw the farming implement followed by a black cloaked figure with a hood over its head. Charlie could not make out any facial features, it was just an empty black hole. He looked again at the tool he was carrying, it was, a scythe.

"Lord help us, it's the Grim Reaper," he managed to utter before fainting, crumpling in to a heap on the floor.

Eric rested the scythe against the display and looked down at the body on the floor.

"Who's this then? Are you still communicating with mortals?" he asked the three ghosts.

"Well, never mind that for a minute, that was a spectacular entrance, Eric. Where did you learn that one?" said an awestruck Wilf.

"Thanks. I've been on an apparition refresher course and picked up some new skills. Who says you can't teach an old ghost new tricks!" They all laughed and applauded as the Reaper took a bow. "So, who is your new earthly friend?"

Charlie groaned and looked up. With a shaky voice he addressed the vision.

"Have you come for me?" he enquired, certain that this was it and he was to be whisked off to the 'undiscovered country from which no man returns'.

Eric looked down at the trembling lad and could now see the badge he was wearing. "Well, no, I haven't come for you, as you politely put it, Charlie, Head of Security. Not this time anyway. Judging by what I see, I'd guess you are a long way down my list."

"Yes, but you know my name," Charlie said leaning on the crisps display to steady himself and stand up.

"That's not difficult when you have it emblazoned on your chest!"

Charlie looked down at the badge, "Oh!"

Eric looked at the others and from under the cloak his bony hand pulled out a bottle of an amber glowing liquid. "Shall we?" he asked, swinging the bottle and pointing to the staffroom.

Wilf and George looked on in wonderment, hypnotised by the bottle of radiant liquid swaying in front of them. They all entered the staffroom and Eric placed the bottle on the table. He then produced four glasses from under his cloak with the flourish of a time served-magician. The three actors still watched in awe while Charlie watched from a distance, framed by the open door. He was still not convinced he hadn't appeared at the top of the Grim Reaper's list.

"You know," Eric continued, conscious of Charlie's presence at the door, "either the living are getting more perceptive or the barrier between our worlds is getting weaker. I'm going to have to report it, perhaps they can change the wavelength or something".

"What, like tuning a radio?" Alice asked taking her eyes briefly off the mysterious bottle.

"Yeah, something like that, I'm sure I've read about it somewhere. I'll look it up when I get back to the office. Anyway, this is a social call, as I happened to be in the area. Anyone fancy a drink?"

Wilf could not contain his excitement any longer. "Is that what I think it is?" he asked, fearing that he was mistaken.

"Ambrosia spirit," Eric confirmed reverently. "Your dead right, Wilf. It was left over from last year's Christmas party and I couldn't think of anyone better to share it with."

Wilf sat down and stared closely at the bottle. "Nectar of the gods," he exclaimed in awe.

As he looked he could see clouds slowly moving around inside the bottle as if blown by an invisible force. "This is exceptional, Eric. I've heard rumours of such a drink but I didn't realise how beautiful it is."

George was less patient. "Never mind that, get it open, and let's taste it!"

Eric carefully removed the foil surrounding the cork and placed the bottle back on the table. "This is a fine vintage," he explained. "It has been maturing in oak vats for over a thousand years. This is to be savoured and enjoyed slowly, so take your time but first watch closely." Eric spaced the four glasses equally around the bottle and stood clear. Slowly the cork travelled up inside the neck of the bottle and rose up into the air where it hovered above the now open vessel.

"Pretty neat trick, eh!" Eric said, picking up the bottle and pouring a generous measure into each glass.

He handed one to each of them and then raised his for a toast. "To good friends and our generous benefactor," he exclaimed and took a sip. "Ahh! This is a fine vintage indeed."

George and Alice watched apprehensively as Wilf then took a tentative sip, after all this was the first time he was able to drink anything since becoming a ghost. The liquid danced in his mouth and he shivered in ecstasy as it slowly trickled down the back of his throat. As it moved down his ghostly form his whole body glowed a golden hue and then slowly returned to its semi-transparent norm. "Ooh, that's amazing, I've never in my death felt a sensation like that."

Having witnessed Wilf's reaction Alice and George quickly followed suit, both cooing with pleasure as the ambrosia did its magic.

Charlie watched from the doorway at the supernatural drinks party taking place in front of him. He could see their ghostly shapes illuminating like a troupe of lighthouses in some freaky sideshow. He determined there and then not to tell anyone about this display in fear that this time he really would be sent to the local asylum. After all, he would be able to share the memory with his three friends in the evenings to come. As they began to relax, the story of the burglary and archaeology were discussed in full. Charlie joined them at the table and was able to regale his story of the police station and his angle on the fateful night of the robbery. He was not qualified to try the ambrosia spirit but instead made himself a nice cup of tea.

"I'm sorry I haven't visited for a while," Eric said regretfully. He was enjoying the company of the three actors and amused by the mortal that had joined them at the table. *'Most unusual,'* he thought but found it rather refreshing. "There've been cut backs in our department. My region has been extended as far as Exeter now, so I've been rushed off my feet! That's why life expectancy has increased in the south west. It's got nothing to do with the success of improved health care or modern technology, I just can't get round fast enough. It's ridiculous expecting someone of my age to cover such an area. Anyway, enough of my moaning, a job is a job in these uncertain times." He took another sip and glowed brilliantly. "Tell you what is coming up. Not that it's the reason I'm here, but I just had a thought. Have you considered moving on?"

The three actors looked at each other. "What do you mean, move on?" George asked on their behalf.

"Nothing horrible," Eric added quickly to reassure them. Not eternal damnation or angel status, this is a genuine opportunity." They put their glasses down and stared intently at him. "You know there's a stately home north of here?"

"What, the one with the wildlife park?" asked Alice.

"Yeah, that's the one... well, it just so happens, coincidentally, that three of the ghosts haunting the place have been promoted to one of the royal palaces. For security reasons I can't tell you which one, but that leaves a gap, or in your case an opportunity. Central office are looking for a trio to replace them. It hasn't even been advertised yet but I just had a thought. Would you be interested?"

There was a long silence as they considered the consequences of leaving their home to achieve stately home status.

Alice, however, had no reservations, she was young and ambitious. "Wow, do you think we'd really be in with a chance, Eric?" she asked excitedly.

Wilf and George were more reserved in their enthusiasm. After all they were just settling back into a very comfortable routine following all the recent upheaval.

"I'd say that the three of you would be a perfect fit. Interviews will be in about three weeks. If you are interested I can put your names forward."

"It sounds interesting but I'd want to know a lot more about the job and accommodation. We are very comfortable here, you know, it's going to take a lot to get us to move," Wilf said cautiously.

George also looked concerned. "What about our friends? What about Molly, Carolyn, Jack and for that matter our new found friend Charlie, here?" George pointed at the only mortal in the room.

Charlie nodded in agreement. He had just started in a new job with the help of these ghosts and couldn't believe they would consider abandoning him just to further their own careers as spirits. It wasn't fair, even spirit friends couldn't be relied on.

"Well, it's up to you, just let me know," Eric said. "Now, duty calls so I must be going, drink up!" They all polished off what remained in their glasses. Once more the room illuminated with iridescent light as they glowed for one final time.

Eric packed everything up, wrapped his cloak tightly around him and looked at them all with a knowing smile. "One last spectacle, watch this."

As they all watched, fascinated, his outline turned into a black dense mist, then revolved faster and faster until it resembled a small tornado.

"You know where to get hold of me," he shouted as his voice became distant. The whirlwind then descended into the floor, swirling elegantly, like water down the plug hole of a bath.

"Say what you like, he's bloody good!" exclaimed Wilf as they all watched the last whiff of smoke disappear.

Charlie fainted again!

Principal cast in order of appearance:

Peter Goodall.............................. Milkman

Wilf Trunnion.............................. Actor

George Shakespeare.................... Actor

Alice Bennett.............................. Actress

Melinda Goodall (Molly)........... Schoolgirl

Joan Goodall............................... Assistant manager (Price Low)

Jack Bonfield............................... Manager (Price low)

Brian Clarke................................ Burglar

Charlie Clarke............................. Burglar

Sergeant Eric Montgomery......... Holeford Police

Constable Ian Dexter................... Holeford Police

Carolyn Jenner............................ Teacher (Holeford Secondary Modern School)

Finbarr Lowe............................... Owner / MD (Price Low)

Michael Jones.............................. Surveyor

Mango Peters............................... Surveyor

Professor Dominic Halford......... County Museum

Father Michael McManus........... Arthur Ray

Archibald Strathmore................. County Archaeologist

Wolf Gore (Charles).................... Holeford Club Captain (deceased section)

Trevor (Gecko) Griffiths............. Heritage committee

Eric.. The Grim Reaper

With grateful thanks to all the other characters involved in making this story possible.

Acting Strangely

Written, produced and directed by........... Andrew Trim

Co-production.. Shareen Trim

Artistic Director... Sam Zambelli (That's Rich Artwork)

Book design and Printing.......................... Chella Adgopul (Honeybee Books)

Pre-production Assessors........................... Steve Ring, Ian Barnett,
Maddy Brown, & Sandra Trim

About the author

Andrew Trim was born and still resides in the beautiful county of Dorset. After a career in construction which took him to all corners of the UK and abroad, he awoke one morning with an idea for a story that developed into his first novel, *Acting Strangely*.

A cornucopia of ridiculous situations and characters for all ages.